Praise for
On the Edge of the Woods

"*On the Edge of the Woods* marks the memorable fiction debut of an author in striking command of all the gripping essentials. Tyrrel offers up likable, compelling characters; vivid settings; a host of stormy and steamy relationships; and a chilling, mysterious thread that keeps the reader turning pages until the shocking twist ending." —Judith Kelman

"Classy, sexy, and deliciously suspenseful. Don't miss it!"
—Linda Castillo

"Readers will enjoy this absolutely enthralling . . . gothic romantic suspense that reads . . . like a modern day *Suspicion*." —*Midwest Book Review*

"A world-class gothic novel." —*RomanceJunkies.com*

Titles by Diane Tyrrel

On Winding Hill Road

A GOTHIC NOVEL

DIANE TYRREL

BERKLEY SENSATION, NEW YORK

THE BERKLEY PUBLISHING GROUP
Published by the Penguin Group
Penguin Group (USA) Inc.
375 Hudson Street, New York, New York 10014, USA
Penguin Group (Canada), 10 Alcorn Avenue, Toronto, Ontario M4V 3B2, Canada
(a division of Pearson Penguin Canada Inc.)
Penguin Books Ltd., 80 Strand, London WC2R 0RL, England
Penguin Group Ireland, 25 St. Stephen's Green, Dublin 2, Ireland (a division of Penguin Books Ltd.)
Penguin Group (Australia), 250 Camberwell Road, Camberwell, Victoria 3124, Australia
(a division of Pearson Australia Group Pty. Ltd.)
Penguin Books India Pvt. Ltd., 11 Community Centre, Panchsheel Park, New Delhi—110 017, India
Penguin Group (NZ), Cnr. Airborne and Rosedale Roads, Albany, Auckland 1310, New Zealand
(a division of Pearson New Zealand Ltd.)
Penguin Books (South Africa) (Pty.) Ltd., 24 Sturdee Avenue, Rosebank, Johannesburg 2196,
South Africa

Penguin Books Ltd., Registered Offices: 80 Strand, London WC2R 0RL, England

This is a work of fiction. Names, characters, places, and incidents either are the product of the author's imagination or are used fictitiously, and any resemblance to actual persons, living or dead, business establishments, events, or locales is entirely coincidental.

ON WINDING HILL ROAD

A Berkley Sensation Book / published by arrangement with the author

PRINTING HISTORY
Berkley Sensation edition / April 2005

ISBN: 0-425-20195-3

BERKLEY® SENSATION
Berkley Sensation Books are published by The Berkley Publishing Group,
a division of Penguin Group (USA) Inc.,
375 Hudson Street, New York, New York 10014.
BERKLEY SENSATION and the "B" design are trademarks belonging to Penguin Group (USA) Inc.

PRINTED IN THE UNITED STATES OF AMERICA

10   9   8   7   6   5   4   3   2   1

Chapter One

I HAD BEEN to San Francisco once before, years ago
when I was a child, but that time I had arrived on a
train. My father had wanted the trip to be special. It
was my first time in a big city, the first time I stayed in a
hotel, the first time I was allowed to wear grown-up stock-
ings and high heels. I felt very sophisticated walking
along the steep streets with my distinguished father.

On our last day in the city, a woman was mugged on
the cable car we were riding. I heard a scream, and people
shouting, and a man ran off into the streets clutching the
purse he had stolen.

For me, the mugging only increased the sense of adventure and thrill of the city.

As my plane made its final approach and I was about
to return to San Francisco, I tried to recall that feeling of
excitement I had experienced as a young girl. But I was
too full of uncertainty, and I was scared. My parents were
both dead now and I was facing this adventure alone.

I knew, from reading a fair amount of romantic literature, what I was about to become. Not a nanny, exactly.
Not a baby-sitter. More like a lady's companion. In the

society of another era, such an occupation was one of the
few honorable professions open to a young woman of
quality with no other means. What recourse had an im-
poverished gentlewoman, having received no other suitable offer?—An offer of marriage, that is, not a vice
presidency. Nowadays girls like me had lots of other options. I'd already used up a bunch of them, having thrown
myself wholeheartedly into classes and crafts and apprenticeships and even relationships that might have
yielded me a comfortable lifestyle if I could have en-
dured them for any length of time. Some of these commitments I had honored for years, but ultimately I had
left them all behind.

A ladies companion. I could just see myself, yarn
looped between my hands, sitting on a footstool before an
elderly woman in a wing chair. I'd actually had a job like
that once, for about three months, until the old woman,
who was 102 years old, died suddenly.

But in the present situation, the lady I had been hired
to be a companion for was a young one, younger than me
by thirteen years. She was, in fact, thirteen years old. Her
mother was gone, through death or abandonment, I didn't
yet know which, but it had been traumatic for the girl, I
had been duly informed. A steadying influence was
wanted. The father had to be away frequently, as his business required him to travel. I did not know what his business was, but it must have been something quite lucrative,
as the amount I had been offered to commit myself to this
position for one year was, by any standards, ridiculously
high. It was so high that I could not say no. It was so high
I questioned my own judgment in saying yes. The information I had about the position was maddeningly vague,
which did nothing to settle my concerns.

Off the plane at SFO, I slung my duffel bag over my
shoulder and found my way through the crowds to the
baggage carousel. I had considered driving my old car up
the coast to my new home and selling it there; but in the
end I decided not to risk breaking down in the old clunker
during my move up the coast. I had driven the damned

thing for the past few years, off and on, whenever it had been inclined to run. I was so glad to get rid of that car. And the scant money I got from selling it helped pay for my plane ticket, which from Santa Barbara to San Francisco is more expensive than L.A. to San Francisco, even though it's closer. Flying had turned out to be a huge hassle, because of all my stuff. Not that I had so much, really, but even a gypsy dabbler like me, with no mate, no career, no possessions of any real value—even I had *stuff.* But I had been informed that, along with room and board and a daily stipend, not to mention that strangely generous salary, I would be provided with a car. In fact, the emphasis on driving was stressed; one of the conditions of my employment was that I could drive well and was comfortable with a stick shift.

"Please, allow me."

I was reaching for the first box down off the chute— besides my carry-on, I had no luggage to speak of, except for these heavy cardboard boxes—when a large hand clamped down on the corner of the box beside my own.

I braced myself for a fight. *Welcome to San Francisco.* But I was no match for his quick strength.

"My God, woman," the young man called over his shoulder as he swung the box onto a cart he had waiting. "What have you got in here? It weighs a ton." He hesitated, brought up short by the fight in my stance. "My aunt told me to come pick you up. You're Sarah Logan, right?" He pointed at the tags on my backpack, with my name spelled out in the block architectural lettering I had learned during my two-year stint in drafting and design school.

"Who are you?"

"I'm Dimitri. Helene's nephew." He smiled at me, all innocence, but I caught the calculated gleam as he ran his gaze up and down the length of my body. "She asked me to apologize for not meeting you here herself, but she had to go out of town for the day. So you see, you're stuck with me." He had a Satyr's wicked look, with black curly hair, bright black eyes, and skinny knotted muscles. He was about nineteen or twenty, I thought, but then I wondered. He might easily have been either older or younger. Certainly too young for me, but the way he was giving me the eye, it was evident he didn't think so. He must be desperate, I thought, if he found me attractive in my current state.

Ordinarily I was a bit vain about my looks, but lately I resembled something the proverbial cat had dragged in. A year earlier, in a misguided effort to make a hairdresser's day, I had agreed to subject myself to a "full makeover." The "artist" chopped off all my tawny hair and dyed the remaining fringe platinum blond. Very chic. Though my friends kindly assured me I was cute enough to pull it off, I thought I looked hideous. I thought maybe I'd like it better when it grew out a little. But then I became ill and lost weight. Not the kind of weight you *want* to lose; this was the kind of weight loss that makes you look, well, *sick.*

My illness baffled my doctors; after months of tests and ineffective therapies, they finally figured out I must have picked up a bug while traveling in South America.

Fast-forward a year. I was slowly recovering my health, and my hair had grown out some, but it was a weird dark-light two-tone scruffy mat that didn't remind me at all of my own once-silky hair. I was still wan and gaunt and hollow where I should have had curves. My skin was strange to me, blotchy and pale, my eyes were too big in their sockets, and I wasn't sure whether I looked older or younger. It was only in recent weeks that had I begun to feel my old energy returning; hopefully, I thought, my looks would come back, too.

Dimitri finished loading up the cart with all my worldly possessions, and we set off through the terminal. I wondered if he had rented the cart, and who was paying for it. I didn't have money for luxuries like a luggage cart; though how we would have moved all my boxes without it, I don't know.

It was weird worrying about money, as I had for so long, when supposedly now I was to be set—if everything worked according to plan—for a long time to come.

The amount I should make in one year was more than I'd scraped up in the past ten years combined. Of course there was a catch. The up-front money was minimal. The contract I had signed guaranteed the big bucks only if I stayed at the job an entire year. I could leave any time I wanted, no questions asked, and reasonable compensation would be issued. If I stayed on for a year, the bonus would be considerable.

Strangely enough, I did not seriously doubt the legitimacy of the offer; the very fantastical nature of the proposition seemed to count in its favor. What worried me was the feasibility of the terms. I knew little about the situation, but I knew enough to know there had to be something wrong. What kind of monster requires such a huge bribe for its caretaker?

Was it the child? Or perhaps it was the master of the house himself who was difficult. Well, I thought, I was soon to find out.

IT WAS A breathless trip to the parking garage. We loaded up a sleek black Mercedes with my duffel bag and all my boxes. Dimitri jumped into the driver's seat, and he had thrown the car into gear before I was able to get my seat belt fastened. He paid for parking, and we zoomed out into the late August sunshine of northern California. The sound system was blasting a bone-vibrating, pulsing beat, some kind of tribal-techno-trance music I'd never heard before. I asked Dimitri what it was, but he merely smiled without answering. Maybe he hadn't heard me.

After a few minutes he said something, which I could not understand over the blare of the sound system.

"What?" I shouted.

"You're not at all what I expected!"

"What did you expect?"

"What?" He turned down the music.

"What did you expect?"

"Someone older."

I decided to take that as a compliment. "So, Dimitri,

how are you connected with the family?" I asked, making conversation.

"I told you," he said. "I'm Helene's nephew. May's mother was my aunt, too. She was my mom's sister."

I was already confused. "Who is May?" I asked.

He looked at me oddly. "May is the girl you've come to care for."

"Thank you," I said. "It's about time I knew her name. So tell me your relationship to her again?"

"May's mother is my aunt. I mean, *was* my aunt."

"So the girl's mother is dead?"

"They didn't tell you that?"

"I knew something had happened to her, but . . ."

"Whether she was dead or had run off with her lover, you weren't so sure, is that it?" A cunning glance. "Well, wonder no longer. She's very dead. Her body was found washed up on the beach."

"Was it a boating accident?"

Dimitri shook his head. "Poor Aunt Lisa." He lost his smile, thinking about her. His voice dropped when he spoke again, as if he feared someone eavesdropping. "I believe it was a murder."

"Why?"

He ignored my question. "I'm not the only one who thinks so."

"But officially it wasn't? A murder?"

"Officially it was a suicide, I think. Or was it an accident?" He scowled, as if trying to remember, but for some reason I had the feeling he knew exactly what it was, "officially."

"The point is," he went on, "nobody knows for sure. Except . . ." He let his voice trail off theatrically.

"Except?"

"Except for whoever murdered her, of course."

"If she was murdered."

"If," he conceded.

"Was she unhappy?"

He gave a shrug as if to say, *How should I know?*

"Well, sometimes you can tell," I said.

"I really didn't know Aunt Lisa all that well, to tell you the truth. I'd only been living here, in the Bay Area, with my Aunt Helene for a few months when it happened."

"And your Aunt Helene is Lisa's other sister."

"Yep. Three sisters. My mom, my Aunt Helene, and my Aunt Lisa, who is dead and whose daughter you're coming to save.

"To save!"

"Well, to teach some manners."

"Ah, yes."

"And all the saving graces."

He was an odd bird, I thought, with his intense black eyes and his flippant remarks. I wasn't sure what to make of him.

"Okay," I said. "Let me see if I've got this right. May's mother was Lisa, and your mother is—"

"Kate."

"Your mother is Kate. But you live with your Aunt Helene."

"Right. We live in Palo Alto. It isn't far from where you're going to be living. Aunt Helene has taken a particular interest in May and the poor widower Gatien. She's actually the one who hired you, you know."

"Yes, I'm beginning to put it all together," I said, thinking of my correspondence with Helene Browning. It had all been very formal and legal and yet strangely quick and decisive. Little information was put forth about the family, but my stepmother, Dorothy, a distant relative of Helene's, had told me about the position, and she told me she could vouch for the character of the master of the house.

If "little" was known about the family, I wondered how Dorothy could vouch for the character of the "master," as she put it. I had voiced my skepticism, particularly when she told me the salary that was being offered.

"It wouldn't be an easy position, Sarah," Dorothy explained. "You would have to be on call for the child twenty-four hours a day, often being the only responsible adult present. You would be expected to pitch in on the household duties as any member of the family. Your job would include shopping, running errands, and chauffeuring. And you'd have to relocate for the duration," she said. "The family lives somewhere near San Francisco."

I had made a quick calculation. San Francisco, a five hour drive from Santa Barbara, my home base. I could deal with that. What did I have to worry about leaving behind? Only Dorothy, my stepmother, but then she was off traveling most of the time anyway. I loved Santa Barbara and I had some good friends there, but I was ready to get away. No, my reservations about this job had nothing to do with the location.

"All right, Dorothy," I said. "What's wrong with the child? She's got to be a creature. Nobody pays that kind of money to a nanny."

"It's more than a nanny job, Sarah. You're to be there for the girl full time. Like—dare I say it?—a *real mother.*"

"So *he's* the problem? The father? What kind of father pays for a mother for his kid? That's just creepy."

"Well, my dear, I think it's a good opportunity and you'd be helping Helene's brother-in-law. I understand he's had quite a hard time of it. He travels frequently, and he's worried about his little daughter. I think this might be just the situation you've been looking for."

"I don't know," I said. "Maybe if I had a chance to speak with him, talk to him about his expectations . . ."

"He's in Europe now, I'm afraid. Or was it South America? Helene's handling this for him. And unfortunately she's got to know right away if you want the job. She's got someone else lined up for the position, but she would prefer to bring in someone connected to the family, so if you think you'd be at *all* interested, Sarah, we need to let her know."

Well, I suppose I *was* connected to the family, though in a rather oblique way. Still, I knew if Dorothy had recommended me, she really did think I'd be right for the part, so to speak.

"Yeah, Aunt Helene is the one who arranges everything," Dimitri was saying. "Actually, I am surprised you passed her test in order to become May's . . . I was going to say *nanny,* but May would hate that."

"What sort of test did I pass?" I asked.

"I don't know. But you can bet she had you thoroughly checked out."

"Well, that makes sense, considering the position. You don't want child molesters or felons, right? But why should you be surprised *I* would pass? You don't even know me."

"All right. Let's just say, I'm impressed. I'd be impressed with anyone who could fulfill Aunt Helene's requirements."

"So she's tough, is she?"

"Nah." He seemed to be reconsidering. "She's just, you know, she has high expectations of everyone."

"Even you?"

"Sure. I just couldn't handle my mom anymore, and she couldn't handle me. I was only sixteen, so they thought I should come here to the Bay Area and live for awhile. I didn't want to, but they made me. It turned out okay. I got one more year of high school, since I flunked a grade, but then I'm out on my own." He seemed almost proud of having "flunked a grade."

"Where does your mom live?"

"Down the coast in Santa Cruz."

"And what about your dad?"

"He's in Michigan. He's got, like, two little kids and a new wife and everything."

"Wow."

"Yeah. Hey, it's all good. You know you can open that vent if you're too warm."

"Thanks," I said. "And what about the child? What is she like?"

"The child?" He looked confused.

"May?"

"Of course. The child. Oh, well, she's fine. She's a good girl. A bit messed up, because of her parents, but otherwise she's all right."

"Her parents—"

"Both of them mad as hatters."

I laughed lightly, trying not to show the alarm this comment raised in me. "Mad as hatters," I said. "Aren't we rather young to be using that expression?"

"It fits. They're like, seriously wack, if you prefer. In different ways. *She* was all right—May's mother—I liked her. Aunt Lisa. Aunt Helene says she was spoiled. But I thought she was a nice lady. I never believed the stuff they said about her."

"What did they say about her?"

"That she was a slut, basically."

I wondered who "they" were, who had said this.

"May's mom tried to be a good mother, at least," Dimitri said, as if he wanted to defend her. "May's father, on the other hand, he—" But here Dimitri cut himself short and flashed a smile at me again, showing his gleaming white teeth.

"Gatien Defalle," I said, not wanting him to drop this theme. "So what's he like?"

"Gatien Defalle . . ." Dimitri chuckled, a private moment of humor that deliberately left me ignorant. "Oh," he said. "You'll find out about *him* soon enough."

"Okay, Dimitri." I ignored what I considered to be his rather childish affectations.

"Hey, forget what I said about May's parents," Dimitri said. "Okay? I was just . . ."

"Kidding? About them being mad as hatters?"

"Well, exaggerating a little."

"That's a relief. Tell me," I said. "Is there anything I ought to know before I start my, uh, new job?"

His eyes left the road and took me in for a second. "Don't be too curious," he said.

"What do you mean?"

"Mind your own business." .

"Right. I'll do my best."

"I don't mean that unkindly. But you *did* ask for my advice."

"Minding your own business is always good advice.

But May and her father *are* my business now, I should think."

"I just mean like, what May needs now is a good future. She needs to forget about the past."

"What about the past? You mean her mom's death?"

He shrugged and nodded halfheartedly. It was a non-answer.

"You think I can help her move on if I don't understand what she went through before?"

"You know what, Sarah Logan?" Dimitri exclaimed. "I think you're going to be great. Just what they need up there. Seriously."

His tone was suddenly too jovial to suit me.

"I just want to do my best for her, you know?" I said. "But I don't know what I'm getting into, so I don't know if I—"

"May's gonna be okay," he interrupted me, staring at the road ahead, and I felt he hadn't even heard what I was saying. "You'll make sure of that, right? Right, Sarah Logan?"

I drew myself in a little. There was something rather creepy about Dimitri.

"Don't worry," he said. "I'm going to help you."

Chapter Two

THE FREEWAY WAS a wide, smooth swath cutting through a long, bucolic stretch of the peninsula south of San Francisco. Broad patches of field and pasture were framed by weathered fences and rows of old eucalyptus, and the rolling oak-studded hills sloped up against the coastal mountain range. It would have been fun to drive it. But today I was a passenger, taking in the sights of this strange new land. Coming from Santa Barbara, I had expected to be disappointed in my new surroundings, but it was much more open and beautiful than I had thought it would be. To the west I could see the jagged fringe of evergreens on the ridges. To the north, a huge bank of fog was rolling in fast, tumbling into the lowlands. As we cruised down the freeway alongside a long blue lake, hundreds of white birds rose up from the dark water, catching the pure light of the slanting sun on their wings. I was shocked at the beauty of it, and my spirits lifted and soared with the birds. I let my apprehensions drop away and felt myself opening to whatever lay ahead.

Dimitri drove well for a kid, and I wondered who owned the Mercedes. I'd dated a guy who had this very same car, and I felt strangely at home in it, with the scent of leather and the air fresh from the vents Dimitri had advised me to open. We got off the freeway at Edgewood Road and dropped down into a wooded canyon on a steep, roller-coaster road.

"You know what that is?" Dimitri asked, pointing out a huge, stark concrete block building down in the woods below the road. "That's an insane asylum. And there used to be this old sanitarium up that road, on the hill. It was like this huge old abandoned brick fortress behind barbed wire. There was a lot of partying going on there, I guess, so they tore it down. That's what I heard. It was before my time."

I almost laughed at the way he said that, "before my time," like he was an old man now or something.

Civilization came into view, and oversized stucco houses suddenly crowded the hillsides across the canyon. But soon the road descended into the woods, and now the only houses that could be seen peeking out from the live oaks and Monterey pines were modest cabins and quaint cottages. A few minutes later we turned off the road and started climbing again on a street that seemed cut into the hillside. The car took the narrow, winding turns with ease, though my heart jumped when we barely skirted a work truck coming down the opposite direction. I glimpsed homes nestled in the oaks, nice houses, but not as huge and pretentious as those on the other side of the hill. Through a break in the trees I could see a slice of blue, which was the bay far below. I saw the cities flanking the water, and the span of a long, arched bridge stretching to the other side of the bay, and the cities alongside the far shore, and the mountains rising above them. Dimitri turned the car up yet another narrow, winding street where the houses were fewer and the woods thicker and wilder.

"This is it," he said. "Winding Hill Road. This is your street."

We wound farther and higher up the hillside.

"Almost home."

Seen through a growth of oak and shrub and wild rose,

an old grape-stake fence leaned slightly, giving way to an ancient stone wall dusted with lichen. As the woods opened up, Dimitri slowed and turned the car off the road. We passed through a wooden gate that stood open, partially hanging off its hinges. As the driveway curved up to the crest of the hill, the house emerged from the woods. It was a modest early twentieth-century California country home, with four gables, wood siding that needed some paint, and old windows reflecting the afternoon sun. Somehow it was not what I expected, which was a relief, though I wasn't sure what it was I had expected.

"And here we are," Dimitri announced, skidding the car to a halt, his one concession to teenage driving.

I opened my door slowly, taking it all in. It was a peaceful place, quiet but for the chattering of birds hidden in the trees, and through the gaps in the branches I could see that stunning view of the San Francisco Bay.

We were met at the door by a small Hispanic woman who, after first looking me over dubiously, as if she suspected Dimitri had pulled a fast one and brought the wrong person from the airport, greeted us warmly and introduced herself as Louisa, the housekeeper for Mr. Defalle. Louisa instructed Dimitri to bring my belongings down to the "little house" as she called it, but when she saw all my heavy boxes, she changed her mind and told him to wait until her husband came up from the gardens to help.

"There's no need," I said. "I'll carry my own boxes in."

This was firmly overruled.

"You don't know how glad we are to see you, Sarah," Louisa exclaimed several times as she led me into the house and sat me down in the dining room to the refreshments she had prepared: iced tea with lemon, oatmeal cookies, and Mexican pastries arranged on a glass pedestal. The room was friendly and informal. There was an old white-painted cupboard filled with mismatched floral china, and a weather-beaten pine table surrounded by benches and various wooden chairs.

"You don't know how happy it makes me," Louisa said, "now you are here." I found out later that she was a great-grandmother. I had no idea, the first day I met her. Her figure was trim and neat in the jeans and cotton blouse she wore, her face smooth, and her hair, which she kept trimmed to her shoulders, was thick and black.

I thanked her and told her I was glad to be there, though I wasn't yet sure if this was entirely true.

Dimitri came in and grabbed a handful of cookies, then disappeared. I was nervous, wondering what he might be doing with my boxes, but most of my attention was transfixed by the view of the surrounding hills and the expanse of the bay beyond, all framed beautifully by the windows facing the northeast. The house was appealing, rustic and pretty, and it appeared that nothing much had been done to it for many years. It was the sort of tired, beautiful old house that needs only some updating and tender loving care to make it a showplace. There were a few pieces of good furniture, several worn but lovely Persian carpets scattered over the plank wood floors, and some very nice expressionist landscape paintings on the walls. What came to mind was "old money," as Dorothy would say; not that I knew much about money, old or otherwise. Still, you can tell. There was worth here, but it was the shabby, unpretentious kind. I felt myself relaxing, and realized how tense I had been. I could feel at home in this place. And yet, some of the details were troubling: the gate hanging off its hinges, the degree to which the paint was allowed to peel off the old outbuildings, the missing shingles. These were things that should be attended to, but hadn't been; they spoke of neglect, not shabby chic. Again I wondered about the character of the man whose home this was.

"You make yourself at home, here," said Lousia, somewhat insistently, as if she had been following my thoughts. "This home is your home now. Your room is in the little house, but you are free to use the main house as well, which will of course be necessary, because you come and go as you please. You rest a bit, I will show you around. May baked these cookies this morning. Very good, yes?"

"Very good." I nodded. "Where is May? I'm anxious to meet her."

Anxious, I thought, was the right word.

"Oh, she runs off and who knows what she is doing now? Don't worry, she will come home soon enough."

"Is she shy?"

"Shy?" Lousia shrugged. "No, I don't think that is one of her problems."

"Does she have a lot of problems?"

"No, just maybe one or two. I think she is maybe too smart for her own good. Like Dimitri, for example."

I laughed. "Oh, is that his problem? He's too smart for his own good?"

"Sometimes I think is better not to be too smart, you know what I mean?"

"I don't know. If that's the girl's worst problem, that she's too smart . . . things could be worse."

"I know. The poor little thing, all she's been through. Her mother, she died so young, and that was only one thing in a list of bad things, I am told."

"Maybe you can help me understand," I said guardedly, hoping to get more information about this family I was suddenly to be a part of. "I know so little of the situation."

A blank look passed over Louisa's face. "I don't know much," she said quickly. "I have been here for seven months only. I came after . . ."

"Is it true May's mother committed suicide?"

"I don't know." She heaved a great sigh. "I came after all that, like I say. Mr. Defalle, he need help with things, he ask me and my husband. We take care of this place very well. Carlos, he fixes things and he works in the garden; I cook and clean and do the clothes. We try to help the girl, but she is too quick for me! You know people talk. The mother kill herself, the mother die in an accident, who knows? It is a tragedy, that's all I know. But maybe she got what she deserved. I don't know."

"What do you mean? Who got what they deserved?" I asked, a bit sharp.

I sensed her draw back a little. "As I said, I don't know."

"You don't mean the *child* got what she deserved."

"No, no, I mean the mother. The poor child, she—but anyway. No, I am talking about the mother. She was . . . *cómo se dice?* She had a reputation."

"She was not a faithful wife."

"As I told you, my husband and me, we came after that. I never see the lady. But people say she courted the attention of men."

"And you think that led to her death?"

"Maybe. No matter what happened, no matter how she died. Maybe somebody gets jealous . . . you know these . . . how do you say . . . crimes of passion? Or maybe she discovered she was in trouble. With her husband, or with her . . . I don't know. If she was very unhappy . . . maybe she did something foolish. Maybe she just slipped and fell into the sea. I don't know. But I tell you one thing . . ." She dropped her voice, luring me into the conspiracy. "That girl, she don't look like her father."

The turn of the conversation left me feeling uneasy. "When will I meet Mr. Defalle?" I asked.

"He is away now. He will be back next week, or maybe the week after. Hard to know when."

"It must be tough on May, having him gone so long. And—frequently?"

Lousia nodded, but something in her expression made me think she wasn't so sure it *was* a bad thing for the girl, that he was gone so often.

"If you are ready," she said, "I will show you around."

I WAS RELIEVED to find the master of the house was not in residence. From what I was learning about the man, he appeared to be fraught with issues. The master of a lovely but crumbling estate. An absent, disinterested father . . . A cold, uncaring husband who drove his wife into the arms of other men? Even if, contrary to rumor, he wasn't a cuckold, his marriage didn't read as the happiest of unions. Maybe he was the innocent victim, but I hadn't heard anyone offering up that particular scenario. Perhaps his wife's infidelities were the result of his own. And his behavior as a father . . . What was the man thinking, leaving his daughter for weeks on end? I felt ashamed of my own part in what must surely be a transgression. Was I to be this man's justification for neglecting his own child?

Louisa took me on a tour of the place, and I found the house was larger than I had first assumed. On the entry level was the vaulted living room and the dining room with the incredible views. Off the dining room was a large, well-equipped country kitchen with pine cabinets and a butler's pantry. Down the hall was a full bath with a door leading into a guest room that had its own entrance and deck. The room was furnished with a queen-sized bed and a sitting area complete with a love seat and fireplace.

I was about to ask if the master often entertained guests, but then I decided that would be a tacky question, given his status as a widower.

On the other side of the house was May's room, with a Do Not Disturb sign hanging on the door. Louisa ignored the sign, opening the door to give me a glimpse of a surprisingly pretty and normal-looking young girl's room decorated with posters of animals and popular musicians. There was a pine bookcase with an admirable number of titles, and a very chic beaded muslin drapery hanging over the bed.

Louisa shut the door to May's bedroom and crossed the hall to another door, before which she paused dramatically, and seemed hesitant to go farther. "This was *her* place," Louisa said. She opened the door quickly, let me look in, and shut the door at once. I had taken in a beautiful room with floor-to-ceiling arched windows and walls lined with well-filled bookshelves, several comfortable chairs, a small sofa, and a large worktable stacked with more books.

"It's a library!" I exclaimed, and Louisa nodded solemnly.

"Mr. Defalle," she said in a quiet voice, "he don't like nobody going in there."

"Oh," I said. "Because it was his wife's place. It is like a shrine for her now, or something?"

"He don't go in there either. Nobody go in there."

It was a warning. She could see my interest in the room. I allowed her to lead me on, and we wound our way down a curved staircase built of gray stone into the side of the hill, to the lower level of the house. We entered a long, wide recreation room with glass doors opening out to a deck. This room had almost the same view of the bay as the dining room above. Here there were big overstuffed couches and chairs and gaming tables, a pool table, and a wet bar, also some exercise equipment. On the other side of the room, through an open door, I saw what I guessed was the master suite: a short, wide hallway that led into a spacious room with a fireplace and a window looking out through the woods; I glimpsed a touch of blue through the gaps in the branches, sky or water, and I could see, reflected in the glass of the open window, a huge bed with a slate colored coverlet and a messy pile of very functional looking pillows.

Louisa did not take me into the master suite. In fact, she closed the door before we continued our tour.

She showed me around the gardens near the house, which were extensive, yet only a small part of the entire property—which she informed me was several acres, an impressive amount of land so close to the city, surrounded by other large, wooded parcels. Most of the land was wild oak woodland and dry meadow, but the house and the gardens were tidy, and the care lavished on them by Louisa and her husband was obvious. I commented on this, and she seemed pleased by the notice. In fact, their devotion to the house and grounds was so apparent, I wondered at the dilapidated condition of the fences and some of the outbuildings, and the other things I'd noticed needing attention around the place.

Just down from the main house we found Dimitri and Louisa's husband Carlos, who were just finishing up hauling the last of my boxes into a tiny cottage that stood in the shade of a circle of young redwoods, its doors and windows opened up to the late afternoon breeze.

Carlos greeted me with cordial warmth. When I commented on his garden and asked him a question about it, he merely smiled and nodded, which meant, I assumed, that he wasn't fluent in English. I was too shy to try my pathetic Spanish with him, so we both resorted to smiles and nods.

"If that's all then, people," said Dimitri, "I'll be off."

"Thank you, Dimitri," said Louisa.

"Yes, thanks," I said. "Thank you for bringing me from the airport, and carrying all my stuff down here, and everything."

"No problem." He flashed me his Satyr's grin, tossed the keys up, and caught them neatly in one hand. "Anytime Aunt Helene lets me drive her car, I am content. So . . . bye, everybody. And good luck with your new life, Sarah Logan!"

He hopped a small stone wall and was gone; we heard the Mercedes engine as he roared off down Winding Hill Road. Carlos had disappeared, too, and I was left with Louisa in the little cottage. Little was the word for it, but it was perfect. White painted siding, windows with blue painted shutters, a tiny front porch with just enough room for a bentwood rocking chair. There was a quaint tiled archway over the front door, and the wood shingles on the roof undulated sweetly. It was truly a storybook cottage, with the fascia boards and window trim cut in fanciful waves, and a tangle of wildflowers growing around. It was just as charming inside, though the tiny sitting room was crowded with my boxes.

Louisa continued her tour.

"Here," she said. "You see the kitchen is no good. That's okay because you eat up at the main house."

I walked through the plastic curtain draped over the doorway into the small, partially gutted space that should have been the kitchen. There were a few builder's tools and a ladder placed neatly in one corner. The old casement window over the exposed plumbing for the sink presented a forest-framed version of that ubiquitous view, the bay and sky glimpsed through lacy redwood foliage.

"But there is a nice bathroom," Louisa called out cheerfully, selling the place like a real estate agent. "Very clean."

I ducked beneath the plastic to get out of the kitchen.

"And the bedroom is fine. Look." We picked our way around my boxes, and she ushered me into the bedroom of white painted woodwork and polished pine floors, the room just barely large enough for the enameled brass bedstead.

Our tour had found its end.

"I love it," I said.

"You love it?"

"It's so sweet. Really. It's great."

"I am so glad you like it." She seemed immensely relieved, looking at me with gratitude, her hand over her heart. "You tell me, whatever you need, Sarah. I want you happy here. Very important. I go now to start my cooking, but you can stay here and rest. I will come back later, help you unpack all these things."

"No, that's okay," I said. "It's mostly all books. I'm going to leave them in their boxes for now."

"Books!" She sniffed, suspicious, peering at the boxes. Then she shrugged and looked away, as if it were no business of hers. "You rest, Sarah. Or maybe you would like to come to the house with me?"

"I think I would like to rest," I said.

"Good. You rest. Dinner time is six-thirty, but I will bring you a snack."

"No, thank you. I'm fine, really. Those pastries did me well. I'll see you at six-thirty."

Louisa paused before going out the door. "You will waste your time if you look for May. She will come when she is ready. You don't look for her."

I waved to Louisa as she went out, wondering how she knew I was planning to look for May.

Chapter Three

I DID TRY to rest, but I was too restless, eager to explore my new home. I knew from what I had seen of the layout of the house and its outbuildings that Louisa had shown me only a part of the place. Should I take this to mean I was only allowed in certain areas? But she had told me to make myself at home. Besides warning me to stay out of the library, and closing off the master suite to my curious eyes, she had indicated that I was free to roam about the place at will.

The late afternoon had brought a chill. I closed the windows and doors of my little cottage, pulled on a sweatshirt, and set out to walk around the grounds.

Narrow pathways and odd little stairways went off here and there over the slope of the hillside through the trees and gardens. It must have been very steep a hundred years earlier, before landscaping had sculpted its flanks, but now the hillside was a series of gentle terraces connected by these charming steps and retaining walls, some of old brick or stone, some of railroad ties, others of weathered concrete. I passed through a vegetable garden, profuse in its late-summer glory, and there was an old potting shed where gardening tools were neatly stored and lettuces sprouted in nursery flats, waiting to be planted.

Down from the vegetable garden the land grew wilder, giving way to a meadow ringed with oaks and the remnants of some ancient fruit trees. The path I was following led in and out of the woods, through the meadow and up again, eventually, to the house. It was possible to get a bit of a workout just walking around the property, which appeared to be partially enclosed by the weathered grapestake fence I had noticed earlier out at the street, and in some places, a crumbling stone wall that might have once encircled the entire estate. In some places the woods opened up to the expanse of amber hills, splendid in the late afternoon light, and I could see the cities along the edge of the bay, and the immense band of water, gleaming in the setting sun. Above and beyond it all, the mountains stretched from north to south, with one big peak, almost due east, rising above them all. I was enthralled by it. Even without the view, the place would have been wonderful. And it was my home! I felt like calling my friends back in Santa Barbara and telling them all about it. See? This wasn't such a crazy move after all! But I wasn't sure yet. After all, I hadn't yet met my young charge. She was, perhaps, the nightmare I was dreading. And what about her father, Gatien Defalle? I walked faster, stomping out the agitation through my feet.

Then I heard the voice. I stopped and stood listening, motionless.

Singing, reedy yet strong, an ethereal, unaffected expression, like nothing I had ever heard before. The song of a fallen angel, otherworldly purity with an edge of sadness, even desperation.

> *How the winds are laughing*
> *They laugh with all their might*

I began to walk toward the sound, and through a glade a tiny cottage came into view, a charming thing, painted white like my cottage, but even smaller. It was another garden shed, or perhaps a playhouse. It had no wheels, but I thought of a gypsy caravan, with its doors flung open and pots of geraniums around the windows.

> *Laugh and laugh the whole day through*
> *And half the summer's night*

I remained hidden in the shadows as the girl appeared in the doorway of the tiny cottage, holding a daisy in her hands. She was tall for her age, for I knew her age to be thirteen; her hair was long and dark and needed a good brushing; her legs were long and bare and brown in baggy shorts. She wore a filmy cotton peasant blouse that added to the romantic look of her; framed by the branches of the oaks, she was a wild gypsy girl in the woods. She absently pulled the petals off the flower but did not seem interested in any message that might be revealed in its numbers. She continued singing her haunting song, and she tossed the button and stem away when she had finished taking the flower apart.

I knew this must be May, and I was debating whether to come out of the woods and make myself known to her when a boy came into the clearing between us. He was perhaps a year older than the girl, a friendly looking, sunburnt young lad with a blond crew cut. When she saw him, she stopped singing.

"What do you want?" she demanded, her voice no longer dreamy and ethereal but rather hard and cold. For a moment I feared she had seen me, and that it was me she was addressing in that challenging tone.

"Nothing," said the boy. I imagined up close he would prove to have freckles and pale blue eyes. He seemed unaffected by her lack of welcome and walked closer, ignoring her, looking at the tiny building with interest. "What's in there?" he asked.

"Nothing," she said. She closed the door and dropped the latch, and stood on the step, as if daring him to come any farther.

He stopped a respectful distance away and said, "I heard there's a lady who's come to live with you."

"Yeah, so?"

"Is she here yet?"

"I don't know. I don't care."

"I heard she's here. She came this afternoon."

"So?"

"Don't you want to meet her?"

"I will meet her sooner than I care to, I'm sure."

"She's here to take care of you?"

"Like I'm not old enough to take care of myself?"

"Your father wants to make sure you're never alone, right?"

"You know nothing about my father," the girl said coldly.

The boy shrugged. "I know more about you than you think I know."

She looked away from him, haughty, refusing to give in and respond.

"See ya," he said, and he moved slowly off into the woods.

She didn't answer, but turned her head and stared after him, staring even after he was gone.

I thought better of making myself known to May at this time.

Instead I walked up toward the house and made a detour to circle around a large building on the west side of the property. When I came to a window that was low enough for me to see through, I peered inside. It was the back of the garage, which, because of the slope of the hill, was loftier than it appeared in the front, and I was intrigued. The building was so beautifully made, I would not have guessed it would have been devoted to something as prosaic as a garage. Inside I saw several cars, but I didn't have a good view and couldn't make out any detail. I was disappointed, having hoped for something more interesting—a mad scientist's laboratory, maybe, or a sultan's seraglio. Then I remembered that I was to have a car, and I looked again. Maybe one of these was my car. They appeared to be expensive European sports cars, three of them, but that's about all I could tell by looking through the window. They looked like collector's cars, sporty and powerful and unreliable. I doubted any of them could be the car I was to drive. Louisa had said nothing about a car during her tour of the house and grounds. With Dimitri and the Mercedes gone, the driveway was empty except for a big work truck, which probably belonged to Carlos and Louisa.

I made my way around the building, passed through a gate, and found the driveway and the front of the garage, its five big panel doors locked up tight.

The rumble of a powerful engine grew louder coming up the road, and a small sedan turned into the driveway. It was a pretty car, a silver Audi sedan with a great sound system, judging from what I heard blaring out of the open window, but the real scene stealer was the man in the driver's seat. He came rolling into the yard way too fast, although unlike Dimitri, this one did not skid when he came to a halt. He stopped neatly, flung open the car door, and leaped out. Also unlike Dimitri, this one wasn't too young for me. He was around thirty, a California golden boy, a surfer or a snowboarder or something else equally fun-in-the-sun sporty and outdoorsy, unsuited to my actual stay-at-home-by-the-fire-with-a-good-book propensities. He was tan and lean, his strength and agility quite evident as he strode toward me. His hair was blond, almost gold, almost curly—but not quite either; the curl was more of a wave, the gold more of a burnished brass.

"Whatcha looking for, lass?" he called out to me in a friendly way.

Good lord, I thought. The master had returned unexpectedly. And he was gorgeous. *It's a fairy tale come true. What* am *I looking for?*

"Um," I said. "I'm looking for my car."

"You're looking for your car?" He looked, puzzled, toward the garage. "In there?"

"I was promised a car," I explained.

He stared at me dumbly for a second, then cried, "Aha!

You must be *her*. You're the lady who's come to look after May!"

"Right."

"Sorry, I was expecting—well, never mind that. Look, I've brought your car!" He opened his arms and indicated the car with a flourish, like a game show hostess. "Here it is. Isn't she *beautiful?*"

"Quite beautiful." I still wasn't sure about all this.

"But what's your name?" He suddenly became soft-spoken, and he moved close to me, which was disconcerting, and he looked into my eyes. His eyes were deep blue. He reached for my hand.

"Sarah Logan," I said.

"Yes. Sarah." He held my hand. "I am Paul."

"Hello, Paul." I gave his hand a firm shake and released it. So this was not Gatien Defalle, the master of the house. I felt deflated.

"So, Sarah, I have brought you your car."

"That's so weird. I mean, I was just wondering where my car was, and—"

"Poof! It appears."

"Yeah."

"Really?" he wanted to know. "Was it really like that?"

I nodded. "You saw it happen."

"I PROBABLY PUT three thousand miles on it in the last week. I couldn't help it. I love driving it. Don't tell Gatien, please, he would kill me."

We were in the dining room, and Paul was finishing off the last of the cookies, which had been replenished since Dimitri had been into them.

"He didn't want me taking it. He wanted to be sure it would be here for you when you came," Paul said. "I told him not to worry. I'd make sure I got your car to you no matter what. I think you'll really like it," he told me again. "Gatien fiddled with it, you know. It's got a bit more power than the stock equipment would provide. It's been, uh, *supercharged.*"

"I would like anything, after the old clunker I've been driving."

"Yes, I am reconsidering my own ride, after all. She is beautiful, but she is treacherous! In the shop again! Another fender bender. Let me ask you something, Sarah. Do you think some cars are accident-prone? Like some people?"

"Yes, I do. Some cars are definitely accident-prone. They get one fender bender, they want another. Yes. That's what the old clunker was about. Smash, smash, smash."

He looked at me, alarmed, no doubt suddenly worried about the car he had come to adore.

"No," I said. "Don't worry. It was never my fault, I swear it. The car was cursed! I am so happy to be rid of it."

"Gatien has a cursed car story," said Paul. "A car he drove professionally. Nobody else wanted to drive it; they said it was cursed. Not because of fender benders, but other problems. He decided to see what it could do, and he won seven Grands Prix in that car."

"Racing?" I said, astonished.

"But of course racing, my beauty. Are you not aware of your new employer's profession? His passion? His, you might even say . . . affliction?"

"Auto racing? You mean like NASCAR or something?"

"Yes, but no." Paul shook his head, affecting a heavy French accent. Or was it Italian? Whatever it was, it was badly done. "Formula One, mademoiselle. Le Grand Prix."

I laughed at him. He was one of those guys who could make something funny just the way he said it. Damn, was he ever cute. "Isn't that in Europe?"

"Exactamo. Europe and other places. South America. Africa. Australia. Even here in the United States of America."

Well, that explained the long absences of the master.

"Wow," I said. "A race car driver. That's like one of those fantasy professions that no one really has."

"Yes," he said. "But in this case, it was no fantasy, it was real. Perhaps *too* real."

"Well, at least your story had a happy ending."

"My story?"

"The story of the cursed race car. You said he won all those races. . . ."

"Oh, you mean Gatien's story. Ah, but that wasn't the ending unfortunately." Paul's tone, so playful and jocular, had changed, and now he was quite serious. "He had recently lost his wife, but he didn't stop racing. Never even missed a race, which cost him some criticism in the press, as you can imagine. He had won seven Grands Prix in that car, and in that car he lost a world championship. Very nearly lost his life. It was a terrible accident. Doctors told him he might not ever walk again, but of course he had to prove them wrong about that."

He would have said more about it, but the conversation was arrested by the soft click of a door closing, and when I looked up, there was the girl I had seen down by the tiny cottage. She came to stand behind Paul's chair.

"May!" he cried, delighted to see her, and it was evident she was happy to see him.

"Hello, Paul," she said. She leaned over him, smiling, and gave him a quick hug with a graceful drape of her thin, long arms, her beautiful dark hair falling over her shoulders. She straightened up and looked at me directly, her smile fading to blankness.

"Hello, May." I took a deep breath. The moment of truth. "I'm glad to meet you."

"You're younger than I thought you'd be," she said.

I wasn't sure if this pleased her or not.

"And you," I said, "look older than I expected."

"If you were hoping for a child to fuss over, you'll be disappointed," she said.

"I'll try not to be disappointed about that, if you won't be disappointed that I'm not an old lady."

A faint smile played over her lips, but she refused to show me the slightest encouragement.

"Well," said Paul in his booming, enthusiastic way, "I

for one am not disappointed in either of you. Now that
there are two beautiful women living here, I have twice
the reason to stop by from time to time and pay a visit."

May indulged him with a soft, knowing laugh; she was
already woman enough to understand male compliments
for what they were.

"Speaking of beautiful women," said Paul, "where is
Louisa?"

"I'm in here," Louisa called from the kitchen.

"What does a man have to do to get some of that famous coffee of yours?"

"It's already on. Give me a minute. Was that May I
heard?"

"Yes, Louisa, I'm here," said May.

Louisa came to the doorway between the kitchen and
dining room, wiping her hands on an apron she had tied
around her trim hips, looking at us all with satisfaction.
"So you have met Sarah, then," she said to May. "Good."

Louisa, I thought, was quite happy to be passing the responsibility of the girl over to me.

"May, Sarah," she said. "Now you will become
friends."

I glanced at May, and she at me, and I think we were
both having our doubts.

Louisa asked Paul to stay for dinner, but he begged for
a rain check, because he still had to get some work done
before he knocked off for the day. "In fact," he said, "if
there is enough time before dinner is ready, I was hoping
I might ask Sarah to give me a ride. . . ." He smiled at me
charmingly, and then at Louisa, who scolded him.

"You were supposed to take care of all that before,
Paul," she reminded him. "You promised Mr. Defalle—"

"But think," he said. "I can teach Sarah all about her
new car on the way, and she can start getting to know the
area. It won't take long, and there's still plenty of daylight
in the sky. We're not going far."

"You live in San Francisco, Paul," Louisa reminded
him.

"But I only need a ride to the office in Menlo Park! I'll

have her back in half an hour. It's either that or a taxi, and I hate taxis."

"I don't mind," I said. "I'd like to give the car a try. If there's time before dinner."

"Paul, you always get your way," sighed Louisa. But she was looking at him with fondness.

"May, would you like to come with us?" I asked.

"No, thank you," May answered politely, not looking at me.

"YOU'RE GOING TO have your hands full with that one, aren't you?"

"On the contrary," I said. "May looks to be a quite capable young woman. I have to wonder if I'm even needed there." I was driving the car, and it was so much more car than I was used to that I was doing badly. The power, the braking—it was all so precise that I nearly gave poor Paul whiplash the first few times I started and stopped. But he was a good sport; he praised my driving and encouraged me, and I began to relax and do better.

"Don't let looks be deceiving," he warned me. "That girl is more needy than she seems."

"So she's had a pretty hard time of it, with her mother dying so young?"

"Of course, that," he said. "She's an unusual child, anyway, I think. And with all she's been through . . ." He was thoughtful. "I think Gatien was correct in having you come. Of course there are the practical concerns. Having someone home for the girl, someone to drive her around. But more than that, I think, a sense of stability, someone to be present for her, day in and day out . . ."

"Are the two of them close?" I asked.

"Who? Gatien and May?" He seemed surprised by the question.

"It's not always a given, is it?"

"No, it's not. With them, it's . . . but the circumstances are unusual, of course."

Because he's gone so much, I thought.

"I can tell you there is a lot of respect between them."

"Respect?" I repeated, puzzled. "Shouldn't it be . . . affection? Respect, too, of course, but . . ."

"Yes, of course affection, but in this case it's more difficult."

"Why?"

"You'll understand as you get to know them," he said.

"Because he's away so much, racing?"

"That's part of it. But no. That's not what I meant." He lapsed into silence.

"You're being rather evasive," I said.

"Well, it's a complicated situation. I could tell you about it . . . but I'm not sure it's my place to get into it with you."

"All right. I can appreciate that. I'll just get all my gossip from Louisa. By the way, that famous coffee of hers was horrible."

"Yes, I know, that's why it's famous."

ABOUT TWENTY MINUTES from the Defalle's, we turned into the empty parking lot of a large office building.

"Just keep on going, all the way down to the end. Almost there."

"Is this where you work?"

"It's one of our offices. I do most of my work in the city."

"I thought you might be a fellow race car driver."

"No. I'm a computer nerd. That's what Gatien calls me."

"And you're not insulted?" I smiled.

"No, hell I *am* a computer nerd, and he's the best friend I ever had, even if he is a Luddite. Besides, he's called me worse!"

"Must have been hard on him, losing his wife. I haven't heard anybody talk about that much. The focus is on May, as I guess it should be, but still . . ." I was fishing here, but he didn't have to know that.

"Yeah. Poor Gatien had to rearrange his whole entire life, it's true."

"And he isn't too happy about it, I guess."

"Well, would you be?"

I answered with a shrug, and he regarded me kindly. "Actually, now that I think about it, it's the same for you, isn't it?" he said. "You have rearranged your entire life to come here."

"Yes, I have. And I hope I'm doing the right thing! There seems to be something strange about the situation." My exasperation was beginning to show. "It's like everyone's holding back some vital piece of information they don't want me to know. Makes me wonder if Mr. Defalle and his daughter need a different kind of help than I can offer them!"

Paul let out a jolly burst of laughter. "You know something, Sarah? I think you are going to be perfect for the job."

Strange, how like Dimitri he sounded just then.

"You're the one who warned me I have my hands full," I said.

"Yes. Well, I think you do." There was that seriousness again. He was able to switch from laughter to solemnity in an instant. "But the important thing is, I believe you fulfill a very basic requirement."

"Which is?"

"You are a damned good driver. Gatien gets really annoyed by bad driving." He pointed to the curb. "Stop right there. I'll walk from here. . . . Can you find your way back home?"

Home. What a strange concept.

"Sure, I think so."

"It's pretty simple," he said. "Just stay on Alameda all the way to Edgewood. But to get out of here, you've got to keep going this way." He waved toward the entrance to the parking complex. "You can't go back the way you came."

"I think I got it," I said.

He patted the dashboard. "Good-bye, you lovely thing. Until we meet again." He looked at me slyly and was out of the car in an instant.

•   •   •

IF GATIEN DEFALLE was a professional driver himself, I didn't see why it should be so important that my driving be exceptional. I could understand wanting a clean DMV, and some basic competence, but beyond that, what was the big deal? I didn't get the impression it was any particular concern for auto safety.

I made it back to the house to find the dining room table set for two.

"Aren't you joining us?" I asked Louisa, but I could see that she and Carlos were getting ready to leave. When I had come into the driveway, he was there, packing up the truck. One of the garage doors was open, and he waved me in. He gave me a remote control for the garage door and showed me how to use it.

"When Mr. Defalle is in town, we go home after dinner is prepared," Louisa explained. I understood. Mr. Defalle was not in town, but I was there as proxy. I thanked them for their welcoming and orientation, and they assured me they would be back tomorrow morning, first thing, which comforted me a little; I realized I didn't feel ready to be in charge here. I hardly knew my way around the place.

As soon as Louisa and her husband were gone, May announced she wasn't hungry and went to her room. I heard the door shut firmly and the click as she turned the lock. I sat down and ate the meal Louisa had prepared, roast chicken and salad and handmade tortillas. Delicious. I hadn't realized how hungry I was.

After finishing my meal, I rinsed my dishes and decided to go to my own cottage. It seemed wrong to leave the girl in the house alone, but that was the setup, and after all, I was hardly ten steps away out the back door. I supposed a teenaged girl and a woman of nearly thirty could handle things alone just fine.

Lying in my strange new bed, my mind played over the scenes of the day. Images moved behind my closed eyes, overlapping, repeating; voices jumbled, the expressions and words of all the people I had encountered that day. Louisa and Carlos. May and the freckled boy who had appeared to her in the woods. Dimitri, my young Satyr chauffeur in his aunt Helene's Mercedes. Handsome, sun-kissed Paul, a bronze statue stepped down from his pedestal—and he seemed like a nice guy, too. Definite possibilities there. Then there was the flight attendant who had served me peanuts on the airplane and the Sikh taxi driver who had been kind enough to help me with all my heavy boxes.

I was uneasy about May, wondering if we would be able to connect in any meaningful way. I was excited about meeting Paul; he was an attractive man, and I sensed his interest in me. But strangely enough, the strongest personality vying for notice in my thoughts was that of the man I had yet to meet: Gatien Defalle.

Gatien Defalle. I didn't think I was going to like him. I was certain I would find him challenging. There were challenges, and then there were challenges. . . . What would make this one worth the effort? As of yet, I wasn't sure anything would. The child, I had found, was a young woman. So far, she seemed somewhat unpleasant, but certainly no monster. The living situation was more than I could have hoped for. But the man, my boss, was still an enigma. My freedom had always been very important to me, and no amount of money could hold me in a place I truly did not want to be. At least that is what I told myself then.

Chapter Four

I WAS AWAKENED from a troubled sleep by an impatient rap on the door of my cottage. I sat up, dug the sleep out of the corners of my eyes, pulled on the jeans and shirt I'd been wearing the night before, and stumbled out to see who was there, knocking louder and even more insistently now.

"May!" I said.

"Who'd you expect, the Pope?"

"Good morning."

"Same to you. When will you be ready?"

"Ready for what?"

"To take me to my game. I'm going to be *late.*"

"Back up, girl," I said. "Fill me in on the details."

"I've got a soccer game at nine. You're supposed to take me to it. That's your job, right?"

"My job is to guide your young existence, and the first thing I must do is correct your manners, my darling. You can't come barging in here, waking me up like that, demanding that I drive you somewhere. It's just not gonna fly, you know? And it sure ain't gonna get you what you want."

"I'm sorry," she said meekly, and she offered me a most winning smile, completely calculated, of course, and I wasn't touched.

"If you had somewhere to be this morning," I said, "you should have told me about it last night."

"Actually, my coach just called this morning. It's only a scrimmage, but he really wants us all there."

I looked at her, waiting.

"Please?" Her voice was wheedling, but I had to give her points for aptitude. "Please will you please drive me to my soccer game, Governess?"

"Governess!" I burst out with a laugh. "You're a little old for a governess, aren't you?"

"*My* point, exactly." Another smile, so fleeting I might have imagined it, but it was the first genuine smile she'd shown me. "But it's a mute point," she added.

"Moot point," I corrected her with a laugh.

"Whatever."

"All right," I said. "I will drive you to your scrimmage. But first I am going to change my clothes and have something to eat."

AT TEN IN the morning the sun was already hot on the field. I had brought no hat, no sunscreen, no folding chair. And more importantly, no book. I brought books with me everywhere as a rule, to read during those downtimes of life, waiting in lines, slogging through boring events. But in my haste this morning, I'd forgotten to bring one. The soccer game wasn't boring, exactly, and I did want to show some support for May when she played, but the coach hadn't put her in the game yet. I paced up and down the sidelines for awhile, then sat on the grass on the outskirts of the field, cheering on the girls.

An old man sitting on an aluminum folding chair motioned toward the empty chair beside him. "You can sit here," he said. "My daughter's coming, but she won't be here for awhile. She had to go up to Marin."

I was about to politely refuse the offer, then thought, *Why not?* I took the chair and thanked him.

"Wears me out, just watching them," he said.

"Me, too. It's such a strenuous game."

A whistle was blown, and May, who had been sitting with several other girls on the grass, jumped up and ran out onto the field.

"You go, girl," the old man called out to her, and I had to stifle a laugh.

Play resumed, and I concentrated on the game. May looked good in her soccer uniform. She had long, slender bones, and she ran with a graceful gazelle stride. But after a few minutes I became disappointed in her; she gave so little to the game. She hung back listlessly, content to let the ball come to her.

A woman walked out to the field from the parking lot and joined us. She kissed the old man on the forehead.

"Hi, Dad," she said.

"This is your chair, I think," I said, rising.

"Oh, please." She waved me back down into the chair. "I've been driving for over an hour. I need to stand up awhile." She was ten or fifteen years older than me, and wore khaki shorts, a T-shirt, and leather sandals. A pile of brown hair was pinned to her neck, and she wore no makeup.

"Did you just get in from Marin?" the old man asked her.

"Yes. Traffic was terrible." She smoothed a strand of white hair off his ruddy forehead. "You're going to get sunburned out here, Dad. Where's your hat?"

"Oh, I guess I left it in the van."

"Is the van unlocked?"

"I think so."

She set off, all no-nonsense strength and unsentimental affection for her father. I thought how nice it was, the obvious closeness of father and daughter. When it gets to the point where the child is more the parent, and the parent more the child, it is sort of sad, but sweet, too. . . . I would never have that with my parents.

I stood up and began pacing again. The woman returned with her father's hat, and she put it on him, tucking it gently over his ears.

"There," she said. "So. How is the game going?"

"We're losing," the old man replied.

AS THE DAY grew hotter, May seemed to go limp. It was painful watching her. Finally the game ended, or so I thought. It turned out to be halftime. The girls gathered in a huddle to eat orange slices and drink from plastic water bottles.

The old man continued to sit and stare at the field as if the girls were still playing. His daughter took three laps around the field, walking with a purposeful stride, and when she came back, she took her chair.

"Hot day," she said to me. I was sitting nearby on the grass.

"I know. I keep thinking about the girls, running around in this heat. Poor things."

"They don't seem to notice it, whether it's raining or sweltering, as long as they can play."

"Some of them, anyway," I said, watching May, who sat just outside the circle, holding her water bottle, not joining in the chatter. It was true that most of the girls, when they were on the field, were completely focused on the play, not noticing the sweat dripping down off their noses. But I couldn't say the same of May. She looked like she couldn't wait for it to be over.

The whistle blew, and the girls stood up and started out to the field. May suddenly ran over to me, and I was pleasantly surprised to be acknowledged. She hadn't looked at me once since we'd arrived.

But she ran past me and went instead to the old man sitting in the aluminum folding chair, embracing him affectionately. "Hey, Grandpa," she said. She hugged the old man's daughter in turn. "Hi, Aunt Helene. Thank you for coming to my scrimmage."

"You're very welcome. Thank you for letting us know you were playing this morning. I got your call on the Golden Gate Bridge!"

"You shouldn't answer your phone on the bridge, Helene," the old man scolded.

"See ya later!" May waved at them. Without a glance for me, she ran off and joined her team.

Without having the least idea of it, I had been sitting in the aluminum folding chair belonging to the woman who had hired me to look after May.

"WELL, YOU DON'T look anything like I had expected," Helene said when I introduced myself, and I wondered when I would stop hearing that refrain. Actually, I liked the fact that I surprised people. People certainly kept surprising *me*.

"I kept looking at that redheaded woman over there, wondering if she was you," Helene said. "I very nearly went up to her and introduced myself!"

"I guess it didn't occur to May that *she* might introduce us."

"I suppose she's been difficult," Helene said. We were strolling together up and down the sidelines, watching the soccer game and talking. Helene was smoking a cigarette. "She won't take to you quickly. You shouldn't expect it. I think the fact that you look so close to her own age might be a plus. But don't let her run you, or take advantage of you."

"I wouldn't dream of it."

"When we talked on the phone, Sarah, I liked your self-possession, your practical intelligence. It fits well with my own style, I think, and I do believe May will come to appreciate it, too, eventually. But I don't minimize the task at hand, and I want you to know you can call on me at any time. In fact, I wanted to be there when you arrived yesterday, but unfortunately, I had to be in Marin. I do apologize. Hope it wasn't too rough a start for you."

"It wasn't too bad," I said. "Louisa was great. She gave me an orientation tour."

"Good. Yes, Louisa is wonderful. And so is her husband, Carlos."

We were down at the end of the field by now, far from the other people, and the girls, who were all running off toward the opposite goal.

"So I gather there is some tragic mystery in the family," I said to Helene, hesitantly, afraid I might offend her. "May's mother . . . your sister, yes?"

"Yes. My younger sister."

"I know it's a sensitive subject, but I feel I should ask, because it concerns May."

"My sister committed suicide, plain and simple," Helene said quietly. "No mystery there. Lisa's death was self-inflicted, the unfortunate action of a very disturbed individual. You're going to hear gossip—all right, I can see you already have—but as far as I'm concerned, it's all a lot of nonsense. Lisa took her own life for her own simple reasons. I am sure in her mind, it was very complicated, but when it comes down to it, it's very sad, but really very simple."

"I'm sorry," I said. "That must have been terrible for everybody in your family."

"Well, yes, it was. But to be honest, Sarah, I have to say that in some sense things are better now that she's gone. My sister caused a lot of trouble, a lot of pain. Things have been easier around here since she's been gone, especially for my father."

"Your father?" I said, showing some surprise I hadn't intended. "I'm sorry, I had thought you were going to say for her husband."

"Of course, he's been very affected, too. But I'm talking about a lifetime of bad choices. Gatien came into our lives only relatively recently, you see. My poor father had to cope with Lisa for thirty-five years. Heartache upon heartache. As a child she would run away from home, scaring everybody to death. She set fires and vandalized buildings. She was doing drugs and sleeping around before she was a teenager. Then there were the pregnancies and the abortions and dragging all manner of riffraff through our lives, criminals and hustlers and drug addicts. She was in crisis constantly. And she got herself in trouble with the law, petty stuff mostly, but it's a wonder she was never sent to prison. And always she looked to my father to bail her out of her troubles."

"Was she mentally ill?" I asked.

"I'm sure she should have been considered as such, though I found doctors to be rather uncooperative in giving us a viable diagnosis. Which *might* have helped," she added in a tired voice.

"And she never grew out of her troubles?" I asked. "Not even after getting married and having a child?"

"I kept hoping. Nobody else can understand what she put him through, really. It's hard to comprehend, unless you've seen it firsthand. I was afraid the stress would kill him."

I was pretty sure she was still talking about her father, not Lisa's husband.

"It must have been hard on May."

"Yes," agreed Helene. "I believe it has been very difficult for her."

"Though if the mother was that unstable, and was so hard on your father, maybe it's for the best that she's not in her daughter's life, either."

Immediately I wished I had not said this; it seemed to lack tact. But Helene didn't seem to take offense.

"It's true," she said. "It sounds awful, but May is probably better off without her. Maybe we all are. I only wish my father would see it that way. He tends to get depressed."

"He's a sweet guy, your dad."

"Yeah, he sure is," she said, looking at him fondly, sitting in his chair.

Helene and I had bonded during the soccer game. She was a little softer toward me now, just a touch friendlier, though she didn't seem the type to be overly affectionate, which suited me fine. I was glad for Helene's insight. She was the first person I'd met since I'd arrived who had presented the family situation straightforwardly and without secrets and mysteries, innuendo and head games. I was relieved, and glad to have met her, and I thought we might become friends.

•   •   •

I WENT INTO May's room that afternoon after the soccer game. She had left her door open, and I found her lying on her bed, brooding.

"Are you upset about losing the game?" I asked her.

"No. I don't care."

"Really? I think you do care."

She suddenly seemed about to cry.

"It's hard when you lose," I said, trying to be philosophical, "after you try so hard. . . ."

"It's not that. I *didn't* try hard. That's the point. I just don't care anymore. I hate soccer."

"Did you always hate soccer?"

She looked up at me with veiled interest, her eyes wary, perhaps wondering what lay behind the question. "No," she said. "I liked it all right when I was a kid."

I sat down beside her on the bed and tried not to smile at that. To me, of course, she was still a kid. "What was different?" I asked.

"I don't know. My friends were all in it, on the same team. I was one of the best players. Now I don't know anybody, and I'm just average, or one of the worst."

"You seemed pretty good to me. Or you could be, if you wanted to be."

"I'm a very fast runner, that's all. Anyway, there are other things I'd rather be doing than soccer."

"Like what?"

"Like whatever I want to do, which is my business."

I took a deep breath. "Well, why don't you just quit then, if you dislike it so much?"

She didn't answer.

"Is it your father?"

She jerked her head up, glowering at me.

"Louisa says he coaches sometimes, when he has time. Is it him you mean to impress?"

To my surprise, she seemed to relax a little, considering the question.

"He likes me to play," she said softly. "He's half French, you know, and they're very big on soccer in Europe. They call it football. He comes to my games when-ever he can."

I was amazed at how her voice changed when she talked about him. *She adores him,* I thought. That should have been a wonderful thing, but somehow something struck me as not quite right. Not quite the way a normal thirteen-year-old talks about her father. I was becoming increasingly curious about this man.

ONE MORNING I was in my bed, half-asleep, trying to re-member my dreams, when I heard a noise in the other room, a loud, persistent banging. I jumped up, dressed quickly, and went out into the gutted kitchen, where I found two workmen crouched down, doing something to the floor. They looked startled to see me, and both of them jumped to their feet. The taller of the two introduced him-self as Nathan the contractor. Daniel, his young appren-tice, seemed shy; he excused himself at once and went outside.

"So you must be the new inhabitant of this little house," said Nathan, with a touch of Southern charm in his mellow voice. "I was told you were moving in over the weekend. Sorry about the noise and the mess," he added. "Did we wake you?"

"Not really. But . . . is this something I'm to expect every morning?"

"Only until we finish the job," he said with a smile of apology. "But not to worry. We're making this job our top priority, and we'll do the work as fast as we can. It's a rush job. The homeowner is very clear about that. Still, things take as long as they take, you know. It'll be really nice when it's finished."

"So Mr. Defalle is a demanding client," I said. *De-manding client, demanding employer,* I was thinking.

"He wants what he wants," Nathan said. "But don't we all? To tell you the truth, you can't say you know a client well until the final stages of the project. That's when the real personalities emerge. Will he be Dr. Jekyll or Mr. Hyde?"

"So you don't know him that well yet."

"Mr. Defalle? Not really, no. I've met him a few times, getting the project off the ground, and all that. Seems like an okay guy, kind of quiet, though he got pretty steamed when the building department delayed the start of the job. I noticed he got his own way fast, considering the circumstances. Never even raised his voice. You can't push these county guys around, but somehow Defalle got them to dance to his tune. But there were other delays, things that couldn't be helped, and here we are, starting weeks behind schedule. He isn't happy about that. He wanted it done by now."

"He's impatient."

"No, I don't blame him. He wanted it done for *you,* I think. But I've had other work to do around the property, getting this place fixed up. Stuff you don't necessarily see but really makes a difference in preserving the structures. He's smart to put his resources toward that. Foundation repair, insulation, getting these old buildings ready for winter. And there's more should be done, a little roof repair, some paint—"

"So he's fixing up the place, then?"

"Sure. He hasn't had the property more than two years, and it was quite the flxer-upper when he bought it. An expensive fixer-upper, but a fixer nonetheless. And then right after they buy it, the wife dies, and then he gets in that wreck—so it's not going as fast as he'd like. But we'll get this little old kitchen done lickety-split, you'll see. It'll be real nice."

"What *is* the plan for this kitchen?" I asked.

"Well, I'm going to move the plumbing and the sink over there, and I'm going to fill in that window and put a new window over *there.*" He unrolled some blueprints on the floor and showed me the plan.

"Why?" I asked. "Why take out that window? Why move the sink?"

"Well, the architect wanted to change it so this counter sticks out like that. And you know, it's an old window. The architect thought it should be replaced."

"But look at the view. And this window, it's still got the old glass—" I tried the window carefully. It was a bit stubborn, but it opened.

"The window sticks a little," Nathan said. "But we could probably fix that. It's actually not in bad shape. It could probably stay. I'll tell you a secret. The architect isn't even working on the project anymore. You could probably keep the window if you wanted."

"And could we leave the sink there?"

"Well, sure. It would actually be easier, from a construction standpoint, to leave it there. But the whole idea was to move it over and put a cabinet on that wall, and pull this counter out, like a bar."

"This room is pretty small to be throwing things out in the middle of it. I'd rather have that pretty old window than the counter sticking out."

"Really? Okay." He looked perplexed.

"I know I shouldn't come in here and try to change everything."

"Well, you're the one who has to live here, right?"

"Right." Only temporarily, of course. From all the stories I'd heard about remodeling, the room might not even be finished by the time my stint here was over.

"Well," he said, "I'd need a revision of the drawings. It means modifying the cabinets a little, and a few other things. And like I said, the architect is no longer on the project, so . . ."

"I could do you a sketch. A scale drawing."

"Well, good. Okay. The sooner the better. We're talking further delays here, you know. And that means more money. But your way would actually be less expensive, and this is the time to make any changes in the plan, before we start the work, obviously."

"It's not really my place to order changes," I said. "I can't authorize that, or pay for it. It's not my place."

"Tell you what. You get me that sketch ASAP, and I'll see what it will cost to change the plan, and I'll call the boss and get authorization. Okay?"

I hesitated, but I thought, *What have I got to lose?* It

would be a shame to lose that pretty little window and the lovely view over the sink. I even had an architect's scale and a few other tools left over from my drafting classes, which I had packed with my architecture books. "Okay," I said. "Does this mean I'm stopping your work today?"

"Not exactly. There are some other things we can do to move the project along."

"I guess I better let you get back to work," I said.

"A pleasing distraction," he replied gallantly. "By the way, what's your name?"

SCHOOL STARTED SEVERAL days later, and a routine was established. Louisa and Carlos came in on weekday mornings before I took May to school. During the day I would do errands or help Louisa and Carlos around the house and grounds. I had a lot of free time for reading and hiking around the hills, and sometimes I drove out into the countryside or to the beach, which was a half hour's drive over the beautiful mountain road. May's Aunt Helene visited several times to make sure I was getting on all right, and the two of us were developing a fine rapport. I was pleased with my new home and I loved my car, but often my encounters with May left me dispirited. She was generally a kind, well-mannered, and intelligent girl, but there was no question that she resented me and did not want me there in her life. Whenever she seemed to soften toward me and I began to feel I was making progress with her, her attitude would change, and she would hit me with a cruel remark or simply shut me out.

Still, as the days passed I began to feel I belonged there, and I felt my own worth, even if I was of little use for May, other than as a chauffeur. I learned to love Louisa, who generously helped me to settle in and plied me with delicious home-cooked meals, and Carlos, who brought up from the garden fresh vegetables and flowers for me to arrange. Louisa exclaimed over the beauty of my floral creations, saying it was the sort of thing she loved to see but never had the time or patience to do herself.

"There is always so much to do around this place," she told me.

"Just tell me what you need help with, Louisa," I said.

"Oh, Sarah, you are more help to me than you can possibly know. But there is always something to do. In fact, you know, I have permission from Mr. Defalle to hire some girls, temporary, some extra help, so I can get the place really clean before he comes home, and I plan to do it now that May is back in school."

I thought the house was quite clean already, except for the library. The one glimpse I had been allowed had shown it to be rather cluttered and dusty, but she seemed to like the idea of having the extra help come in, and she deserved all the help she could get, so I didn't argue with her. I enjoyed helping Carlos in the garden, harvesting and weeding and cleaning out the spent plants, and I liked being inside with Louisa, tidying the house and decorating it with flowers and things I found around the house, like a grouping of May's childhood paintings I framed and put on the wall in the hallway, or the cozy seating area near the fireplace I created with a small sofa and an easy chair that had been pushed against the wall and seldom used.

I fell in love with the house—with its rustic simplicity and surprise ramblings, the beauty of the surrounding woods and gardens—and I drank in the distances available through every window in every room, the changing moods of the weather and wildlife as late summer mellowed into early fall. And I fell in love with my car, a throaty, punchy little thing with more power than I needed, but which I enjoyed immensely. The response of the engine when I touched the gas pedal and the way it rounded the corners, climbed the steep hillsides, and navigated the mountain roads with so little effort made me feel like I could fly.

I had more freedom in this new position than I would have dreamed possible; more freedom here than I'd ever had before in my life. I had wings, I had wheels. I had plenty of pocket money and whatever I needed for household expenses. I made my own schedule, although I tended to May's schedule first. Louisa and Carlos would have deferred to me in anything I desired; I came to realize they were relieved and happy to give over the ultimate responsibility for running the household to somebody else, and right now that somebody was me. Because I did not attempt to meddle in their business, that is, the kitchen and the gardens, they were willing to allow me any other liberties I might claim. Louisa was very particular about how the rugs and upholstered furnishings were to be cleaned, but she had no feeling whatsoever for decorating and could have cared less about rearranging furniture. Carlos encouraged me to cut flowers and fill my basket with tomatoes any time I wanted, but I wouldn't dare argue with him about compost and mulching or natural pest control; those were his areas of expertise. It turned out to be a fine arrangement, the two of them and me. We worked well together. My only complaint was that Louisa was feeding me so well and regularly that I feared I would gain back too much of the weight I had lost, though she assured me I was as yet much too thin.

I could have been perfectly happy if I thought May was happy, but I knew she wasn't. Louisa told me often what good I was doing for the girl, and her sincere support helped, but I couldn't see that I was doing all that much for May, besides driving her around. Another thing that bothered me was the suspicion that this position, seemingly so ideal, with all the freedom and ease I could want, might suddenly change when the master arrived home.

Chapter Five

I HAD BEEN living in my new home for almost three weeks when Gatien Defalle returned.

He gave no warning of his impending arrival, or none that I received. It began as a day like any other. The fog burned off early. It was a Friday morning in mid-September, and I drove May to school as I did every weekday morning. As I pulled up to the curb to let her out, she said to me casually, "Oh, by the way, Louisa called this morning. She asked me to tell you she isn't going to be over till later, 'cause she's got some shopping to do."

"Yeah, I wondered where she was this morning."

As she climbed out of the car, May added, "And I'm supposed to tell you we're having some people over for a barbecue tonight, okay?"

"Uh, okay," I said.

Who could it possibly be, I wondered, *coming over for a barbecue?* May had dashed off before I had a chance to ask. Louisa and Carlos never stayed for dinner. May didn't seem to have any friends. None of my friends were in the area. That didn't leave many options. Maybe I had misunderstood. Maybe *she* was going to a barbecue, at her Aunt Helene's, for example. Helene would not invite herself over to our place for a meal, but she might invite us to her place. But I knew Helene would have invited me, too, and she probably would have made a point of asking me herself.

I didn't think about it much after that. I drove home and relished the stillness of the house and grounds, which were even quieter than usual with Carlos and Louisa gone. I realized how seldom I was actually alone on the property. The day wore on, and still I was alone.

In the early afternoon I wandered through the house, taking advantage of the unusual solitude. I could walk into any room, check out any secret corner I had a mind to. I thought at once of the master bedroom, a reflection in a mirror, the large bed with a slate-colored coverlet. What would I find if I looked in the drawer of his bedside table?

I went, instead, to the library.

The door stuck a moment, and I thought it was locked, but then it creaked open, and I went inside. Leaving the door ajar, I switched on one low lamp. The room was stuffy, the tall windows all shut tight and shrouded with draperies. It was a beautiful, well-proportioned room with (I peeked behind the drapes) views of the hillside across the valley. Everywhere, jammed into shelves, piled on the floor, stacked on tables, were books. I began to examine the titles and found a curious jumble. Classic literature, history, philosophy and science, many volumes in German and French, and books on book collecting and rare manuscripts. There were a few a collector of antiquarian books might own, prized more for their age and rarity than their readability. I was amazed at this treasure trove; as a book lover I was impressed by the sheer wealth of reading material, and as a book buyer, by what such a collection might be worth.

I was standing at a table in a darkened corner, examining an ancient, leather-bound volume of Arthurian romances, slowly turning the soft leaves, marveling at the lovely old typeface and the luminous illustrations, when I heard the front door banging shut and voices in the front part of the house. *Carlos and Louisa have arrived,* I thought, disappointed. I had hoped to have more time alone to explore this forbidden room. Not that I was terribly worried about being discovered. I didn't really care if Louisa found me in there, looking at the books. I wasn't doing anything wrong, and having established myself securely as part of the household, I knew I could overrule Louisa's objections to my being in the room, at least for a few minutes.

Then I forgot about Louisa and Carlos. I was engrossed in what I was looking at, and I didn't hear the door open behind me. Startled out of my reverie by the unfamiliar male voice, I very nearly knocked the book off the table.

"I would prefer this part of the house to be left alone, please." A low, resonant baritone. "There's no need for you to clean this room."

I looked up through the gloom of the dimly lit library and I saw him, very nearly in silhouette so that the details of his face were at first indiscernible, and I was startled by the quiet power of his presence. At just over six feet tall, he gave the impression of slender grace, and yet there was significance in the volume of his musculature, in the broad build of his shoulders and his arms, in the weight of his groin and thighs. But the impact of his presence was more than the size of him; it was some force of personality, a combination of inner fire and poise—though it was only later that I came to think of it like that.

"I wasn't cleaning, actually. I was looking at the books." I heard my own voice, articulate and calm, though my heart was suddenly pounding hard in my throat. I knew without question *this* was the master of the house, and I was a trespasser in a place I had been expressly forbidden to enter.

Before either of us could think of something more to say, May, full of energy, charged into the room.

"May!" I was astonished to see her. "What are you doing home? Why aren't you in school!"

"I *knew* you'd be home by now!" she cried, to the man, not to me, and I thought with alarm that she might throw herself at his feet. There was, instead, a curiously bumbling embrace. Gatien Defalle returned his daughter's affection awkwardly. But May didn't seem to notice his stiffness; she spun around in a graceful pirouette, and her happiness at seeing him was almost pitiable.

I had never seen her so high, and I knew at once the presence of this man had infused her with this restless, dancing joy. I understood completely. It was suddenly the same for me.

"I cut my last class and ran home, because I wanted to see you," she confessed to him.

I said, "You did *what?*"

"Oh, I see you've met Governess," May said with a pretty pout, as if noticing for the first time that I was standing there. "How disappointing! *I* wanted to be the one to introduce the two of you. Governess, this is Gatien Defalle. Gatien Defalle, this is Governess."

"Governess?" He looked confused.

"Like in a book," she explained. "Penniless spinster, not particularly good-looking, nothing else going on in her life, why not? She's come to turn my life around. And marry you, of course. Isn't that what governesses do? We couldn't keep calling her 'the lady who is going to be living with us until May starts high school,' now, could we? And *babysitter* is so degrading and humiliating, for her—and more importantly, for me. So I call her Governess!"

"I see," said the man.

With that, May ducked out of the room, leaving me alone with him.

"It's better than *Nanny,* I suppose," I said.

Gatien Defalle took me in with an imperious sweep of a glance. "You're not the girl my housekeeper hired to help clean the place?"

"No, I'm the one *you* hired to take care of your daughter."

"Well then. I am pleased to make your acquaintance," he said formally. Actually, he seemed anything but pleased. He was embarrassed, and he was perplexed, but he had the manners to attempt to hide all that. I wasn't what he'd expected, that was sure. He was about the only one I'd met since I'd come here who didn't say it.

I gave him my hand, and we shook awkwardly. His hand

was large, and warm, and I could feel the strength of him in it, though he held my hand gently, and only briefly.

"I'm sorry," he said, "but I've forgotten your name."

"Sarah," I said coolly. "Sarah Logan." *Quite a father,* I thought. *Doesn't even know the name of his daughter's . . . whatever I am.*

"All right, then, Sarah. How are you and May getting on?"

"Fairly well, considering the situation," I said. "There are some things I would like to talk with you about."

"Anything of great urgency?" he asked politely.

He's mocking me, I thought, bridling. "I suppose that depends on how you define urgency, but no. Nothing of great urgency."

"Your accommodations are adequate?"

"Very much so." I found myself falling in with the formal style of speech he had adopted for this conversation, as a form of hostility, or at least of distancing, which was how I felt he was using it on me.

"I would like to talk with you more and see how you're getting on with May," he said. "But I'm afraid that conversation will have to wait, because I have guests here now."

"Very well, sir," I said, and from the droll expression he leveled on me, I knew my sarcasm was not lost on him.

"After you," he said.

I was being dismissed.

In the hallway, I was about to head off in any direction opposite of him, when he hesitated, and said, "And my original orders stand. The library is not to be disturbed."

"As you wish, sir," I said, tightening my teeth at the word *orders*. "But with all due respect, I must disagree with you about one thing."

"And what might that be?" he asked, and I could have sworn he was holding back a smile.

I blew a spot of dust off my fingers. "That room," I said, "actually *is* in need of a good cleaning."

THE STATE OF equilibrium I thought I had achieved in recent weeks had been overturned in a matter of moments.

I heard Louisa in the kitchen, talking to Carlos, and I heard other voices as well. The master, as I thought of him with just a touch of spite, had brought home with him friends, male and female. May was already home from school—no thanks to me, her chauffeur—and with her father home, I figured my formal obligations for the day were fulfilled. I slipped away down to my own cottage where, I decided, I would indulge myself for the remainder of the afternoon, curled up in bed with *Middlemarch.* Or rather, a portion of *Middlemarch,* as I had torn up my paperback copy of the fat book into manageable chunks. I knew May wouldn't miss me, and with her father's friends around, I would only be in the way.

I heard the construction noise in the cottage before I walked through the door.

"Looks like you're going backwards," I said, poking my head through the plastic sheeting over the door to look in at the job.

"Yeah, well," said Nathan, "we found a little rot we hadn't expected, so we have to fix it before we move on. Speaking of which, since the homeowner is back, I'm going to be talking with him in person about your ideas. We have a meeting set up for tomorrow morning."

I was tempted to tell him to forget about it, but I realized I was just nervous, now that the master of the house had decided to make an appearance. I had worked for hours on that drawing, and I knew my plan was better than the one they were set to go with; better for me, anyway. I was the one living in the cottage, but it was his property, and he could do whatever he wanted with it. He could shoot down my ideas if he wanted to, but I swore I wouldn't be intimidated before he actually said anything.

"Okay," I said. "We'll see what happens tomorrow morning."

"I look forward to it," Nathan replied.

Not only was the little cottage crowded and noisy with the work going on, but now there was a terrible smell coming from the job site, which was, Nathan explained apologetically, due to a chemical he had applied to the floor to prevent further rot. I gave up on my plan to read in bed and took my book outside, but the fog was already rolling in over the hills, bringing the cool wind from the ocean. I heard laughter and smelled the barbecue up on the back patio, so I circled around the house in the other direction and let myself in through the guest room door.

Like every other room in the house, this one was blessed with simple charms: a plump bed, the riverstone fireplace that shared its chimney with the fireplace in the living room, the cozy love seat turned toward the hearth. I chose the love seat for my reading, wanting only for a lamp beside me, but since there was still some daylight glowing from the muslin-curtained windows, I made do without.

Middlemarch is one of my favorite books, but it is a dense read, and usually I fall asleep whenever I attempt it. This time was no different.

I woke suddenly to the sound of low murmuring, an excited, rapid exchange of words between a woman with a husky voice and a man whose deep baritone I recognized instantly, though I'd spoken to him only once before—not an hour earlier.

"I don't know why you always do this to me," the woman was saying. "I don't know why. . . ."

The room was dim; the sun had gone down. I realized they couldn't see me, that I was concealed by the back of the love seat like Rhett Butler at Twelve Oaks when Ashley and Scarlett played out their passionate china-smashing drama.

"I haven't seen you in ages, Gatien," she went on. "I would think you might miss me once in a while."

"You said there was something you had to show me in here, Theta," came the reply, and there was something strained in his voice. Impatience? Or annoyance? But he controlled whatever he was feeling and did not express it.

"You know very well what I'd like to show you, Gatien."

"All right, then," he said softly.

There was a short silence. I heard the rustling of clothing. My heart was drumming, and I was afraid to breathe.

"Wait, wait!" the woman cried. "Please don't go. There *is* something I need to discuss with you."

He let out a long, low groan. "Theta, if this is—"

"It's about May."

His sigh was audible. I heard the creak of the bed; perhaps he was sitting down to listen to whatever it was she wanted to tell him.

"Is it that painful for you, being alone with me?" There was a plaintive note in her husky voice, and a touch of humor that made it very seductive.

What should I do? I was desperate. I had to make myself known to them at once. My God, she'd already got him onto the bed. How long would it take her to complete the transaction? But I was mortified, and I could not bring myself to stir.

"Don't." She laughed at him, gentle and teasing now. "Don't say anything. I know what this is about. I know how *wretched* you are. I know what it is you're trying to avoid; why you run off to the ends of the earth, chasing the races, even though you can't drive worth a damn anymore, can't win anymore—"

"Theta, my dear, sometimes I think if you were a man I'd lay you out."

A soft, feminine giggle. "But I'm not a man, am I, darling?"

Before he could respond, she changed tactics with a sudden shift of tone. "Seriously, Gatien. I wanted to talk to you about May. I'm concerned about this girl you've brought in to take care of her."

"I didn't bring her in. Helene did."

"Anyway—"

"And Helene has the perfect right. It always falls on her shoulders, all the responsibility when I'm away, and she did what she felt was best for May."

"But the girl is ultimately *your* responsibility, Gatien. And do you really think this waif, who looks like she's barely out of high school herself, is suitable for the kind of—"

"To be honest with you, Theta, I don't know how I feel

about this girl. I've only just met her this afternoon—in fact, I mistook her for a maid—and by the way, how do you know how she looks? Have *you* met her?"

"Paul told me about her, and I saw her earlier, down in the garden."

"She *is* striking, isn't she?" he murmured. "That's what's got you all fired up. Paul likes her, doesn't he?"

"I don't care what Paul thinks of her. It's what *you* think that counts with me."

"Right. Now, if you're finished—"

"No, I am not finished. I told you there is something I want to show you."

I'd had about enough of this. *When they start talking about me and whether or not I'm suitable, that's it. I can take no more.*

I sat up.

By the dim bedside lamp I could see Gatien Defalle sitting on the edge of the bed. Theta, a lush brunette and one of the most beautiful women I had ever seen, was in the process of swinging one of her amazing legs over both of his, effectively straddling him, lowering herself down into his lap. During the same graceful choreography, she unsnapped the front of her blouse to expose her round breasts to the man, presenting them in a low-cut lace bra just inches from his mouth, two perfect ripe fruits cupped in a pair of doilies like a delivery from the Fruit of the Month Club.

What might have happened next I can only imagine, because it was then, at that moment, that my presence in the room was discovered. I don't know if I made a sound, or if they caught the movement when I sat up, but they both suddenly turned their heads and locked eyes on me.

"Good God," said the master of the house.

The woman, Theta, was shameless. She lingered over Gatien as she slid her body off of his, watching me with dark, bold eyes, until a thick lock of dark hair fell over her face, which she didn't bother to brush away.

"What are you doing?" Gatien demanded of me. I knew he was embarrassed. More so than he had been in the library an hour ago when he had mistaken me for a house-keeper.

"I fell asleep." My own voice sounded as husky as Theta's. I lifted the book, or rather one chunk of it, to show them. "I was reading."

"Why the devil were you doing it in here?" He was angry, not even bothering to conceal it now. He had risen from the bed, and he seemed to have forgotten Theta, who stood waiting by the door, slowly fastening up her blouse, watching us, one eye still veiled by that hair.

"I'm not allowed in the library," I said pointedly, struggling to keep my own passions subdued. I would not let this man stir me. "There is a very smelly construction project going on in my own cottage. There is a party going on here in the main house, and it's too cold to sit outside, which left me this option. So here I am."

I was proud of how I controlled my temper, but my eyes were flashing fire, no doubt, same as his were. Some current seemed to leap through the air between us, but it wasn't arcing only through the eye contact; it was a high-voltage exchange from the top of the thighs.

He suddenly looked away, and when he turned to me again, he had changed, the current had been rerouted, and there was a quizzical humor in his expression.

"Right," he said. "I see your point."

I was disarmed. I was at a loss. I realized I wanted to be fighting this man. Anything to catch another secret glimpse of him, of that burn beneath the cool self-possession.

The door to the hallway was thrown open, and there stood Paul, the bronze god who had delivered my car the day I arrived at the Defalles, but for a moment I could only blink at him, wondering who on earth he was. I had known I would see him again, but I had not expected it to be like this.

"Ah, there you are!" Paul cried, to none of us in particular. He looked at me, and an expression of delight suffused his already beaming countenance. "Sarah!" he boomed out. "I was *wondering* what happened to you. Do you know Louisa has been looking for you? She's afraid you might be starving to death. I see you've met the indomitable Gatien and my lovely wife, Theta."

His wife? Saints preserve us.

"Yes," I said sweetly. "I was just being introduced."

"She's excellent, isn't she?" Paul demanded, putting this question to Theta and Gatien about me, now, as if I wasn't standing there with them. "Louisa says she's an angel from heaven."

"Gatien thought she was one of the girls helping with the housekeeping," Theta said with a pretty giggle.

"Actually, I am," I said. "I *do* help with the housekeeping. And gardening, and cooking, and shopping, and mending, and chauffeuring, and"—I glanced at the master—"your daughter's homework. All according to my contract." I couldn't keep a hint of scorn from creeping into my voice.

"Keeps you quite busy," Gatien said. He was mocking me again. If he had been caught off guard earlier, he had quickly regained his composure.

"Yes, it does keep me busy," I said.

"And yet it seems you find plenty of time to read books." A pointed volley.

"I like to set a good example for your daughter," I shot back, and a sense of triumph flared in me when he nodded his approval, and his laughing gaze lingered over me a moment before he turned away and ushered his guests back into the other room.

That night, alone in my cottage, I had trouble sleeping. The dense chemical odor still hung in the air, and I could not find the off switch for my thoughts, which were stuck on continuous playback. I kept hearing the master's deep voice, and everything he had said. Every change of tone, every word.

No doubt about it, the serene new life I thought I had achieved had been proven a mirage. The arrival of Gatien Defalle had changed everything.

Chapter Six

"HEY THERE, SARAH, good morning! I brought you coffee."

I was still in my robe when Nathan popped his head through the plastic drapery over the kitchen door. I accepted the coffee eagerly and sat down on a box of books to enjoy it. A fresh breeze blew in from the front door, which I had opened to air out the place, because I could still smell the chemicals Nathan had used to treat the floor joists.

"The coffee is a peace offering," he said. "It's Saturday morning, and you're probably sick of me."

"Well, the faster you get it done, the sooner it will be done, right?"

"Well said." He lifted his cup. "That is a good attitude to take."

"But when *is* your day off?"

He gave me a comical look. "You askin' 'cause you really *are* sick of me, or 'cause you wanna know when I'm free to take you out on a date?"

I didn't answer that. I tried the coffee. It was good coffee. Rich, dark, and strong. Quite a treat after Louisa's famous coffee. I took another look at Nathan. He was able-looking. He had a casual charm, which was easy to roll with. And he appreciated good coffee. Definite possibilities there; I would give a full report to my girlfriend Mallory when next we spoke.

"We're going over your plan this morning," Nathan said. "Maybe you'd like to sit in on the meeting."

I balked at that. A meeting with Gatien Defalle? "I don't know," I said.

"You could—" He stopped. "Well, speak of the devil. Here he is now. Come to check out the job and have our little meeting."

I turned around, and there he was, the master of the house. He rapped on the open door and entered my cottage without waiting for an invitation. It was the first time I'd seen him in bright daylight. We looked at each other and, fascinated, I studied his face in the split second he held it for me to view. He wasn't a handsome man, I thought. But there was something arresting in his expression, and I found it impossible not to look at him, even after he had turned away. He was, in fact, beautiful. There was the classic broody strength about the mouth, an aspect of melancholy in the dark slate eyes. The planes of his cheekbones intersected improperly, which gave him an odd, pieced-together look. An ugly scar raked over his nose, across his cheek, and all the way down to his jaw. His hair was straight and shaggy, the same dark slate color as his eyes. His neck was graceful and strong, his powerful throat exposed at the open collar of the white oxford shirt that he wore over faded jeans.

"Am I late?" he asked, and that strong, broody mouth parted slightly in what might have been a smile. The focus of his gaze moved from Nathan to me, where it rested and seemed to take me in as a whole, from my unbrushed hair to my ratty old robe, gathering some compendium of information and then moving on, dismissing me, it seemed, for his attention was now back on Nathan and the job site.

"We were just talking about the project," Nathan said.

"So, how's it going?"

"Well, slower than we hoped, but then I always account for that." Nathan spoke in his easy, confident way. The men moved into the kitchen, leaving me sitting with my coffee in my tiny living room filled with boxes of books. I listened to them talk, especially attuned to the master of the house, who asked several technical questions. I tried to place his accent, but he didn't say enough for me to get it. He could pass for all-American, even Californian, if there is such a thing, I thought; and yet if he was, why did I hear something in his speech that didn't belong there, something exotic and carelessly elegant, made wholly mesmerizing by the slow vibration of that deep, resonant voice?

I went into my bedroom and dressed. I brushed my hair and took extra care to get it smooth, though it didn't want to cooperate. The bleach-damaged ends tended to frizz and stick out, but my hair was long enough now to be worn tied back. I felt frustrated, looking at myself in the mirror. I did look like I was barely out of high school, as Theta had pointed out. I could try taking that as a compliment, but actually it just meant that I was skinny as a post with no breasts or hips, and my eyes were overlarge, like those pathetic paintings of orphan kids and animals. Then I remembered *he* had said I was "striking," and I wondered what that meant. Something striking wasn't necessarily a thing of beauty. If my looks stood out in any way, surely it was because of my strangeness, the unusual, translucent pallor of my skin. And then I felt annoyed with myself fretting like this over my appearance, something I didn't ordinarily do. The presence of the men working in my cottage had inspired me with girlish energy, which I did enjoy, but it was this particular morning that I found myself taking extra care and attention over what I looked like. It was ridiculous, I decided, and I turned resolutely away from the mirror.

THE MEN WERE outside, down the hill from my cottage, looking at something on the hillside, a post where a bundle of electrical wires converged. I saw them through the little kitchen window I liked so much, and I saw the plans were laid out on a makeshift worktable in the center of the room, my drawings included. I looked out the window again and watched the men climb slowly back up the hill, engrossed in their discussion. For the first time I noticed that Gatien Defalle walked with a limp, as if one of his legs refused to bend the way it should. The limp gave a pathos to the strength that emanated from his presence, and I was captivated. I could not stop looking at him.

I was seized with a sudden urge to flee, to run up to the main house, to check on May, anything to excuse myself from the impending meeting. But I knew she liked to sleep in on Saturdays, when she didn't have an early soccer game, and there was no point bothering her now. So I waited for the men to come back into the kitchen and steeled myself to hear what the master of the house thought about my revised kitchen plan.

"And here she is," said Nathan. "The designer herself."

I felt Gatien's eyes on me, his cool appraisal. How unlike friendly, amiable Nathan he was. Gatien kept his thoughts and feelings to himself. He didn't speak for awhile, letting Nathan go on. Nathan ran his hands over the papers on the table, smoothed out the drawings, and pointed out the differences between the plans and my sketch, though I was sure we all knew what these differences were already.

"Well, what do you think?" Nathan asked at last, looking from Gatien to me and back again.

"How much longer will it take if we do it this way?" Gatien wanted to know, indicating my drawing with a nod of his shaggy head.

"Depends on the building department, more than anything. We'll have to get the changes approved, but that shouldn't be a problem. This is actually an easier plan, so all in all, it shouldn't take much longer or cost much more."

"It shouldn't," Gatien remarked with a cynical smile.

"There are no guarantees in this business," Nathan

said, refusing to be any more specific than that, and I liked him for not making empty promises.

I still had no idea what Gatien was thinking. Was he irritated, having this decision thrust upon him? Nathan had said he was impatient to get the job done, and here I was, slowing things down. Was he annoyed with me, the upstart stranger, coming in and imposing my will on the situation?

"Where did you learn to draft like this?" Gatien asked, turning his attention on me, which I found unsettling.

"I took some classes at a community college," I said.

"Well," he said, "your plan looks better to me than what I got out of that useless architect."

"I'm just the builder," Nathan said. "But I think she's right. This plan makes more sense."

There was a short silence during which time Gatien studied the drawings, evidently making the comparisons again in his own mind.

"Well, then," he said presently. "Let's get on with it, shall we?"

MAY WOKE UP around nine, and at nine-thirty she came to me dutifully and asked me if I wanted to go to breakfast with her and her father and Paul, who had arrived shortly after the construction meeting, without his wife. I could see May was inviting me only because she had been told to do so, and I begged off, as I did once again a few minutes later when Paul sought me out to personally invite me himself.

I was out in the garden, picking tomatoes.

"You disappoint me," he said. "I finally have an excuse to see you, and you turn me down.

I laughed, flattered by his attentions, but they meant something different to me now that I knew he was married. I was actually surprised that I had not been more disappointed to learn he had a wife. I had thought he was the most attractive eligible bachelor I had met in some time. Well, scratch the eligible bachelor part. I knew of married men who were heavy flirts, never letting it go past that,

but given the behavior of Paul's wife with Gatien, I had to
wonder if Theta and Paul didn't have some sort of open
marriage arrangement. But whether they did or not was
of no consequence to me, for I wasn't interested in becoming part of a triangle. Or would it be a rectangle, in this
case?

"Come on, please, Sarah," he said. "It will be so lonely
without you."

"Then maybe you should have brought your wife."

"She's working," he said without flinching. "She has to
work weekends a lot. She's a videographer. She's taping a
wedding today." He spoke of Theta with pride and affection. Maybe he wasn't trying to hit on me. Maybe he was
just super friendly.

Paul finally gave up on me, and when they left, the
house and grounds seemed strangely empty and quiet. It
was Carlos and Louisa's day off. Even Nathan had disappeared. I wandered up to the main house, looking for a
chunk of *Middlemarch,* which I had set down somewhere
and forgotten. As I passed through the hallway, I noticed
the door to the library was open, just slightly, and perhaps
that was the reason I went into the room. Or maybe it was
just a perverse compulsion to do exactly the opposite of
what I had been ordered.

Things looked exactly the same as before, the room
dark and quiet and dusty, and I longed to throw back the
heavy draperies from the beautiful windows, air the place
out, and dust off the tables. For a book lover, this forbidden library was a tease and a torture. I walked slowly
around the room, examining the bookshelves, reading titles. On a lower shelf, a row of notebooks caught my eye.
They were the sort of black speckled cardboard-covered
books used by science students to do their lab work. I
drew out one of the notebooks and opened it.

It was a personal journal, densely written in dramatic,
feminine handwriting. The entries were dated; this journal
appeared to have been written nine years earlier. With
guilty excitement, I began to read.

July 17

What a party last night! I am picking up some very bad habits. Drank too much, flirted too much, talked too much, but what's the use of denying it? I had a fabulous time. Fang got into this big argument with Uther about socialism and American imperialism and the way he talks, you'd think he hated Americans. Does that mean he hates me? He looked incredible in his dinner jacket last night, by the way. I had the handsomest man there, I have to say! I couldn't wait to get my hands on him after the party. Not that he minds.

He's fighting me about this school thing for May. I think she should go to the American school. She gets enough of the French thing here all the time. He gets annoyed with me and my tirades. So what? I'll fight for my way, if I think it's right. I'm going to do what I think is best for my daughter. She is half mine, isn't she? and I don't see why she shouldn't embrace that part of her heritage, too.

So, I was reading the personal diaries of the dead woman whose child I was here to watch over.

August 1

God, the dressmaker was so rude on the phone this morning. You would think she didn't appreciate all the business I throw her way. Of course, I haven't paid my last bill yet, so I can't really blame her for being crabby. She did agree to see me at 3. I hope I can get out of Renee's by then, because Adrian's really going to be put out if I'm late.

She went on about her struggles with the dressmaker, and a cursory flip through the next few pages showed more of the same, so I closed the journal and put it back, took out another one. The pages were filled with passionate, wordy entries describing incidents and encounters, thoughts and feelings; I read a few pages, curious and amazed at the honest, unfettered emotions and opinions expressed. She spoke frequently of the man she called Fang; apparently it was the nickname she used for her husband. Her feelings for him appeared to be mixed; she was obviously crazy about him, but there was a current of tension there, too.

I realized I was looking for evidence of the crazy sister Helene had described. There *was* a sort of manic frenzy suggested by some of the journal entries; Lisa threw herself into certain pet projects and schemes with all her energy; then, only a few pages later, the emphasis would shift, and another object of devotion would take its place, described just as passionately and soulfully.

I put the book back into its place and selected another. I found a similar theme. The writer seemed fixated on her emotional life, which revolved around her child and husband, and her busy, chic social life, but she wrote of other things as well, the arts and politics, musings of a spiritual nature—*What is my purpose? Why am I here?* kinds of things. It was rather touching, but ultimately unsatisfying and dull, as far as I was concerned. I was looking for clues to the present.

I jumped ahead in time, checked out the journals from a more recent era—they were placed on the shelf in chronological order. Each diary held the entries for one year, January to December. I was looking for Gatien's name, and I was not disappointed.

March 23

  Gatien placed third today, very frustrated with his car. He wanted me to be with him at the circuit, but I refused. I just can't watch it anymore. I told him third place is very good, and at least he's accumulating points, but he is only satisfied with winning.

April 4

  Paris. We had a picnic today, but then it rained, forcing us inside. I get so sick of hotel rooms. Gatien says if the

*team can't do better with the car, he'll quit. But of course
he'll never quit, and of course someone else will offer him
a spot. Ferrari has expressed interest, and anyway he's so
high in the points right now, I think he's just frustrated with
the managers and blowing off steam. I do wonder about
that car, though. I hope it won't betray him. . . .*

Prescience? I wondered.

THE SOUND OF the doorbell jolted me out of this other
world I had entered; into which I had trespassed, it would
be more accurate to say. I thrust the notebook back into its
place on the shelf. I let myself out of the library and went
out to the entry hall to answer the door.

It was Helene, May's aunt, the woman who had hired
me, and for this reason, perhaps, she intimidated me a little. I wondered what she would think if she knew I had
just been reading her dead sister's diaries.

"Hi, Helene," I said, holding the door open for her. I always felt I should address her by the name Mrs. Browning, but she wasn't a Mrs., and she really wasn't that much
older than me. "Come on in."

"I can't stay but a minute," she said. "Did Gatien return
home yesterday?"

"Yes, but he isn't here now. They went out for breakfast."

"They?"

"Mr. Defalle, and May, and Paul."

"Oh, I see. Well, I'm glad Gatien made it home safely
once again. And how is May?"

"She's fine, I think. She seems happy to have him back.
But she cut school yesterday and walked all the way
home, just to see him."

"*Did* she?" Helene seemed to be impressed by this, and
not in a good way.

I felt guilty for not having had a better handle on May's
actions.

"Well, that sounds like May," she said in a tired voice.
"It's not your fault, Sarah. Sometimes I wonder if his

presence is good for her, or if he does more harm than good, throwing her off balance the way he does."

I thought the presence of a caring father in a child's life could never be anything but positive, but I understood how the inconsistency might cause problems. Helene wasn't interested in my opinion on the matter, however, and she was already moving on to a new subject. "I wanted to talk to Gatien about this trip we're planning, to my father's beach house up north," she said. "Has he talked to you about it?"

"No, he hasn't."

"We have it scheduled for the last weekend of the month, because May has that Friday off school. You'll be coming with us, of course."

"I don't know," I stammered. "I hadn't heard anything. . . ."

"Well, you will have to come," she said. "They'll need you to drive. I'll be bringing my father."

"I don't have any plans," I said, faintly annoyed. "If I'm invited, I'll come."

"I hereby extend to you a formal invitation," she said with a faint smile. "I think you'll like the place, Sarah. It's quite beautiful, right on the ocean."

"Sounds great. But I wonder if May would prefer having her father to herself for the weekend."

"She might at that, but it's not that sort of occasion. There will be a number of us, family and friends. And that means you, too, Sarah. You're part of the family now."

She was trying to be kind. I didn't know how to respond. I wasn't sure the master of the house would want my company on a family outing. It wasn't like May needed constant supervision, like a toddler.

"Listen, don't you worry about it, I'm arranging everything," she said. "I've got to go to a doctor's appointment now, but I'll talk to Gatien this evening, and I will let you know the exact dates and times."

"All right," I said. Anyway, a weekend at a beach house sounded fine to me.

After seeing Helene out to her car, I went back inside

and considered returning to the journals, to read more. I wanted to know how Lisa and Gatien had met, how their romance had progressed, how they had come to be married and have a child together. And I was curious to know if she had truly been unhappy enough, at the end, to finish it off in the dramatic manner she appeared to have chosen. But it was getting late, almost noon, and I knew they would all be back from breakfast soon because May had a game at one, so I refrained from returning to the forbidden library, though I did go back to make sure the door was left open, just the way I had found it.

I DIDN'T SEE much of Gatien Defalle the rest of the weekend, which was all right with me. When I saw him in the gardens, I went into the house. And when he came into the house, I stole away to my cottage. He made no effort to seek me out; maybe he even avoided me, as I avoided him. And so things went on, almost as before. It seemed he would not be an obtrusive employer, which was a relief. I certainly had no desire to be with him. The problem was, May *did* want to be with him, and he almost seemed to be avoiding her, too.

He spent a lot of time in his garage or out and about on his estate, cleaning and fixing things. May would join him for a few minutes, then wander away. They didn't seem to have much to say to each other.

Monday morning Louisa was back in the kitchen, even more cheerful than usual, singing along to the romantic songs playing on a Spanish-language radio station. She was, I suspected, touched with the same feminine excitement that had infected the other women in the house. No one was immune to the powerful aura of the master. I caught myself singing along with Louisa.

After taking May to school, I came back to the Defalles' and parked in the driveway. I brought out from the house a portable vacuum and some cleaning supplies so I could give my car a wash. I'd never had such a nice car of my own, and felt the pride of ownership, even if I didn't really own it. Wearing old shorts and a T-shirt, I tied my hair up in a bandanna, turned on the radio in the car, and went to work vacuuming the seats and carpet.

"Excuse me, miss."

I was in the backseat of the car, vacuuming, and so I hadn't heard the car come into the driveway over the sound of the radio and the vacuum. I gave a start to see two dark-eyed men staring at me through the windshield. I switched off the machine and the radio and waited to see what they wanted. I thought at first they must be selling something, or wanting to talk about their religion, though we didn't get a lot of that sort of traffic up here at the top of the hill.

"I am Moshe Yaron, and this is Ira Meyer," said one of the men. He spoke with a heavy accent. "We would like to talk with someone about the books belonging to the late Mrs. Defalle."

"The books?" I wasn't sure if he was talking about books, as in books, or as in accounting practices.

"Yes. We have been trying for some months now to get access to her library."

"She had an extensive library," the other man, who sounded like he might have been from Brooklyn, added.

"Oh, I know," I said. "But you would have to talk to Mr. Defalle about that."

"He refuses to talk to us, miss."

I nodded sympathetically. "I believe you."

"It is very important," said Mr. Meyer, who was the taller of the two men, with a fierce, ascetic scowl that seemed to be etched permanently across his brow. "Is there any way you might intervene on our behalf, so that we might have a chance?"

"I don't think I can help you," I said. I was about to tell him I wasn't allowed to look at the library, either, but then I didn't know who these guys were or what they really wanted.

"Please, miss. It is imperative—"

"Can you tell us, please?" his partner interrupted. Moshe Yaron's face was narrow and delicate, his mouth wary. "Has anything been sold from the collection?"

"I really wouldn't know," I said. There was a strange intensity shining forth from the two of them, and it was rather odd and unsettling, the way they were fixed on me with their big, dark eyes. "I don't know anything about it. What are you looking for?"

"We are looking for—"

"It doesn't matter what you're looking for." A new voice cut him off. This one was a melodic baritone and so velvety calm it was more powerful than a shout. "I have asked you not to come around here." It was the master of the house, and he did not look pleased.

He had appeared from who knows where—I hadn't seen him at all that morning—and now he walked toward us across the driveway with his strange limping stride, and there really was something daunting about him, a self-possessed determination that shone from him. I couldn't blame the two dark-eyed men, both of whom were considerably smaller than Gatien Defalle, for backing up a bit, and looking alarmed.

"Forgive me, sir," said Moshe Yaron. "But you must understand, we—"

"I understand enough," said Gatien. "And I want you off my property."

He said nothing more, and did nothing more; he stopped a measured distance away and watched them in silence until they had retreated to their own car, which was parked out near the gate. I gazed after the men, wondering what on earth it was they had been so intent about in that library. When I looked back, the master of the house was gone.

SO THERE WAS something valuable in that collection of old books. I had thought perhaps Gatien Defalle didn't want the room disturbed out of respect to his late wife's memory, but now I wondered whether his motives weren't a bit more mercenary. Maybe the master didn't want anyone else getting their hands on something he intended to cash in on himself.

He appeared again after I had washed my car, as I was cleaning out my bucket and rolling up the hose.

"If you're about finished with this," he said to me, "I'm going to need you to drive me downtown in a few minutes."

I stared up at him, astonished.

He limped off, and I carefully hung the hose on its hook by the garage. Had I heard him correctly? I was pretty sure I had.

The more I thought about it, the more steamed up I got. By the time I was back in the kitchen, putting away the sponges, I was furious.

I turned to Louisa, who was cleaning out the pantry cupboard, and said, "I can't believe he just ordered me to drive him down the hill, just like that! Why doesn't he just drive himself?"

"Who?" she asked, surprised at me. "Mr. Defalle?"

"Yes, Mr. Defalle."

"Well, you see, he cannot drive. That's why he needs you, Sarah."

I understood at once, and was appalled at how dense I could be.

"His leg, it got crushed in a race. He can drive no more."

I thought about it, and no, he hadn't driven anywhere that I'd noticed. After his long absence, he had arrived home with friends, Paul and Theta, in their car. There was that comment Theta had made about him not being able to drive and win races, which I had taken to be some sort of insult to his manhood, not a statement of fact. And when he'd gone out to breakfast with his daughter, Paul had driven once again. Apparently Paul was some sort of designated driver for Gatien. And now it made sense, all the prehiring emphasis on my ability to drive.

Gatien gets really annoyed by bad driving.

It wasn't just for chauffeuring May around. I was to be the master's driver, too. "If he doesn't drive anymore, then where does he go all the time, when he goes away?" I asked. "What does he do?"

Louisa shook her head and looked at me strangely. "I don't know, Sarah," she said.

I WAS REALLY nervous when we got into the car together. It was such a small, intimate, enclosed space, and his presence was so commanding. And yet he was guarded. He kept quiet. Knowing I had to drive the car with him sitting beside me, judging me, well, that made it worse, of course. *Gatien gets really annoyed by bad driving.* He was a professional race car driver! Or had been. How was I supposed to live up to that?

"I'm nervous," I said to him. We were sitting there in the driveway together, and I had just turned the key in the ignition.

He laughed, a surprisingly generous, hearty sound. That was the first time I ever heard him laugh.

"Why?" He really wanted to know. He stopped laughing. "Why are you nervous?"

"Why do you think?"

"Don't worry," he said. "I used to drive for a living. If you have any trouble, I'll be happy to give you some pointers."

I let out a long breath, disarmed once again. I couldn't help grinning. I pulled the car into reverse, and we were off.

"Used to?" I said, when we were on the road.

He cocked his head, not understanding me. His right leg was stretched out long in front of him. The car seemed very small and intimate with him in it beside me.

"You used to drive for a living. Past tense."

"That's right," he said slowly, in that familiar mocking way of his, and I knew I'd blundered. "Past tense."

That was all he said about it.

"So who were those guys who wanted to check out your wife's library?" I asked.

"Sarah, please," he said. "Just leave it alone."

I didn't ask any more questions.

I took him around town on errands. We went to the bank, the post office, and the vacuum cleaner store, for

Louisa. We stopped at the nursery to get something for Carlos, and the bakery, to get something for May. Sometimes I accompanied him, sometimes I waited in the car. Gatien was very efficient, jumping out of the car and running in to do his business. He might not have been able to drive, but his bum leg did not prevent him from getting around quite well on foot, though once or twice he seemed to stumble. Once, when we were coming out of the post office and going down a flight of concrete steps, he lurched a bit and grabbed for the handrail, and I reached for him instinctively, my arms around him for a split second, and I was suddenly self-conscious and hyperaware of this man, of the warmth of him, of the hardness of his belly, and the unmistakable shudder that ran through his body when I touched him.

"Silly girl," he murmured. "I don't need you to help me walk." The encounter was sensual, as well as awkward. I sensed his embarrassment, but there was something else there, too. We both ignored it and were quickly back in the car, on to the next errand.

"What are all those boxes you've got?" he asked me when we were driving, in between stops.

"What boxes?"

"In the cottage. All those cardboard boxes. What have you got in there?"

"Oh, so you can ask me about my personal stuff, but I'm not allowed to ask you about yours?"

"You can ask me anything you want."

"Maybe I'm not interested anymore," I teased him.

"I think you wanted to ask me about my racing career, and whether it's over, and I would have to say yes. But I think that is pretty obvious, given that I can't even drive a street automobile in my current state, let alone a Formula One race car."

"So are you getting physical therapy, or something?" It was a clumsy question, and I regretted my words before they were out of my mouth.

He gave a laugh of derision.

"I mean, are you trying to get back to it? To racing?"

He gave his head an impatient shake.

I stumbled on, making it worse: "You wouldn't be the first athlete to come back from terrible odds. Medical science is pretty amazing these days, and if you have enough drive and ambition to get back out there—"

"And just what do *you* know about drive and ambition?"

His cool presumption infuriated me, and I was about to spit out something rude, but I decided I'd done enough of that already. I let the emotion settle back a little, then said quietly, "Well, maybe not much. But then I haven't been lucky enough yet to find out what it is in life I really love."

He was silent. I parked the car in front of the hardware store, our next stop. He jumped out without a word, leaving me behind.

When he returned to the car, he said, "You know something, Sarah? Traditionally, all of the women in my life—my mother, my stepmother, my sister-in-law, my wife, even May—they've always tried to convince me to stop driving. You're the first one who has ever argued I ought to try to get back to it."

"Is that so?" I started up the car and studied him for a moment. "Could it be that maybe they know something I don't know? Maybe you are simply a bad driver."

He laughed at that. "No," he said with a faraway look. "In fact I was a very good driver."

The mood had changed between us. We were more relaxed with each other now, and at the same time energized by something that sparked when the two of us came together. It was a hot afternoon in mid-September, skies clear but for an orange haze over the East Bay hills. In the evening that cool breath of autumn would steal into the air, but for now, in the midafternoon, it was summer. We had the stereo on loud for Third Eye Blind, and the windows rolled down, the wind blowing through the car.

"It's books," I said.

"What?"

"In those boxes, in my cottage. You asked what they were. They're books."

"What kind of books?"

"All kinds. Novels. Nonfiction. Reference books. School books. History, poetry, anthropology. Architecture, design. Anything I've ever studied, and I've studied a lot of different subjects. I love books. I always think I should get rid of some of them, but I just seem to gather more."

"I've got a lot of books, too," he said without enthusiasm, looking out the window. "They were my wife's, mostly."

"I know," I said drolly. "It's an amazing library. What I've seen of it."

"Yeah, I guess."

"You guess!"

"That library represents something to me I would forget if I could. My wife was rather obsessed with . . ." His voice trailed away.

"I'm obsessed with books myself. It's one of my joys in life." Then, thinking my comment may have been tactless, considering what I'd heard about how troubled his wife had been, I added in a rush, "But of course, I don't know your situation."

"Lisa tended to get obsessed by things," he said. "Always something different. Her latest obsession, before her death, happened to be old books and manuscripts. We always had books, but it started to get out of hand. These books were like rare art. They weren't the kind of things you actually *read.*"

"And you didn't share her interest," I said.

"Me? I like a book for the sake of reading a book. But something just to sit on a shelf and be old? I don't see the point. If it's worth anything historically, it belongs in a museum. But she was a collector, and for her, it was . . . it was not good." He had been about to say something else and changed his mind. And then he said unexpectedly, with a soft vehemence, "Stay away from those guys who came to the house today, Sarah."

What could I say? It wasn't like I was going to go seek them out or something. But I *was* curious about the encounter. "They *did* seem to believe there was truly something of value there, in your wife's library," I said. "Are you sure you don't want to have it checked out?"

"Just stay away from it, Sarah," he said softly. "Please."

I was perplexed. There was a pleading in his voice.

I was about to say sure, okay, but instead I was silent, remembering how I'd already transgressed, had already gone into the room when I wasn't supposed to, had already read the journals. I was already guilty.

"Let's go out to the ocean," he said suddenly.

"The ocean?" I cried, as if he had suggested the moon. "I can't, I've got May."

"You've got what?" He looked confused.

"I've got to pick May up from school," I said with exaggerated patience. "You know, May? Your daughter? School?"

"Right. What time?"

"In about an hour, at three o'clock. The same time as last year. And the year before that."

He didn't seem to pick up on my snide tone. "All right," he said. "We'll get Louisa to pick her up."

"Louisa's got enough to do without me giving her my job on top of it," I said. "I'm not going to ask her on such short notice."

"Ah, she won't mind."

For some reason his cavalier attitude put me off. Was it his utter lack of interest or knowledge of his daughter's schedule? Or his dismissal of Louisa's time as unimportant? Or that he seemed to think I would drop everything on a whim, just to be with him?

"Well, I do mind," I snapped.

He sat back in his seat and put up his hands as if to fend off an attacker. "Okay!" he said. "Forget it. I didn't realize you took your job so seriously."

"Well, of course I take my job seriously," I said with exasperation. "Wouldn't you expect me to? Anyway, it's more than the job, it's about people depending on you."

"I don't think I need a lecture from you about people depending on me."

"Oh don't you? I just think it's a good thing your

daughter wasn't depending on *you* to make sure she gets home today, because obviously it never would have crossed your mind."

"I noticed how well you kept track of May on Friday, when she just showed up at home on her own, an hour before school ended."

He hit a sore spot there. I had wondered what he had made of that! But that wasn't my fault! "Well," I said sweetly, "I wonder what motivated her to do that? The poor child is so desperate for her father's attention she cuts school and walks three miles home and all the way up that damned hill just to see him!"

"A three-mile walk is hardly going to hurt the girl."

"That's not the point. You leave her for weeks on end, and then you blame me for her actions, when she's made it quite clear all she wants is to be with *you.*"

"And you have made it quite clear that you do not," he said preemptively. "So forget I ever mentioned going to the beach. Let's just go home."

I WAS MISERABLE. I realized I had come to feel very much at home in the Defalle household. I liked my job. I liked the challenge of May. I liked my cottage and the neighborhood and the people I worked with. I liked the money and the freedom and the sense that I was finally doing something with my life, however mundane and temporary, that mattered. Because I could see I was making a difference in the lives of these people. But now maybe I had gone and made one difference too many.

I could not believe I had spoken in that manner to someone who was supposedly my boss. I say supposedly, because I was sure I had gone and lost the position for myself. The way I had lashed out at him, he would have every right to fire me, no bonus included. After all, the conditions of my employment were to be there for a girl whose father was frequently out of town. What business did I have, then, criticizing him for that very thing?

That evening, May came down to my cottage.

"He wants to speak with you," she said. "As soon as possible."

I FOLLOWED HER up to the main house, but she disappeared before I could thank her, or ask her where I might find her father. I heard music coming from the rec room, so I went down the stairs and found Gatien there, shooting pool.

"Ah, Sarah, come in," he said. There was something of the formality about him that I had noticed the first time we'd met. "Would you like a drink?"

I noticed a short glass of something the color of amber sitting on the edge of the pool table, so I nodded. "I'll have one of those."

He handed me the stick and went to the bar. He poured whiskey over a couple of ice cubes in a glass and brought it to me, and we made an exchange: the cue stick for the drink.

The drink was shocking and bracing and good. I stood by the French doors, looking out at the lights on the bay. God, it was beautiful. The view of the bay at night was just as spectacular as the view by day.

He expertly finished sinking the balls.

"I want to apologize," I began.

"Please don't."

"If I could take back what I said to you today, I would. It's no business of mine—"

"That's where you're wrong, Sarah. It *is* your business. I should be glad I hired someone strong-willed enough to make it her business, because that's what you're here for, isn't it? I can see now Helene was right. And you were right. But it's going to take some time. I've got some loose ends to tie up. Some things just can't happen overnight. And there are things I can't control. . . . And that's why May needs you. That's why I need you."

"I'm sorry, you've lost me," I said, flushing, from the alcohol, probably. I could feel the heat on my cheeks and my neck.

"No." He shook his head. "I can't believe that."

"No, I mean, I'm not sure I understand what you're saying. Loose ends?"

"Never mind," he said gently. "I just wanted to tell you I have to go out of town again tomorrow. We can talk more when I get back."

"So . . . you're not going to fire me?"

"I've been trying to think of what I could do to get you to stay."

"You don't have to do anything."

"I am a man of action," he said, and now it seemed his familiar mockery was turned on himself. "It is often difficult for me to do nothing, when I could be doing something. But sometimes doing nothing is the best thing. Don't you agree?"

He looked at me sadly, and I felt he was trying to impart some message through his cryptic words, his sober expression, and his body language, which was much more standoffish and formal than it had been just that afternoon. He was asking me to stay, but he was letting me know that if it was to work, we must maintain a businesslike relationship.

I agreed. I finished my drink a little too quickly, declined his polite offer to play a game of pool, and went back to my cottage. I felt slightly buzzed and floaty. Something of his melancholy had touched me, but I was at peace, just knowing I was to stay on.

Chapter Seven

I LOVE THESE flowers," I said. "The way they grow wild and tangled alongside the road."

May and I were walking along Winding Hill Road together as the sun was setting behind the hill. We had just reached our own gate when we stopped to admire the brilliant colors of the flowers, coral red and yellow and orange. I liked the messy tangle of stems spilling over the wall, and the lily pad leaves.

"Look at this one, it's like a yellow skirt with bright orange stripes." May stopped to pick the flower. "What kind of flowers are these?"

"I can never remember what they're called," I said.

"They're nasturtiums." This information was given to us by a woman who was walking her dog past our gate. I recognized her as one of our neighbors from down the hill; I had seen her walking her collie on a number of occasions. She cut a stout figure in her tweed jacket and linen skirt, her just-starting-to-gray brownish hair chopped thick to her shoulders. "The flowers are good to eat, you know," she added.

"Are you serious?" May scrunched up her nose with distaste.

"Oh, quite serious," said the woman. I could hear in her voice the remnants of what I guessed had once been a thick Scottish brogue.

"I think I've heard that," I said. "They're supposed to be good in salads."

"I dare you to eat it, Governess!" May thrust the flower at my face.

I took the flower in my fingers and looked it over. "No bugs," I said. "And Carlos never puts pesticides on anything. Why not?"

May squealed as I ate the flower. At times she seemed very young. "What does it taste like?" she asked.

"Like tender lettuce," I said. "It's good. You should try it."

"No way. Some deer probably peed on it." She giggled. She ran on ahead into the house, while I stayed and talked to our neighbor for a few minutes. Her name was Ellen Bruce, and she was a repository of information, well-versed in the history of the hill and its residents. She seemed to know more about the Defalles than I did.

"Shame about the child's mother," she said with a sharp cluck of her tongue. "She was a lovely lady, not that I ever got to know her well. They hadn't been living here a year when she passed. Then, what—a month later? The child's father had that horrific accident. He was in the hospital for weeks, and when he finally came home he had to have a man to help him around. The doctors said he'd probably never walk again, but within three months that attendant of his was out of a job!" She shook her head, clearly impressed. "Though why anyone would do such a thing as drive a car at those speeds, I can't comprehend. All right, then, Mac," she said to the dog. "I see you're eager to be getting on." She rested calm gray eyes on me and patted my arm. "I know the child's father is gone much of the time," she said. "You call on me if you need help with anything. I'm in the white cottage, you know the one, down past the fork in the road."

"Yes, I know the one. Thank you," I said. "I appreciate that."

"I do wonder about you two girls all alone in that house. . . ."

Her concern was touching, and I liked her friendly solidity. I realized I was happy to know she was there, just a quarter of a mile down the road.

IT HAD BEEN arranged that Friday morning May and I would pick up Gatien at the airport and continue on up north to the beach house. All through the week, I felt May's anticipation and excitement, and though I really didn't want to be, I was excited, too.

It was the idea of a little vacation at the beach that I was so looking forward to, I told myself. I'd been at the Defalles' for over a month now, and it would be good to shake up the routine a bit. I decided the occasion would be a good excuse to take May out shopping for a few new things to wear.

I was wary, wondering how she and I would do together; it was such a potentially loaded activity, shopping for clothes. But I needn't have worried. We were like girlfriends, trying on clothes together, sharing our thoughts about what looked good and what wasn't working. I found she had a good sense of style and expensive taste. She wasn't afraid to voice her opinions, and she seemed to want me to express mine.

"Why do you always wear those baggy T-shirts?" she demanded, rejecting some of the pieces I had elected to try on. "You have a nice body. You ought to show it off more."

Ah, a compliment. My clothes were all too big, it was true; though I'd gained back some of the weight I'd lost when I was sick, my old clothes still hung on me, and I had a tendency to pick out the same sort of thing I'd always worn. Trying on some new jeans and tops, even a dress or a skirt, I began to feel like a new person. Some of my curves had returned, thanks to Louisa's good cooking, and the clothes May picked out for me showed them off.

Of course, finding clothes that looked nice on May was easy, with her willowy figure and long, graceful bones. To my surprise, she rejected anything for herself that was overly tight or suggestive. I thought it just as well that a beautiful thirteen-year-old girl was content to dress conservatively, though it seemed odd. I had been wondering if I'd be challenged to censor her choices, but I ended up encouraging her to be a little more daring, just as she did with me. She seemed pleased with what she had chosen, and by the time we headed back to the car, loaded with shopping bags, we were both in excellent spirits. During our time at the mall, I began to feel we were actually making progress in our relationship. I never thought I'd say it, but—hooray for the mall!

We got home from our shopping trip to find a bunch of flowers propped up against the front door. They were unusual, large, bell-shaped flowers, tied together with a bit of twine. May stopped when she saw them, staring at them with distaste.

"What's this?" I said, picking up the bunch of flowers and smelling them. They had a pungent, sweet odor that was oddly affecting.

"Must be from your secret admirer," May said.

"Or yours," I quipped back.

"Why don't you eat them?" she said. "You like to eat flowers so much."

"Maybe I will. *Yum.*" I lifted the flowers and opened my mouth as if to take a big bite of one of the waxy white bells.

"No, lady."

I was startled by the sudden appearance of Carlos, who materialized beside me on the porch and slapped the flowers away from me.

"Poison," he said. "Very bad. To kill you."

Where in the heck had *he* come from? I'd had no idea he was there, watching us. I felt silly, and irritated with Carlos, because he had scared me, appearing like that so abruptly, knocking the flowers out of my hand, like I was really going to eat them, which of course I wouldn't, not knowing what they were.

It was a little thing, but for May and me both, it was off-putting. Neither of us wanted to pick up the bunch of flowers, which were lying on the porch now, looking a bit ragged for the struggle.

Carlos bent and picked up the flowers. He held them away from himself, looking uncertain.

"You want to put them in water?" I suggested. "They're pretty."

"No," said May. "Throw them away. Please, Carlos. Just get rid of them."

GATIEN WAS WAITING for us outside the terminal when we drove up. He was dressed well, businesslike yet with some casual flair that I attributed to his European connections. He wore a dark brown suit with a wide pinstripe, but instead of a shirt and tie he had on a dark blue sweater with just a hint of a white T-shirt collar showing, which set off his masculine, beautiful neck. He looked dashing and elegant and yet casual and offhanded, as if he had just thrown on whatever was lying over his bedside chair; but I was sure it was calculated. His hair had been cut since I'd seen him last; he was no longer shaggy, and there was that familiar formality about him he seemed to cultivate.

His attitude toward me brought to mind the deliberate distancing we had tacitly established the last time we were together. He greeted me with cool politeness. Toward May he was scarcely more demonstrative; the hug they shared was awkward and brief. But May didn't seem to find anything lacking in him, and without being asked, she graciously hopped into the back so he could have the front passenger seat, which was more comfortable for his leg. He seemed in good humor, happy to be out of the airport and on the road.

Conversation between the three of us was halting, at first, and it was difficult with May being in the back, so we mostly just listened to music, and sometimes May sang. I absorbed that haunting soprano of hers right through my pores. There was something clumsy about the three of us together; we had never been captive in each other's company for any length of time, like this. The music helped dispel the awkwardness between us. We took turns picking CDs from a well-stocked case; Gatien picked *The Joshua Tree,* May went for *Mozart's Greatest Hits.* When it came to my selection, I put on Loreena McKennitt, whose pure, mystical singing voice reminded me of May's. We were nearly finished with that one when we reached our destination, and I realized for the first time I had let myself relax in Gatien's presence. Then we arrived at the beach house, and it was time to become part of the larger group.

THE PACIFIC STRETCHED out blue and huge and high to the horizon. The shingle roof of the house was the size of a postage stamp against the immense expanse of ocean as we dropped down from Highway 1 into the little clifftop hamlet, where the Browning vacation house was nestled in a grove of wind-bent cypress and Monterey pine. The narrow driveway leading from the highway to the house cut briefly through the woods, and between the criss-crossed trunks of the trees ahead, I caught a glimpse of a fleeting Satyr with dark, curly hair. By the time we drove past, he had vanished.

"Was that Dimitri?" I asked, but neither Gatien nor May had seen him.

"You can park right there," Gatien said, directing me to stop in front of the detached garage, where another car was already parked. I recognized Helene's Mercedes.

"How old is this place?" I asked, looking about appre-ciatively at the sweet rustic buildings and the ocean, huge and present beyond the grove, triangles of blue behind the dark pattern of tree limbs.

"I don't know," said Gatien. "It's old."

"From all the little details in the woodwork and the construction, I'd say it must be nearly a hundred years old."

"Are you some sort of building expert?" May asked, challenging me.

"No," I said, "I'm not an expert at anything. I worked for a construction company for a couple of years. We specialized in vintage house restoration."

"Were you a carpenter?"

"Not that year, no," I said, unruffled, knowing she was making fun of me. "I worked in the office, typing proposals and invoices, drawing up contracts, handling customer service, accounting, ordering, answering phones, scheduling jobs, bookkeeping . . ."

"Is that all?" Gatien teased me.

"So, the prodigal granddaughter has arrived!" It was Helene; she had just opened the front door and stood waiting for us to come up the flagstone path. She was dressed in baggy jeans and an army-green T-shirt, her faded dark hair pulled back in a bun at her neck. Helene was a puzzle to me. She did nothing to make herself look attractive, with her hair or makeup or dress, and so probably looked older than she was. Despite that, or maybe because of it, I thought she was a very beautiful woman, especially her eyes, which were cool and gray and steady.

"May," she said, "your grandfather has been asking after you every ten minutes since noon. He keeps saying, 'Where *is* she? Where's May?' "

"Here I am!" May called out. She seemed younger than usual today, and happy, dancing along the path with her graceful tiptoed leap, her slender arms like wings stretched to catch the wind. She hugged Helene quickly and ran into the house.

"How was your drive?" Helene asked us.

"Beautiful!" Gatien and I said it at the same time, looking at each other. His injured, unusual face was shining. We all laughed, and I felt a rush of heat up my neck, and I turned away from them to look out at the ocean.

"This place is fantastic!" I exclaimed.

"Come in, Sarah," said Helene. "Grandpa wants to say hi to you."

•   •   •

I HAD ESCAPED out to the terrace after paying my respects in the living room to Mr. Browning, Helene's father, May's grandfather. He was a sweet old man, but rather difficult to get away from, once he had you. Gatien had disappeared as soon as we arrived, May was in the kitchen fixing herself a sandwich, Dimitri had not reappeared (assuming it was Dimitri I had seen), and Helene was making sure all the beds had enough blankets. That left me to sit with Mr. Browning.

When I asked him what the weather was supposed to be like for the weekend, his response somehow led into a dissertation on the weather patterns of the north coast of California. That led into a story about a leaky roof, which generated a detailed catalog of all the repairs he had made to the beach house and its outbuildings during the forty-odd years he had been custodian of the family compound.

"You have a house beside the ocean, you're asking for trouble," he told me. "You know some of these places have been completely lost, eroded away. The cliffs collapse beneath the house. It all just goes. Here, so far, we've just had the usual tussles with the forces of nature. Shingles and shutters ripped off in gale-force winds. Salt damage. Rot. But the forces of nature, they take their toll, you know. . . . Mother Nature changes everything, eventually."

I wondered if he was thinking about his daughter, a victim of drowning. Forces of nature taking their toll.

"Lisa, now, she was the most powerful force of nature of all!" His chuckle seemed forced, and I was startled when he mentioned Lisa just like that, when I was thinking of her, but maybe that was just the natural progression of thought, in this case.

"You should have seen the repairs we had to make to the place after the vandalism," he said. "She was the worst thing ever come through, more than any storm. But you have to remember she was only fourteen years old at the time. She ran away from her mother's home in Nevada and hitchhiked out here by herself. She was resentful, because she thought she wasn't getting her fair share of

things. Helene got to come to the beach house quite frequently. That's just how things were. But you know how
children are about things being fair."

I nodded, wondering why one sister got to come to the
beach house frequently, and not the other.

"Looking back," he said, "there're a few things I would
have done differently. Then maybe things would have
turned out differently. Makes sense, right?"

My interest was aroused when he spoke of May's
mother, but he went back to the topic of household main-
tenance. Finally Gatien reappeared, and I used the break
in conversation to withdraw to the terrace. Outside it was
windy and cool, and I could see a faint whitening of the
horizon that I knew meant the fog was on its way. But for
now the sea and sky were shades of deep, faded blue, and
the air was sweet and wonderful to breathe in. I leaned
over the stone parapet that looked out over the cliffside,
down to the beach far below.

I felt the warm hands clap over my eyes, felt the heat
of his body near mine.

"Guess who?" he said, but I had already guessed
wrong. I spun around, practically falling into Dimitri's
lean, sunburned arms.

"Hello, Sarah Logan," he said.

"Hello, Dimitri."

"I turned eighteen three days ago."

"Happy birthday."

"Thought you should know."

"Why?"

"I'm no longer jailbait." He slyly arched one black
brow.

"I'll keep that in mind."

"Do you like our little enclave here by the sea?"

"It's fantastic."

"That's where the body was found." He pointed toward
the north, where the cliffs jutted into the ocean and
formed a small cove.

"You mean May's mother?"

"They weren't even really sure it was a drowning.

There was some speculation the victim was killed else-where and the body dumped into the ocean. But I discount that theory."

"You mean May's mother?" I repeated, sharper this time.

He looked at me coolly. "The body was too badly de-composed to be sure."

I didn't like his brutal telling of the story. What if May overheard? Or Gatien? Or perhaps Dimitri didn't even bother to spare them what he felt free to say to me. But he *must*. Gatien would never put up with it, not around May.

"What's the matter, Sarah?" he asked innocently. "Did I say something to upset you?"

"Are you trying to upset me?"

"No. I only wondered how much they've told you."

"*They* have told me virtually nothing."

"Aren't you curious?"

I thought about that. I *had* been quite curious at first. But lately I found I was more apprehensive than curious about what I might find out if I was too inquisitive. I was beginning to like these Defalles, and I didn't want any-thing to mess that up.

Coward, I said to myself.

"You *are* curious," he said before I could think of some way to reply. "Despite my warning on the day we met."

"To mind my own business."

"Yes. So you *do* remember. My warning is vaguely pulling at the edge of your consciousness, a faraway bea-con. But you've come to the land of the lotus eaters. You've eaten the drug, and now you want to be like them."

"Dimitri, you're weird."

"Thank you. Don't worry, Sarah Logan, I will protect you."

"That is a great comfort to me."

He ignored the jibe. "I protect May. And I will protect you, too. Farewell for now!"

He jumped up on the wall and then leaped off on the other side. It appeared he had leaped over the edge of the cliff, but when I moved closer, I saw the land leveled off just beyond the footing of the wall before dropping down to the sea, and I saw a trail there, leading into the woods. But Dimitri had vanished.

I HEARD THE slam of car doors, and I walked around to the front of the house. Theta and Paul had arrived, she with her long dark hair pulled back in a scarf tied beneath her chin like a '50s starlet, he with bronzed waves, a golden lion's mane, such a beautiful couple they were, a perfect contrast, the shining and the dark.

"Hello, Sarah!" Paul shouted, and I waved. Theta looked through me and walked into the house.

Paul lingered behind. "When did you arrive?" he asked me.

"Not an hour ago."

"Good drive?"

"Great."

"Gatien not too hard on you, then."

"No, why? Should he be?"

"He always nags at me about *my* driving."

"Well, if he did that to me, I'd leave him behind," I said.

"I think you would," he said approvingly.

We went into the house, and Paul instantly enlivened the place with his boisterous humor and flirty friendliness. Gatien came to greet him, and the two men embraced with enthusiasm. Gatien turned to Theta and let her kiss him on the cheek; if he felt awkward with her, it was hard to tell. May and Helene came into the living room; there were greetings all around. After what I considered a polite interval, I drew away and wandered off. I was an outsider within this intimate group. I felt welcomed, mostly, but if I were to really become one of them, it would have to happen gradually.

I found the stairway down the cliff, and I took my shoes off and left them at the top before descending. Down on the beach the tide was coming in, and walking along the edge of the broken waves, I found I had to dance to keep out of the water, which was shockingly cold. The water was so cold it seemed to stop the blood in my legs when it rushed up the beach, swirling around my bare feet and ankles. The beach was steep and fell away abruptly. I felt the sand give way beneath my feet. The pull of the water was surprisingly strong, like it wanted me, wanted to take me out to sea.

At last my way was barred by the incoming waves churning onto the rocks at the end of the curved beach. I climbed up on some boulders near the cliff and sat on the rock with my arms on my knees to watch the endless succession of waves.

Growing up in Santa Barbara, I never tired of looking out at the ocean; I sometimes thought I would be content to simply look out at the broad, mutable horizon forever, like gazing into the eyes of a lover. But this coastline was unfamiliar to me. It was wilder, the cliffs higher, the rocks more jagged. Even the sand was coarser and darker. This ocean had a different spirit than the waters off Santa Barbara. I felt at home on beaches from Rincon to Gaviota; there was something distinctly different about these north coast shores. Like the difference between domestication and wildness. Wildness was danger. I found it powerful and primitive and extraordinarily beautiful. A great surge of happiness rose in me, just to be there.

Down the beach I saw him, walking along the shore, looking almost dejected. Something in Gatien's awkward stride always pulled at my heart. It wasn't so much pity as wonder at how he managed to be so virile and graceful, despite his limp. Was he in pain? He never let on.

In a few moments, he would be close enough to notice me sitting perfectly still on the rock. I wondered if he would maintain that formal reserve with me, even here on this wild, rocky beach.

But before I could find out, another figure appeared in the distance. It was Theta, slender and agile, hurrying along the sand to catch up with Gatien. He lifted his head and turned at the sound of her approach. When he saw her, he backed up a few paces, almost stumbling into the foam of an incoming wave. She reached out and grabbed his hand in hers, trying to reel him in to her, but he was too strong for her, and he managed to hold her off. He was laughing, and the contact was playful. She surrendered to his superior strength; they dropped hands, turned away from me, and walked away together, side by side, and soon they were out of sight.

"THIS PLACE HAS been in our family a long time," Helene said. "My great-grandfather—or was it my great-*great*-grandfather? Well, he owned a lumber mill where the river meets the ocean, near Mendocino. He got rich from cutting down the huge old redwoods, and he built himself a grand mansion up north a ways. The family sold that house off eventually, but they kept this place on the beach. It's called Flotsam, and the annex is Jetsam, because the original cabin on the site was built from logs that washed in from the ocean. Here, May, I think they'll need this about now."

She instructed May to bring a platter out to the men, Gatien and Paul, who were tending the barbecue on the terrace.

May's grandfather wandered into the kitchen. It was the first time I'd seen him out of his chair since we had arrived.

"When do we eat?" he wanted to know.

"It's almost done, Dad," Helene assured him. "They're taking the chicken off now."

"Smells good," he said. "Do you want that water running in the sink?"

"I got it," I said. I turned the water off, and then I went into the dining room and surveyed the table, upon which was set everything we could possibly need for a buffet-style feast. Salads, vegetables, and bread, plates, flatware, napkins—

"Helene, what about salt and pepper—?" I turned and nearly collided with Gatien, who held a platter of hot meat and roast corn.

Why did I want to read significance into every look he

leveled upon me, every time I encountered him? Maybe he gazed at *all* the ladies with that enigmatic, melancholy expression of his that seemed to convey so much yearning. He swerved smoothly around me and set his platter on the table, and I went back into the kitchen.

MOST EVERYONE HAD filled their plates, and they were eating, perched in various spots around the dining room and terrace. I stood talking with Helene in the kitchen.

"Looks like it's Dimitri and May," she said. "The next generation. I only hope they can continue to keep up the place. The pressure is on to tear down these old cottages and put up multimillion-dollar mansions."

"I don't know about Dimitri," I said, "but I know May loves it here. I'm sure that runs in the family."

"Yes, her mother had a thing for the beach house, too. Lisa didn't get to know this place and love it the way I did, though. She lived in Nevada with our mother for most of her childhood."

"You lived apart from your sister, growing up?"

"Yes, after my parents split, when Lisa and I were quite young, she went to live with my mother. I got my dad."

"What about the other sister? Dimitri's mother?"

"Kate. She came along later. She's actually my half sister, born after my parents divorced, to my mother and her new husband. The two of us weren't terribly close, as girls, which I suppose is no surprise, since we grew up living apart. But I am enjoying having her son live with me, and I think it's been good for him."

"He says so."

She looked at me, surprised. "Does he?"

"Yes. First time I met him, he told me it's worked out well for him to come live with you. He told me you were 'cool.'"

"That *is* a compliment, isn't it?" she said, pleased. "I never had children of my own, and up until quite recently I never thought I'd regret it. Never any children, never married. But I've had the consolation of taking in Dimitri, and May, for a time, when her father was injured. . . ."

"You might still have your own," I said. "You're young."

"I'm nearly forty and too set in my ways, I'm sure. When I was in my twenties, my father was ill for several years. I took care of him, and I think I spent a lot of my time with him when I might otherwise have been socializing, you know, going out with friends, meeting people. Dating. But of course it was worth it; my father got well. I learned to be very self-sufficient. And I always felt he was very grateful for my help."

I nodded, thinking about what a devoted caretaker I'd had in Dorothy, my stepmother, who had let me live with her when I was sick and had lost my apartment because I couldn't pay the rent. I mentioned this to Helene, who was connected to my stepmother as a distant relation.

"She had even canceled plans for a trip to South Africa," I said, "because she didn't want me to be left alone. That's something I can never repay."

"It's often assumed we have only to make up our minds to know exactly where we're going in life." Helene said. "But sometimes there is only one path we can take, or should I say, only one option, which is no choice at all. I had no choice but to take care of my father."

"Did you get much support from your sister Lisa?" I asked.

"If you had known Lisa, you would know why that is almost a funny question," Helene answered. "She was rather more of a taker than a giver. Even before she moved out of our mother's house, she was draining my father of his resources, financially and emotionally. She was his baby, you know, five years younger than me. It killed him to let her go, when my mother took her away. But it was either give her up, or give up the both of us. That was the deal. I don't know if it was such a good thing to do to one's children. I don't think my father ever felt happy about the way things worked out. Later in life, Lisa took advantage of his feelings of guilt, I suppose. Or perhaps it was our mother who was to blame." She smiled ironically. "But after our mother's death—by that time Lisa was practically grown up—it was even harder for my father. Lisa showed up one day, announced she was going to live in California, and demanded his support. That was just the beginning. Of course he couldn't deny her anything. Didn't want to deny her anything. He'd been deprived of her for so long he wanted to shower her with every good thing. Can't blame him for that. And I guess you really can't blame her, either, that she took advantage of it."

"Is it difficult for you?" I asked, thinking of what Dimitri had told me. *That's where the body was found.* "Coming here, to your family's beach house, with all the associations?"

"You mean, because she killed herself out there? I'll tell you, Sarah. It wasn't the first time she'd tried it. She took a bottle of sleeping pills in my father's house in Palo Alto when she was sixteen. At the age of thirty-three, she finally carried out her intention. And there were other attempts in between. So I've got the associations, everywhere."

"That has to be hard."

"Well, yes. But it is all over now. Isn't it? If only my father could accept that." She sighed, and I sensed her anxiety for the old man. "Well," she said. "Let's go eat. You must be starving, and me babbling on about my family."

I went to the table and filled my plate, thoughtful. I had a feeling about Helene—she wasn't as stoic as she pretended to be. Her sister's suicide troubled her more deeply than she wanted to admit.

What *if,* I thought. What if it could be proven Lisa's death was an accident? Wouldn't that be some comfort to Helene, her sister? To her daughter, May? To Gatien, her widowed husband? It would have to be better, knowing someone you loved had left the game of life not of her own free will, but unwillingly. Accidentally. What if it could be proven?

The diaries, I thought. Lisa's journals. What if her diaries reflected the truth? What if she had kept a written record of her thoughts and feelings, right up to the time of her death? There would have to be a clue there.

And I bet I wouldn't be the only one who had thought of this.

But what if no one else had? What if it was I, Sarah Logan, who was to discover the pivotal journal entry for the date immediately preceding Lisa's death? *Dear diary, I love life and I intend to live forever with my wonderful husband and child. I can't wait to see what tomorrow will bring. . . .*

But then that would bring up another question. If Lisa didn't do herself in, was it possible, as Dimitri liked to insinuate, that someone else had done it for her?

Dimitri was so far-fetched in his manner and with the remarks he made that I took very little of what he said seriously. Still, it was obvious he knew something of what had really happened. How much of what he said was actually true?

"Don't tell me you're not going to try the chicken." The voice was low and seductive in my ear. It was Paul, who had joined me at the table to load up his plate a second time.

"I am. I just haven't got to it yet."

"Thank God. I feared you were a vegetarian. Theta's a vegetarian, poor thing."

"I take it you're not."

"Indeed, no."

"Did you grill this meat, then?"

"I like to think I helped, but nah, it was Gatien. He's quite handy with fire, you know."

"I don't doubt it."

"And remember, Sarah. You must fight fire with fire."

I glanced up at him, alerted. Did he know about my clashes with Gatien? He was studying me carefully, but I couldn't tell what he was thinking.

He speared a small morsel of meat on a fork and brought it to my lips. As I opened my mouth to accept it, Gatien walked into the room.

"Hey," he said, "she can feed herself, can't she?" The annoyance in his tone was obvious. He grabbed a bottle of wine off the table and left the room abruptly.

Paul and I looked at each other.

"Were we being rude?" I asked.

"I don't think so," Paul said.

"I understand he's quite particular about table manners. According to Louisa. And May."

"Don't worry about it; come on, let's go sit down. Just remember what I said: fight fire with fire."

Most everyone retired early that night, myself included, though I was too keyed up to sleep; overtired, probably, from the long drive up the coast and settling in to the strange surroundings. May slept soundly in the bed next to mine. Gatien, I knew, had the room beside ours, sharing with Dimitri. Helene and her father each had a room, and Paul and Theta had the small annex just off the main house, the cottage called *Jetsam*.

How had Lisa died? I kept thinking about it, asking myself the same questions. Was it possible to prove her death was not a suicide? What did Gatien know about his wife's death? What was he hiding beneath his enigmatic exterior? He never spoke of her, not to me, anyway. I thought of Theta, beautiful Theta, how she made no bones about her desire for him. He fended her off, but was that just for show? It was certainly inconvenient that she had a husband . . . a husband who was Gatien's good friend. Had they found it even more inconvenient, when Gatien had a wife? Were they secretly pleased he no longer had a wife?

These were disturbing thoughts, and I tried to shut them out, tried to stop thinking.

Finally, I fell asleep.

I heard the moaning through the thin walls of the beach house, and I sat bolt upright, fully awake. It came from the room next to mine, a deep, guttural groan. It was Gatien. I heard a sudden outburst of swearing, in which I recognized the voice, if not the vocabulary. He did not habitually use those words. I was awake in an instant, my ears straining to hear more. And so I did. It was the sound of a man in the throes of some savage exhilaration, his physical passion too intense to control. The involuntary "Ah—ah—ahhhh—" hit me so strongly I was up out of bed in a single motion, pacing the floor, listening, horrified and fascinated.

The moaning died away.

I let myself out of my room, disturbed and disoriented. My first thought was that it had been Gatien and Theta in the room next to mine, making violent love. But what about Dimitri? Wasn't he sharing the room with Gatien?

But when I got to the living room, I saw Dimitri sprawled out on the sofa, innocently snoring. I got a drink of water in the kitchen and went out to the terrace.

The air was biting and wet. Mist swirled around the buildings and through the trees, white and glowing and softening the roar of the breakers on the rocks below. The sky was completely blotted out, and all that remained was this close, cold presence, the fog.

Here I stand, in a cloud, I thought. I could not figure out why I felt so bereft. So severely disappointed. I had only known Gatien Defalle for three weeks. Three months ago I had been unaware of his existence.

Why did the actions of this man, this virtual stranger, affect me so? Why was I so sorry to know he was sleeping with his best friend's wife? Would I have preferred it if he were sleeping with someone else? Yes, I thought, I would. I was very drawn to this man, and I wanted my interest and attraction to be justified. I did not want him to be a man who cheats a friend, or weakens himself in the face of temptation.

But wait, I said to myself. *This is all circumstantial. There is no proof. . . .*

And then suddenly, from out of the passageway between the house and the cottage, the woman was there, moving silently through the mists, walking away from the main house. Theta.

Damn.

No proof? Well, there's your proof.

Did it have to get any clearer than this? It was three o'clock in the morning. There was Theta, leaving the scene of the crime.

Paul appeared at the doorway of the cottage, waiting

for his wife. He stopped her when she would have walked past him through the door.

"Hey," he said, and his voice was hard with anger. "You know you piss me off when you do this shit, Theta."

She ignored him and pushed past him, and he followed her inside the cottage. The door slammed shut.

Raised voices filtered out into the mist, but it wasn't long before they died away, and the light in the cottage went off.

Not a terribly big fight, considering the transgression. Poor Paul must be getting used to this sort of thing. I was so stirred up myself, I found it incredible that they had turned the lights out and gone to bed. I stayed out on the terrace until the cold drove me inside. I walked through the living room where Dimitri lay on the couch, in his big baggy shorts and a surfer T-shirt, looking very young and vulnerable, sleeping with his mouth open. I walked past Gatien's door, and slowed to listen; all was silent from within.

THE BEACH HOUSE weekend wasn't as fun for me after that. I avoided Gatien and Theta without difficulty. I spent Saturday morning reading, and took a long walk down the beach in the afternoon with May and Paul. It was invigorating, being there so close to that grand agitation, the Pacific Ocean. I won back my old spirit by Saturday afternoon, thinking, *To hell with them. I'm going to enjoy myself!* It was a bitter resolution, but firm. The evening was cool, and I sat contentedly by the big brick fireplace, playing cards with Helene and her father. Paul joined us for a few hands. He sat down across the table where I had to look at him constantly. He knew how good-looking he was, his eyes so blue against the dark tan of his skin, and his hair, which had turned golden from a couple days of sunning. I considered him, my eyes enjoying the taste of his looks, like a butterscotch sundae, so pleasurable on the tongue for a moment, so regrettable in the long run, if you allowed yourself to indulge.

Who knows? I thought, letting Paul hold my gaze.

Maybe he's for me. She *doesn't seem to want him.* But when I tried him on for size in my mind's eye, I just couldn't picture it. There was something missing from my attraction to Paul. Though he had a wife, he didn't seem very married; but the less married he appeared to be, the more I became convinced we should just be friends. Or maybe it was simply that when Gatien walked into a room, I didn't see anybody else.

"Sarah, can I talk to you a minute?"

I looked up, startled, to see Gatien standing there. "Sure, it was a lousy hand anyway," I said. I laid my cards on the table.

We went out through the kitchen, which was tidy and dark, down a flight of steps to a mudroom. I hadn't yet been in this part of the house. He opened a door, and suddenly we were outside, and the night was clear, startling with stars, and we were alone together in the darkness.

"Want to walk?" he asked.

I nodded, not sure at all, and we set off. Uneasy, I wondered what this was all about. For a few minutes we walked along in silence.

We stopped on a promontory where one lone cypress leaned over the cliff. Below, the ocean was in close, bashing itself against the rocks. We stood together without speaking, looking out toward the west.

Finally he said, "You told me the first time I met you that you had some things to talk with me about. In regard to May."

"Oh—" I wasn't prepared for that. I looked at him and laughed. This was so unexpected, I was at a loss, unable to think of a single thing I had been concerned about on the day we met. I could think only of his deep resonant voice, how strange and passionate it had sounded when he had cried out last night. Tonight his voice was controlled and quiet, and questioning. Tonight I could see stars, and I felt guilty for something. I felt hunted. I had an impulse to look around furtively, to see if we were being followed or watched.

A funny look passed over his face, one I couldn't read.

"I'm sorry," he said. "We're on a holiday here. I guess I shouldn't be talking about this sort of thing now?"

"Don't be ridiculous."

We walked slowly along the top of the cliff, up toward the sparse grove on the north side of the property.

"It's just that I told you we could talk about it later," he said, "when you first brought it up, but we never have."

"No. I know."

"You said it wasn't urgent, depending on your definition of urgency." There was that mocking amusement again, creeping into his tone.

"I think I was just looking for some insight, how to do my best for May."

"Me, too," he said lightly. "That's why I hired you."

"That's all well and good, but it's you she craves."

"Me?" A visible recoil. My remark had hit some nerve.

"Yeah. You."

"But she's thirteen. She's not supposed to want a parent type around anyway, right?"

"She had a big tournament last week, you know."

"I know."

"She was really hoping you would be home in time to go. But I suppose you had something more important to do."

He was silent a moment, then he said, "Yes, I guess I did."

"Did you know May hates soccer?" I turned and faced him. We were close enough to see into each other's eyes in the dark.

"She doesn't hate soccer," he said.

"She only plays to please you. Though I can't see why. You hardly ever go to her games or show any interest."

He was silent. I moved off, boiling.

"She wants to quit?" he asked, following me. We were headed back toward the house.

His voice was tentative; he was wondering, I think, what I wanted of him. In that moment I felt both tender with him and terribly frustrated by his responses. If he had gotten angry, defensive, argued with me, I would have felt better. Why did he act, sometimes, like he had suddenly become a father, instead of a man with thirteen years' parenting experience? Had he really been that absent from her life? I found it exasperating. I could never share my life with a man such as this—such an inept parent! I was relieved by this thought. It was something to keep me from running headlong into his arms, as if he would even have me. That was completely impossible.

"No, she doesn't want to quit," I said. "She wants to finish out the season."

"So what is this about, Sarah?"

"It's about your daughter," I said, my voice chilly. "It's about what's going on with her. You brought up the subject, remember?"

"All right." He was clearly confused.

"May needs you," I said.

"I know."

"You might contact her, once in awhile, when you're out of town. You know, like, phone calls, letters, E-mail?"

"Well, thanks for the suggestion."

"You're pretty distracted, it seems to me."

A bitter laugh escaped him. He let another silence gather around us before he spoke again. "I know."

We parted, and I was left feeling an oppressive uneasiness. Would that he had opened up to me, if only with the anger I had seen from him once or twice before. His quiet acceptance of my criticism was maddening to me. His wrath would be more welcome to me than his indifference.

I had to ask myself if I had baited him on purpose, to get a rise out of him, like some addict looking for a fix. If so, I had failed, and I was left without satisfaction. But there was no satisfaction to be had, for I could think of nothing that would have made me feel at ease.

In my room I fell into a deep, dreamless sleep. During the ride home Sunday, the three of us were tired and quiet, and May made no protest when Gatien announced he was leaving again the next day.

Chapter Eight

I T WAS FROM then on our real rhythm emerged. Gatien went away, and then he returned, days or even weeks later. Sometimes he asked me to pick him up at the airport; sometimes he arrived home with Paul or in a taxi. He was a hard man to know. Always he was polite and deferential, not only to me but to everyone he encountered. He treated me no differently than anybody else, or he was perhaps less affectionate with me than he was with others, but then, why wouldn't he be? He had his daughter, and his sister-in-law Helene, and his father-in-law, and his friends, not only Paul and Theta, but many others as well. People dropped by all the time, looking for him. He was good to all of them, dividing his time between them, doing his duty to all in his warm yet formal way.

When he was home he was often meeting with people, or doing business on the telephone. He paced across the terrace, the phone at his ear. He tended to talk too loud when he was on the phone, so it was difficult not to eavesdrop. He was involved in a number of business dealings having to do with Formula One racing. I heard talk of car design and development, investment in racing teams, deals with sponsors, and lots of other stuff I knew nothing about. But never did I hear Gatien talk about getting back into a car and racing again himself.

And yet I would see him sometimes, and wonder. I found a book in the dining room, *Competition Driving,* by Alain Prost. I knew it wasn't May or Louisa reading that book. I knew he was working out faithfully, running every morning, and he was down in that rec room, whenever he was home, lifting weights, using a rowing machine, and, I was pretty sure, doing yoga. I heard a message on the answering machine from what sounded like a physical therapist, confirming an appointment— though he never asked me to drive him to that appointment. I didn't always know what he was up to, because he was often with Paul, and they would take off in Paul's car to who knows where.

Oh, Gatien! I would think sometimes, wistful without really knowing why. I didn't mind that he had his own life, and I had mine. I didn't mind.

"OKAY," I SAID. "They want your home number and address. What's the zip code here, again?"

I was sitting at the dining room table, filling out some school papers with May one evening in late September. She was about to answer, when Gatien came into the room.

"We're not having our address and phone number put out like that," he said.

"But it's for the school directory—"

"We've got an unlisted phone number, and I don't want the address posted either. Right there. Check, 'I do not wish to be listed in the directory.' "

I looked at May, wondering if she thought this was odd, as I did, but she was busy cleaning her fingernails.

I shrugged. "Suit yourself," I said, and I finished filling out the forms.

GATIEN DID ATTEND May's soccer games when he was in town. There was usually a contingent of us there to cheer her on. Besides Gatien and me, Paul often came, and Helene usually arrived late with her father. Paul didn't pay much attention to the actual game. He spent most of his time shooting the breeze with Mr. Browning. But Gatien was intensely focused on each play. He paced the sidelines, silent, scowling, and broody. The first time I heard him shouting—with encouragement for May—I was startled. When he got really excited, he switched from English to French.

I stayed busy running May around to soccer practice and games, helping her with homework and school projects, and I got involved with the kitchen remodeling in my cottage. Because the architect was no longer working on the project, the choice of finishes fell to me. I got to pick out tile and appliances and flooring and paint colors and anything else I wanted to get involved with. Nathan, my stalwart contractor, came to me on every point. He consulted me in such trivial matters of detail, I began to suspect he was looking for excuses to seek me out.

Well, why not? I said to myself. I liked his tall, lanky good looks. His goofy humor. He seemed to enjoy life and his chosen career. He was at least moderately successful, from all appearances, and of seemingly good character. I knew he liked me. It was really Nathan who made me feel pretty again. I wondered if he was a good kisser.

Rolling that idea around, the thought of Gatien instantly interfered. *Okay,* I thought. *Consider Gatien. Would* he *be a good kisser?* But I couldn't. There was no knowing about it. I could hardly imagine it.

Nathan, on the other hand, I could bring to mind, his detergent smell, the way his voice would sometimes rise up an octave as he talked, and the texture of his lips would be . . . spongy?

There was definitely something spongy-looking about his lips.

I thought of Gatien's mouth, the hard line of it when he was annoyed, the way it drew back like a snarl when he parted his lips in a smile, how white his teeth were, how wide he could open his mouth, like a roaring lion, when he was shouting at the television during a football game. American football, with quarterbacks and everything. He loved it passionately.

He would kiss passionately, I was certain. *Yeah, well, why don't I just ask Theta?* I got so annoyed with myself when I went off daydreaming about Gatien. Back to Nathan.

What would it be like with Nathan? Sure, I could imagine it. . . .

MAY, MEANWHILE, SEEMED to have a suitor of her own: the sandy-haired boy I had seen on the day I arrived. She had yet to tell me his name. He was a good-looking kid, I thought, and I teased her about him sometimes. He sauntered past the gate, lingering, glancing through the trees at the house. She did nothing to encourage him, and in fact I saw her abandon her usual good manners one afternoon and tell him off. *"Just leave me alone!"* she yelled at him from a window.

Poor fellow, she crushed him with her withering contempt. I knew how he felt.

I stopped teasing her about it when I realized it made her uncomfortable. That he found her attractive actually seemed to infuriate her. I had to remember how young she was.

But May didn't seem to mind the attentions of one young man she knew, and that was Dimitri. Dimitri worried me a little. He was already a man—a rather immature man, but a man nonetheless. May looked up to him, and I wondered if she didn't have a crush on him, though she would have cut her tongue out before admitting it. I noticed him hanging around the Defalles' quite often, appearing unannounced, and I sometimes had no idea how long he had been there or what he'd been doing. I saw him with May, wandering about in the woods. I was nervous, thinking about them. May was only thirteen, and though I wouldn't exactly encourage her with anyone of the opposite sex, I would have been happier to see the interest she showed in Dimitri shifted toward the neighbor boy who was her own age.

I kept an eye on them. That was my job, after all.

GATIEN CAME HOME from the airport one afternoon to find Nathan and me together in the new kitchen of my little cottage, grouting the tile countertop. Paul, who was with Gatien and apparently playing chauffeur today, let out an appreciative whistle—at the sight of the new kitchen, I thought, not at me in my cutoff shorts and my hair tied up in a messy ponytail.

"I thought we had money in the budget for subcontractors," Gatien commented, looking at the two of us busily working. Nathan and I were having a lot of fun, working in close proximity on a cool October day, flirting as we toiled. I guess it probably showed. I suddenly felt self-conscious.

"Well, it's such a small job," Nathan said, "we decided we could do it ourselves, and I discovered Sarah here is experienced—she worked as a handyman for a couple of years."

"Handywoman," I corrected him.

"She continually surprises me," Gatien said.

I kept my attention focused on the grout line I was sponging. Some of my easy good mood had fled in the face of the master's unsmiling, unexpected presence, but a strange joy rose through me in its place, pulsing like adrenaline, making me giddy and anxious. He hadn't been home for nearly a week.

"Looking good," Paul said.

"Yeah, the job looks good," said Gatien grudgingly.

"I wasn't talking about the job, I was talking about Sarah's legs."

"Watch it, buddy," Gatien warned.

I turned my head to hide a blush.

Paul retorted, "But why shouldn't I say it? They're very fine legs."

"Yeah, especially since she's put a little meat on those bones," said Nathan.

"Come on, Gatien," Paul needled his buddy. "You gotta admit she's a gorgeous girl."

"Guys," I said, "I'm *grouting tile* here."

"Sarah's all right," Gatien said, and the way he said *all right,* it meant something more than just all right. "I thought she was all right the day I met her, and I think so now, and I'd still think so if she was eighty years old and weighed two hundred pounds."

I laughed. He was so sincere, so matter-of-fact. "That is the most beautiful compliment anyone has ever paid me," I declared.

"I stand by my comment regarding your legs," said Paul.

THAT EVENING MAY and I walked down Winding Hill Road to a Halloween party at Ellen's house. We were both dressed as witches, wearing black skirts and shirts, clothes we already owned—and two tall witches' hats I'd picked up from the drugstore. There was a low, reddish light around the oaks tonight, an eerie, autumnal gleaming. I was excited and stirred by the beautiful, sweet-smelling evening, especially knowing Gatien was home. I wished it didn't make a difference, but it did.

When Gatien said it was okay for May to go to the party, I was almost surprised. He seemed very protective of her in some ways, and I couldn't help remembering his strange insistence about keeping the family's phone number and address out of the school directory. Perhaps he simply liked his privacy, I thought. And yet I sensed there was more to it than that.

But he had no objection to her going to the party, especially when I told him I was going with her. I suppose I was disappointed again, almost hoping he would forbid it so I could challenge his decision. But apparently he agreed with me that it would be a good thing for his daughter to get out in the neighborhood. May asked him if he wanted to come, and he just laughed it off and told us to go have a good time.

•   •   •

"THERE'S A SCOTTISH custom I'm going to tell you about," said our stout neighbor Ellen, offering May and me each an apple from a big wooden bowl. "On Samhain, if you eat an apple and look into a mirror, you just might see the man you're going to marry."

"What's Samhain?" asked May.

"Samhain. Halloween, child."

"Go ahead, May, try it," I urged. "Let's see who you're going to marry."

"I will if you will," she said. "Where's a mirror?"

"Go look in the entry hall," said Ellen. "There's a perfectly lovely looking glass there."

So May and I went, and she insisted I go first, but then she decided to go first, and she stood in front of the old oval mirror, munching away at her red delicious. "I don't see anybody but myself," said May. "But the apple tastes good."

"So, it didn't work, huh?" I said, disappointed, when she had finished off most of her apple and turned away from the mirror.

"No, but that's probably because I have decided never to marry."

"Ah. Well, you didn't say so before. I suppose that was a good test to see if this technique with the mirror actually works."

"Your turn!"

"A Jonathan for me," I said. "Or will that limit me only to Jonathans?"

"Better a guy named Jon than a guy named Pippin," May said.

I took my place in front of the mirror, bit into the apple. "Ooh. It's sour. Maybe I should have picked the Pippin. Wouldn't you rather be married to a Pippin, May? If he was sweeter? But not too mushy?"

"Shhh," May scolded. "You have to concentrate. I'll dim the lights."

Now the room was in darkness but for the glow of jack-o'-lanterns sitting on the porch, just beyond the open door. I stared into the mirror a long time, until my own image floated away for a moment. I chewed the apple slowly, looking into the glass, becoming mesmerized. I closed my eyes for a moment, and when I opened them, I was looking into the face of a stranger, a familiar stranger with enormous eyes and dramatic cheekbones, wearing a pointed black hat. It was me, but I was no one I recognized. *Must be the overdone makeup,* I thought. In that moment I had a sense that I could be anyone or anything I wanted to be, and that I was at a crossroads. And then suddenly, just above my reflection, staring back at me out of the glow, was Gatien, with his wary eyes and his strong, soft mouth, and I took in a start of breath, to see him there beside me in the glass. For one bare instant I thought I was having a vision, looking into a magic mirror. But he was really there. He had just walked into the entry hall behind me.

"Sarah's looking for her husband in the mirror," May explained. "If she eats an apple on Halloween while looking in a mirror, she's supposed to see him there."

I turned around with a self-conscious laugh, the spell broken.

"Any luck?" he asked softly.

"I didn't see anybody," May said, "when I tried it. But that's because I'm not going to get married."

"I see." He considered that. "Makes sense. And what about you?" He looked at me.

"Well, I would like to have a husband, someday," I said.

"So, did you see someone?" May wanted to know.

I hesitated. "Yes, I did."

"Who was it?"

"I'm sure I'm not supposed to tell you."

"But will you marry him?"

"Only time will tell, won't it?" I lifted my apple to Gatien. "Want a bite?"

He was saved by Ellen, our hostess, who came at that moment to greet him and welcome him to her party. But I think he had been about to go for it.

•   •   •

THANKSGIVING CAME, AND all through the long weekend the house was filled with people. Helene and Dimitri
came for dinner Saturday because Dimitri was at his
mom's on Thanksgiving day. Though they had the holiday
off, Louisa and Carlos came by with a basket of home-
made tortillas. Paul and Theta were in and out, and Ellen
brought us an apple pie and stayed most of Saturday afternoon, showing May and me how to make bread.

We were about to sit down for our post-Thanksgiving
feast when I realized we were short a couple of chairs. I
found Louisa in the kitchen, standing at the stove, stirring
gravy. I thought I might always see Louisa in my mind's
eye thus, standing at the stove, stirring something. The air
always smelled heavenly when she was in the house. I
told her we were short of seating and asked her if she
knew of any other chairs in the house we could use for the
occasion. "I got a couple from the library," I told her, "and
one from downstairs, but we still need two."

"Yes," she said. "I know of some chairs. I'll go get
them, you stir this, please."

"Oh, no, I'll go get them. Just tell me where they are."

She shook her head and handed me the spoon, which I
accepted automatically, and when I stood there stupidly,
she motioned me to the stove with a sharp whirl of her
small hand.

"No, really," I said. "I'll get them if you just—"

"Stir," she commanded, and there was a cold-steel determination in her, to get me to do her bidding. It was unusual, for her. I obeyed her without a word as she hurried
away.

Now that *was strange,* I thought, stirring idly. *Louisa
must be stressed with all these people in the house.* I
thought I could probably turn down the heat a bit and not
stir the pot so faithfully, but after that look she had given
me, I dared not try such a thing.

I savored the moment, listening to the music of the
household. There was the muted roar of the football game
in the living room. Music filtering up from my cottage; I
had left my radio on, tuned to an R & B station. May's

voice calling out from downstairs, Gatien's delicious deep reply from upstairs. How I loved his voice. His rare laughter. Now it was Dimitri, shouting something, then Paul, yelling even louder. They were raising such a ruckus, I figured they must all be in the living room watching football. Gatien joined in, perhaps the loudest and most passionate shouting of them all, his English sliding into French, as it would when he was particularly emotional. It always startled me when that excitement came out of him; he was ordinarily so quiet.

I heard Louisa's voice now, and I turned my head automatically and looked out the kitchen window toward the sound. I saw her crossing the garden, calling for Carlos. He emerged from the potting shed, lifted his cowboy hat, and wiped his brow with his bandanna, waiting for her. *Dear Carlos,* I thought. Even on his day off, he couldn't resist going down to his gardens. Louisa hurried toward him, motioning with her arms, and they huddled together, talked a moment. He asked her a question, and she raised her voice in a sharp, singular reply. She clearly had the authority on this one, and he shrugged, tossed something into the shed, and followed her. They walked around the corner of the building and I saw them no more.

Five minutes later Louisa and Carlos carried two dusty Chippendale side chairs into the dining room. Louisa instructed Carlos to wipe them clean, and then she came to me in the kitchen and took back her spoon with a smile. I tried to get her to look at me—because there was something going on with her, I was sure of it—but she wouldn't.

ON A COLD, clear Saturday morning in early December, May and I were hanging Christmas lights around the front windows of the house. Gatien had been gone since Thanksgiving. I knew he had come home last night in a taxi, but he hadn't made an appearance yet this morning.

"He's doing something mysterious in the library," May said.

"What?" I asked, from my perch on the ladder. She

handed me a strand of lights after I finished tapping in the nail that would hold them to the corner of the house.

"I don't know. He's dusting up or something. He's been in there all morning. He came home late last night, you know."

So we were both thinking of him. "Well, good," I said. "It's time that room was cleaned up."

"My mother loved that room," May said.

"It's a beautiful room. I'm rather drawn to it myself."

I had withstood the temptation to go back into Lisa's library. The master of the house had asked me to stay out of there. Was I the type of person to go snooping about in other people's business?

Well, maybe . . .

I knew very well I was simply afraid of what I might discover in those journals. I wasn't sure I wanted to know what I might end up finding out. I also knew that eventually I'd be back in there again, unable to resist.

"Good day, ladies." Speak of the devil. It was Gatien, and he looked cheerful. He was wearing jeans and a grimy T-shirt, and there was dust in his hair. May and I looked at him with surprise, to see him so untidy. He walked out on the driveway to take a look at our lights.

"Good day," we both answered.

"How have you been?"

"Very well, thanks," said May.

"Sarah, I was wondering if I might be granted permission to move your boxes of books."

I looked down on him from my height on the ladder.

"Your cottage," he explained, "is practically uninhabitable, due to the large number of boxes you have in there, and I was wondering if I might put them in the library, where I have cleared a space just for your books. Can I do that for you?"

I was astounded. I was tempted to ask, sarcastically, what good my books would do me in a room I wasn't even supposed to enter, but he was being so gallant with his offer, I couldn't. "Uh, sure," I said. "That'd be fine."

I hadn't even bothered to open most of the boxes yet,

anyway. What did it matter where they were stored? If he wanted to move the boxes, fine.

May and I gave each other a bewildered look as he marched off to carry out his mission.

"Don't *even* ask him if he wants your help!" she warned, reading my mind, and I burst out laughing.

We spent more time together than usual in the weeks before Christmas, Gatien and me. I drove him around frequently, and we made a point of going Christmas shopping for May several times.

"May's mother used to do this," he said to me one afternoon, when we were driving home after a trip to the mall. "I was never much of a shopper."

"You did pretty well today," I teased him.

"Hey, she's going to love that Monopoly game," he said.

"I think you bought that as a Christmas present for *you.* You know she wants a nose ring."

"She does?" He turned to me, shocked.

"No, no," I assured him, laughing at his expression. "She's never mentioned it. I was just kidding."

"Good," he said in a low voice. "Though God knows a piercing would be the least of my worries with that girl."

"I don't know what makes you talk like that," I said. "May is a good girl, not half as difficult as everyone makes her out to be."

"She is a good girl," he agreed. "But there's more there than meets the eye, with that one."

"How so?"

He glanced at me shrewdly. "Has she told you anything?" he asked. "About her past?"

"She's a little young to have a past, isn't she?" I joked, but it fell flat.

He waited for my answer.

"She hasn't said anything about losing her mom," I said. "She doesn't talk about it. Neither do you, for that matter."

"It's hard to know what to say about that. One day you're living your life, and then suddenly you're in a whole new world, having to deal with it all on a new level. I'm afraid I'm making a mess of it."

"You must really miss your wife."

"I do miss her," he replied slowly, emotionlessly.

We drove in silence for awhile.

"She didn't kill herself, Sarah."

I froze, waiting for him to explain. But the silence went on as before.

I said, "So you think it was an accident?"

"I don't want May growing up thinking her mother took her own life."

"Is that what May thinks?"

"I'm not sure what May thinks. That's why I asked you."

"Sometimes I worry about her, what she hears from people. Some of the things I hear Dimitri say . . ."

"What does Dimitri say?"

I shrugged. I didn't want to repeat what Dimitri had said, that Lisa's death might have been a murder; it sounded so callous. "I don't know. Just talking about May's mother, and her death, in a way I wouldn't want May to hear."

"So you're leaving us after Christmas."

And you're changing the subject rather abruptly, I thought. "Yep. I'm going to go hang out with some old friends down in Santa Barbara. I'll be gone most of the week between Christmas and New Year's Eve. I've got everything set up with Louisa. She and Carlos are going to look after the house, so you won't even have to think about it. It'll be good for May to get away and go snow-boarding with you and Helene and Dimitri."

"Yeah. But we'll miss you."

These words of his warmed me, and I felt I must be blushing. I kept my eyes fixed on the road.

"Don't worry," he said. "I'll watch Dimitri."

ONE AFTERNOON a few days later, when Gatien and May were out with Paul, I went into the library. I wasn't sure if Louisa was in the house then or not, but I figured if Gatien had made a place for my books in his late wife's library, it would be okay if I went in there once in a while, and besides, I knew by now that Louisa didn't care if I went in the library; that was between me and the master of the house.

The place was less dusty than I remembered, and the drapes had been pulled aside to let in some sunlight. There were my books, no longer in their boxes, all lined up neatly in one of the bookcases. But I went directly to the journals.

I had avoided them after that one sneak peek. But talking with Gatien the other day, and his insistence that his wife had not committed suicide, had confirmed my conviction that it was at least worth a look to see what Lisa's state of mind had been in the days leading up to her death.

But when I went to the last journal, I found it was finished about seven months before Lisa had died. Since each journal was written over a year's duration, I concluded that just one journal—the last journal Lisa had worked on, the one she would have been writing at the time of her death—was not with the collection.

I flipped through the journal, wondering if I might find some insight there anyway.

There was evidence of conflict in the words Lisa had written; frustration that Gatien wasn't around enough, unspecified worry about May. Lisa expressed her fears that she might be making mistakes in her dealings with her husband and her daughter. But what was a journal for, if not for voicing frustrations and worries? I didn't see anything that indicated an unusually troubled personality.

Then I came across this entry:

November 12

I told Gatien we needed to get May back into therapy so she can work through what happened. I thought he would fight me. But he surprised me.

November 17

   I'm so worried about her. I feel so helpless. And I can't help thinking it's all my fault. I know I should have done something more.
   Sometimes I'm afraid Gatien doesn't realize how serious this is. Her life may be ruined, and he's asking me to pass the potatoes. But he's so far away, even when he's here. I want to scream at him and pound him with my fists, I get so angry. Sometimes I think I'd be better off without him. That it would be better for May if we just went away somewhere. Then I think, what would we do without him?

   And then it was back to the more mundane descriptions of daily life.
   I slipped the journal back onto the shelf with its mates, feeling glum. I had more questions than ever. What was this about May? I had assumed that her so-called problems stemmed from losing her mother at such an early age, and not having her father around enough. It was true, I'd heard hints that she had other strikes against her as well, but nobody had told me what they might be. Now I was filled with apprehension. Something had happened to the girl when she was—how old? There might well be an explanation in the earlier journals. . . . I laid my hand on the journal that sat beside the one I had just looked through. But I hesitated, aware of a certain cowardice in myself. Cowardice warred with curiosity.
   "Sarah!" Louisa was calling my name.
   "I'm here," I called, letting myself out of the library.
   "It's Nathan," she said, coming out of the kitchen, her smooth face rosy and damp from standing over her cook pots. "He is looking for you."
   As usual. "All right," I said. "I'll go down and see what he wants."
   My investigation would have to wait.

Chapter Nine

Y OU DON'T HAVE to cover for us, you know."
I dried the platter I held in my hand and put it
into its slot in the cupboard.

"It's sweet of you, but it isn't necessary." Theta stood
with her hip cocked against the cabinet, regarding me with
a mixture of amusement and disdain.

Paul and Theta had come to the Defalles' for an early
supper on Christmas Eve. When we finished eating, Paul
and Gatien set up a game of chess in the living room. I
was in the kitchen doing the dishes when Theta joined me.
She didn't offer to help.

"What do you mean, covering for you?" I turned to her
and asked pointedly, though we both knew exactly what
she meant. I wanted to hear it from her, since she brought
it up.

"I've been waiting for you to say something to Paul,"
she said. She plucked a decorated cookie off a plate, tested
it with her teeth. "But time goes by, and you keep your
lips locked. Why is that, I wonder?"

"What's between you and Paul is your business."

"And so is what's between me and Gatien."

The warning in her voice had my hackles rising. "Whatever that is!" I replied.

"Well, whatever it is, I know you're jealous of it."

I burst out laughing. "It's beginning to sound a bit like sixth grade here, don't you think, Theta? Can't we get past the cattiness? I have no quarrel with you."

She conceded this with a tiny smile. "Okay," she said. "Truce?"

"I don't trust you for a moment."

"Then you're smarter than you look."

"You have a sweet husband," I said. "Why don't you appreciate what you've got?"

She made a face, twisting her lovely features until she was actually ugly for a moment. "Oh, of course you think he's great. *He's* the one you shouldn't trust."

I picked up a freshly washed bowl and went through the motions of drying it.

"He's still really messed up, you know," she said, composing herself. "I wouldn't try it if I were you. You'd just be sorry in the end."

"Are you taking about Paul or Gatien?"

"Either one, really! But no. I mean Gatien."

"So he's the one you're worried about!" I was incredulous. "I wonder if you would even care if I went for Paul."

"I think you already have, but that's beside the point. No, I'm talking about Gatien, because I really feel you should be warned. He's a broken man. In more ways than one. He didn't love his wife, and that makes it worse, do you know what I mean? She might have figured that out. She was a smart lady. Instead, she focused on his job. She ended up hating what he did for a living. At first she romanticized it. But then she started realizing it was for real, and she might lose what she had, which was more than she expected to get out of him in the first place. She couldn't believe her own luck when he agreed to marry her, but that's another story. She tried to get him out of racing. She tried to wreck his career, but it was the accident that did that. She got her way in the end—he had to stop racing. But by then she was already dead."

Theta was looking out the window, gazing off down toward my cottage where a string of white lights twinkled on the eaves.

I dried the dishes and listened to her, fascinated. It seemed like everyone who had known Lisa had a different take on her.

"You know they suspected Gatien was the one who killed his wife? But they had no evidence. No proof. Well, if he didn't do it, he probably would have, eventually! I knew them both, and I saw it. She was driving him crazy. You know what I think? *I* think he did do it." She turned and looked at me slyly. She laughed at the expression on my face, knowing she'd finally got to me, and walked out of the room.

Theta was a charming person, ordinarily. Aside from being beautiful, she was witty and intelligent and vivacious, and I could see why people, especially men, were attracted to her. She was amiable and easy with May, polite to Louisa, gently flirty with old Carlos, and, except when no one was looking, a perfect lady with Gatien. With me, she was a bitch. Usually with more subtlety than what she had displayed this evening, but she was always an antagonist. I knew her attitude toward me was due to some insecurity, some specific threat she felt. I had thought it was about Paul, but now I realized it had more to do with Gatien.

She's the one sleeping with him, I thought, out of sorts. *Why harass me?*

But *was* she having an affair with Gatien? Though the signs would indicate it, I questioned it. Argued it. I suspected it was my own wishful thinking trying to argue me out of what was obvious. And why should I care, anyway? It didn't affect me. As long as they kept it from May . . .

But deception wasn't good for May, hidden or otherwise. I felt very righteous about that; but of course that wasn't the real reason it bothered me.

I finished the dishes, wiped down the counters, and turned off the overhead lights, leaving just the glow from the stove light on to warm the room. I was standing alone, staring out the window at the lights of the city below, when Gatien came into the kitchen.

He came up behind me, and I felt him standing close, gazing out the window to see what I was seeing.

"You look like you'd rather be anywhere but here, Sarah," he said.

"On the contrary," I replied, matching my low tones to his. "There's nowhere else I'd rather be." We stood together for a moment, not speaking, and in that fifteen or twenty seconds, I was certain there was no Theta, no other, just the two of us, almost close enough to touch, not speaking, only being together.

"Oh my *God!*"

We both started at the girlish shriek, and we turned around to see May in the doorway between the dining room and the kitchen, her face full of mischief. "Don't you two realize you are standing under the mistletoe? You must kiss!"

But Gatien and I had taken immediate action to move apart, actually stepping away from one another as we looked up to see the bunch of dusky leaves and berries tied above the door with a red ribbon.

"Come on!" she demanded. "You have to! It's Christmas Eve. You need to get into the spirit." But she could see she would get nowhere with us. We were both embarrassed and shy.

"Oh, what's the use!" she cried. "You two are hopeless."

We laughed about it awkwardly and went together to join the others in the living room.

Well, that was clumsy, I thought, and I wondered: *Why are we so formal and tight with each other? Why freeze up at the idea of a friendly kiss?*

I knew why. There was a current that zapped between us like a bolt of wild electricity whenever we got too close to each other, though sometimes I swore I could feel it just as strong even when he was on the other side of the planet. Only a fool wouldn't recognize that as dangerous and approach with caution. I wasn't sure what Gatien felt for me, but I knew what he'd chosen to do about it, and that spoke volumes. And I was okay with that. I knew it was actually better this way. The ethics of the situation alone demanded it. But it annoyed me. I'd been living with him for four months. I wanted to feel easier about the whole thing. I didn't like this tension between us. If it was to be this way between us, reserved and formal, fine. I understood that. I accepted it. But I wanted us to be friends, easy and affectionate with each other. Was that impossible? I had thought we were getting there in recent weeks, but maybe I was wrong.

In the living room I watched him interact with Theta. He didn't initiate contact with her, but I noticed he didn't avoid it, either, as he seemed to do with me. And yet, what was that about, a moment ago, when he had stood so close to me? He hadn't made a move to touch me. He never did.

Was that why I longed for him to do it? Maybe I should just get it out of my system. Seduce him and be done with it. But I couldn't imagine seducing Gatien Defalle. I could only imagine him seducing me. And yet in real life he did not seem inclined to do that at all!

As is only right, I told myself. *He is May's father.*

The doorbell rang, and May ran to open the door.

"Merry Christmas, everybody!" It was Nathan with a big basket of Christmas treats. "Something for everyone!" he cried. There was candy and rum cake; a bottle of whiskey for Gatien, and for May, a box of hair ornaments.

"And this is for you, Sarah," Nathan said, presenting me with a small foil-wrapped box. "Merry Christmas."

I sat on the edge of a chair, holding the present self-consciously.

"Open it!" he urged.

It was a necklace of crystal beads, very pretty, and I murmured my thanks. It was a lovely gift, but it was excessive for the level of our relationship, and instead of finding it pleasing, it made me uncomfortable.

"Of course it is customary for the contractor to give gifts to clients," Gatien said sardonically. I knew he sensed my embarrassment, and I could see he was teasing me, a sly grin on his face, but with Nathan he seemed annoyed.

Helene and Dimitri dropped by, and the level of noise in the house rose to a party pitch. I sat near the fire, fingering the crystal beads of my necklace. I had a feeling I ought to return the gift, that it wasn't right to accept it; if I accepted it, I was accepting something else, it seemed.

"Do you like it?" Nathan dropped down beside me.

"I think it's very pretty," I said.

"I think it is, too. I thought of you when I saw it."

"Thank you."

"Do you have a number where I can reach you next week? I know you're going to be out of town, but just in case . . ."

"Nathan, the job is nearly done. I mean, it is done, or will be, as soon as that punch list is complete, which it practically is, right?"

"Yeah. This is one job I really hate to see end." He looked at me meaningfully.

"It turned out really nice," I said.

"Did it?" He stared at me. "Is it really finished, then, Sarah?"

I didn't give him any help one way or another. I still wasn't sure what I thought of him. I wanted to give him a chance, a chance to grow on me. I liked him. He liked me. He was available.

But still he didn't make a move or ask me out. I don't know if he was waiting for some signal from me, but for all his hinting, he had yet to get around to suggesting an actual date. I was neither disappointed nor relieved.

Dimitri appeared beside me and put something in my hand. It turned out to be a small shiny pebble with a turtle carved into it.

"It's for protection," he said. "Merry Christmas, Sarah Logan."

LATER THAT EVENING I drove Paul and Theta to the airport. Gatien sat by my side; Theta and Paul were silent in the backseat. They were flying to Reno for the holidays.

"You don't have to go to the airport," I had told Gatien politely before we left the house. "You can stay here with Helene and May."

"We're leaving soon, anyway," Helene said. "Don't worry about us." Nathan took the hint and went home. Dimitri kissed May on the top of her head, and he went off with Helene amid a chorus of hearty *Merry Christmas*es.

Gatien insisted he would accompany us to the airport, and I thought maybe he just wanted that much more time with Theta before they parted. May assured us she would be fine at home alone.

At the airport, Gatien and I helped Paul and Theta out at the curb and said our good-byes. The mood was subdued. I saw no spark of longing between Gatien and Theta when they parted, at least not on his side.

What does it matter? I asked myself ruthlessly. *Who the hell cares what they do?*

I turned the car onto the freeway, headed south toward home, and I heard the question come out of my mouth: "Are you in love with her?"

He looked at me, startled, and gave a laugh, a sort of deep chuckle, from nervousness, I thought. "What?" he said.

"Are you in love with Theta?"

"In love?" He blew out a breath of disdain. "I don't even know what that means."

"Haven't you ever been in love?" I asked.

"No."

His answer surprised and saddened me. So he had not been in love with his wife, as Theta had said.

"Don't get me wrong," he said. "I know what it is to love. I have loved people, a few of them very deeply. I have loved animals." He smiled. "I have even loved certain machines. But this bit about being in love is meaningless to me. Sorry."

We were getting off the subject here. I had really been asking, I suppose, if he was sleeping with Theta. Having sex with her. But I found this conversation rather interesting, too. Until he turned it on me.

"What about you?" he asked. "Have you ever been in love?"

"Yes, of course I have." My voice sounded defensive.

"And yet, you aren't married. Didn't he love you back?"

I thought of Anthony, my high school sweetheart. Oh, yes, he had loved me back. And Shane, my sophomore heartthrob when I was a student at Santa Barbara City College. If that wasn't mutual love, I don't know what was. So what if it only lasted seven months? "Yeah, I think they loved me back," I said.

"They?"

"There were one or two in my past. To me, if you aren't loved back, it isn't real anyway," I declared. "It's a vain crush. It's based on an illusion, or something. Real romantic love is an exchange. But my experience of love is the puppy-love variety, I think. Love, as in till death do us part? No, I haven't ever had that. But I think I understand what it would—what it would—"

"Feel like?" He tried to supply the words.

"Yeah, I guess. But not just *feel* like ... but what it would *be*. Like you would know it, even when you weren't necessarily *feeling* it."

"That I understand. I know what it is to make a commitment," he said. "And to live by it. It doesn't have much to do with feelings. You make a decision, you stick by it."

"You make it sound so ... legalistic."

"Well, it is. That's what marriage is. Isn't that what you were just talking about? It isn't about feelings. It's a decision you make."

"What about the heart? What about passion?"

"Of course, I am a man, and I've lived a man's life. Sex is a fantastic thing."

"And marriage?"

"Quite useful, at times."

"But you separate the two. The passion and the commitment."

"Yes. There is the logical mind, and then there is the beast. My father used to talk about something that he called sitting on the beast, that is, himself. Always being in control of his actions and his emotions. When I thought about that, when I was beginning my career, I decided that is what I would do. Learn to ride the beast. It's not about taming it, or breaking its spirit—because then you've lost its fire, and it's no longer of use. To me, it's about using the power, harnessing it, controlling it."

"And so you do."

"I taught myself to do that very early in life, and I have applied it to every part of my life. The beast does not control me. I control the beast."

"Always?"

"The beast is always there, underneath everything. That's passion. Desire. Primal animal hunger, if you will. I honor that. I see it coming at me. But I don't let it run over me or devour me. I get on it and I ride it, let that force carry me where *I* want to go."

"And how does that relate to being in love?"

"It relates to any relationship I have with anyone. Sexual desire is a primal force. One of the most powerful beasts imaginable. But it doesn't rule me, and I never make decisions based on what the beast wants."

"Never?" I felt a delicious urge to tease him. "Sounds like a pretty bland life to me."

"No, because the passions are still there. That's the point. Life is rich with emotion and feeling, and often it's these that fuel the thing. What I'm trying to say is, no matter how tempting something might be, if it doesn't go along with my plan, I don't let it happen. And, um, lest you think I am avoiding your question, what I can tell you about Theta is . . . she is my best friend's wife. And because she is my best friend's wife, that is all I am willing to say about her."

"How very gallant of you." I laughed.

I still didn't know for sure about him and Theta. The more I thought about it, the more it seemed he had danced around the question. But more significantly, I felt he had been trying to tell me something else. Not about him and Theta, but about him and me. He might acknowledge the heat between us, but there was no chance he was going to act on it, because that wouldn't fit in with his agenda. His plan. Want to get ahead in life? Don't be distracted by messy temptations. Don't sleep with the baby-sitter.

IT WAS A relief. I might laugh at his self-control, his conscious erection of boundaries, but I was glad for them. I don't know what I would have done if he had put the moves on me. I was definitely attracted, but playing out that attraction was another matter. He was May's father, and that was a sensitive relationship. Casual sex would do more harm than good in this situation. I wasn't into casual sex anyway.

May had set out a plate of cookies and a glass of milk, "For Santa," she told us with emphasis, and was just brushing her teeth for bed when we arrived home. She came out and kissed Gatien good night, then came to me and gave me a quick embrace. She had never done that before, and I was absurdly touched.

"Good night, May," I said.

"Don't get all choked up," she warned me. "It's like the cookies and milk. I know when to kiss ass."

"May." Her father rapped out a warning.

"Good-night!" she sang out gaily. "Merry Christmas!" And she twirled off to bed.

The look Gatien and I exchanged was priceless. One glance held pride and alarm and delight in that moment, and it was something to know we shared that with each other. I looked away quickly, the feelings stirring inside me, pleasing me, annoying me, scaring me. I realized I was not only attracted to Gatien in a physical way, I was beginning to desire something I had not previously been aware of wanting, except in the vague, distant future: a family of my own.

Gatien and I stayed up late together that night, making sure everything was just right for Christmas morning. We stuffed May's stocking and set out the presents we had bought for her. I wrapped some presents for Louisa and Carlos, and finally, about midnight, we were finished.

"It's bedtime, Sarah." Gatien's voice was soft. He stood in the doorway to the master's suite.

"Good night, Gatien," I said. I was sitting on the carpet in the rec room staring at the lights on the Christmas tree, where we had created a fantasy scene with gifts for May. "I'm going to sit here for a few minutes, if that's okay."

"Stay as long as you want."

He pulled his door partway closed but didn't latch it. I heard him moving around in his room, then the light went off, and there was only silence.

I grew so sleepy, looking at the lights, but I didn't want to move. I climbed up on the couch and closed my eyes.

I was riding in a sleigh, and Gatien was driving the reindeer that were pulling us through heavy snowdrifts. He looked at me, the wind whistling through his beard— his *beard?*—no, there was no beard, only that clean, strong jaw and that odd broken cheek, and when he smiled it was like bright stars falling around me. We came to a lodge by a frozen lake and I ran upstairs looking for him. I heard him making love in the room next to mine. I knew he was with Theta. I could tell by the noise he was making. I'd heard that sound before, that startling expression of groaning, painful ecstasy—

Or was it simply pain?

I came awake, riveted, horrified.

I knew the sound. It was the same moaning and groaning I had heard the night at the beach house. But I had thought he was making love with Theta that night! And I was pretty sure Theta wasn't in there now, since I had dropped her off at the airport hours earlier with her husband.

Someone else? A man like Gatien Defalle would have many lovers, no doubt. But if he had another woman in his room, she had crept into the house and walked past me sleeping on the sofa sometime after midnight on Christmas Eve. . . .

Rather unlikely.

My God, I thought, struck to the heart as the passionate

groaning rang out again. *That's not a cry of pleasure.
That's a roar of pain.*

Without thinking further, I jumped up and ran into his
bedroom.

Gatien was lying on his bed, naked but for a pair of
white boxer shorts which were drenched in sweat and
twisted like a rag around his slender thighs. He was
writhing about, clutching at his lame leg, his face con-
torted, his body thrashing on the sheets.

"What is it, Gatien?" I asked, keeping my voice low
and calm. "How can I help you?"

"Nothing, go away, it's just a cramp."

"Here, give me your hand." I grabbed his hand in mine.
"Lie back down."

"I can't."

I pressed my thumb into a certain spot, a pressure point
on his hand. "Blow out your breath," I commanded. "A
long exhale, as long as you can, then take in another
breath, slowly and deeply. . . ."

He collapsed back on the bed pillows with a grunt. I
laid one hand on his leg, and I felt the muscles begin to
lengthen and shudder out of the cramp. I covered him with
the blanket, except for where I was working on him.

Instead of fighting it he began to work with it, breathing into it, and the cramp loosened up a little more.

"That's good." I breathed with him.

He stopped clenching, and I let go of his hand and
began to rub the calf and ankle of his leg with firm, long
strokes. I could feel the ridges of a huge and terrible scar
running along the shaft of bone.

I massaged the leg until I could feel the heat flowing
beneath the skin.

"I'm going to do the other leg, now, to balance it," I
told him.

"Right," he said. He was calm now, lying with his arms
at his sides, his legs splayed in the blankets, his breathing
full and deep. "Where did you learn to do this, Sarah?" he
asked, watching me from his cushion of pillows. The

room was dark, but I could see the gleam in his eyes. "Another one of your many apprenticeships?"

"I worked as an assistant to a massage therapist for a couple of years," I said.

"You certainly do have a wide range of experience, for one so young." He said this with his familiar mockery. "God, but you *are* good."

I shrank away from him, hurt by his flippant words.

He grabbed my arms, guided my hands back to their work. "Please, don't run away. I don't mean to embarrass you." All the teasing mockery was gone. "You don't know what you saved me. You have healing hands. I'm indebted to you," he added sincerely.

He leaned back to watch me, and my hands fumbled on his warm skin. I worked more self-consciously now, and I realized I would have to end it very soon. I had done my job. I became acutely aware of the feel of his flesh between my fingers, the volume of his muscles, the heat of him, the pulse of blood through his veins and arteries. *This is Gatien,* I thought. *This is his body. In my hands. Close enough to touch, and I'm touching, close enough to smell, and I can breathe him in, his animal, male scent. Close enough to taste. Oh, God, what am I doing?*

What I felt moving through me was desire—my own, and also his—an appallingly powerful wave.

I lifted my hands from his body and slipped off the bed.

He didn't say anything, but he was staring at me, his chest rising and falling rapidly now.

We parted without words.

I ran down to my cottage, half-fearing, half-hoping he would come after me. I reached my front porch, and my hand hesitated on the door handle. My spirit would not be contained, not yet. Instead of going inside, I turned and walked up another pathway that led to a stairway up the hillside. The night was cold and starry, like in my dream. Instead of fog, there was only one strange blaze of cloud, a long pale stripe across the dark sky.

When I came to the top of the first rise, I turned and looked down on my cottage, and I saw Gatien, naked above the hips, on the pathway between the main house and mine. He was walking down the hill with his awkward, potent stride, wearing only his jeans in the cold December night, and he was headed straight to my door. There was one small glow coming from behind the curtains in the cottage. It wasn't exactly welcoming, nor was it discouraging.

I stood still and silent, watching him. His naked chest was wide and flat, and his arms were tightly muscled. He stopped before my porch.

I could see him clenching his fists, fighting something in himself, maybe, just as I was fighting something in myself, watching him. I came so close to calling out to him, I almost did it unthinkingly. But if I did that, I'd scare him away, like a wild animal. I was crazy with curiosity, but I could only watch and wait and see what he would do.

He hesitated a good long moment, then he turned around and walked back up the hill to the main house.

"Good," I said aloud in a quiet, shaken voice. "It's too soon." *And if this is what I think it is . . .*

I felt alive and washed clean by the stark, cold Christmas Eve and my emotions, which had suddenly cracked like an egg to allow something completely new to emerge. Something had changed for me. All the assumptions I'd made about Gatien, they all fell away, and I was ready to find out who he really was. I felt something stirring—no, rather going off like an explosion—and I warned myself to be careful. Even more careful than before.

Chapter Ten

I LEFT FOR Santa Barbara in the evening of Christmas Day.

Christmas morning had been hurried and embarrassed. May was politely pleased with her gifts and truly appreciated most everything she was given, but it was clear her enchanted childhood days were past, and we were not a cohesive family unit with understood traditions. So much for my homey fantasies of the night before.

"So, this is your second Christmas without your mom," I said to her. We sat together next to the tree after opening our presents, with Gatien in the room, close enough to hear us, to be part of the conversation, if he wanted to be. If I mentioned Lisa in that house, I always felt I was trespassing on some unspoken taboo. But I felt it was important, for May's sake, for us all to get past that.

"No—" May jumped to correct me, then realized my reckoning was accurate. "That's right. Last year we were on the cruise with Aunt Helene. It didn't seem like Christmas. It was like we missed it or something. Mommy died that September, you know."

"Yes, I know," I said.

"It doesn't really seem like Christmas without her."

"What did you do on Christmas morning when your mother was alive, May?"

"We'd have pancakes and bacon and put off opening our presents as long as possible, to keep the suspense."

"We always rushed to see who could open all their presents the fastest," I said.

"Really?" May was wide-eyed. "That's disgusting."

"Yes, I hated it. It was my two stepbrothers, actually; they're very uncivilized. But what could I do? They outnumbered me. I had to join in, because if I went slowly, they'd finish theirs first and start opening mine!"

"Oh my God. That is so rude."

"*Oh my gosh* being the more socially correct form, if you please."

"Oh my *gosh,*" she said exaggeratedly. "And your parents—your dad—? Let them get away with it?"

"My dad died of a heart attack three months after he married my stepmother, when I was twelve. Almost your age. We had just moved in with them, like, six months earlier. Sold our house, and everything. Then my dad died, and there I was. Living with my stepmother and two stepbrothers."

"Just like Cinderella!" May was impressed. "Wow. At least *I* don't have to put up with a stepmother and stepbrothers."

"Not yet you don't."

"What?" She flashed a bright, hard glance at me, suspicious. Gatien looked up from his reading.

"Well, your father's a very eligible man, isn't he?" I winked at her. "Some woman will find him irresistible—and he will find her irresistible, and then—voilà."

"Yeah, I know," May said glumly. "It's bound to happen. So what happened to your mom?"

"She died when I was five, of cancer. I barely remember her."

May regarded me with a new respect. Gatien did not say anything. But I sensed I had gained ground with both of them, simply through telling that story. I had earned my way in to a deeper acceptance, paid my dues with my own semitragic history. But I sensed there were episodes in their family saga they weren't ready for me to know about just yet.

Louisa and Carlos dropped by later in the morning with their granddaughter Flor, a friendly girl a year or two older than May, bringing us baskets of the handmade tortillas I loved and exclaiming with requisite delight over the candy and nuts and popcorn we'd packed for them in the tins May had painted by hand. We went to Helene's for an early supper, and the rest of the day was spent among a small crowd. Gatien never glanced my way.

He had given me no Christmas present, except that of an employer to an employee: money. Formally and in an envelope with a Christmas card signed in his handwriting, *With many thanks and best wishes for a Happy New Year, The Defalle Family.* I knew Louisa and Carlos had received one exactly like it.

When it was time for me to leave for Santa Barbara, he had gone off somewhere and we didn't say good-bye to each other.

I wasn't sure what it was I had wanted from him; I only felt the empty, aching absence of it. I pondered the question as I drove through the fallow fields south of Salinas. It was Christmas, after all; but what should I have expected? The cash bonus I received was beyond generous, and yet I could bring myself to feel no joy when I considered it. So what would have worked for me? I asked myself. I would have been embarrassed by jewelry, as I was with Nathan's necklace; disappointed with chocolates or flowers, or anything too cute, or too precious, or too practical.

That didn't leave much, true, but that wasn't the point. I realized it wasn't any material thing, any boxed gift that I had been looking for. It was some symbolic form of special recognition I had wanted. A lingering look. A brief touch of his hand on my shoulder. A short, significant note. Something from him that communicated to me that he was aware of what was there, undeniable, between the two of us. Or could it be I was simply deluded? Because he seemed to be denying it.

I could not believe that something vital had not passed between us last night, that I had imagined it or exaggerated its significance. But of course I probably had. I forced myself to replay the conversation we'd had on the way home from the airport, when it seemed he had been trying to tell me he would not be drawn into a frivolous relationship with me. I had listened dispassionately, amused more than anything. But I had been a different person then. That drive home in the car seemed so long ago, ages ago, when I had yet to be hit with the thermonuclear thunderbolt; that had come later, after midnight. Standing on that hill in the starlight, looking down at him, a half-naked, crippled centaur, shy and wild and too magical to be tamed with the usual techniques, I knew. Nothing between us could be frivolous.

For five hours straight I drove; I had the freeway practically to myself. On a rock station just north of San Luis Obispo I heard the Pretender's *"Criminal,"* the live version, a beautiful song I couldn't remember hearing before, and it hit me with such poignancy and sadness, I began to sob. No longer thinking of Gatien now, I was thinking about my father, and how I *had* felt like Cinderella after he died, even though my stepbrothers were never as horrible as her evil stepsisters, nor was my stepmother ever evil at all. I hadn't cried like that, thinking of my father, for years. I cried for my father, then I cried for my mother, whom I could not remember, except for some vague, dreamy impressions, then I cried for the stupid mistakes I had made, with friends and with the men in my life, how I had hurt the ones who had loved me or humiliated myself with the ones who didn't, and how I might be on the verge of doing it again with Gatien, and I realized how hopeless it was, this fantasizing about the father of my precious charge, May, who was really the most important part of the picture, I reminded myself again. I was in danger of putting my own desires over what was best for her. Thank God Gatien was a gentleman. I certainly couldn't trust myself.

By the time I pulled into my stepmother's driveway, my eyes were puffy, and I had poured out all manner of self-pity and yearning and frustration and loneliness and sadness and regret, and the emptiness was slowly filling up with peace. I had put almost three hundred miles between myself and the Defalles.

WHENEVER I GO away from Santa Barbara and come back again, I'm always amazed at how beautiful it is. It's the combination of small town and cosmopolitan city atmosphere, the university and colleges that bring in gorgeous people from all over the world, the stunning geography of the great blue ocean and the Channel Islands on one side, and the big purple mountains so close on the other, and the climate so temperate that flowers bloom in profusion all year round, and palm trees grow along miles of beaches.

I loved being back in town again, but once I was there, I found I couldn't wait to get back home.

Home, I thought. *Wow.* I really felt at home at the Defalles' now. I warned myself how dangerous that could be. I decided not to worry about it.

"GOD, YOU LOOK good," said Mallory, my best friend.

"Thanks," I said.

"No, really, it's great to see you back on your feet, Sarah," she said. She was sitting across from me in a booth at Moby Dick's on the wharf, staring into my eyes with her own big brown ones, framed by small, stylish glasses and her curly, dark hair. "I have to tell you, I was worried about you."

"Yeah, well, I was starting to wonder if I was gonna die," I said. "You weren't the only one who was worried."

"So what . . . what did they say it was, exactly? Did they ever . . ."

"Yeah. It was a nasty little critter I brought home with me from my travels."

"Well, it sure is amazing how you've been . . . transformed."

"I know, well, if someone had told me I'd get a bad hairdo and be sick for a year, but I'd end up twenty-five pounds lighter and with all new hair, I can't say I'd have taken the deal."

"Twenty-five pounds, huh?"

"Yeah. I lost more than that, but I gained back some. That's how it's kind of leveled off, I guess."

"Wow." Mallory was clearly impressed. "I wish I could ask how you did it, but you've just told me your secret. I don't think you can bottle that."

"No, and I wouldn't want to. I wouldn't wish that on anybody."

"So how's your love life? You must be attracting men like flies to dogshit."

"Uh . . . Well, actually . . . it's okay. Enjoying the scenery in the Bay Area, if you catch my drift."

"Any notable specifics?"

"Well . . . let's see. There's my boss's best friend, Paul. He's flirty, funny, very fine, and very married."

"Hmm. Of *course* he is."

"Well, maybe not *very* married, but married enough. And there's Nathan, an attractive and eligible contractor who's been working on the kitchen in my cottage, and he's got what appears to be a crush on me. He's a really nice guy."

"Okay, so *he's* out."

I laughed. "I know. It's too bad, isn't it?"

"What about your boss? The little girl's dad?"

"The little girl is thirteen and a woman grown, my friend."

"Ow."

"Exactly. She's a challenge. But she's cool. I think it's working."

"What's *he* like? The father?"

I shrugged, remembering I had asked Dimitri something of this sort the day I arrived, and he had not wanted to answer, and now, neither did I. To put Gatien into a few

simple words was impossible. If I could have sat up all
night with Mallory, drinking wine in front of the fireplace
in her Trout Farm cabin, I might have had a go at describing him, analyzing him, dissecting his every move. But
the truth was, since high school we didn't spend a lot of
time doing that sort of thing anymore. However, about
Gatien, and with Mallory, my best friend since seventh
grade, I was tempted to regress. Good thing we only had
this supper to spend together. Dorothy was expecting me
back early that evening.

"Sarah? Hello?" She snapped her fingers in front of my
face.

"I'll bet you'd like him," I said.

"Who? Yes, I bet I would. Your boss? The girl's dad?
Is he—?" She stretched out the word *he* meaningfully.

"Very much so," I replied.

"I see. So he's good-looking."

"In a tragic sort of way. He's got scars, and everything."

"Money?"

"Some, I think. And you'd like the fact that he's half
French. His name is Gatien Defalle."

"What is his profession?"

"He's a race car driver."

"My lord. You're kidding, right?"

"Former race car driver, I should say. Maybe retired.
I'm not sure. He had a big accident. Doesn't drive anymore. Won't talk about it."

"And it's a romantic, tragic story, too. Terrible accident. Can't race anymore. Lost his wife . . ." She frowned.
"How, exactly?"

"Supposedly she committed suicide by drowning herself in the ocean."

"Supposedly?"

"Yeah. Some say it was an accident. And some say"—
I paused for dramatic effect—"she was *murdered.*"

"What's *his* version of the story?"

"He told me just a short time ago that she would not
have killed herself. He seemed pretty adamant about it."

"Adamant, huh? I distrust adamance."

"I know. Me, too, but . . . is that a word?"

"You like him."

"What?"

"But you *like* him."

"Yeah. I do like him."

"Oh, God, girl. Goddess help you, darling. He's your *boss.* You're taking care of his *daughter.*"

"I know."

"But to tell you the truth, Sarah, I don't really see any intrinsic evil in the governess bonking the child's father. It happens all the time in gothic romance novels, right?"

"Yeah, but only after the governess *marries* him, the master of the house."

"Right. Otherwise, the governess is just a slut. No better than the scullery maid."

"What would *you* do, Mal?"

"You know exactly what I'd do. I'd have already seduced him by now and overwhelmed him with my undying love and enthusiastic appreciation of all his merits, and freaked him all out and scared him witless. He'd want to keep sleeping with me, but he wouldn't want me around because I'd make him feel guilty. So it would limp along for a few months, like for about the duration of my term of employment, and we would be making a big mess of our lives and would meanwhile also be messing with his daughter's head because of our own selfish preoccupations, and when it was over, he'd dump me and not pay me. I certainly wouldn't marry him, because he'd never have me."

"So, is that your recommendation?"

"I never recommend, only suggest. What does *he* want?"

"Nothing."

"Bullshit."

I shrugged, helpless.

"He's got a girlfriend?"

"I don't know."

"You would know. You've lived with him for what? Four months?"

"Well . . . he travels a lot."

"I didn't ask you if he was sleeping with someone else. I asked if he had a girlfriend. You know, a reason *not* to be with you."

"No. I guess not."

"He isn't gay?

"No, I don't think so. I mean, he dresses really well," I said with a laugh, "but still, no."

"He was unhappy with his wife." She said this with complete conviction.

"What do you mean? Why do you say that?"

"An attractive, happily married man, if he loses his wife to natural causes, he'll be married again, pronto." She snapped her fingers. "Inevitably."

"Well, it hasn't been that long. A year and a half . . ."

"And there's no girlfriend?"

"His best friend's wife throws herself at him periodically."

"Okay, but no available girlfriend, right? After a year and a half, he should at least be tagged. How old is he?"

"Mid to late thirties, I guess."

"A little old for you. Maybe he just hasn't noticed you yet. Though I find that hard to believe."

"I love you, Mallory," I said.

"I love you, too, dah-ling, and that's why I'm cautioning you against this one."

"What!" I cried. "On the basis of his age and—what else?"

"He's trouble. I can sense it. He's flawed."

I was about to come back at her with one of my snappy rejoinders, but the words stuck in my throat. *Flawed.* It was too apt. I could not respond.

I sat quietly, and she signaled the waiter for the check.

I DROVE UP north a day earlier than I'd planned, and I arrived back at the Defalles' to an empty house. For the first time since I had started my new position, I really had the

place to myself. No Gatien, no May; they had gone to
Tahoe with Helene and Dimitri.

I thought I would go straight to the library and do some
sleuthing, but I went downstairs instead. I stood before
Gatien's door, and I saw it was unlatched and standing
open a few inches. If the door had been shut, I don't know
what I would have done. But the door was not shut. I
pushed it open and went in.

As I walked through his room I was beset with a
strange but familiar feeling, like walking into a church or
a temple, the stillness of the space generating some force
of its own, quieting the spirit with its coolness, its scent,
and its silence; and I felt peculiar and empty but for a sad
guilt, for violating something, for being here in this place
where I didn't belong but could not resist entering. The
colors of the room were muted but striking, and I had to
wonder if Gatien consciously matched his surroundings to
his own coloring, slate wool carpets and the simple cotton
spread on the frameless bed. The only item of decoration
was a framed photograph propped on the dresser, a beautiful car streaming out of focus across the picture plane, a
blue rocket with big black wheels, the cockpit open, just
the suggestion of a helmeted pilot, and I guessed it was
Gatien himself driving the car, though later I found out it
was his father. There were no other photographs or art in
the room, which was spare, sparse. Ascetic, like a cell in
a monastery, but the view from the tall, plain windows
gave it spectacular, sensual beauty.

I learned nothing about Gatien in his room. Perhaps
there were clues in the drawers of the bedside tables or his
dresser; in his medicine chest or in the big leather trunk
that stood at the foot of the bed, but I didn't search them
out. Walking through his room was one thing, rifling
through his drawers was another.

I was letting myself out of Gatien's suite when I noticed the stack of books in a pile on a shelf in the corner
by the door, and I moved closer, curious to see what he
was reading. The book on the top of the pile was the one
on racing technique I had seen in the dining room. An-

other book was the novel *Cold Mountain,* in hardcover, and beneath the books, there was a stack of perhaps a half-dozen news magazines and mail order catalogues for men's fine clothing.

I saw the edge of it poking out, the speckled cardboard of a lab notebook, and I reached down automatically and pulled it out of the pile. It came out neatly, not even disturbing the stack. I blew a light coating of dust off the edge of the book. It was marked on the front cover with the beginning date, as were all the others, but there was no ending date.

It was the missing notebook—the one Lisa had been writing before her death. I opened it, and there was her handwriting, dramatic and beautiful, same as in all the other notebooks. I felt a cold prickle run down the back of my neck. What if I was being watched? In this era of nanny-cams and hidden spy equipment, I'd be a fool not to consider the possibility that anything I did was subject to preservation for posterity. I stood there with the notebook in my hand and considered my options. I could put the notebook back where I found it, forget it ever existed. Or I could take it and read it, cover to cover, in the privacy of my own cottage. If I took it, I was taking something that wasn't mine and sticking my nose in something that technically was none of my business. If I put it back and forgot about it, I might be passing up an opportunity to learn something important, something that could help this family I was learning to care about, this damaged, mysterious family. What if, hidden in this notebook, was proof that Lisa didn't kill herself? Okay, so it was a far-fetched notion. It would actually be easier for a diary to prove she *had* intended to kill herself. Either way, I wanted to know.

There was another option. I could go to Gatien and tell him what I had found. I wondered if he had looked in the journal himself. If he even knew it existed. How long had it been sitting there, in that pile of books and papers? Some of the catalogues and magazines were old, dating from before the time of Lisa's death. Was it possible he didn't even know this journal existed? Or perhaps he was well aware that it existed and had deliberately separated it from the others.

But it only made sense that the journal would not be with the others. It had been a living document at the time of Lisa's death, her current personal record. She would have kept it close to herself . . . in her bedroom. Perhaps she had left it on her bedside table. It had been there the day she died, untouched until someone cleaned the room and stacked everything neatly in a pile to be placed on a shelf, and there it might have stayed for months.

How thoroughly, I wondered, had Lisa's death been investigated? If there was any question of foul play, a journal left casually lying around would certainly have been treated as evidence.

I jumped, guilty, as I heard the doorbell ring, and I stuffed the journal between a couple of magazines, as I had found it, and went upstairs to the entry hall.

"MRS. DEFALLE?"

"No, I'm Sarah," I said. "Can I help you?"

"Are you his girlfriend?" He huffed out a laugh. He spoke with a British accent, but I didn't think he was British, for some reason.

I shook my head, but he wasn't looking at me anymore, didn't seem interested in the answer anyway.

He was handsome, or had been once. His face was well-built and sensual, his skin pockmarked, his thinning hair still dark. He couldn't have been more than ten years older than me, but he seemed dissipated. Though he was tall, he stood slightly hunched and vaguely unsteady on his feet. The slacks and shirt he wore hung on him in a rather elegant way because of his tall, slender proportions, but they seemed wrong for him, didn't fit him, as if they were borrowed from someone larger. But the most striking and unexplainable thing about him was the sense of recognition I felt the moment I looked at him. And yet I could not remember ever having met him before.

"Are they here?" he asked, with a demanding, somehow frightened stress on his words. He took out a pack of cigarettes from his pants pocket and lit one with shaky hands. He didn't look at me when he spoke. "Guy by the name of Defalle? Dark-haired girl named Anna May? Or maybe just May . . ."

"No, they're not," I said, instinctively protective. I didn't care for this man or for the familiar, disrespectful way he spoke of Gatien and May.

"But they live here, right?" He suddenly looked at me, piercingly, for a moment.

For some reason, he scared me, looking me up and down, sizing something up. With icy politeness I drew myself up and said: "Whom shall I say has called?"

"You tell him the Lone Wolf was here," he said in a quiet voice. "And I want him to know something else. You give him the message. I don't care how much money he's got. Or whatever else he's got going for him. You tell him that for me. I'll have what is mine. I know where he is now, and I *will* have what's mine."

I shrank into the doorframe and pulled the door closer to me, like a shield, my prim strength cracking, but he was, in a sense, oblivious to me. He spun on his heel and strode off down the driveway. I heard him whistling as he walked away.

EVENING WAS COMING on. I walked back into the house and lit a lamp. I had thought I would enjoy being alone, but now that I had the place to myself, I felt lonely, and the rooms seemed big and empty. The meeting with the strange man had left me feeling jumpy. What kind of a weirdo was he, anyway, with his handsome, pockmarked face and his strange words. *I know where he is now. . . . I'll have what's mine. . . .*

The Lone Wolf. Good grief.

And why did he seem so familiar?

I wished that Gatien would suddenly walk through the front door. I would tell him all about the strange man, and he would laugh off the incident, explaining that the Lone Wolf was actually a friend of his, an old Formula One buddy, a fellow driver, who had the championship but lost it to his friend and rival Gatien Defalle, and who vows to race to victory, to take back the title. I'd seen his photograph around the house. That's why he seemed so familiar.

Sounded good to me.

And I would tell Gatien about the journal and explain to him my reasons for wanting to read it. And he would say, *Sure, go ahead. I never thought to read it myself, but what the hell. Let me know if you find anything significant.*

Right.

I took a deep breath. I walked around the house and locked all the doors. Then I went down to Gatien's room and got the journal.

I THOUGHT BETTER of staying in the house, and I brought the journal down to my cottage. I made myself a cup of tea in my newly remodeled kitchen and settled down in the overstuffed chair to read.

It really was nicer in here, with the construction work complete and without all the boxes cluttering up the place; I now had a comfortable and charming sitting room. For a few minutes I sat there with the journal unopened on my lap. Finally, I opened the cover and turned immediately to the last entry.

I had to flip back through a number of blank pages before I reached the final few sentences. Theoretically, the last words Lisa had written before her death.

September 7

Autumn is here again. The days are warm still, but even in the midafternoon you can feel a menacing chill in the air. The season is nearly over, and Gatien will have his way, if all goes as it has been the last few months. I suppose he deserves it. I've decided to stop running after him. He might even like me better for it. Bittersweet surrender.

Helene has invited me to come to the beach house this weekend with May and Dimitri. Maybe I'll see if Paul and Theta want to come along.

I'm off to the seashore!

That was it.

I read the passage over again and pondered it. Interesting, I thought, if unrevealing. I was struck by how it might be read any of a few different ways. As the final statement of a woman about to commit suicide? Not inconceivable. The last words of an unwitting murder victim? Perhaps.

Bittersweet surrender.

Or, maybe Lisa's journal showed she was simply another unlucky casualty of Mother Nature's dispassionate wrath. *I'm off to the seashore!*

Who could say?

I read backwards through the journal.

In the second to the last entry, Lisa bitterly denounced the president of the United States and his foreign policy. Would a person on the brink of suicide be thinking of such things?

The entry previous consisted of a list, everything she had eaten that day, and a complete, detailed self-examination and psychological profile of herself in relation to her food choices. Entry after entry, as I went backward through the journal, it was the same, either politics or diet. She was either expounding on her political views or obsessing with her weight, which was apparently within ten pounds of where she wanted it to be, but that was a very heavy ten pounds for her, and it seemed to occupy much of her thinking. I sympathized, but it wasn't what I was interested in reading. My disappointment grew as I read.

Patience, I told myself. *Keep on slogging.* Just because I had turned to the last entry and found—well, nothing—that was no reason to give up on the idea that I might have something significant here. Or in the other journals. Somewhere in the hundreds and hundreds of pages . . . there must be something. I was afraid of missing something crucial.

August 15

    Ray brought up the SORE SUBJECT again tonight. It's a joke. It just isn't there. I'm tired and bored of the whole thing, I feel like a fool, and Gatien would kill me if he knew what I've actually spent on this mad quest of mine. I feel like boarding up my library and never going back in there.

    Now *there* was something. A mention of the library. The mysterious, forbidden library. Okay, semiforbidden. What mad quest was she talking about? I continued reading backwards through the journal. More politics, more dieting. Ray was mentioned again a week or two later, or earlier, as it were:

July 29

    I promised Ray I wouldn't give up, not yet, but I think I just said it to be nice. I should never have gotten involved in this. Maybe the old count was delusional, and maybe so am I for falling for his story. I know I'm being paranoid, but I'm starting not to trust anybody.
    On the other hand, Ray and Isaac are wonderful, and I wouldn't have gotten so close to them if I hadn't done it.

    The passionate discourse on the political situation and dieting died away as I flipped backward through Lisa's journal.

June 21

    What a fool I've been. Nothing.

June 7

    The longer it takes, the more I think I may have been the victim of a con. Funny, this time I really thought I was going with my instincts, and when I do that I'm usually okay.

May 15

I've just got to be patient. Things take time.

May 8

Waiting and waiting for more to arrive.

April 9

Brought the books to the Shiptons.
Something of a letdown.
Isaac told me what I do have is actually quite valuable, so I shouldn't be so disappointed. But I thought I had something special there.
Anyway, it was only the first shipment. There's supposed to be lots of others. We'll see.

April 5

The first box has arrived!
I bid too much for the lot, but they're just the most beautiful old books. I can't wait to see what Ray and Isaac have to say.

March 21

I feel like I'm on a treasure hunt! I haven't felt this alive in so long. The Shiptons are very conservative, the best of the best in the business, they say. If I've really got something here—and if the count is an honorable man, I must—the Shiptons will know it.

I was intrigued, thinking of the men who had come asking about Lisa's library, and Gatien's odd behavior in regard to them. I turned to the front of the journal and began to read from the beginning. The obsession for old manuscripts seemed to have grown out of an interest in antiquities, which had begun with a visit Lisa had paid, accompanied by her sister Helene, to a museum in San Francisco, a trip described in excited detail near the beginning of the journal. Lisa also detailed her sister's patient exasperation with her; this fixation on antiquities, the manuscripts in particular, was apparently merely another in a long line of passionate interests, including English horseback riding, sailing, collecting rare orchids, golf, and Persian cats. Lisa acknowledged her own fickle heart and her short attention span, but her self-awareness did not prevent her from jumping wholeheartedly and with what seemed to be a rather generous budget (thanks to the combination of a generous father and an indulgent husband) into what was to be her final obsession, a fascination for rare manuscripts. It seemed to me the only real thread of continuity among her various interests was the fact that, as hobbies go, they were all rather costly.

I turned the page again, and a white business card with elegant gold embossed lettering fell out of the journal.

Shipton Antiquities. Rare books and Manuscripts. Appraisals.

The card listed an address on University Avenue, in Palo Alto. I set it aside and began to read again.

January 24

Home again. Though it's hard when I'm away from Gatien, cutting back on all the travel has been good, for May's sake. But I'm so glad I went this time. What an incredible time we had! And Eduardo is such a sweetheart. Charming, handsome, and sexy. At dinner, he leaned over and said in a low voice, "Do you trust me, Lisa?"

I looked at him, about to reply with a joke, but then I saw he was completely serious, looking at me with his opaque dark eyes. "What do you mean?" I asked.

"You've told me you want to invest in fine manuscripts, rare things. I see you have the passion, and the where-

withal, and you know enough to get the best in the business to help you."

I nodded.

"My dear, would you be willing to be entrusted with something far more priceless and rare than anything I've shown you yet?"

"Of course. You know I would be, but—please, explain what you mean."

"What I am about to propose to you, Lisa," he said, *"would require a great commitment on your part. Of money. Of time. But especially of heart."* He leaned toward me and gazed at me like a lover. I looked at Gatien to see if he was jealous, but he was just smiling at us, as if something amused him.

"But you must trust me," Eduardo said. There was something softly insistent in his voice. *"Can you trust me, Lisa?"*

"Yes, Eduardo," I said. A strange excitement rose in me. *"Yes,"* I said softly. *"I trust you."*

Hmm, I thought. Was this the beginning of Lisa's extramarital dalliance, such as the rumors had spoken of? But Lisa wrote no more of Eduardo on that date, and the next few journal entries were of no help in the matter. The Defalles were moving into a new home high on a hillside in California, and her energy and focus turned to that. Then, on February fifteenth, Lisa wrote:

Helene found out Daddy gave me money for the shipment. I know she wasn't very happy about it. She thinks I'm wasting his money on my frivolous obsessions. I hope I can prove her wrong this time. But even Daddy said, "I don't understand what you find so fascinating in all those dusty old books, Lisa!" And I said, "I know, I can't believe I'm over here lusting after a bit of old vellum like it was a string of pearls or something."

Gatien just says, "If it makes you happy, Lise . . ." If he doesn't care, why should they? Most of the money I spend is his, anyway.

It's really like an oyster, more than a pearl. I open each one, thinking I'm going to find that pearl inside. So far I haven't. Not the pearl of great price anyway. At least not after you deduct the cost of the oyster! But I've got a good feeling about this latest acquisition of mine. . . .

I closed the journal at last, my eyelids heavy and my brain saturated. *I'll find it* I thought. *Something of significance. I'll find it. It's just going to take time.* But I was beginning to wonder.

LOUISA CAME IN early the next day, filling the house with the delicious smells of her cooking. I ran errands and helped Louisa prepare the house for the return of the family, so I had no time to pick up Lisa's journal again. In the late afternoon Helene's Mercedes pulled up in the drive. Gatien and May had returned. I was curiously excited to see them again. They all got out of the car rather stiffly and stretched— Dimitri, who had been driving, Helene, who looked a little sore, rolling her back and shoulders; Gatien, who had no word of greeting for me, only an enigmatic smile; and May, who, to my complete surprise, ran up to me and gave me a quick hug and said, "I missed you, Governess!"

"I missed you, too, May!" I said, and it was true. We all walked into the house together, everyone talking at once. May and Dimitri were particularly excited about their snowboarding vacation, and they had a lot to tell me.

May said, "We were trying to talk them into staying another day, weren't we Dimitri? But *some*one wanted to get home!" She smiled with a pointed look at her father.

"Well! I for one had had enough!" declared Helene. "I'm getting too old for skiing!"

"Come on now," Gatien said. "You're in the prime of life."

"Yes. And the prime of life is too old for skiing!"

"I wish you had been there, Governess," said May, her eyes shining. "You would have loved it."

"I'm sure Sarah had a fine time visiting in Santa Barbara," said Helene.

"Yes, I did," I said. "But I'm glad to be home." I said

it before I could catch myself. Calling the Defalles' place *home* seemed presumptuous.

"I'm glad to be home, too," said Gatien, with a guarded look at me.

"Really?" Helene sounded surprised. "I've sometimes wondered if you think up excuses to stay away from home, Gatien."

He responded to that merely by picking up some of the bags that had been piled by the front door and carrying them off down the stairs.

"I gotta get back up on the slopes," Dimitri declared. "I need to fix into my brain what I've learned this week so it doesn't slip backwards."

"Yeah, right!" May laughed. "Give me a break. You are *so* good, Dimitri. Sarah, you should see him. He is awesome on a snowboard. He does jumps and flips and everything."

I was amazed at May's energy and excitement, glad to find her more open and happy than I'd ever seen her before, but I was uneasy about it, too. I couldn't help but wonder how much of her excitement had to do with Dimitri. I was pretty sure she was infatuated with him. It might be difficult for her, if he didn't share her interest; but if he did, that would be worse. They were cousins; but would that be enough of a taboo to keep them apart? I remembered him telling me, when he had turned eighteen, that he was no longer jailbait. I hoped he kept in mind that she still was.

Louisa had refreshments ready in the dining room. May and Dimitri went in together, still laughing and arguing about their snowboarding experiences. Gatien had disappeared. Helene went outside on the terrace to have a cigarette, and I joined her.

"It was a successful trip, judging from the sound of it," I said.

"Yes indeed," she agreed, taking a deep drag of her cigarette, letting it out with a certain relief. "And how was your vacation, Sarah?"

"Nice," I said. "Good to see old friends."

"And Santa Barbara is so beautiful."

"It is that."

"Well, I for one will be happy to get home. I'm going to finish this cigarette, pull Dimitri off cloud nine, and get going."

"Before you go, Helene," I said, "there's something I wanted to talk with you about."

"Of course. Anything."

"This is personal, I know, and I apologize for that, but . . . you know I've thought a lot about May's mother . . . your sister, Lisa."

"Yes?"

"Well, you've made it pretty clear that you have no doubt about her death being a suicide."

"Right."

"But wouldn't it be . . . I mean, wouldn't you rather know that it had been an accident? Wouldn't that be easier for everyone in the family? Especially, I would think, for May . . ."

She laughed dryly. "We can't decide these matters based on what we'd *rather* they be."

"I know. Of course you can't. But what if there was some sort of evidence proving it wasn't a suicide? As it is now, there are all these rumors surrounding Lisa's death. You know what they are."

"Yes."

"I don't think that's good for May."

"What sort of *evidence* are you talking about?"

"Did you know Lisa kept a journal?"

She nodded, let out a breath of smoke, a smooth, controlled exhale. "Yes, I know she dabbled with her writing, but . . ."

"Look, I realize this is none of my business. I'm poking into something that maybe I shouldn't, but I can't help but wonder. . . ."

"You've seen her journals?"

"Yes," I admitted. "I've looked at them. I've read a few entries."

She gave me a long, wise look. "That's all right, Sarah. I've got a curious mind myself. I understand." She sighed heavily. It seemed to be painful for her, discussing her dead sister's effects, and I couldn't blame her for that. But I was glad to be confiding in her. It hadn't felt right to me, keeping it to myself.

"The truth is," she said, "I went through all those journals myself, looking for the very same thing. And what I found, I'm afraid, only confirms my own convictions on the matter. My sister, God love her, was a mixed-up individual. If there was a journal closer to the day of her death, it might be different, but everything I found was written at least a year earlier, so even if—"

But that's just it, I was about to say. *I found the last journal in Gatien's bedroom.* No, I couldn't say that. I held my tongue, suddenly afraid that if I told her I had it, she would ask where I found it. I knew better than to start lying. Lies beget lies. So I withheld the information, and I did not tell her about the journal, though that had been my purpose for bringing up the subject.

"I suppose it would be interesting reading, at any rate," she said, and I wondered if she was being facetious.

No, actually, it was rather dull reading for the most part.

"Anyway," she said decisively, "I don't think there's much hope of finding that magical narrative that would change the way history is perceived."

That was probably true enough.

We looked up to see Dimitri standing outside the door. I wondered how much of our conversation he had heard.

"Dimitri," said Helene. "Are you getting anxious to leave?"

He shrugged. "Sure. Any time you're ready."

"Anyway . . ." I watched Dimitri as he moved to the railing, casually leaning against it, looking off across the peninsula, out beyond the East Bay hills and the hazy mass of Mount Diablo. He didn't seem to be paying attention to Helene and me, but we dropped the subject of Lisa's journals. Helene finished her cigarette, and we made our way out to the car.

"May!" I called. "Come say good-bye to your Aunt Helene, and thank her for taking you to Tahoe."

Helene turned to me before she got into the car and said quietly, "So tell me, Sarah, why did you mention this, about Lisa's journals? Have you found anything of significance?"

"Well, no," I said truthfully.

She nodded. "Well, I hope you're not too disappointed."

"I wondered if I should talk to Gatien about this," I said.

"Well, I would, certainly, if there was a good reason to bring it up. But you know how prickly he is about anything to do with Lisa or that library of hers. I think those journals are a part of that."

"I know. That's why I thought I'd bring it up with you first."

"That makes sense," she said.

May and Dimitri joined us.

Gatien came out to stand on the porch and see Helene and Dimitri off.

Helene gave me a brief, stiff hug, like someone unaccustomed to showing physical affection, and whispered, "Thank you, Sarah. Your concern for my family is very touching." She called out to the others. "All right! We're off."

May waved as the Mercedes pulled out of the yard. I looked at Gatien and found him watching me. He turned and went back into the house. His coolness exasperated me, but I shrugged it off. My little family was back together again, and I was content.

Chapter Eleven

THE NEXT DAY was New Year's Eve, and I was surprised to be suddenly in the middle of preparations for the big night. I would have thought everyone would be tired, having just gotten home from a week at Tahoe the previous day, but May announced at the breakfast table that we were expected to help Helene cook and decorate for a party that night.

"That's only if you want to, of course, Governess," she said with exaggerated politeness, looking up at me earnestly. Sometimes, I thought, May was too slyly calculating to be trusted. I was never quite sure of her motives. "But Helene would like to have you, if you would come," she added.

"She didn't say anything about a party when we talked last night."

"It's just something she does every year. Except not last year, because of my mother."

"What does she need help with?"

"We're going to make chili and cornbread and cookies and ice cream and set up videos in her family room."

"Chili and ice cream? It's New Year's Eve, not the Fourth of July."

"Get dressed. She wants us over there early."

"Now? Why do we have to go so early?"

"Get things done; we can take naps later so we can stay up really late. And we need to go shopping for something special to wear. To get dressed up."

Well, I agreed. May and I went to Helene's, where we spent the morning stirring and chopping and sifting, and then Helene sent us on a shopping spree at Stanford Mall with a credit card and a firm admonition to make sure we looked fabulous at her party that night. She made appointments for us at her hairdresser's in Menlo Park and booked us a table at a café in Palo Alto for lunch. It was a fantastic day, all in all, though I had been reluctant to leave the house. I wanted to stay home; to be near Gatien, if the truth be told. I had missed him. I should have been used to being away from him, because so often he was gone for days or even weeks at a time, but this latest separation had been different. He wasn't the only one who had gone away. And now we were both home and yet still apart.

In the weeks leading up to Christmas, Gatien had been home much more than usual. I suppose I was getting used to having him around. In December we had started having breakfast together, Gatien, May, and me, before I took May off to school each morning. We ate leftover tortillas grilled over the open flame on the gas stove, with cottage cheese and hot sauce. Or I made my specialty, French toast, and we teased Gatien about it being "his" toast, because he was half French, and he'd scoff and declare he'd never seen anything remotely resembling my French toast in France, but he seemed to like it anyway, and he ate slice after slice of it, dripping with butter and real maple syrup, until he groaned and said his stomach hurt. It was about the only undisciplined thing I ever saw him do.

We always ended up laughing and laughing. May had a sophisticated and wicked sense of humor. She was so perceptive and mature for her age, I would catch myself speaking to her in a way that I would only speak to someone of my own age, a little more frank than appropriate for my role as guide for her young soul. Sometimes I had to remind myself she was only thirteen.

Gatien's sense of humor was dry, and there were times I didn't realize he was kidding around with me until after the fact. May seemed to understand him; the two of them got along well and seemed to enjoy each other's company. In fact, it seemed to me that over the months I had known them they had grown closer right before my eyes, opening up to one another as father and daughter, even as both May and Gatien were opening to me in another way.

I was becoming addicted to him. All the while I was away from him in Santa Barbara, I had thought about him. I remembered the way he smiled when he let his guard down, his strangely formal gentleness with May, his patience with her. How playful and teasing he was with Louisa, how respectful of Carlos. His friends loved him, that was sure. Helene doted on him, Paul practically worshiped him, and Theta obviously couldn't get enough of him.

I had mixed feelings about this New Year's Eve party. I was looking forward to spending an evening with the Defalle family and friends, but I was troubled. I wasn't sure why, but when I analyzed it, I was amused to realize it was the whole kiss-at-midnight thing that was making me anxious. If it hadn't been for Gatien, it wouldn't have made any difference if I didn't get kissed. But tonight, at midnight, I would be in the same room with a man I really wanted to kiss.

That's it, I thought. *That's all it is!* It was so simple, I didn't know why I hadn't thought of it before. I just really wanted to *kiss* him. The idea of actually making *love* with him was too scary to contemplate. Well, not to contemplate, but to actually follow through on, it would be. He was just way too intense for me, in a very cool kind of way. Sex with him would be too fraught. I would worry about what he thought of my body. I would worry about how it would change everything between us—or wouldn't. I would worry about being worried about it.

But a kiss. A kiss was more innocent. A kiss could be a single moment in time, never expected nor expected again. *Yes,* I thought. *Kissing him would be . . . not unimaginable, as I had once thought. A kiss might be . . . interesting . . . exciting . . . dreamy . . . and . . . nice. How I would love to just touch his lips with my own. . . .*

Then again, a kiss can be disappointing if it's slurpy or dry or just lies there. A kiss usually involved the hands in some way. I loved Gatien's hands. They were strong and bony, with big knuckles, but they were slender and grace- ful, too. So a kiss would mean his hands were gently grasping my arms. Or sliding around me, a quick em- brace. Or cupping my face as his lips touched my lips. Or sliding into my hair, one strong arm pulling me against him as he crushed his mouth into mine, romance novel–style, and made me know him completely, if just for a moment.

Just a kiss, that's all I wanted.

So it was New Year's Eve, and I wanted to kiss this guy so badly I could taste it. But I was only tasting the desire. I wanted to taste *him.*

All the while we prepared for the night to come, I was doing it for him. When I carefully sifted the flour for the rolls, it was because Gatien liked fresh-baked bread. When I tried on silk slacks and short skirts at Blooming- dale's, I wondered which ones Gatien would like. When I got my hair cut and styled, I kept it long because May had told me he liked long hair.

But all the while that I was laughing and chatting and planning and shopping and baking, I was fretting, and un- derneath it all, uneasy. It was because of what had hap- pened between Gatien and me on Christmas Eve, that moment in the darkness as I massaged his cramped leg.

I knew if I hadn't gotten up and walked out of his bed- room when I did, we would have been naked in each other's arms in about thirty seconds. And from that moment on, Christmas Day and ever since, Gatien had raised the old formality between us.

It was New Year's Eve, and Gatien wasn't going to kiss me at midnight.

Deal with it, Sarah.

AS MAY AND I walked down University Avenue after our Helene-sponsored lunch on the afternoon of New Year's Eve, looking in the shop windows, I was looking at the addresses. I had not deliberately set out to look for it, but being in the area, I couldn't help but consider it. When an embossed brass placard mounted on the corner of a commercial building caught my eye, I saw the familiar name, between the law firm of Nickerson and Tate, and Drs. Benson and Shute: *Shipton Antiquities.* It was the name on the card I had found in Lisa's last journal. Accompanying the names was a brass arrow, pointing down an ivy-draped, cobblestone alleyway housing the entries of several quaint shops and upscale offices.

"May, come here a sec," I said, pulling her into the narrow side street with me.

"What are we doing?"

"Hold on." I continued a few doors down until I came to the name again, this time in fine gold lettering on a glass door between two shops, a chic haberdashery and a gift boutique.

Shipton Antiquities. Specializing in Rare Books and Manuscripts, Appraisals.

"That's it," I said.

"What are we doing?" May asked again.

"May, would you give me a moment to check something out?"

"Yeah, sure. Could I look in the gift shop?"

"Yes. Stay in there until I come back. I'm just going in here for a minute or two. Wait for me in the shop or right outside the door here."

"Okay."

"Don't go anywhere else."

"Okay.

We parted; she went into the shop, and I tried the door. It opened to a stairwell, and looking up I could see light from a room upstairs. I heard music, reedy flutes and drums, and a man's voice, loud and argumentative. I almost turned back.

I took the steps tentatively and found an open door at the top. I looked into a large, open loft filled with tables covered with books. There were bookshelves on every available wall, counters loaded with pottery and sculpture, bins and cubbies, cabinets and closets, all bulging with relics and materials, art and archeological specimens and books and manuscripts, and against the back wall, something that looked like a giant refrigerator. A young man with a spiked Mohawk was sitting at a counter in the corner, looking through a microscope, and in the center of it all was a dark-haired, fierce-looking giant wearing eggplant purple overalls and talking on the phone.

"Goddam it, Pedro, you told me you'd have it finished for me by Tuesday! Blast your ass! I don't give a damn about holidays. All right, then." There was a short pause. "Yeah, buddy, you know it. Next. Yes. Right! Friday. Copy that. Over and out!" He slammed the phone into its cradle on the wall, and turned to look at me, having already spotted me standing there, imposing on his domain.

"May I help you?" he shouted.

He was vivacious and huge and handsome, with a black beard, fierce eyes, and white teeth. He bared those teeth, looking at me from across the room, waiting for an explanation of my presence.

"Are you Isaac Shipton?"

"And what's your purpose for wanting to know?" He approached me, dodging around the various worktables and cabinets with a bearlike grace, regarding me with suspicion.

What was my purpose for wanting to know? I hardly knew the answer to that myself. "Do you appraise manuscripts?" I asked.

"Do you have a manuscript you want appraised?"

"I was just curious what makes a manuscript valuable,"

I said. It was kind of a stupid question, but he had caught me off guard.

"Depends on what it is, who it was written by, and when. Condition. Documented history. If it has any"— here he paused, both in his speech and in his movement, for he had come to stand very close to me, his head at an angle—"historical significance."

"I see."

"What are you interested in?"

We looked at each other.

"Actually, it's for a . . . friend," I said.

He burst out laughing. "Excellent. And what can I do for your . . . friend?"

"He's a man I work for, actually. His wife was interested in old manuscripts and collected them, before she died. She left behind a rather impressive library. It's all sort of in limbo now, and it's kind of a shame, because there's some interesting stuff there."

"What sort of books does she . . . did she have?"

"I'm not sure the extent of it. Her husband is sensitive about the whole thing. He doesn't like anyone poking around in there, so I don't really know."

"Well, if the owner is dead, it seems to me if there was anything of value or interest there, the family would have snapped it up. If you have anything of specific interest that you would like me to take a look at, we can make an appointment. There is a list of my hours and fees, there on that desk. You may take a flyer."

Nothing like being summarily dismissed.

"All right," I said. "Thank you." I turned and went toward the door. I nearly passed on the flier for Mr. Appraiserman's services. But I didn't, and as I was reaching for one, his voice boomed out again.

"What did you say your employer's name was?"

"I didn't." I picked up the flier, studied it casually.

"There was a young woman who lost her life rather tragically a year, year and a half ago," he said, his voice lowering and portentous. "Wasn't much of a serious collector, but she came into some interesting merchandise from an estate lot she bought in Spain. She happened to be there with her husband who was there on business. He was a race car driver."

He was watching me keenly.

I nodded. "Yes," I said. "He was. So you are familiar with the collection?"

"The lady brought me one or two things to look at. She told me she was expecting to bring me something very special, but then . . . such a shame. She was so young."

"She mentioned you in some writings she left behind. She said you were really good at what you do. The best."

"Did she ever get more of that shipment she was expecting?"

"I don't really know," I admitted.

"Do you know there are those who would kill to get a good look at what you have there, in your employer's library?"

I thought of what I had read in Lisa's last journal. She had been waiting for a shipment of books. She had grown discouraged, given up. There was no record of her ever having found what she was looking for, whatever it was. So whatever it was in Lisa's library that interested these scholars, my guess was it didn't exist.

"Who would they kill?" I asked uneasily.

"You work for him, you say?"

"Yes, I'm the nanny. Or as May says, the governess."

"What's the nanny doing asking questions about the Defalle library?"

"I have books of my own, shelved there," I said coolly. "It's a beautiful library."

"I know of several individuals who have already made quite an effort to gain entrance to Lisa Defalle's library."

"So do I. What I want to know is, why? What are they looking for?"

Crossing his arms over his huge chest, he leaned back against the cabinets and regarded me with a new interest. "You tell me," he said.

"Can you give me a hint?"

"You really have no idea?"

"I don't know much about antiques," I said. "And I don't know anything about rare manuscripts."

"And have you explored this library at all?"

I thought about what I had explored the few times I had actually been in Lisa's library. It wasn't the rare books and manuscripts, no. It was Lisa Defalle's personal diaries. I felt ashamed, like someone with literary pretensions being caught reading the *National Enquirer*. But then, if I hadn't snooped I wouldn't have found Isaac's name.

"Not extensively," I said.

"I figure by now, it would have been dismantled anyway. Things sold, divided, given away, looted." He gave me a surprising, kindly smile. "Am I right?"

"I don't know. I don't think so."

"Really?" He was thoughtful.

"So what are they looking for?"

"I can't comment on that," he answered.

"But you know, don't you?"

"Hey, listen, whatever your name is," he said, talking to me almost tenderly now. "Want my advice? I'll give you some, free of charge, the first three minutes. Forget about the whole thing. Get rid of anything that's left. Have a garage sale."

"Strange advice from a guy in your profession."

"Hey, I guess that's just 'cause I like you. You seem like a nice girl, and I wouldn't wanna see you get hurt."

"Hurt?"

"Like Lisa Defalle." He looked at me long. "She got in over her head."

"Sarah?" I heard May's voice echoing up the stairwell.

"I'm coming," I called down to her.

"Just some friendly advice . . . Sarah," Isaac said.

"I'll consider it," I said. "Thanks."

I descended the stairs and met May on the sidewalk outside the building. She looked at me expectantly. "Ready?" she asked.

"Yep. Let's go."

The door opened behind us and Isaac came out. "Sarah," he said. "I want you to have my home number, in case you need to get hold of me." He handed me his card, which was exactly like the one I had found in Lisa's journal. On it he had scribbled a number beside his shop number.

May was watching us intently.

"Okay," I said. "Thank you."

"Happy New Year, Sarah," he said softly. He went back into the building.

"I do love men with beards," May said.

THE HOUSE GLOWED with the lamps lit in the living room, and the windows were frosty, making it all very cozy. The three of us were busy getting ready for the party, running through the house, somewhat disorganized because we had all been gone the previous week. I was excited about getting dressed up and going out to a party, but I would have preferred to be staying home, sitting with Gatien in front of the fire.

I came face-to-face with him outside the guest room, where I had gone to get something from the packages May and I had brought home that afternoon. We had stashed the bags on the bed in there to get them out of the way.

"How dressy is it going to be?" I asked nervously, smelling his fresh-washed body so close. He was wearing casual cotton trousers, but the fabric was so fine it was silky, the cut perfect over his lean, solid thighs. He wore no shirt, only a towel draped over his ropy, tanned neck. His belly was hard and bare, the muscles of his arms knotted and compact. His hair was wet and stood up like the pelt of a wolf.

I was wearing a long velour dressing gown, zipped up to my throat, and suddenly I was glad I was well-covered. His partial nakedness was disconcerting to me, here in the hallway on this cool winter's night.

"It's casual," he said to me. "Don't worry about it."

"What are you looking for?"

"My silk pirate shirt. I think it's in here."

"Your idea of casual is rather elegant, I've noticed," I said.

"I accept that." He added, with a smile, "Do you have a problem with that?"

"I like it."

"Hi!" said May, popping up between us. "How do I look?"

"You look smashing," I said. And she did, dressed in white bell-bottoms and a paisley silk peasant blouse, her dark hair long over her shoulders, her pure, innocent beauty so becoming with the chic retro '70s style.

"Very nice," said Gatien. "You remind me of my mother."

"Is that a good thing or a bad thing?" May wanted to know.

"She was very beautiful. But she was a heroin addict."

May's eyes grew wide.

"Didn't I ever tell you that?"

She shook her head.

"She died of an overdose in an elegant apartment in Milan when I was sixteen."

"How sad," said May.

"Yes. But I was ashamed. I barely knew her."

"That's even sadder!"

"What about your father? How did he take it?"

"They were divorced already, for five years. My mother hated the racing. But it was what my father did for a living. When she died, I quit school and began to race cars."

"Your father was a race car driver, too!" I said.

"Yes."

"Is he still alive?"

"Yes. He lives in the south of France."

May was listening, riveted, as if she had never heard any of this before, which seemed strange to me. It didn't make sense. It was a colorful bio, but any normal thirteen-year-old would have heard this family history stuff a million times already from her old man. Was she just so thirsty for his attention she would drink in every word he said?

"Your mother was a model, right?" May asked.

"She was. She was a drug addict, but she knew how to dress!"

"So it runs in the family," I said. "Uh, I mean, the part about knowing how to dress. Speaking of which, I'd better get on with it."

"Get on with it, then," said Gatien.

"And just what is it *you* are you wearing tonight, Mr. Defalle?" May asked her father.

"I'm wearing these pants and my pirate shirt."

"Oh, no, not that pirate shirt again!" she cried.

"Don't you like my pirate shirt?"

"Billowy shirts on men are like, so *out*. It actually said so, in the style section of the newspaper last week."

"We'll have to go by that, then," said Gatien.

"Let's see this pirate shirt," I said.

He switched on the light in the guest room and went to the closet, opened the door, and took out the silk shirt. He slipped it off the hanger, pulled the towel off his shoulders, and dived into the shirt. He straightened himself up, and I stepped up to help him, pulling the silk down over his back, and he gave me a quick, surprised look, that I would take the liberty, but I ignored him.

"There," he said. "What do you think?"

"I like it," I said. "I've got a weakness for pirates."

"Oh, jeez. You don't even care if you embarrass me." May threw up her hands and marched out, disgusted.

"Well," Gatien said, watching me intently. "What's the verdict?"

"The shirt stays on," I said.

"As you wish." And he bowed to me.

I laughed, grabbed up the bag I had come for, and turned away from him.

"Where are you going?" he demanded to know.

"Down to the cottage to dress!"

"Oh. Right. See you soon."

I ran down the steps behind the house, through the gardens, and into the redwood grove, where the little shingled cottage peeked through the straight trunks of the trees with their curtains of needly leaves. My cottage felt

small and solitary, and I wanted to be back up in the house
with May and Gatien. At the same time, I was grateful for
this place of refuge, a place of my own. I felt so happy,
and yet I felt a certain anxiety as well. My joy was neu-
rotic, too dependent on whatever Gatien said or did. But I
decided I would have a fantastic time tonight, no matter
what. I dumped my new black silk pants out of the bag
onto a chair and I picked up the blouse to try on.

It was a romantic blouse in sheer clingy white jersey,
with a dozen tiny mother-of-pearl buttons running up between the breasts, generous sleeves, and a pretty, open
collar. Chaste and yet sexy, too, because the fabric hugged
my curves so nicely and because it was rather low-cut,
showing a hint of cleavage. With the black silk pants, it
would go well with what Gatien and May were wearing. I
dressed quickly, and when I saw myself in the mirror, I
was even more pleased than I thought I'd be when I had
bought the clothes. I was almost twenty-seven years old,
and tonight I might have been eighteen, or thirty-five. I
looked timeless, ageless, and a little out of this modern
world.

Now I no longer wanted to curl up in front of a fire in
my dressing gown. I wanted to go out on the town, show
myself off—for *him*. Why not admit it? I wanted to drive
him mad.

And anyway, if that didn't work, I just wanted to have
fun.

"So, WHAT'S YOUR new boyfriend's name, Sarah?" May
asked. We were in the car on the way to Helene's party.

I looked at May in the rearview mirror. Maybe I hadn't
heard her right.

"That guy you were with this afternoon, with the black
hair. The one who gave you his phone number? So who
was he? What's his name?"

I glanced at Gatien, who had leveled a look of dispassionate interest upon me.

I was about to retort to May's question with some
quick lie, but then I stopped myself. A little white lie

would have been easy enough to come up with. I was fairly adept at white lies and not adverse to using them now and then. But May had asked me a question, straight out, and a lie would be a lie. I was caught short by my own conflict. I was in a parental role, here, with May. Would I lie to my own child? Sure, about Santa Claus maybe. But this was different.

I didn't answer.

"Are you going to see him again?" she prodded mischievously.

If she had asked me if I was planning to go out with him, which was what she was insinuating, I could have responded with a hearty *no*. But I had already thought of questions I wanted to ask him, and I had been considering giving him a call or going back to see him.

May laughed at my hesitation. "He was handsome, wasn't he?"

"Yes, he was," I agreed.

"And *huge.*"

May was making a big thing out of the encounter on purpose. Gatien was silent.

May tapped me on the shoulder. "I could tell he had the hots for you."

"May, that's enough," said her father.

THE PARTY WAS a strange one. Not many people had shown, and those who had seemed uneasy. Gatien, who had been full of humor earlier, at home, was quiet, almost sullen. May was disappointed that Dimitri wasn't there; he had disappeared shortly after we arrived. Helene explained that he had gone out for more ice, but he had been gone a long time. Helene herself seemed frazzled and tired. I couldn't blame her. After all, she hadn't been back from Tahoe a day. Her father was there, sitting in a chair in the living room, watching television. She didn't get much help from him. Paul came in, without Theta. He had the most downcast aspect of all, very uncharacteristic of him.

"What's going on? Are you okay?" I asked Paul when

I had a chance to get him alone. We sat together on a large padded footstool in a secluded alcove off the living room.

"Theta and I are separating," he said.

"Oh, wow. I'm sorry." He looked so sad, I truly was sorry.

He stared glumly down at his expensive casual shoes. "I couldn't make her happy, Sarah."

"Sometimes you just can't, I guess. But maybe with some time apart, she'll see how good she really had it."

"Maybe." His voice raised hopefully. "But then," he added, "I don't know if she makes me happy, either."

"Well, you know, you're not supposed to be in charge of making another person happy."

"You're not?"

"Nope. The new psychology confirms it. And so do all the talk shows. You've got to make your own happiness. No one can do it for you."

"But having a mate who loves you sure can help."

"Well," I said. "I guess I'd have to agree with that. Though I really wouldn't know."

"Poor Sarah." He draped his arm over my shoulder. "Hey, I'm single now, too. Perhaps we ought to give one another solace."

I took a deep breath. His sad, golden beauty was only mildly tempting. "You're awfully quick to seek solace with another woman," I said. "Maybe that's part of your difficulty with Theta."

He laughed, forgetting his troubles for a moment. "It probably is. It probably is."

As his arm slid off me, Gatien joined us in the alcove, a drink in his hand, a scowl on his broken face.

"What's going on, buddy?" He greeted Paul in a friendly way, but there was an edge to his voice.

"Theta wants a divorce," Paul said.

"Oh." Gatien's scowl deepened. He thought about it a moment. "She doesn't mean it."

Paul grinned, stood up so that he was eye to eye with Gatien. "I'm afraid she does, pal."

"We'll see," Gatien said. "Is she here?"

"Nope. She's not coming."

"She'll come. Mark my words. Hey, let me get you a drink."

Gatien slung his arm around his friend and herded him toward the kitchen. They seemed to have forgotten all about me.

DIMITRI ARRIVED ABOUT an hour later, but May was already tired of the party by then. There weren't many young people there. Dimitri was with a friend, another young man around his own age, and they disappeared into Dimitri's lair to play games on the new computer Dimitri had gotten for Christmas. The men gravitated out to the carport, where they stood together, leaning against Helene's Mercedes, telling stories and drinking beer. I helped Helene with drinks and food. In the kitchen a tall, dark-haired woman was standing at the sink, washing vegetables for a dip.

"Hello," she sang out. "Do you need to get in here?"

"No, I'm looking for the napkins."

"Right over there."

"Thanks."

I came back into the kitchen a few minutes later, and she had finished up her washing. She was chopping the vegetables on a board.

"You look familiar to me," I said. "Have we met?"

"You're the girl who's looking after May, aren't you?"

"Yep."

"I'm May's Aunt Kate."

"Oh, you're Helene's sister."

"Half sister, right. Would you hand me that platter there? Thanks."

So this was Dimitri's mother. Now I knew why she looked familiar, with that tall, lean build, the dark hair, the mysterious eyes. She was an older version of Dimitri! She looked too young to be his mother.

"Your son is a very talented snowboarder, I've heard," I said, picking the first thing I could think of to make conversation. I wondered how she felt, having her son living away from her.

"Yeah. I'd just as soon not even know about that!" She laughed. "Makes me nervous to think about what he might be doing out there."

"Oh, I'm sorry I brought it up, then!"

"Guess it's better than *some* things he could be into," she said. "Now, what did I do with my towel—oh, there. So, how is life at the Defalles'?"

"It's . . . it's nice," I said. "I left for the week, to visit friends, and when I got back, I was really glad to be home. Like I belong there now. I think May and I have come to an understanding."

"Really!" She looked surprised. "Well, that's great. My little niece has been through a lot. I'm glad you've been able to bring back some stability for her."

"I'm sorry about what happened to your sister."

"Lisa? Oh, I know. Isn't it sad? She was so young. And look what she left behind."

We looked out together through the kitchen window to the carport, where the men lounged about, and there was May, coming to ask something of her father. We couldn't hear them, but we could see him earnestly considering whatever it was she was asking him about. I could not figure him out. Sometimes he was so good with May, but other times he was so stiff with her. And how could he stay away from her so much? I realized I could exchange myself with May and ask the same questions. How could he stay away from me so much?

"He's had it hard, too," Kate said absently, staring at Gatien.

"I'll bet he misses your sister a lot."

"I'll bet he does!" she agreed with a sober laugh. "He got a bit more than he bargained for, didn't he!"

"All right," said Helene, bustling into the kitchen. "I think we've got almost everything out on the table. Kate, are the veggies ready? Oh, have you two met?"

"Yes, we just met," said Kate. "Except I don't know your name," she said to me.

"Sarah," I said.

"Pleased to make your acquaintance, Sarah."

"Now," said Helene, "if everything here is under control, I'm going upstairs to take a pill. My back is killing me."

"Don't worry," said Kate. "We'll cover for you."

THE PARTY DRAGGED on. Gatien and Paul stayed outside for what seemed like hours, talking with a handful of other men. May skulked around the house, manifestly bored. Dimitri and his friend didn't leave the computer room. Helene's father did nothing but watch television, waiting for the ball to drop in Times Square. By now it had actually happened in Times Square, but we were watching the tape delay.

"What do you think of Gatien?" Kate asked me, her voice quiet. We were alone together in the kitchen again later that evening.

"Gatien . . ." I said.

"He's awfully sexy isn't he?"

I was too surprised to answer.

"I'm rather perplexed that he hasn't been snapped up yet, if you know what I mean. But then, he doesn't have much liking for *amour,* you know, his experience of women being that they're usually more trouble than they're worth. And I don't think my sister was much help in dissuading him on that point. He's had some extremely beautiful and glamorous women, you know, models, wives, daughters of politicians. And politicians!" She laughed. "There's even a rumor he went out with Rania. You know, that beautiful queen of Jordan?"

"I had no idea he was such a . . . such an eligible bachelor."

"Well, of course he is. Gatien was the top American driver in Formula One before his accident. He was world champion, what? Twice? Three times? He was the best in the world and was going for another world championship when he had his big *shunt,* as they say."

"What are you, his press agent?" It was Theta, coming in with a bunch of flowers in her arms.

Kate let out a snort of laughter. "Hey, Theta. Long time no see."

"Has it been *that* long?"

"Theta, you know Sarah, of course?"

"Oh, yes, I know Sarah."

"Sarah," said May, slinking into the room. "Do we have to stay until midnight?"

"That's up to your dad," I replied.

"Well, don't say hi, stranger."

"Hi, Theta," May answered dutifully. She went through the kitchen door to the carport, and we heard her ask her father if it was necessary to stay until midnight. The door shut before we heard his response.

"Where's Helene? I brought her some flowers," said Theta.

Ah, I thought. So the flowers weren't a peace offering for her husband.

"Here," said Kate. "I'll put those in water." She took the flowers from Theta and began rooting around in cupboards for a vase.

Suddenly everyone was in the house, all gathering around the food table, as if some inaudible bell had gone off. The men tromped in from the carport, as did the boys from the computer room, and Helene's father, and a number of others I hadn't yet met, people who were even now arriving. The house was filled with clamor, and I was happy, for Helene's sake, that her party wasn't a bust after all.

By now the large, sprawling house was filled with people, but I was feeling less and less sociable. I had one glass of champagne and figured I'd better have another, just to loosen up. But it would take some doing, getting through that crowd to the drinks table. I decided to go to the bathroom instead, and I headed down the hall. I was waiting outside the bathroom door when I heard the voices, raised in anger, coming from a room at the end of the hallway.

"Damn you to hell, Defalle!"

A door slammed against a wall, and Paul burst out into the hallway, followed closely by Gatien. Both men were of high color, vibrating with emotion. Paul pushed past me without even acknowledging me.

Gatien grabbed my arm. "Find May. I want to leave right now."

"She'll be pleased to hear it," I said. "And since it would seem I have no say in the matter, let's go."

He stopped, exasperated. "Please, Sarah," he said. "Please take me home. You can come right back. Just take me home, please?"

"All right," I said, my voice calm, and I patted the hand he had clamped on my arm. He let go abruptly, realizing how tight he'd been gripping me. "Let's go."

I asked Kate to give our apologies to Helene, because I didn't have time to hunt her down myself. May was so ready to leave she didn't seem to know there was a problem with her father. Gatien didn't say a word during the drive home. May nearly fell asleep on the way, and I knew some of her ill humor was simply exhaustion. Maybe it was the same for him. We arrived home, and she went straight into her room, to bed.

"You go on back to the party, now," Gatien said to me brusquely.

I shook my head. "I don't think so."

"I've ruined it for you, eh?" he said.

"No, I'd had enough anyway."

Gatien stomped down to the rec room, and I heard the clink of glass. He was making himself a drink. I went downstairs to join him, wondering if I would be welcome there, but he didn't seem to notice me as he stood at the little counter that served as a bar. I went to the pool table and began to set up the balls, keeping my eye on him.

Gatien was doing a very poor job of making himself a drink. He fumbled with the ice, dropping it all over the counter, and then he ran into trouble when the bottle of bourbon he was pouring emptied out after just half a shot.

I heard him mumbling curses to himself in French.

"Gatien," I asked, "are you drunk?"

"Yes," he answered. "And I intend to get even drunker. If I can manage it."

"I don't think that's going to do it."

"No, it's not. Wait, I know! I know where there might be more. That bottle I got from your suitor, Nathan, for Christmas. I didn't want to drink it, so I put it in Lisa's library. We used to keep the drinks things in there, before she went into the manuscript business."

He walked past me and stomped up the stairs. I went after him, feeling almost responsible for him, as if he were a child. He was, on the surface, very calm and collected, but I knew this was the most upset I had ever seen him.

We walked together along the hallway, and he turned to me. "You following me?"

"Yes," I answered.

He considered this, nodded curtly, and we went on. We looked in on May; she was sleeping soundly, tucked in her bed. At the doorway to Lisa's library, he paused. "What time is it?" he asked.

I looked at the wristwatch I seldom wore. I had put it on just because it was New Year's Eve. "It's ten till midnight," I said, wondering why he'd asked. "Almost the new year."

"Okay." He pushed open the door, flipped on a light.

We both gasped out loud.

The room was strewn with books and papers. Entire shelves of material had been pulled out, left dumped on the floor, on counters and tabletops. Lisa's library, which was ordinarily a bit untidy, had been thoroughly trashed.

Oh my God, I thought. *This is my fault.*

I thought of my visit to Isaac's studio. The things I had spoken so freely about, to a complete stranger! Things that were none of my business. And those things I had said and done had led to this. I was sure of it.

"When did this happen?" I asked, my voice shaky. "When was the last time you were in here?"

"Just this evening, before we went out," he said. "I was

looking for my pirate shirt. I knew it was in one of the closets upstairs, and I looked in here first—"

"And the room didn't look like this, then."

"No."

For a brief moment, I wondered if I could believe him. *But why would he lie?*

I stared all around me, aghast, wondering what, if anything, had been taken. Lisa's journals looked to be all there, though they had been tossed off of their shelf, like most everything else in the room.

"I don't like this," he said. He was angry and sobering up fast. "I don't like this at all."

We walked around the house together, rechecked on May, examined all the doors and windows, and found everything was in order. There was no sign of a break-in, besides the ransacked library. We went back in the room and stood staring at the mess.

"Gatien," I said softly. "I have to tell you something."

"All right." He directed me to sit on the leather sofa, while he took a wooden chair from beneath one of the tables and set it in front of me. He seated himself and gave me his full attention.

"That man, the one May was talking about tonight. The one I saw in Palo Alto today?"

He nodded, waved at me to continue.

"He's a manuscript appraiser. We were downtown today, and we happened to be near his studio, so . . . we stopped by. I just wanted to ask him some questions, about what makes old books valuable. I knew his name, because . . . of Lisa. She had his business card, and I found it. . . ." My voice trailed off. I didn't want to tell him I'd been reading her journals.

"A manuscript appraiser?" he asked, his voice sharp.

"Yes. I was curious about Lisa's library—"

He was suddenly laughing to himself.

"What?"

"Nothing. Sorry. Go ahead." He smiled at me. He seemed happier all of a sudden, happier than he'd been since we'd arrived at Helene's party.

Poor man's gone bonkers, I thought.

"Go ahead," he said again.

"Okay, so, when we were in Palo Alto today, I went to his studio. Well, the thing is, we got to talking. I asked him some questions, he asked me some questions. I didn't tell him, but he guessed whose library I was talking about—"

"My wife's," he said.

"Yes. And he said there were people who were very interested in what she had. Scholars, or collectors, I guess. He said there are those who would kill to see what was in her library. But he wouldn't tell me why."

He nodded, listening. He looked at me, to see if there was more.

"One other thing I should tell you. Before you got home from Tahoe, a man came to the house. He was sort of strange, and he asked about you and May. He said to tell you he knows where you are. And that he's going to have what's his. Or something like that. He was sort of scary to me. I don't know why. He called himself the Lone Wolf."

Gatien swore again. I had never heard him swear so much.

"So do you know this guy?" I asked.

"Yes, I know him," Gatien replied. He offered no explanation, looking around the room with disgust.

"What is it?" I asked. "What's got everyone so fired up? What are they looking for?"

He looked at me, and he looked tired. He took a deep breath and seemed about to confide in me, then he seemed to think better of it. I wanted to shake him.

"What are they looking for?" I asked again. "The law codes of Hammurabi?"

He gave me a funny look. He didn't want to tell me what it was. Nobody did.

I sighed. "So did they get it, whoever it was who rifled through this room tonight? Did they find what they were looking for?"

"I've already taken care of the most valuable stuff," he

said. "I had an expert from a museum in San Francisco take some things to be archived."

"Well, that's good," I breathed, relief making me weak. "I'm really glad to know that."

"Yeah. But it pisses me off, knowing someone has been in here. And how'd they get in? The place was locked. There is no sign of anyone breaking and entering."

"We should call the police, Gatien."

He nodded. "Yes, I guess. I'll do it." He got up from his chair and started for the door. He paused and looked back at me across the room with a troubled expression. "Hey," he said. "What time is it?"

"Oh, I completely forgot. It's—after midnight!"

"Ah, so we missed it. Happy new year, Sarah."

"Happy new year, Gatien."

THE POLICE TOOK a long time to come; I guess they had more pressing problems on New Year's Eve than our van-dalized library. Gatien and I sat together in the living room, waiting.

"So what were they looking for?" I asked him again.

He looked up at me blankly. Was he pretending not to understand what I wanted to know?

"You're really not going to tell me!" I let my indigna-tion sound in my voice. "You're not going to tell me what everyone is so all-fired up about in that dusty old room! You know, when Louisa first told me you had forbidden anyone to go into your late wife's library, I thought it was because you wanted to leave the room just as she'd left it. In honor of her memory. But now I understand. Now I know you're just holding your cards close to your chest. You want whatever it is for yourself. You know it's sup-posed to be this priceless thing, and you want to make sure no one else cashes in but you. Or maybe you already have. Well, why not? It's all yours. You're entitled." I watched him, waiting to see if I could get a rise out of him.

"Are you finished?" he asked.

"Yes. I guess I'm not getting any answers from anybody."

"Any other questions?" he prodded me, sarcastic.

"Yeah. What was going on with you and your comrade there, at the party? Don't worry, I don't expect you to answer that, either."

"He accused me of sleeping with his wife."

I waited to see if he would add anything; he did not. "Well, then," I said. "I suppose we're lucky there wasn't bloodshed."

"Fucking guy is my best friend."

"How long have you known each other?"

"Since we were teenagers. We went to the same high school in L.A."

"Los Angeles? But I thought you grew up in Europe."

"I did, but my dad insisted I live here, too, some of the time. Mostly to get to my mother, I think."

So that was how he was able to fit in so well, here, as an American. Despite his continental elegance, and that slight trace of an accent.

"So you and Paul go way back."

"Yeah. Almost twenty years. And half that time, he's been with her."

"Well, it's not surprising that this comes up now. He's just distraught because she left him. He's taking it out on you. He's not thinking straight."

"Sarah, Paul's not the only one who isn't thinking straight."

"But the jealousy really has nothing to do with you, Gatien. Or"—I couldn't help asking—"does it?"

"His jealousy doesn't," he said.

I looked at him questioningly, not understanding that.

"I could have defused the situation," he said, more to himself than to me. "I could have—"

"Well, you've been friends a long time. You won't let a woman come between the two of you."

He regarded me with his melancholy expression. "I hope we don't," he said.

Gatien escorted me down to my cottage that night to

make sure everything was all right. Upon entering the still, small space, I had the feeling someone had been in my rooms, but there was nothing I could point to. Maybe it was just because the police officers had been inside, taking a look. Everything was just as I'd left it.

"You sure you don't want to stay in the guest room, Sarah?" Gatien asked me for the third time.

"No," I insisted. "I'm okay here."

We parted awkwardly, without touching, though the strangeness of our shared experience that night seemed to call for some ritual exchange of intimacy, an embrace or at least a handshake or something, but there was nothing.

I looked around the cottage again, checking every closet and cupboard, not even sure what I was looking for. Lisa's journal was sitting on the table next to the bed under my ripped-up copy of *Middlemarch*, just as I'd left it.

Chapter Twelve

I WAS FRUSTRATED that Gatien wouldn't tell me what it was everyone was so interested in, in Lisa's library. What could it be? He must know more than he was saying. And why didn't he trust me enough to tell me? Things like this reminded me what strangers we were to one another. He hadn't told me who the "Lone Wolf" was, either.

And yet, New Year's Eve had brought us closer, like Christmas Eve, but in a different way. I sensed Gatien's concern for both May and me. The week after New Year's Eve, he had a fence contractor come and do estimates for repairing the fence around the entire property. He had an alarm system installed, and he insisted we all use it. He even had my cottage rigged. I found his concern touching, though I was annoyed with the hassle of increased security. It just made things less convenient, and I didn't feel a whole lot safer with it, maybe because the break-in hadn't made me feel unsafe as much as personally violated. I didn't think whoever it was that broke in wanted to harm anybody. And they'd gotten what they'd come for, or they found out it wasn't there. Either way, I didn't think they'd be back. I hoped they wouldn't be back.

May wasn't particularly frightened either, though she did seem angry about the vandalism. Perhaps the most upset was Helene, who seemed to think it was her job to worry about Gatien and May anyway, and she tried to offer her services in getting the room back in order, but Gatien told her firmly he would take care of it.

I didn't like the alarms, though it warmed my heart to see Gatien protective of May and me. But whenever I forgot myself and started to relax into my friendship with Gatien, he would raise something between us, just enough of a curtain to keep me from touching him. *Ah, Gatien,* I thought. *You frustrate me.*

I TOOK ON the project of cleaning up the library. Louisa wanted nothing to do with it, May was back in school by that time, and Gatien seemed to want to ignore the whole thing. At first he dismissed me and my offer to help get the room back in order, as he had Helene. He put on his familiar *The room is forbidden* scowl and scared everyone with his dark expression. But I didn't let that faze me, and I asked him about it again. Some days had passed, and he hadn't done anything about it. The third time I brought it up, he gave in.

"Sure, go ahead and clean it up, organize it, do whatever you want to do, Sarah," he said, resigned. He knew I was eager to get into Lisa's library and have my way with it, and so, reluctantly, he finally left it to me.

I launched into my new project with vigor. I was thrilled to be given carte blanche in the room at last, to be able to poke and pry to my heart's content.

One of the first things I did was to restore Lisa's journals to their place on the shelf. I placed them there in chronological order, one at a time, ending with the last one, the journal Lisa had been writing when she died.

After the police had finished in the room on New Year's Eve, as soon as I could manage it unobtrusively, I had slipped Lisa's last journal, which I had kept in my cottage, into the pile of journals where they were lying dumped on the library floor. I felt guilty for having it, and the break-in had spooked me. I didn't want the journal in my possession any longer. I couldn't put it back in Gatien's room without going in there, and with him in the house, that was impossible. So I put it with the others, and after a quick glance at the unexamined portion of it—just to see if I had missed something glaringly interesting—I didn't read any more.

Now the journals were all in place. I stared at them, at a loss. Equal and opposite forces pulled at me. *Read them,* said one. *Leave them alone,* said the other. I suddenly remembered something Dimitri had said to me the day he drove me to my new post: *Mind your own business. Don't be too curious.*

There didn't seem to be anything of great importance in those journals, anyway. Certainly nothing that shed light on Lisa's death.

Now Gatien's voice echoed through the hallway outside the room, and something in me warmed, just to be reminded that he was there. I wondered when he would be going away again, as he inevitably would. He had been home much longer than usual this time. It couldn't be long now before he was off again.

I pushed a brass bookend in the shape of a sailing ship closer to the row of journals, securing them in place. For now, at least, I would take Dimitri's advice and mind my own business.

IN THE MIDST of my library cleaning project I found some photographs of Gatien in his racing days. *What a gorgeous man,* I thought, studying one photograph in particular, and I realized I was looking at an image of Gatien before something catastrophic had changed him, rearranged the planes of his face, crushed his leg, and damaged his spirit. There was something different about the man in the photo, and it wasn't just the bones of his face. It was something shining in his eyes that I had seen only in sharp flashes, guarded, just often enough that I knew it

was real, it was there, it existed. Here in this portrait, that
spirit was beaming out like a powerful wave of light and
seemed to touch all those who gathered around this good-
looking cowboy in his flameproof racing suit.

"What are you doing, Sarah?"

Gatien sounded annoyed. I looked up to see him looking down at me, as I sat on the floor going through his
photographs.

"I'm just organizing things," I said with all the innocence I could muster.

"I think maybe you are a bit of a snoop."

I rose to my feet, faced him, put my hands on my hips,
and nodded. "Yep. I am. But you know what? I happen to
be interested in you and your family! Pardon my curiosity! I don't know what's going on in May's mind half the
time. I *never* know what you're thinking. I don't know
what your wife had in this library that so many people
seem to covet. You won't talk about your accident, or your
injury, or if you ever plan to race again! You never open
up to me about anything—"

"Sarah, Sarah." He clasped my arm with one big, warm
hand and laid his mouth on mine to shut me up. It was so
unexpected that I let out a gasp as he drew away, and he
put an end to that gasp with another forceful, deliberate
kiss. It turned hungry almost instantly; we kissed raven-
ously. And then we pulled apart just as violently as we'd
suddenly become joined, looking at each other with startled, frightened eyes. It was a shock to both of us, I think.

"I'm sorry," we both apologized at the same time—me
for my rambling rant, which had led to the impetuous kiss,
and he for the impetuous kiss. He drew himself up, and
the formal Gatien suddenly appeared, all trace of passion
gone. "I do apologize, Sarah. I shouldn't have done that."

I felt my cheeks burn with a blush. I was mortified that
he was apologizing for kissing me. It made me know he
shouldn't have done it, had done it for the wrong reasons
(in his mind), and so he considered himself guilty. I felt
insulted and stirred, and even more so when afterwards he
acted like nothing had happened.

• • •

WE HAD DINNER together that night, the three of us.

"He won't stop bothering me," said May.

"Who won't?" asked Gatien.

"Slughead."

"Who is Slughead?" I asked.

"Don't call him that," said Gatien disapprovingly.

"Okay. *Danny,*" May said with distaste. "He's that annoying neighbor of ours. He lives down the hill. He just won't stop *bothering* me."

"Danny . . ." I said. "What does he look like?"

"He looks like a dork. He's got like, short blond hair, and, I don't know . . ."

Danny. The boy I had seen in the woods around May's cottage.

"What does he do that upsets you?" I asked.

"He always wants to hang out with me."

"That *is* terrible!" I said.

"Well, what if someone was coming on to *you?* How would you feel about it?"

I glanced at Gatien, then looked down at my plate. "I don't know," I said. "Depends how I felt about him, I guess. What do you think he wants from you?"

May sat silent a moment, thoughtful. "He wants—he wants *me,* I guess."

"And you don't want to give him you," said Gatien.

May shook her head.

"He doesn't just want *you,*" Gatien said with a faint smile and a flicker of a glance my way. "He wants to give himself to you, too."

"Well, I don't want him," May said with finality.

"But, lady, won't you please reconsider?" Gatien teased her with a gallant charm.

May burst into laughter. "What? You *want* me to go out with Danny?" She stared at him, incredulous.

"I only meant that you should consider the pain of a lonely heart," he said with a serious expression.

"No way. Not a chance." May laughed again, and I thought how much she was opening up, how much she

had changed since the beginning of the school year. And
Gatien, too, was easier with her, joking with her more.

"I have something to tell both of you," he said when
our laughter had died away.

May sat up straight, readied herself for an announcement.

"I'm going out of town again," said Gatien.

"Oh?" May slumped, pouted. "Do you have to go?"

"Yes. I'm afraid I do."

"The racing season hasn't started up yet, has it?" May
challenged him. "Why do you need to go now? Why do
you have to go away for so long and so far away? I like
having you around here."

"I like being here," he answered. "And I'm arranging
things so that I can be here more. But I have to do this—"

"It's been a long time since you've gone away from us.
How long will you be gone this time, exactly?"

"I'm not sure," he said quietly. "It might be awhile."

May swooned dramatically, slumping down in her seat
as if stabbed with a knife in the heart. *My sentiments exactly,* I thought. But unlike May, I kept my feelings to myself.

FOR THE NEXT two days Gatien avoided me. The humil-
iation that had flared in me when he had apologized for
kissing me smoldered and burned. I had no idea what he
was thinking or feeling. His silent avoidance was driving
me crazy. What was really driving me insane, however,
was the memory of that kiss. Over and over in my head,
we kissed. Every sensual detail was alive in my mind, my
body. I could smell him, and I could feel the heat of his
body and the strength in his hands as he hauled me against
him. I knew the shocking thrust of his tongue, the unfamiliar taste of his mouth, heard the deep rumble of the
moan that had escaped him.

By the time he was to leave it was a relief to me, to
know he was going. He probably would have liked to
avoid asking me to drive him to the airport, but he was no
longer relying on Paul. Silently we loaded his gear into

the trunk and set out. May was busy with homework and had elected not to come with us. We drove up the freeway in the twilight.

"You might hit some traffic on the way home," he said. I didn't answer.

We drove in silence. A few miles from the airport, the freeway slowed to a crawl.

The way home, my ass, I thought.

The silence between us seemed to swell as the car slowed down. I felt something akin to despair. Here we were, in the final moments before parting for days—maybe even weeks—with nothing to say to one another. The slow traffic was maddening, and yet I was grateful for it, for keeping us together that much longer. But after awhile we were completely stopped, and it seemed Gatien might miss his flight. I began to feel panicky.

At last we began moving, and a few minutes later we passed the wreckage of an accident, a motorcycle and a van mangled by the side of the road, an ambulance flashing its strobe, a firetruck, policemen and paramedics, a man standing as if in shock, staring into the darkness.

WE REACHED THE airport. I pulled up to the curb outside the terminal and got out to help him with his bags. He was cutting it very close. He was in a big hurry, but he stopped suddenly.

"Sarah," he said. "I don't want this silence between us."

"Well, what *do* you want between us?"

"What I want and what I can have are two different things."

I shook my head, annoyed. "Gatien, I don't know what you're trying to say to me."

He smiled at that, broke into a laugh. "God, I'm gonna miss you, girl." He grabbed me in a big, vigorous hug that had little sensuality in it, just affection and something epic, like the farewell of two adventurers about to embark on separate journeys, not knowing when they might meet again. "Take care of May."

"I will."

"And take care of yourself, and don't fall in love with Paul! Or anybody else!"

"What?" I cried, smiling and frowning at the same time, and he grinned at me and limped off into the terminal with his bag slung over his shoulder.

Chapter Thirteen

NATHAN CAME OVER one morning to tie up some odds and ends on the kitchen project. A light fixture we had ordered months ago had finally come in, and he stopped by to install it. He asked me if I wanted to go to lunch with him, and we ended up in downtown Palo Alto, and that gave me an idea. I was too much of a coward to go back to Isaac on my own and confront him about the break-in, but if I had a big construction guy backing me up, maybe I could be brave. After lunch I told Nathan I had an errand down the street and asked him if he'd like to take a walk with me, and of course he said yes, making a big show of using his cell phone to postpone an appointment for the next hour so he could be with me.

"So what's this errand?" he asked as we walked along, dodging some Stanford students who were eating pizza beneath an umbrella at a table on the sidewalk.

"I need to see someone who might appraise some books for me," I said, keeping it vague. We reached Isaac's building and went upstairs together.

There was the man himself, and I wondered if Nathan

would actually be any protection against a guy like this. As May had said, he was huge. And handsome, with his fierce eyes and his black, black hair and beard. Poor Nathan looked skinny and pallid next to Isaac.

And the contrast increased when Isaac jumped up and came to greet us, his great booming voice filling the room. "Hello!" he hollered. "It's Sarah, right?"

I introduced the men, and they regarded each other dubiously.

"What can I do for you, Sarah?" Isaac asked me.

"I'd like to talk to you about something," I said. "It's um, it's about what we talked about last time." I lowered my voice, and Nathan, bless his heart, took the hint.

"I'll just wait outside," he said, and darted down the stairs.

"So, what's up?" Isaac asked when we were alone. I noticed there was no Mohawk-adorned assistant hanging about today.

"Long story short?" I said. "My employer's house was ransacked on New Year's Eve, hours after I spoke to you," I said. "Specifically, the library. I wondered if you knew anything about it."

He folded his arms and looked at me directly. "I warned you, little lady."

"Oh, please." The *little lady* annoyed me. "Talk to me," I said.

"Okay." He sighed, opened his arms, and shrugged. "Seriously, honestly, I have no idea."

"What is it?" I asked.

"What is it?"

"What are you all looking for? I want to know."

"I'm not looking for anything!" he said hastily. "I told you. You shoulda had a garage sale. Accepted your losses."

"So you know there were losses? Whatever it is didn't amount to much, did it? The big mystery thing didn't pan out. I don't know why everyone's so excited."

"I don't either."

"I think you're full of shit."

"Lisa Defalle was a dilettante. She was a nice lady, and I hate to speak ill of the dead, but there you are. She had no business poking about in matters that didn't concern her. She let herself be conned and maybe worse. Rumors get started, and people being what they are, legends are born. I don't think this secret library exists."

"Secret library?"

He looked annoyed with himself. "Yeah. That's what they call it."

"So, is it a geographical place?" I asked. "Like a hidden room?"

"Don't think so. It was books or manuscripts of some kind. Something really special. Supposedly something Lisa Defalle bought from an abbey in Spain. She brought in some stuff to show me, nice stuff, but nothing to justify the hoopla. There. That's all I know."

"And you have no further curiosity about it?"

"Not enough to break into someone's house, if that's what you're asking."

"And you can't help me? You have no idea who might have broken into the house? It happened hours after I talked to you, Isaac."

"An unfortunate coincidence."

"What about your—assistant? The guy with the Mohawk? He was listening to us talk that day."

Isaac waved that off as ridiculous, or perhaps he just didn't want to consider it. "What good would it do, anyway, even if I did know who it was?" he asked. "You gonna go confront them, next? What if they're not nice, like me?"

"That's why I brought Brutus, down there," I said with a smile.

"Give me a break," he snorted. "Your boyfriend?"

"No. He's a friend. I just brought him along as insurance."

"Some insurance. Are you Defalle's woman, then?"

I laughed at that, a rather bitter sound. "He's the boss. I'm the employee. Does that make me his woman?"

"You could do worse. The wife and I had dinner with

him and Lisa once. Pleasant evening. Good guy. It's too bad about the lady. Nice lady. A little flighty, but good-hearted. I was sorry to hear about what happened to her."

"Yeah," I said, studying him. There was something genuine about the great man. "So you're married, huh? May will be disappointed to hear it. She was trying to do some matchmaking between the two of us."

"Obviously she has a good eye." He smiled good-naturedly. "Yes indeed. Very married, ten years. But I'm flattered by the suggestion. Anyway, I don't know how we got on this subject."

"I do. You asked me if Nathan—I mean, Brutus—was my boyfriend. Then you asked if I was 'Defalle's woman.' None of which is any of your business, incidentally."

"True. But I just wondered." He added, looking me up and down appraisingly, "Just thought he might have started a new life. Nothing wrong with that, right?"

I nodded, embarrassed.

I left Isaac's studio feeling even more confused than before. Either he was the world's best con artist, I thought, or Isaac was a regular, nice guy. I just couldn't help but like him. I didn't totally trust him, though. Maybe he didn't orchestrate the break-in, but I wondered if he knew who did.

Nathan was waiting for me downstairs. "Another satisfied customer?" he said with a rueful nod toward Isaac's studio.

I shrugged. "Not completely, no."

"My aunt is an expert on old books," Nathan said. "She's an antiques dealer. She does appraisals, if you ever need anything like that. And she's trustworthy," he added disdainfully, as if to imply that Isaac wasn't.

"I'll keep that in mind," I said, amused.

TWO WEEKS AFTER Gatien left I got a call from a woman named Betty Wilson, a guidance counselor at May's school. "I'm calling because I'm concerned about May," she told me. "She has no friends. I see her alone all the time. At lunch, she's always alone."

She asked if I had some insight. How was May's behavior at home? I told her I was aware that May was a loner, but she didn't seem terribly unhappy. Sure, she was moody at times, but what teenager wasn't? What adult wasn't, for that matter? We talked for some time. I told her of our situation, that I wasn't May's mother, and her father was out of town frequently. She told me I could call her any time, and I thanked her for her concern.

"I'm glad we talked," she said. "I had a heck of a time getting hold of your phone number. I finally convinced the powers that be I had a legitimate reason for wanting it!"

"Well, I'm glad you persisted," I said. "I'm glad we talked, too. Sometimes I feel like I'm in this game alone."

"Well, you're not," she assured me. "Remember, you can call me any time at the number I gave you."

I thanked Betty Wilson once again, and after I hung up, I kept thinking about the conversation. I thought about it all day. Here I thought May had been making progress, opening up, and then I get this phone call from a school counselor. I knew how busy they were. May must really stand out in the crowd at school to have drawn attention to herself to the point that the counselor was calling with her concerns. I was worried, worried for May's sake and worried about my own performance on this job. What could I be doing for May that I wasn't? Or what was I doing that I shouldn't be doing?

Immediately my guilt presented itself: *Gatien.* I was devoting way too much of my energy toward him, mental, emotional, even a sort of physical energy. I had come here for May, and I was focused on her father instead.

I pondered it for a long time, and I resolved to change.

I was determined to be a better guardian for May, but after a few days I realized I was already doing what I thought was best for her, moment by moment, every day, and that was really all I could do. She was thirteen years old, a loner by nature, and she was proudly independent. She didn't mind being alone; in fact, she seemed to prefer it, and after all, we had that in common. I could sit her down after school and question her about her day, but if I pushed it, she just gave me that disdainful look of hers, and turned her head away, ignoring me and anything I said until she decided to forgive me. I came to the conclusion that what was best for May was not for me to obsess about her happiness, but for her to see me happy and independent and busy. To be a good, healthy role model. I did resolve to stop focusing on Gatien; obsessing about a man was not good for me, nor was it a good example to set for a young girl, even if I did hide it from her. At least I hoped I did.

I continued cleaning and organizing the library. This project I had thought would take me a couple of days had turned into a major undertaking, lasting weeks, partly because I devoted only a small amount of time to it each day, partly because it was a big room and there were hundreds of books and papers to be cleaned and classified. But I had made steady progress, and I was almost finished. My goal was to have it complete by the time Gatien got home, which I hoped would be soon.

One morning, having accumulated a large pile of outdated magazines, I was looking for a box or crate to pack them in. I went into the garage and checked out the storage closet, to see if there were any boxes left over from Christmas. And that's when I found it.

I'd been in the storage closet before on a number of occasions, for various reasons, and it had been sitting there all along, a dusty cardboard box with the shipping labels all intact and the packaging untouched. It had never been opened. I hadn't noticed it before, but I noticed it this time, because I was looking for boxes. Empty boxes, which this one was not. It was a package, shipped from Spain, postmarked a year ago last October. Could it have been sitting in that storage closet for over a year?

My heart beat with excitement as I moved the box to my cottage. It was just a little heavy for me. I had an hour and a half before it was time to pick up May from school. I locked the door, pulled out a knife from a drawer in the little kitchen, and sliced open the cardboard.

Inside there were no scrolls of ancient text, neatly rolled and stored in earthenware jars, packed in biodegradable peanuts. But there were several old books, including a beautiful illuminated manuscript that looked very old to me, and I knew it had to be valuable. There were several other books that looked like they might be of the same vintage, accounting books of some sort, bound in leather, not illustrated or decorated in any way.

Maybe these books were valuable enough to offset the financial outlay for the collection. Maybe I could present them to Gatien as a sort of gift. But would he simply be annoyed with me? He had already told me I was a snoop.

But how could he blame me for this? I was organizing the library with his consent. I had run across these books legitimately, unlike the journal I had taken from his room. Still, I had the feeling this new discovery would stress him rather than please him. But I didn't have to think about that now, anyway, since he was out of the country.

Chapter Fourteen

"C AN I GO to the movies tonight?" May asked as we
pulled into the driveway later that afternoon.

I thought about it. Friday night, nothing else to
do, why not? "Sure," I said. "Will you help bring in the
groceries?"

"Of course."

We were just getting into the house, arms full of grocery bags, as the telephone rang. I practically dropped the
bag I was carrying as I lunged for the phone. I expected
Gatien's call from the airport any day now.

"Oh, hello, Helene," I chirped, trying not to let my disappointment sound in my voice. "How are you?"

"Pretty good. My back's been a bit stiff, but what else
is new? What are you up to, Sarah?"

"Oh, we just got in, stopped after school to pick up a
few things at the grocery store. It's Louisa's day off."

"I thought she had Saturdays and Sundays off."

"It's flexible," I said. "You know Louisa. She's her
own boss! So what's up?"

"My father is here, and we thought we might play cards
tonight. Wondered if you and May would like to join us."

"Oh, sounds great, but I promised May we'd go out to the movies this evening."

"That sounds fun. What are you going to see?"

"I have no idea. It's up to May. Well, within reason it's up to May."

"Right!" She laughed. "Well, another time, then."

"Yeah, for sure. Oh, and Helene, there's something I wanted to tell you about."

"What's that?"

"I found something today. Something rather interesting." I was about to go on, but May wandered into the kitchen.

"Tell me," Helene said, catching my excitement. "What is it?"

I hesitated. I wanted to tell May and Gatien about what I had found when the three of us were together. Perhaps I hoped May would impart a little excitement about the discovery to her father when I made my announcement. But first I wanted to find out how valuable and significant my discovery was.

"Listen," I said. "I'll talk to you later, okay?"

"I understand. May's right there, isn't she? Is it something to do with my sister and her library?"

"Yes, as a matter of fact it is."

"You found something in her library?"

"Well, sort of—"

"I'm sorry, I'm asking too many questions."

"That's okay."

"I'm just concerned about that library, you know. What with the break-in—"

"I know. But we've got the alarm system now, and besides, it's not in the library, it's in my cottage. I'll give you a call tomorrow and tell you all about it. I haven't had a chance to check it out myself. And tonight we're going out, so—tomorrow!"

"All right. You two have fun tonight."

"We will. Thanks again, Helene." I hung up, energized but uneasy. I wasn't sure why, but I felt as if I had betrayed someone. I wished I had waited, not told anyone about the old books I'd found, until I told Gatien. But I was so excited, I was eager to tell someone. I wished I had asked Helene not to mention my discovery to Dimitri.

"What movie are we going to go see, May?" I called out to her.

She walked out of her room with a dramatic, worried expression on her mini-Madonna's face.

"What is it, May?" I cried. "What's wrong?"

"Promise you won't be mad?"

"No, I cannot promise you that."

She moaned, patently miserable.

"May, just tell me what's going on."

"It's just that . . . we were going to go to the movies. I mean, me and some other people."

"Other people?"

"From the team."

"Your soccer team?"

"Uh-huh."

"Oh, *I* get it. You don't want me to come, right? People under sixteen only?"

"Well, yeah." She smiled up at me gratefully. "Leslie organized this sleepover at her house. Everyone's getting dropped at the theater by their own parents, or, as in my case, their own caregiver, and then her dad and mom are going to bring everyone to their house to spend the night and then bring us all home in the morning."

"Leslie from your team?"

"Yeah. Can I go? The whole team's invited."

"How are they going to transport all those girls?"

"They have a van and a car."

"With enough seat belts?"

"I don't know! But yeah, probably."

"I've met her mother several times, haven't I?"

"Yes, you have. She's the one who always cheers really loud."

I thought about it. There was no manual here for me to follow. I didn't know what Gatien allowed in cases like this. May had never asked to spend the night at a friend's house, that I knew of. Ironic that this should come up now, right after the concerned counselor's call. I decided to take it as a positive sign.

"Everyone on the team is invited," May said again.

"Sounds all right. But I'd like to give Leslie's mom a call first, and talk to her."

"Sure," said May. "I'll get you the phone number. It's on the team roster. Which is . . . do you know where the team roster is, Sarah?"

"It's in the drawer by the phone in the kitchen."

So I called and chatted with Leslie's mom and found the movie proposal to my satisfaction. "All right," I said to May. "You can go. I'll drop you off at the theater in an hour, so be ready."

She was so pleased, she gave me a quick, shy hug. "Thank you, Sarah," she said. "I'm sorry you won't be coming. Really."

"Yeah, right." I laughed. "Why don't you make yourself a sandwich before you go?"

"Okay. After I get dressed." She ran off to her room to get ready.

I picked up the phone and dialed Nathan's number.

"SARAH," HE SAID. "You don't know how long I've waited for this call."

"Nathan? Are you all right?" I questioned him, concerned. He sounded drunk.

"Sarah? That *is* you, isn't it? Calling me on a lovely Friday evening."

"Yeah, hi. I was just wondering if I could get that number from you. You said one of your aunts is an antiques dealer. . . ."

"Oh, you're calling to get my Aunt Edith's phone number! Oh! Okay. I just thought—oh, never mind. Just a sec." He went away from the phone, came back, read off two phone numbers. "The second one's her shop. It's downtown on Broadway. She's usually there until about six. Maybe you can catch her right now."

"I will try to do that," I said.

"You got some books you want her to look at, huh?"

"Uh, yeah," I said. I had blithely told him I had some books I wanted appraised when we went to Isaac's shop. Then it had been a pretext. But now it was true.

I dropped May off at the theater, and instead of heading straight home, I drove downtown and turned onto Broadway. I parked, picked up the shopping bag I had packed with the books I'd found in the storage closet, and made my way down the street.

The shop was not actually on Broadway but in a tiny, dark, dead-end alley off the main drag. On the smudged glass windows, faded fancy lettering shone in the glow of the streetlights: *Madame Curio's: Antiques and Rare Books*.

In the shop's window an odd vignette had been created: a silver tea service was laid out on an upholstered stool beside a large wing chair. Beside the chair, a Victorian cane stand was filled with canes, with handles of carved dragon heads and geese and ivory elephants. There was a walnut chest of drawers, on top of which stood an old globe of the moon, a deep sea diver's helmet, and a fossilized fish lying on a black velvet cloth.

I pushed the door open, setting off a strange, shimmering bell chime, and I entered a dim room cluttered with antique tables and chairs, china cabinets and hutches, and bookcases filled with old leather-bound books. Objects crowded every available surface, figurines of porcelain and silver, paperweights and tea sets, seashells, billiard balls and ostrich eggs piled in wooden bowls. There was a human skull in a glass case and a stuffed raven on a perch. To the side of the room was an old apothecary's chest, and on the back wall, a beautiful mahogany bar, behind which were rows of glass shelves stocked with hundreds of small opaque glass bottles, all labeled and printed with tiny handwritten letters.

The place seemed to be deserted; there was only one light glowing dimly from the back. I very nearly walked out.

"Hello?" I called out.

There was no answer. I moved about the room slowly,

taking it all in. It was an incredible collection, each object rare and interesting and beautiful, but there was a strangeness about the way they all lived together in that dark room, like a set piece for a horror film.

"How may I help you, my dear?"

At first I couldn't tell where the voice was coming from.

I turned around.

"What have we here?" Her voice was surprisingly deep for someone so small.

I turned again, and she was beside me, no taller than my shoulder. "Hi," I said. "Are you Edith Kirkland?"

"I'm called Madame Curio," she said with a strange smile. She might have been joking; I wasn't sure if she really wanted me to call her that.

"My name is Sarah Logan. Your nephew gave me the referral. He said you appraise old manuscripts and books."

"Yes. Which nephew? Percy?"

"No, Nathan."

"Ah, Nathan . . . yes." She brought her attention to rest on the bag I carried. "What did you bring me?" Her eyes seemed to glow as she asked, and she opened her long thin hands.

I set the books in her arms, one by one.

"Ah, yes," she said. "Very interesting. How very beautiful." She laid them out on the one bare surface in the shop, a dark cherry claw-and-ball-foot table in the center of the main room. She opened the books, one at a time, and perused them reverently. "Mmmhmm," she nodded.

"What do you think?" I asked at last.

"You must leave them with me," she said. "I can't tell you for sure until I verify a few things, but . . ."

"But?"

"I believe you have something very lovely here. I can't say for sure until I thoroughly check them out."

"When will you know?"

"It's Friday, so . . . it will be, say, by Monday afternoon."

"You need to keep the books that long?"

She gave a shrug. "It's up to you. That would be the fastest and easiest way. I'm leaving town in a week, closing up my shop for a month or two, while I travel, so I haven't much time for appraisals right now, but if you could leave them, I might be able to do something over the weekend. Of course I would give you a receipt."

"All right," I said. "I'll take that receipt, and I'll be back here Monday afternoon to get the books."

"They're wonderful books," she said. "I don't think you'll be disappointed."

I was full of turmoil about what I was doing. I was unsettled by the strange little lady, and as I left the shop, I couldn't figure out why I had just handed over these potentially priceless books to a woman I had known for five minutes. It was as if I had been hypnotized and made to do something I would never have done otherwise. I consoled myself with the thought that the lady was Nathan's aunt. She wasn't a perfect stranger.

My feeling of disorientation increased when I nearly ran into two men who were entering the shop just as I was leaving it. They mesmerized me, each in turn, with their big dark eyes. There was something so familiar about them I stopped short. I turned around, startled at the odd encounter, and looked back. But they had already gone inside the shop.

It came to me, how I knew them, only after I was in my car and headed home. They were the two dark-eyed men who had come to the Defalles' house months ago, when I had first moved in, the men who had asked me to give them access to Lisa's library. The two men Gatien had thrown off his property that day and warned me to stay away from.

I DROVE HOME slowly. I felt extremely sleepy. I knew what I had done was wrong. I had no business leaving those books with a stranger. If they were lost or stolen or otherwise abused . . . and what about those two characters showing up there? Ironic, I thought. It was actually them—or the intense interest in Lisa's library that they represented—I had sought to avoid when I went to Nathan's aunt to have those books appraised, instead of to Isaac. So what were they doing there, at Madame Curio's shop? My head was pounding with it.

If anything happened to those books . . .

But Gatien claimed he wasn't interested in Lisa's old books anyway. What, really, was the worst that could happen? He didn't even know the books existed. I tried to comfort myself with that thought. I drove home, put my car into the garage, walked down to my cottage, and went to bed early.

The silence of the night surrounded me. I was all alone on the estate. *When will he come home?* I wondered, drifting off. *When?*

I SMELLED SMOKE. Something wasn't right. I tried to get up. I wanted to get out. But I found it impossible to move. *This languid heaviness of my limbs.* Even in my dreams, I tried to get away, to escape.

I am trying . . . but something is coughing me up. I am filled with agitated people, all in my chest, all trying to talk at once.

How long?

How long can I go on? I am so tired. So sleepy.

I BECOME AWARE of him.

He is holding me, carrying me in his arms.

Can it be? That he's here. He is here. At last. But it's too late. It's too late. . . .

Gatien.

His arms are strong and his arms surround me. He holds me so sweetly and tenderly, sweet as a soft wind kissing bare skin. He is laying me down on a prickly soft blanket, the blanket of the earth. Helping me to breathe. His hands stroke me and caress me. My arms, my face.

"Sarah . . ." His deep baritone goes through me, his words so gentle and worried, touched with the panic he is trying to control. "Stay with me, Sarah," he says, over and over. "Stay awake. Stay with me. I'm here. I'm here with you, Sarah."

He is bending over me, his lips so close to mine I can smell his panicked breath layered over the smell of smoke in the air, and I believe he is ready to breathe into me if need be, but it seems I am breathing all right on my own, now, though I'm coughing and coughing.

"GATIEN," I SAID, wonderingly. "You're really here. You're really here," I whispered, and closed my eyes.

"Open your eyes, Sarah, look at me."

I obeyed him and opened my eyes, and he was staring down at me, his eyes brimming with tears. I wanted to reach up and brush away the tears, but I couldn't lift my hand. I was too tired.

"Is it really you?" I managed.

"Is it really *you?*" he asked back, gently mocking. "Do you know who you are?"

"Yes."

"Who are you, then?"

"Sarah."

"Yes," he cried, hugging me tightly. "Yes. Thank God. She's going to be all right."

"What happened?" I asked. "Why did you come?"

"Your cottage caught fire, Sarah. But you're all right."

"May . . . May."

"May's all right."

"May . . . spent the night . . ."

"Yes," said Gatien. "There's a message from May on the machine in the main house, saying they finished the movie and they're all at Leslie's house for the night."

"Okay. Good." I closed my eyes.

"Sarah, don't go to sleep."

"Why not?"

"Because," he said. "I want to keep looking into your eyes. I haven't seen them for so long."

I tried. But it was hard. I was so sleepy. I began to cough again.

There were others around me, uniforms. Light and

dark. Somebody wanted me to go to a hospital, but I clung to Gatien and pleaded with him not to let them take me.

"Don't worry, Sarah," he said. "I'm staying with you."

Chapter Fifteen

THE HOUSE AND grounds were busy with people for days. Family and friends and neighbors and journalists and police and fire investigators. Helene and Dimitri were in and out frequently. Gatien was there. Gatien was home.

Nathan came on the Monday after the fire to see the burned-out cottage and assess the damage. He brought me flowers and visited me in my new quarters, the guest room in the main house. I was lying down on the love seat listening to music when he arrived. I still felt so tired. I didn't know if it was something physical, left over from the smoke inhalation, or something psychological, but I felt so sleepy all the time. All I wanted to do was crawl into bed, slip into a dream, and stay there. I would close my eyes and feel myself swirling into soft darkness, where Gatien would find me and dance with me in his arms.

"So they're saying it was arson, huh?" Nathan said, with concern in his pale blue eyes. He pulled up a stool and sat facing me.

I really didn't want to talk about it, but I didn't want to

be rude, so I nodded and said, "Yeah. That's what they're saying."

"Damn, missy. Thank *God* you're okay."

I forced a smile for him. "All that work you put into the place," I said. "Up in smoke."

He shrugged. "No big deal. I'm hoping to get the job of fixing her back up."

"Is anything salvageable?"

"Sure. The roof's totally gone, and the place is pretty much gutted, but the foundation's not really touched, and some of the framing is okay. Just smells really bad right now."

"The pretty little windows were all blown out. But the redwood trees are all right. Another few minutes, they tell me, and they would have gone up. Might have taken out the main house . . ."

"Yeah. So what did you lose? Everything?" He regarded me with compassion.

"I lost some clothes. Some personal stuff, papers, you know. All I really own, anyway, is books. And my books were in the main house. So none of them were harmed, because none of them were in the cottage, except *Middlemarch*, which I already finished anyway!"

"I'm just glad you're all right. And I'd like to find whoever did it and put them out of their misery."

"How did you get in here, by the way?"

"The lady let me in."

"Helene? Is she still here?"

"Yeah, she's who, now?"

"Gatien's sister-in-law."

"Right. I thought I knew her. I used to see her around her dad's place now and then, when I did his addition. I think Helene and Louisa are in the kitchen making some kind of huge Mexican feast."

"They've both been so great through all this," I said. "They were both pretty upset. Helene really worries about May, who wasn't home that night, thank God. And I think Louisa feels the same way you do. She'd like to find the perpetrator, if you know what I mean."

"I know exactly what you mean."

"It's a terrible feeling, you know, knowing someone has it in for you. To that degree. I'm kind of dazed, to tell you the truth."

"Well, sure you are. But can they be so sure it's arson, already?"

"The investigator said it was pretty obvious the fire was set with gasoline, all around the perimeter of the cottage—"

"I want to help you, Sarah. I want to be there for you."

"I know. Thank you, Nathan."

He leaned toward me, his big white hands knotted together, looking down on me with a serious, compassionate expression. I wished he would go away. Talking to Nathan seemed to require more energy than I had to spare.

Helene poked her head in the room. "How are we doing in here? Anybody hungry?"

"Something smells awfully good," said Nathan.

Hint, hint, I thought.

"It's going to be another few minutes," Helene said, "so I expect you to sharpen up that appetite!"

"You got it!" he exclaimed.

She went back to the kitchen, and he turned his attention to me once again. "How about you?" he said. "Are you hungry?"

"Not really."

"Are you sure you're okay?"

No, I thought. *I just told you. I'm not okay. I came very close to suffocating to death in my bed.* I could still feel the heavy ache in my lungs.

Helene popped her head in again. "Someone else here to see you, Sarah."

Gatien? I wondered, hopeful, my attention suddenly awakened. He had been home since the night of the fire, and now we lived in the same house; but I felt I was with him more often in dreams than in waking life. He was there; he was around me. I smelled his aftershave and I heard his voice, calling from another room. But I wanted to see him there before me. I wanted to touch him. He was so elusive, keeping to himself. He had stayed with me, faithfully, until I had come to myself again after the fire, and had no need of him. *(No need of him!)* Then he withdrew into the background and let everyone else come to me, Helene and May, Louisa, Nathan . . .

And now, Paul.

I smiled weakly. I did love Paul, although not in the way he seemed to want me to love him.

"Howya doing, Sarah?" He looked like Apollo in a business suit.

"Hey, Paul."

He bent down to give me a hug.

"Have you two met?" I asked.

"Think so," said Nathan. "What's up, man?"

"Not much." The guys shook hands.

"Here, Paul," I said, drawing my legs up beneath the tartan throw I was using as a blanket. "Sit down."

Paul sat beside me on the love seat and Nathan sat on his stool.

We sat like that for a moment, awkwardly, nobody saying a word.

"Haven't seen you for a long time," I said to Paul.

"Yeah. It seemed best to lay low for awhile. But when I heard about the fire, I had to come. Damn the consequences!"

"Such courage." I laughed.

"So, buddy," Paul said to Nathan. "You got plenty of insurance, right?"

Nathan looked at him, baffled.

"In case it turns out to be faulty electrical wiring."

"They've already determined it to be arson," Nathan said, dignified.

"That's what I'm saying," said Paul.

"Paul," I said. "What's this about?"

"I'm pissed off, and I'm worried about you, Sarah! Arson! Jesus Christ. When I read about it this morning in the paper, I just about came apart."

"Well, don't take it out on poor Nathan."

"Yeah, all right. Hey, I'm sorry."

"That's okay, man," said Nathan. "I'm pissed, too."

"So, how are you and Theta doing?" I asked Paul.

"We *have* come apart."

"Seriously?"

"Seriously. Completely undone. She moved out."

"Oh, I am sorry."

"You are?"

"Well, I don't know. Are you happier now?"

"Not yet." He looked from me to Nathan, and back again. "I mean, look, I lost my wife and my best friend on the same day. How do you like that?"

"You lost them together, eh, my friend?" said Nathan.

"Exactly. Tell me how a man is supposed to deal with that?"

"With a duel, traditionally," Nathan said.

"A duel. Hmm." Paul appeared to be giving the matter serious thought. "A duel . . ."

The door opened, and there stood Gatien, not the tallest man in the room, nor the most classically handsome, but his presence filled the space as did neither of the others. The mention of a duel, and the sudden appearance of Gatien Defalle, had us all stopped short. I was certain Gatien had heard what Paul had been saying. I felt very self-conscious, there on the love seat, wrapped in a blanket, with Paul so close, and Nathan sitting on the stool, leaning toward me, wringing his hands. Gatien stood above us, looking from Paul to Nathan with lordly contempt. He didn't seem to notice me at all.

"For which woman do you propose a duel, gentlemen?" he asked. He cut the question with a pirate smile, and the men laughed awkwardly. Nobody answered.

"IT'S ALL OUT on the table, buffet-style," said Helene, "So help yourselves, everybody."

The dining room was full of people; May and Dimitri were there, Paul and Nathan, Helene, Gatien and me— Gatien had even persuaded Louisa and Carlos to join us for the meal. May's grandfather was there, too, and He-

lene had to scold him into getting himself a plate. He said
he wasn't hungry.

"Do you want me to make you a plate, Dad?" she
asked.

"No, I'll do it myself." The old man reluctantly got in
line at the table, looking down on Louisa's fantastic Mexican dishes with a dubious frown.

"He worries me," Helene said to me in a low voice,
watching her father. "I used to have to get after him about
keeping his weight down. Now I have to nag at him to eat.
He doesn't seem to have much of an appetite lately."

Me neither, I thought. An appetite is a funny thing. I
watched Gatien and Paul, fascinated. Neither of them
were eating. Paul claimed he wasn't hungry (first time I
had ever seen him not hungry), and Gatien told Helene he
would eat when everyone else was served. It cracked me
up. Gatien, it seemed, would allow Paul into his home,
and here was Paul, actually daring to step foot into Gatien's space, but still they refused to break bread together.

"I failed you, Sarah Logan." Dimitri stood beside me,
holding a plate heaped with chicken mole, green salad,
and rice. His black hair was bleached almost white, cut
short, and spiked all over his head. He had one earring, a
silver stud, which seemed conservative with that hair.

"Explain to me how," I said.

We walked outside onto the terrace with our plates of
food and sat down together at the picnic table.

"I told you I would protect you, and I failed you," he
said, lowering his voice, though we were alone on the terrace. "Your cottage burned down, and you nearly died."

"I don't blame you, Dimitri," I said. "Should I?"

"I'm redoubling my efforts. I won't see you become
another Lisa."

"What do you mean, another Lisa?"

"Another murder victim."

"Your concern is very touching."

"So then why are you upset with me?" He looked at me
pointedly. There was hurt in his huge, dark eyes.

I didn't trust the little Satyr.

He was right. He made me angry when he talked about Lisa's murder, if that's what it was; and he really pushed some buttons when he talked about mine.

Helene came out on the terrace to have a cigarette. "So how are you holding up, Sarah?" she asked me.

"I'm okay," I said.

"You still sound a little hoarse."

"Yes. My head aches, and I'm still coughing up black stuff from my lungs, but I'm not feeling so sick to my stomach anymore."

"It makes me shudder," she said, "to think what might have happened."

"And everything you owned was destroyed!" said Dimitri, wild-eyed.

"Thank God for Gatien," I said quietly.

"If he hadn't come home then, smelled the smoke, if he hadn't gone looking for you . . ."

"I know. If he hadn't found me when he did . . . After he got me out, the place just went up. It was like, a matter of seconds."

"Speaking of seconds, I'm going in for some." Dimitri announced. "Can I get you ladies anything?"

"No thanks, Dimitri." We both shook our heads, and he went in and left us alone on the terrace.

"Well," said Helene, "I do feel badly for you, Sarah. You'll be needing new clothes, and I want to help with that."

"It's okay. I had been planning to buy a new wardrobe anyway. None of my other stuff fit right anymore, except for what you bought me on New Year's Eve."

"I suppose most of what you had in that cottage was unsalvageable."

"Yes." It occurred to me that Helene probably assumed the books I had told her I'd found had been lost in the fire. If I hadn't taken them to the appraiser when I did, they surely would have been.

"You know how I told you I had found something interesting?" I said.

"Yes," she said in a low voice. "Do you know what you had there? Did you get a chance to look at it, before . . ."

"I think one of them was a fourteenth-century illuminated manuscript," I said. "The other three were accounting books of some sort, dated from around the same time."

She looked thoughtful. "Really. What a loss. Where did you find these books?"

"In the storeroom in the garage. The box had never even been opened. Helene, I have to tell you the truth."

"I certainly hope you will!" she exclaimed.

"The books weren't lost in the fire. They're sitting downtown, in an appraiser's shop."

"Well!" She laughed. "I was just going to say we had better find out if they're insured!"

"My problem is, I took those books without telling Gatien about them. I was hoping to surprise him with some exciting news about how valuable they are."

She smiled. "Sarah, your secret is safe with me. And just between us, I think you're handling it correctly. If there's something there, present it to him. Otherwise, don't bother him about it. You know how he is."

"Yeah, well, there's *something* there. They are beautiful old books, no question. . . ."

"He's not all that excited about beautiful old books, I'm afraid."

"No," I said. "I know he isn't." I looked up and saw Dimitri at the kitchen door, looking out at us through the open window.

TOWARD THE END of the Mexican feast, I was in the kitchen when the phone rang. I picked it up and was surprised to hear my name. Usually I took my calls on the phone in the cottage. But of course the phone, not to mention the cottage, was no longer with us.

"Sarah?"

"Yes?"

"It is me, Edith Kirkland. Madame Curio. I expected to hear from you by now, about the books you left with me, and so I called my nephew, who told me your house burned down! I'm so sorry."

"Yeah, thanks. I've been a little distracted."

"Yes, yes, I'm so sorry for you. That explains why you haven't been answering your phone, doesn't it! My nephew told me about it, and he gave me this number to try. I hope you're all right."

"Yes, I'm fine now."

"I was wondering why you didn't come to pick up the books. But I suppose now I know why you haven't!"

"I'll come to your shop as soon as I get a chance," I said.

"Come as soon as you can, because I'm leaving for Europe—"

"Sarah, do you want more?" Louisa appeared at my side with an almost empty basket of tortillas. Gatien came into the room behind her, carrying dirty dishes.

"I'm sorry," I said into the phone, shaking my head at Louisa, trying not to look at Gatien, who went to the sink and began to scrape the dishes.

"Sorry. What was that?" I said into the phone.

"So will it be tomorrow?" Madame Curio asked.

"Yes," I said. "I think so."

"All right, then. I'm very much looking forward to talking with you."

"Me, too."

Gatien, I felt, was curious to know who was on the phone, but of course he would never ask. At least I hoped he wouldn't ask.

I felt like a sneak, a thief, a liar. Which of course I was. I was wishing I'd never found that box in the storeroom. I could not bring myself to tell Gatien what I'd done. I kept thinking I was going to tell him, but the time just was never right. And the more time that passed, the more not right the time seemed to be. I resolved to go first thing in the morning, get those books back, and end this folly. Besides, I was curious to know what Madame Curio would tell me about them.

Chapter Sixteen

I WANTED TO get to bed early that night, but it was after eleven when everyone finally left. I planned to get May off to school the next morning at eight, get some things done around the house, then go "do some errands"—that is, go and get those books—around ten. I didn't think Gatien had anything planned, and I was hoping I could get out of the house alone without having to say anything specific about where I was going. I lay awake in the guest room bed, the one on which I had once seen Theta straddle Gatien's lap.

It was past one in the morning when I finally slept.

I thought I was dreaming when I came to consciousness with his hands on me. He was whispering my name. I could smell him, his clean breath, his subtle, expensive aftershave. Intoxicating.

I breathed him in deeply, stretching and turning, and I opened my eyes to see him bending over me, everything still dark in the room with the shades drawn.

"Don't wake up, Sarah," he said. "You can sleep in. I'm taking May out of school today. We're going up to the city. We want you to come with us, but you don't have to.

Helene said she'd drive, if we needed her. But we'd rather have you."

I lay there, wondering if I was indeed dreaming. But I didn't think so.

"What do you say, Sarah? Will you come with us?"

I lay there motionless, trying to wake myself from a dream into a dream.

"Nod yes," he commanded.

I nodded.

"Good!" He sounded happy. "Go back to sleep."

Right.

WE DROVE UP 280, and Gatien instructed me to get off at the Pacifica exit. We cut over the peninsula toward the ocean, climbed the bluff, and suddenly we could see the ocean off to one side and the city on the other, and Gatien pointed out the orange vermilion towers of the Golden Gate Bridge peeking out of the fog to the north.

We hit the coast highway and cruised alongside the dunes, the ocean to our left, the edge of the city to our right, miles of boxy beach houses sitting side by side, windows facing the water.

"This might take a little longer than Nineteenth Avenue, but I like it better," Gatien said.

I didn't know the city at all, so it didn't matter in the least to me.

"You still haven't told me where we're going," I said.

"I'm just going to take you and May any place that strikes my fancy, or yours," he said.

"Sounds good to me!" said May. "What about you, Sarah?"

"I'm always up for an adventure!"

"Gato, where do you go when you go so far away, for so many days?" May asked him.

"Well . . ." He hesitated like a man about to confess a career in espionage. "I go to be with the Grand Prix. There's one in—"

"Why do you go now, if you no longer race?"

"For business. I'm working with some up-and-coming

constructors. We're creating the fastest, most beautiful car in the world. And there are other things I have to do, to be in it, like dealing with sponsors. Helping teams raise money. And also, I go to—"

"To make commercials," said May.

"What?"

"Aunt Helene says you do TV commercials and maga-zine ads. But I never see you in them."

"They're mostly in other countries."

"She says you're a big star in other places, like Europe and South America. That when you walk down the street in France, people take your picture and ask you for your autograph. Is that why you go there so often?"

He glanced at me and blushed.

"Well, partly," he said. "And also because of my loved ones there."

In the rearview I saw May, nodding gravely, as if she understood.

My loved ones . . . A woman, I thought. I was instantly on edge, waiting for him to explain. And if he didn't, May would ask. She would surely pursue the issue. I was cer-tain she would, knowing her as I did.

She didn't. Perhaps she *had* understood.

"So have you made a lot of money racing cars?" she wanted to know.

"Yes, but I've had to spend a ridiculous amount, too, and sometimes I worry about the difference."

"You *had* to spend?" I asked ironically. "Isn't the spending always your own choice?"

He thought about that, laughed. "No! I wish it were, but it's not."

May supported him. "No, it's not always his choice," she agreed. "Except that he *chooses* to help others. Mr. Defalle, here, is responsible for many financial responsi-bilities."

I burst out laughing. "I see you have a champion, here, Gatien!"

"What do you mean, a champion?" May frowned, thinking of soccer champions, I think.

"Champion," I said. "Like a defender. A knight defending a damsel in distress."

"Oh. Okay." She frowned, thinking. "Am I the damsel in distress, or the knight?"

"Everybody's a bit of each, aren't they?" I said.

We stopped at the Cliff House and sat by a window high above the beach, watching the waves come in while eating buttery-crisp popovers with jam and marmalade; then we drove on up to the Palace of the Legion of Honor to see Leonardo's *Lady with an Ermine*, which was there with the Polish exhibition. I was amazed at May's interest in the art; I had expected her to be bored.

When we came out of the museum, we hiked the trails around the edge of the bay. The Golden Gate Bridge was close, and the fog had gone; the colors of the bay and the pines on the shore were crisp and vibrant.

We drove through an elegant neighborhood at the tip of the bay, and Gatien indicated a stunning mansion with a wave of his hand. "That's Paul's house," he said. I could see the water sparkling in the old mullioned windows. We drove past slowly, without stopping.

"I'VE GOT AN idea!" said May.

"Let's hear it," Gatien said.

"Let's go over to Sausalito for dinner."

"Dinner?" I exclaimed. "Aren't you stuffed yet? After that shrimp cocktail at Fisherman's Wharf and that hot fudge sundae you just ate at Ghirardelli?"

"But I *love* Sausalito. Sarah, don't you love Sausalito?"

"Sausalito," I said, trying to muster up my Bay Area geography, which was still rudimentary. "Isn't that on the other side of the Golden Gate Bridge? Yeah, I think my dad took me there once, when I was little! We had ice cream and walked along the waterfront . . . there's a candy store, and a toy store, and lots of art galleries. . . ."

"Yes." May turned to Gatien imploringly. "Can we go?"

Gatien hesitated a moment before answering. "Sounds like a great idea, but I have to get back home soon."

"Why?" May wanted to know. She didn't want to accept no for an answer.

"I'm going out tonight," he said. I heard a touch of Gatien's mysterious, courteous *Don't cross me* tone, which had been absent all day, up until now.

Going out? Going out where? I wondered. Ordinarily if he had somewhere to go, he needed me to drive him. And, ever since the first time, he had always let me know in advance if he had something scheduled; if it was spur-of-the-moment, he always asked politely. He hadn't said anything about tonight.

"Going out where?" May demanded, asking the question I wouldn't.

"Out," he said. "With a friend. It's a fund-raising thing."

She groaned.

"It's a school night, May," I said, feeling awkward about this turn of events and trying to flow with it. "We should get going back anyway."

"School night!" she said, disgusted. "I hate school."

"Well, you know," I said. "Spring break is coming up soon, and you're going to Santa Cruz, where you can forget about it for awhile."

"Yeah, but that is like *so* far away in the future."

"Only a couple of weeks."

"I was thinking of taking off for a few days, myself," said Gatien, "when you're in Santa Cruz, May. Maybe do a road trip. Cruise up the coast a ways."

"A road trip? What about the driving thing?" May asked with concern.

"Well, I have to ask Sarah about that," Gatien said. "Sarah, I was wondering if you have any plans for spring break. Are you going to Santa Barbara, or . . ."

"I really hadn't given it much thought."

"I wonder if I might persuade you to be my driver. Time and a half and all expenses paid, of course." He grinned. "What do you think?"

I was wounded a little that he would put the idea of us taking a trip together in terms of employment and compensation. Why didn't he simply invite me to come along with him? I kept my eyes on the road ahead of me as I drove, troubled by my own ferocious desire to jump at such an offer.

"No fair," said May. "*I* want to go, too! Why are you doing it just when I'm going to be away?"

"Well, I'm taking that week off so I can be home for Easter. It doesn't mean we can't do another trip, later, when you can go, too," Gatien said. "And I've been thinking I'd like to bring you to France this summer, May."

"Cool." She seemed satisfied by this. "We haven't been to France in a long time."

"Come on, Sarah." That sexy baritone was softer now, and I realized he had more emotional investment in my answer than he would have it seem. "Would you do this for me?"

"Of course," I said evenly. "You're the boss."

"SINCE YOUR DAD'S going out tonight, why don't we just make a pizza?" I said to May. "I think there's one in the freezer."

May hooted her approval at that.

"Why don't you get your shower taken before dinner?" I said, sliding into what I was beginning to think of as my mom mode. "I'll put the pizza in."

"Okay."

I turned on the oven, took the pizza out of the freezer. I heard the sound of May starting her shower, the water rushing through the pipes in the walls. I hadn't seen Gatien since we'd arrived home an hour earlier, but I had heard the sound of *his* shower, through the walls of the house.

Who was he going out with? Who was driving him, if not me?

I put the pizza in the oven without bothering to preheat. I didn't care how the pizza turned out. I wasn't hungry. I took it out again at once and set it on the stove to wait, feeling guilty for May's sake. *Let the oven heat up.*

Should have let her do the pizza. She's better at it than I am, anyway.

There was a knock on the door. I walked through the living room toward the wavy image in the glass front door behind the sheer curtain. I opened the door.

"Hi," said the bright voice. "I'm Courtney." She held out her hand and smiled like a Texan, big teeth and great warmth. "You must be May's—I'm sorry I've forgotten your name."

"Sarah," I said.

"Hi, Sarah." Her hand was hot, her grip strong, but not as strong as the power of her smile. I was nearly knocked over by it. But just before she overwhelmed me with the sheer force of her dazzling white teeth, she shut her mouth and finished the smile demurely, and let her big brown eyes express her sincere delight at meeting me. That's when I noticed how pretty she was, how doelike her cameo face, how lustrous her long brown hair, how perfectly made she was in every detail, from her delicate hands and feet to her long, flared nose. I had already noticed her figure through the glass, so lean and elegant, draped in a very expensive-looking silk thing that looked like a nightie with a tiny jacket over it. The skirt barely skimmed the tops of the sleek columns of her legs, legs that came up to my chin, but that was partly because her heels were so high. She was a few years older than me, and so sophisticated I could eat my heart out.

"Where is Gatien?" she asked. "I want him to see me on time for once."

"I don't know," I said. "I think he's getting ready."

"Such a bore, these charity things, and on a weeknight!" she cried, exasperated. "He's such a sweet boy for saying yes. I know he hates them."

"Well, he sure is a sweet boy," I said.

"Uh, thank you for that."

I turned my head, galvanized by the sound of Gatien's deep voice. He was emerging from the stairwell, moving from darkness into light. He wore a dark suit with a white shirt and a simple dark silk tie. His hair was longer now.

It had grown out some since he'd cut it, and it lay smooth for the evening against his beautiful head. His brow was set with a look of fierce determination.

"Gatien!" Courtney crossed the room in a furl of silk to meet him halfway.

I watched them kiss, fascinated. They were sweet, cool, affectionate with each other. She said to him, almost too quietly for me to hear: "Those roses were lovely, hon, thank you!" She tweaked his ear playfully, and I was wounded to the quick.

He glanced my way, and he must have seen it in me, for I had no time to lower my eyes. He looked away and seemed flustered, as if he wasn't certain where to set his gaze.

"Shall we then?" said Courtney.

"Where's May?" Gatien wanted to know.

"Taking her shower," I answered mechanically.

"Well then, say our good-byes for us."

"Yes, do, please," Courtney said to me. She took Gatien's arm. "Too bad. I would have *loved* to see your May again. Well, next time!"

She waved at me in a friendly way.

They walked together to the door, and he stood aside for her to precede him out. He hesitated a moment, staring at the floor, as if he'd just thought of something he'd forgotten. I stood, unable to move, waiting for him to leave.

He lifted his chin, but he didn't look at me. He didn't say anything else, either, and went out the door. As he crossed the threshold he seemed to falter, probably because of his limp, but he recovered himself gracefully and was gone.

Chapter Seventeen

I WAS UP earlier than usual the next morning, pacing the floors, waiting for May to get ready for school. Gatien did not make his usual appearance. Louisa and Carlos arrived, and he still wasn't up. I did not pour him a cup of Louisa's coffee, as I had been in the habit of doing lately.

"Gato is sleeping in late this morning!" May remarked, spreading cream cheese on her bagel.

"He must have stayed out late with Courtney last night," I said. *If he even came home.*

"Courtney!" May exclaimed. "Is *that* who he went out with?"

"Yeah. Why?"

"Oh my *God.*"

"What?"

"Nothing."

May's mood darkened considerably.

I was relieved when it looked as if we would get out of the house without meeting up with Gatien. I intended to go see Madame Curio as soon as her shop opened—and I wasn't going to come home first as I had planned.

But as we were going out the door he appeared at the

top of the stairs, looking dark-jawed and rumpled and cranky, all rather out of character for him.

"Finally, you're up!" May ran and gave him a kiss on the cheek. "Bye-bye."

He made no sign whatsoever, and my heart swelled with indignation for May's sake. I went out without looking back at him.

I DROPPED MAY off, rather dark of temper myself, though I had tried to pretend that everything for me was normal, for her sake.

When I got to Madame Curio's I found a note in the window which read: Closed For Vacation.

I couldn't believe it. I hadn't expected the shop to be open just yet this morning, but I certainly didn't think I'd have to wait weeks! I dug into my bag and got out my cell phone, which Gatien had given to me after my cottage was burned, and I called Nathan.

"Sarah! Hi!" He was always so maddeningly happy to hear from me. And right now, that was a good thing.

"Nathan," I said. "I need to get a hold of your aunt, Madame Curio."

"Oh, but you can't. She went on a buying trip to Europe. She left this morning, in fact. I took her to the airport."

He was silent in response to my sudden outburst of swearing. "My apologies, Nathan," I said. "But she has something I gave her that I was *really* hoping to get back."

"I know. She told me she had expected you yesterday. She said she told you she was leaving town, and if you didn't pick up the books, she would have to wait and meet with you in a few weeks. She told me she warned you."

"Maybe. Yeah, I think she did. She called me during dinner the night before last, when we had everybody over to the house, remember? You were there. I didn't hear everything she said, and I just figured I'd go the next day, as we agreed, but then I couldn't make it yesterday, and so . . ."

"Don't worry, you'll get the books back, Sarah. My aunt is very trustworthy."

"It's just that it's . . . they're not mine, Nathan. They actually belonged to Lisa Defalle. Gatien doesn't even know about them. I wanted to surprise him, but I wanted to see what they were first, you know, have them checked out. . . ."

Nathan listened avidly to my tale of woe. He wanted to be my knight in shining armor; he wanted to save me. He thought of a way. "Listen, Sarah," he said. "I think I might be able to help you. Can you meet me down at the shop around five-thirty this evening?"

"Sure," I said, wondering if I could.

"Let's see—actually, let's make it six. I'll see what I can do for you, okay? I'll see if I can get you into the shop and get your books back. Then I'll take you out to dinner. Deal?"

"Okay. Thanks, Nathan."

"I'll pick you up?"

"No," I said. "I'll meet you down there."

I HUNG UP, standing in front of the shop in the early morning quiet, peering in the windows of Madame Curio's. *Now what do I do?* I wondered. I didn't want to go home. I didn't want to see Gatien. I couldn't bear the thought of seeing him with some sort of morning-after glow. Though I had to admit he had looked more growling than glowing. I couldn't stand the thought of being anything but nonchalant with him, and I wasn't sure I could pull that off just yet. It was almost unbearable, I thought, living with him, especially now that we were actually in the same house. If he was going to bring women home . . .

Snap out of it, Sarah!

I shook my head, trying to clear my brain. What I needed was that good old metaphorical slap in the face. Well, that seemed to be exactly what I had gotten. I started walking down the street toward my car.

Look at the situation logically, I thought.

I got in the car, started up the engine, threw it in gear, and roared off. I didn't know where I was going, but I was going to get there fast. When I got out of town and hit the country roads, I stepped on the gas, rolled down the windows, opened the sun roof, popped in a CD, and let my hair fly.

Gatien Defalle had hired me, Sarah Logan, to look after his child for the duration of one year. Gatien Defalle was my boss. He paid me to live in his house. When my term was finished, my job complete, I would take the payment due me and move on. The man had been a perfect gentleman with me, notwithstanding one out-of-control kiss, quickly controlled. I could find nothing with which to reproach him. No promise, no hint, no indiscreet word or deed besides that one hot kiss. He was a man, as he had once informed me himself. He led a man's life. He was a widower. He had the perfect right to have a lady companion. Or companions. And it was none of my business.

IT TOOK HOURS of soul-searching and a drive down the coast highway at a considerable speed to straighten myself out, mentally and emotionally. Luckily, it was a weekday morning, and I practically had the road to myself. The colors of sea and sky were saturated, vivid sapphire beside the topaz and emerald cliffs. I could have kept driving and driving, but by midmorning I had reasoned out that if I didn't come home all day, it would look like I was sulking, and that would be worse than confronting Gatien himself. I was too proud to let him know how affected I was by the beautiful woman he had accompanied out on the town last night. So I turned the car around and drove up the coast and over the mountain toward home, but when I got there around noon, the place was silent, and Gatien didn't appear until after May had come home from school.

"AREN'T YOU EATING?" May asked me. She and her father were serving themselves from the casserole and cook pots Louisa had left on the stove in the kitchen.

"Actually, no," I replied. I was searching in the kitchen drawer for something I could use to tie back my hair. "I'm going to go see Nathan—that is, if there's no pressing need for my services here," I added ironically.

"Nathan?" May looked at me oddly. "You're not going out with him!"

I shrugged. "We're going to go get something to eat."

"There is suddenly a lot of dating going on around here!" May said primly.

"It's not a date," I said. "We're just getting some dinner."

"That's a date."

"No it isn't." I found a rubber band and twisted up my hair, horribly self-conscious. Gatien was looking at me. I was mortified to think he might assume I'd run out and gotten myself a date just because he had.

But I couldn't very well explain the real reason Nathan and I were getting together. Not unless I wanted to suddenly start telling the truth about certain things, which I definitely did not.

NATHAN WAS ALREADY there at his aunt's shop when I arrived. He had the door unlocked, the alarm disabled, and the lights on.

I was impressed. "Did you break in?" I asked.

"No," he said with a modest laugh. "Not exactly. I have the key, and the codes. I take care of the shop when she's out of town. Come on in."

He slipped his hand over my shoulder to guide me in.

We gave the shop a quick perusal and didn't see the books. He showed me into the office.

"I think she keeps the things she's appraising in here," he said, unlocking the door. The room was outfitted with a desk and bookshelves, with an adjoining storeroom. In the storeroom was a large safe.

"I don't have the combo to the safe, so if she put them in there, we're out of luck," Nathan warned me.

After a half hour of searching the entire shop, office, and storage area, I concluded we were out of luck.

I was having some terrible visions. Maybe the books had proven to be so valuable, Nathan's aunt had skipped town and run away to another country to live out her life in the lap of luxury! Or she'd been murdered by blood-thirsty rare book scholars, the same bad guys who had murdered Lisa!

The books were probably just tucked away in the safe, Nathan assured me, and I had to believe that. I would just have to bide my time and hope Helene didn't mention something in passing to Gatien about a box of books from Spain that snoopy Sarah discovered in the storage area. And then took upon herself to give away. Too bad I didn't just say the books were burned up in the fire.

Why was I being so apprehensive about Gatien finding out what I'd done? If I hadn't brought them in to Madame Curio when I did, they *would have* been burned in the fire.

Was that fire meant to destroy those books? I suddenly wondered. Who knew—or thought, rather—that they were in my cottage at the time? I had told Helene. Only Helene knew. Unless she had told Dimitri. Unless Dimitri had overheard . . . "There, there, little Sarah," Nathan crooned, putting his arms around me, patting me. "You seem so upset." We were standing together in the doorway between the office and the storeroom. I rested against him for a moment, enjoying the comfort of his tall, warm presence.

He pressed his hands on either side of my face, and made me look at him. He was gazing at me adoringly. He leaned in and kissed me tenderly on the mouth. His lips weren't spongy, as I had imagined they might be. In fact, they were rather cool and hard, and surprisingly insistent, and growing more insistent by the second. His hands moved down over my shoulders, and his arms slid around me, encircling me with a surprising vigor. I was inflamed with physical frustration and emotional confusion, added to a chronic paranoia, always looking over my shoulder, wondering who was out to get me. I was not thinking clearly. Except for one thing, one thing that hit me over the head and drove everything else down. I began to cry.

"Hey, hey!" murmured Nathan, his gentle, ardent expression changing into one of alarm. He withdrew his arms from around me, caressed my cheek, and thumbed away a teardrop. "What's going on, Sarah?"

"Oh, Nathan," I sobbed. "I'm so sorry. You're so nice, and attractive, and everything. It's just that . . . oh my God. It's true. I'm in love with my boss."

He opened his mouth, and a comical look of understanding came over his face. "Ah . . ." he said softly. "I get it. And . . . does he love you?" He shook his head sadly, and added, "Sure he does. How could he not?"

"No," I replied dully, through my tears. "I don't think he does."

"Hmm." Nathan was thinking. He was probably as confused as I was, but he was a man, and he was busy at once, trying to think of a solution to this problem.

"So, basically, what you're saying is, you like me all right, but you're kind of already into this other guy, so . . ."

"Yeah. I guess."

"So you can't think of me in that way, because . . ."

"Yeah."

"Because you're hung up on him."

"Yeah."

"But you don't have any *commitments* between the two of you, right?"

I shook my head.

"So what I gotta do is simply drive that man out of your mind and then—"

"Nathan."

"I know. I'm coming on too strong. I've been afraid of doing that all along, with you. But then I was afraid that if I didn't let you know how I feel, I'd miss out because I didn't act when I should have."

"You sure are nice."

"Look. He's had the advantage. You live there, he lives there. If you got to know me like that, maybe you'd see that I'm the one for you."

"Yeah, maybe." But as soon as I said it, I knew I wasn't

being truthful with Nathan. I knew, deep in my heart and soul, that for me, Nathan could never compare to Gatien. Maybe nobody could.

"So I'm not going to give up," he declared, more to himself than to me. "Besides," he added. "I saw you first."

Chapter Eighteen

S O I HAD several weeks to wait until Nathan's aunt returned from her trip before I could get the old books back. What choice did I have? I thought about relaying the status of things to Helene, but she wasn't thinking of the books anyway; her father had taken ill and had to go into the hospital.

Gatien and May were of course very concerned; Helene was beside herself, though she kept it together and was strong for her father. She decided that she or someone else in the family should be at his bedside at every moment, and so everyone was pressed into service. Gatien, May, and I took turns relieving Helene, who bore the brunt of it. We were in the car, driving back and forth to Stanford Hospital for weeks. It was early spring; the buds on the trees lining the streets were beginning to quicken.

It had started as pneumonia, which was under control now, but Mr. Browning simply wasn't getting back his health and was plagued with various other ailments, which threatened him because he was so weak from the pneumonia.

"I don't know what to do for him, Sarah," Helene told

me one evening. "The doctors say it's as if he's lost the will to live."

Mr. Browning finally went home. He seemed to be getting better, but after a week he was readmitted. He died several days later.

I was most concerned for May. She had lost her mother such a short time ago, and now her grandfather. It was a lot for a child to process. And my heart went out to Helene: first her sister, then her father. Helene and her dad had been very close, and I knew what it was like to lose a beloved father.

I was touched when she came to me for support. "I can't believe he's gone, Sarah," she said, her voice hollow. "I hardly know what to live for, anymore."

I knew Gatien must be hurting, too. He had been fond of the old man. Helene asked Gatien to do the eulogy, which I thought was a strange request until Gatien asked May and me to be his practice audience. He had prepared a few remarks in a small spiral notebook, but he barely glanced at his notes. His words were simple, heartfelt, and delivered with a professional assurance that astounded me. It was as if he were a different person, standing there before us, speaking with gentle wit and poignancy. There were tears on both May's and my cheeks when he was finished.

I STOOD IN the shade under a pergola, waiting for the church to fill. Helene and Gatien were busy greeting all the people they knew. Dimitri came to stand beside me beneath a rain of fragrant purple wisteria blossoms. "Poor little May," Dimitri said, following her with his gaze. "First her mommy, now her grandpa. At least *he* wasn't murdered, I don't think."

"Dimitri," I said sharply. "You're always insinuating that May's mother was murdered. Why are you so interested in promoting her death as a murder?"

"Because I think it *was* a murder."

"Why? Why are you so sure she was murdered? Who would have had a motive to murder Lisa Defalle?"

"Her husband, for one."

"Oh?" That answer startled me, though I should have expected it. I looked at him blankly. "Why would Gatien want to murder his wife?"

"There are those who say she was not faithful to him. Or that she annoyed him in other ways. Drove him to do her in."

"And just who, exactly, are *those* who say this? Why do you get off on attacking him? What did Gatien ever do to you?"

"How staunchly you defend him," Dimitri murmured. "I'm jealous. I'd love to inspire such devotion in you, Sarah Logan." He smiled at me sweetly. What a handsome little Satyr he was. Not so little. Almost six feet tall. "But Sarah, I'm not trying to disrespect Gatien, or insult him."

"Calling him a murderer isn't insulting him?"

"I didn't call him a murderer. I only said he had a motive. The husband almost *always* has a motive. That's murder 101. But that doesn't mean I think he's the one who did it."

"Then why do you say it at all?

"You brought it up, Sarah."

"So you have other suspects as well?"

"Well, let's see. Who might have had a motive to wish Aunt Lisa dead?"

"Theta," I said, watching her come in from the entryway across the courtyard.

Dimitri followed the direction of my gaze. "There you are," he said. "Theta. Another suspect with a motive."

I looked at Dimitri, and we both started laughing, trying to suppress it immediately, out of respect for the occasion. I guess I wasn't the only one who was aware of Theta's interest in Gatien.

Theta was gorgeous as always, in a tan skirt, black spike heels, and a black top with ties in the back that cinched the blousy fabric close to her trim figure. She looked around, saw Dimitri and me, and dismissed us; she got Helene in her sights and torpedoed over to offer her condolences.

And then suddenly, there was Nathan. I felt disoriented for a moment, seeing him there, and I probably blushed, remembering our overly emotional last encounter. "Nathan!" I said with surprise.

He didn't notice me there, beneath the pergola, and he wandered off toward the sanctuary.

"Ah, yes, there's another one," Dimitri said.

"Nathan? A suspect?" I whispered, incredulous.

"Sure."

"What possible motive could *he* have? And what's he doing here? I didn't even think he knew the old man that well."

"Oh, yes, he knew him very well. He did a big remodeling project for him, lasted over a year."

"Oh, right, I think I knew that, but . . ."

"Nathan became like part of the family. He's the one Gatien's wife is rumored to have, uh . . . *you* know. Cheated on her husband with."

"Oh, no! You're joking. Not *Nathan.*"

"Yeah. I mean, no, I'm not joking. It seems Lisa paid quite a few visits to her father's house while it was being remodeled. If you get my meaning. Obviously Uncle Gatien never heard the rumors, or I don't think he would have hired Nathan himself."

"Or maybe he *has* heard the rumors and didn't give a damn about idle gossip."

"Okay, okay, calm down. I forget how sensitive you are about him."

DIMITRI WENT TO help Helene move some flowers, and Paul sought me out. He was looking better than the last time I'd seen him. He seemed to be getting his old verve back.

"How are you and Theta doing?" I asked him.

"Well, we're legally separated now," he said. "We haven't filed for divorce, but I think it's inevitable. And I'm okay with that. To tell you the truth, I think I'm better off without that woman."

"Well, then I guess it's good you're doing this."

"Definitely. Yeah. But you know, I don't want to make it sound like I'm all happy about it or anything. For a while I was kind of depressed, Sarah. And I think this bullshit with Gatien has been just as bad as losing Theta."

"What about that?" I said. "Gatien says you accused him of sleeping with your wife."

"I did," said Paul.

"I can see why that might cause a rift between you."

"That's not what caused the rift."

"It's not?"

"No. When I accused him of sleeping with my wife, he just laughed. That pissed me off, of course. But the big blow-out wasn't about Theta, it was about *you.*"

"Me!"

"Yeah. He told me to leave you alone. I told him to mind his own business. Except I used different words. He used the same words back at me, stressing in no uncertain terms what he'd do to me if I defied his wishes."

"Why?" I demanded. "What business is it of his? Why would he care if you and I—?"

"Don't ask stupid questions, my dear."

When I continued frowning at him, baffled, his expression changed.

"I don't believe it. Are you telling me you and he aren't—you haven't—?"

"Haven't what?"

"You know very well what I'm asking you."

"It's none of *your* business, either, but no. We haven't."

"My God. Then . . ." He broke into a rakish grin. "And I've been holding back all this time? There's got to be a statute of limitations on these things. Besides, if Gatien and I are going to remain enemies anyway, I might as well . . ." He leaned forward and grasped my hand, tried to kiss it.

"Paul," I said, pulling my hand away. "You and Gatien are *not* going to remain enemies. There's no good reason for that."

"You could be an awfully compelling reason, my lady."

"That's absurd. There's nothing between us. Not between you and me, nor Gatien and me. So how does that make me a reason for you two to be feuding?"

"My God!" He threw up his hands dramatically. "It kills me. He's forbidden me to court you, and yet he doesn't take you for himself?"

"Take me?" I exclaimed, offended. "I might have refused *him,* you know."

"Ah! So you were waiting for me?" he asked hopefully.

"I liked you when I first met you," I admitted with a laugh. "But then I learned you were married, and by the time you and Theta separated, I . . ."

"You what? You what? I know. You lost interest in me. Admit it. It's because of Gatien. You do like him, don't you? I knew it. Damn it."

"I didn't say that."

"Well, is it true?"

"He's got others he prefers, I think," I said cruelly.

"Theta?"

"You tell me."

"You're playing with my head, aren't you?"

"As you are with mine."

"You do me an injustice. To tell you the truth, I just can't be sure about Gatien and Theta. I hate to say it, but I've always trusted him more than I trusted her. Sometimes I think she'd sleep with him if she had the chance. But what would *he* do? I used to not even think about it, but now I'm just not sure. Especially lately."

I was thoughtful, and he became suspicious when I didn't say anything.

"You know, don't you?" he said. "Tell me, Sarah. Are they having an affair? My wife and my best friend?"

"I really don't know," I admitted.

"You really don't know?" He seemed to find that hard to believe.

"Paul," I said, "do you remember that night we were at the beach house? The first night we were there? In the middle of the night, I saw Theta coming out of the passageway, walking from the house to the cottage . . . and I wondered, I thought maybe she and Gatien, the two of them, that night . . ."

"Yeah, I know the night you're talking about," he said, with some bitterness. "And no, I can tell you there was nothing like that going on. I know because I was with her. Theta and I were up all night long, talking."

"Talking?"

"Well, arguing mostly. At one point, she yelled at me, told me she wanted a divorce. But she always said that whenever we had a fight. And it always pissed me off. Anyway, the night dragged on, and so did the fighting. She said it again. *I want a divorce.* I told her to get the hell out if she really wanted a divorce. I opened the door for her. So she walked outside, around the main house, and came back to the cottage a few minutes later, which actually surprised me, that she came back so soon. Usually she goes off and pouts for a few hours. When she came back, we got back into it a little, and then she was suddenly real quiet, and she stopped fighting me, and she said she knew it was unfair, how she flings around the word *divorce* like a weapon, but that she was beginning to think she really did want a divorce. That's when we really started to discuss things soberly. We hardly slept at all that night. We just lay together in bed with the lights out, talking about what if. What if we really did it. After that we went on as if nothing had happened for awhile. But that was really the beginning of the end."

It was time to go into the sanctuary. Gatien appeared, ignored Paul, took my arm without saying a word, and led me in to sit beside him and May.

"YOU DON'T NEED your notes, Gatien," I whispered.

He looked at me and gave me a smile, and as he stood he handed me his little spiral notebook to hold for him. I promptly dropped it on the floor. I was torn between wanting to bend down at once to pick it up and wanting to watch him stride up the aisle toward the altar with his distinctive, rocking limp. The limp was actually less noticeable lately, I thought. Or maybe I was just getting used to it. My eyes lingered on him, then I remembered myself and bent to pick up the notebook. As I fished it up from beneath the pew in front of me, the notebook fell open to this:

> *I can't make love with you, Sarah.*
>
> *God knows I am dying to. That I dream about you every night and can't get you off my mind all day. But we can't.*
>
> *You think it is because you are not "part of my plan." In the beginning, yes, that is what I told myself. It wouldn't be right to take advantage of my position as your employer and touch you in the way I wanted to touch you, and I imagine you want me to touch you (though I'm never sure what you're thinking).*
>
> *It's far beyond that now. It could only be good, and right, to hold you in my arms. Except for one thing. It is very difficult to talk about, and I realize now I should have been candid with you from the beginning, but it is not my decision to speak of. I feel it would be too insensitive to her to do this. Because of*

Because of?

Insensitive to whom?

Theta? Courtney? The memory of his beloved dead wife? Someone in France?

I turned the page, but that was it.

One unfinished paragraph in Gatien's small square handwriting was enough to put me into a spin. I kept it discreetly sheltered from May's eyes.

Gatien stood at the altar and began to speak to the congregation with perhaps even more poise and effectiveness than he had during his practice run, but I was in a daze and having trouble getting out of my own self-centered world long enough to concentrate on his words or even on why I was there in church. I had to read what he had written one more time, before closing the notebook on my lap to await his return.

Chapter Nineteen

FIRST THE HOLIDAYS, then the fire, then the death of May's grandfather, and now Easter was nearly upon us. I wasn't sure what ordinary life looked like anymore.

Madame Curio wasn't back from her trip yet; Nathan told me she had decided to stay an extra week or two in London. Gatien was out of town, and May was busy finalizing her vacation plans. She was going to be staying with Dimitri at his mother's house. May and Dimitri were hoping there would still be snow in the mountains, and they could talk Kate into taking them snowboarding for a few days. I warned May that it was unlikely the snow would be any good that late in the season.

"I don't care," she replied. "If there's no snow we'll just stay at his mom's house in Santa Cruz. It's near the Beach Boardwalk, you know."

When she and Dimitri had first come up with the plan, I was dubious.

"I don't know, May," I had said to her in private. "I'm not sure how I feel about this vacation you want to take with Dimitri."

"What do you mean, you're not sure?" May said darkly. "You don't need to be sure. It's nothing to do with you, Sarah. I'm going, and you have nothing to say about it!"

Her sudden defensive posture shouldn't have taken me by surprise.

"Actually, I could have quite a bit to say about it, and I think your father would consider my opinions very carefully," I told her. "Look, May. I know you really want to do this, and I *want* you to do what you want to do. But only if you're going to be safe doing it."

"Safe!" She was puzzled by that.

"You're a beautiful young woman," I said carefully. "And Dimitri is an eighteen-year-old, red-blooded young man—"

"What do you mean by red-blooded?" she asked with a suspicious frown.

"Well, when I say red-blooded in this context, it means a person has a healthy sexual appetite."

"Oh."

"So what I'm saying is—"

"I know what you're saying," she said quickly. "And you do not need to be worried about anything like *that*. I will never do *that* with anyone. *Ever.*"

I almost laughed, but she was so resolute I decided it was best to respect her feelings, however childish and unrealistic I might think them. I said, seriously, "It isn't just about you, May. I don't know Dimitri well enough to know what kind of pressures he might put on you."

"Oh, Sarah." May shook her head and looked at me pityingly. "You don't know Dimitri at *all* if you think he would do something like *that.*"

I sighed. "All right then. Helene and your dad seem to be okay with it. I just felt I had to voice my concerns."

Her face was transformed with a bright, shy smile. "That's actually very nice of you, Sarah," she said, and patted my arm. "Thank you for caring."

•   •   •

FRIDAY AFTER SCHOOL was out for spring break, Dimitri and his mother Kate drove up to the house to collect May.

"So do you think you're bringing enough stuff?" I asked May.

She rolled her eyes, loading her gear into the back of the car, one bag at a time. "Well, Governess, you know I am going to be gone almost a whole week."

"And you're bringing enough for six months."

"I say, be prepared for any eventuality!" Gatien cried, jumping over one of Carlos's planter boxes to join us. He really was looking more limber lately, and happy. He had a grin on his face. I was beginning to realize he was younger than I had once thought him.

While he helped May with her luggage, Kate came to stand beside me and murmured discreetly, "You've done wonders for those two, Sarah."

I looked at her, surprised.

"I'm not kidding. May has *blossomed.* And Gatien, I can't even begin to—"

"Mom!" Dimitri was shouting. "Let's go."

She heaved a sigh and shrugged. "Well, the boss has spoken!"

"Mother," Dimitri scolded her. *"You're* supposed to be the boss."

"I always forget that," she said.

"I guess." He sighed, shaking his head indulgently. I watched him bound to the car, his mother following along behind. There was another delay as they began to argue about who would drive.

May ran to me and threw her arms around me. "Bye, Sarah," she said. "Have a great vacation."

"You, too." I squeezed her. "Love you, May." The *love* just popped out spontaneously, and I was rather surprised at myself for saying it without first analyzing the consequences of such a statement.

I think May was surprised, too. She drew back and looked at me carefully, as if to make sure I wasn't joking. Then she smiled and patted me on the shoulder, murmuring, "See you in a few days, Governess." For the first time

I felt she was using the title as a term of endearment rather
than an indignity. She ran to Gatien and gave him a quick,
affectionate hug, but he had his hands in his pockets, and
he didn't hug her back. "Bye, Gato, I love you!" she sang.

"Have fun, May," he replied.

I stared at him, waiting for him to respond to May's affectionate farewell with some small demonstration of
warmth, but that was as far as it went. She ran off to the car
and jumped into the backseat. Kate was driving, with a dis-
gruntled Dimitri riding shotgun, his mother apparently not
being quite the pushover she made herself out to be.

When they had gone, Gatien brought his bags out to the
driveway. He seemed eager to get on the road, too. But
when I went to open the trunk of my car, he shook his
head and was already opening the garage door. "Let's take
this one."

He unlocked the driver's door of a gleaming black
Porsche and held it open for me.

WE WERE BOTH quiet for the first hour of the drive. I
didn't know where we were going; I didn't ask, and he
didn't offer to tell me, except to instruct me to head north
on 280. We drove into San Francisco and ran into traffic
through the city on Nineteenth Avenue, clutching and
shifting in the strange, marvelous car.

I was amazed at how out-of-sorts I felt. The fog was in
over the city; it was gray and cold, the radio was full of
commercials, and I had thoughtlessly packed the CDs in
the trunk. I should have been glad to have time off from
my so-called job, but I only felt a nagging sense of guilt
and uneasiness, like a mother who has sent her child off
with a stranger.

Of course! I realized. *That's exactly what I am.*

I was worried about May and Dimitri. I was worried
about entrusting a thirteen-year-old to a woman about
whom I knew nothing, except that she couldn't handle her
own teenage son well enough to keep him home with her.
I was worried that Dimitri had evil designs on May. I was

angry that I was the only one worrying about this. Gatien didn't seem to share my reservations.

But I was surprised, most of all, by my own lack of enthusiasm for this road trip. It was such a typical fantasy of mine: Gatien swoops me up for several days of tripping around the back roads of California; we're alone, just the two of us; the weather is perfect (well, it would be, once we got out of San Francisco); and the car is responsive, willing, and eager. I felt disoriented, now that the dream was actually coming true. But this wasn't the way I had imagined it. Not with me in this hired-chauffeur role for a man who had some previous commitment and so couldn't make love to the nanny, and why would he bother anyway when he had other more beautiful and sophisticated women at his disposal? This cold, secretive brute who couldn't even hug his daughter when she was leaving him for a week. *What on earth am I doing?* How was I supposed to act in my role as chauffeur-about-the-state? How could I stand being so close to him, day after day after day, without ever touching him or being touched by him? Why was I even attracted to him? A broken-down grump who walks with a limp, can't drive and is out of a job, except being in commercials (and how long can *that* last?). During this charmed moment of my existence, when there happened to be no lack of men in my life, why did I go around brooding about the one who *wasn't* interested, which was obvious by his actions, whatever romantic notions I might cherish, whatever silly notes I may discover while snooping, however accidentally.

I was, apparently, a textbook case of the emotional mess who chooses a target of infatuation for its very unavailability.

Finally we made it over the Golden Gate Bridge, and climbing into Marin we passed through the rainbow tunnel and burst into bright sunshine.

"Well," Gatien said. "Now it's up to you. You can continue up 101 on the freeway, or we can cut over to the Pacific Coast Highway."

"The coast," I said.

"It's a spectacular road, but it's treacherous and long."

"I know. Let's do it. If you're not scared."

He laughed. "I'm always scared when I'm in a car. I know too well what can happen."

So we drove alongside the bay, and Gatien pointed out the houseboats, and we nearly missed our turn to the coast because we were watching a little plane land on the water with pontoons.

We stopped at Stinson Beach and shared a sandwich, got the CDs from out of the trunk, stretched a little. The spring sunshine warmed the sandy concrete sidewalk outside the deli, and the wind from the ocean was stirring and fresh. I was cheering up in spite of myself.

"This place is pretty nice," Gatien said. "But I'm itching to get back on the road. Let's drive up to Mendocino for the night."

Mendocino, I thought. A small, picturesque village on the north coast of California, isolated and wild and romantic. Or so I'd heard. I'd always wanted to go there.

For the night.

I balled up my napkin and sent it flying neatly into a trash can. "All right," I said. "Let's go."

The coast highway was indeed spectacular, with its winding curves cut into the cliffs above the ocean, but it was slow, and there was quite a lot of holiday traffic. By the time the sun was setting we were still a long way from Mendocino. Gatien could see I was getting tired; he announced we were going to stop for the night. Several times during the day he had asked me if I was tired of driving, and each time I had said no. But now I was grateful he had made that pronouncement. But when we checked out the next little hamlet along the highway, everything was booked. He came back to the car, looking disappointed.

"They're all full, all the places here. It's spring break, so they're pretty busy. I hadn't thought of that."

We continued on. I was getting hungry, and the road, fun to drive and amazing as it was, did take its toll. We were so far out in the middle of nowhere, towns so few and far between, I began to fear we might not find a place to spend the night. What few lodgings we passed were already booked up.

It was completely dark when we rolled into the next little village perched on the cliffs. We got out of the car, and it seemed impossible to think of moving again. We went into the roadside bar where we had parked and asked the bartender about a place to stay.

"I think everything's full," he said. "If you go on up to Mendocino, you'd probably find something around there."

"I can't drive another mile," I said, slumping onto a barstool. "Are you sure there's nothing?"

"You know, Sarah—" Gatien began.

"Hang on a sec," the man said. He disappeared into a back room. Five minutes later he returned with a key.

"You're in luck," he said. "Someone just canceled. It's number seven, out the back there."

"Thank you," I said.

"You can settle up in the morning, here at the bar. Breakfast will be left outside your door at nine, or later if you leave a note on the kitchen door."

"Nine will be fine," Gatien said, looking at me for confirmation of that.

"All right, then. If you're planning to eat out tonight, the place across the street is open, but you'd better not wait; things close down early around here."

"Thanks." Gatien took the key, and I followed him out the side door, where we found a gravel driveway leading to a cluster of white-painted wooden cottages, all huddled on the edge of the cliff looking out to the ocean.

"Number seven," said Gatien. He unlocked the door, and we entered the cottage. It was tiny and charming, with a queen-sized bed and an upholstered chair, a woodstove, a little bathroom, and not much else.

I suddenly felt panicky. This was a mistake. Gatien and I could not share such a small, intimate space for the night. It simply would not do.

But I knew we had been lucky to get this room. There was no chance we would find another here in this village.

"We could continue on up to Mendocino," said Gatien, who was clearly reading my anxious expression.

But he could read my response to that just as well. I didn't want to get back in the car.

"Listen, Sarah. I want to tell you something I should have told you before. You don't have to dr—"

"We'll make this work," I interrupted him. "I like it here." I walked to the window and opened it for the fresh ocean air. In the daytime, we would be able to see the ocean. Now it was night, and moonless, and completely dark.

"You'll take the bed, of course," he said. "I'll sleep on the floor, or in the chair. I'm sorry, Sarah. This is my fault. I should have set it up better. But I just wanted to strike out, without making plans, you know?"

"An adventure," I said.

"Right. So—we'd better go eat. Before the town closes for the night."

"ARE YOU GOING to tell me what's going on?"

He looked at me across the table, his eyes on me, his attention completely focused on me.

"What are you talking about?" I asked.

"I know something has been troubling you all day, maybe longer than that, I don't know. You look like you'd rather be anywhere but here, with me."

"On the contrary," I said. "There's nowhere else I'd rather be."

"I believed you when you said that to me on Christmas Eve. Tonight I don't."

I sighed. I was very tired, and emotions seemed close to the surface. I didn't trust anything I was feeling in this state. But he was right. Whatever it was, it had nothing to do with how long the drive had been or how late it was or how exhausted I felt. But I wasn't sure exactly what it was, or how to explain it.

He signaled the waiter for the check. He seemed disturbed now, and I struggled, guilty, wanting to give him something, since he had risked asking.

"I'm sorry, Gatien. I don't know if . . ."

He watched me, waiting.

"I'm afraid this wasn't such a good idea, me being your driver. It just feels awkward, and I don't know how to . . ."

"To what?"

"To be. To simply be your driver."

"I don't need you to be my driver, Sarah. I don't need you to drive me anywhere, anymore."

I looked at him oddly, not understanding that.

"I started to tell you earlier. Something I've been wanting to tell you. I can drive."

I found this absurdly funny, and I began to laugh.

"I've been driving, Sarah," he said seriously. "Practicing. Training. I didn't want you to know until—well, there's a good chance I may get a place on a team. I wanted to surprise you."

"You're going to race again."

"I was planning to keep it a secret until I could make it happen, and then . . ." He stopped himself, frowned. "I guess that's stupid."

"No, that's great! I'm—wow. I'm in shock. That's great. Congratulations."

"It's because of you, Sarah. What you said to me, months ago. About getting myself back together, trying again. Made me feel like I was being a big baby. Made me feel I could do it. Had to do it."

"You never said a word."

"At first I was afraid. That I would blow it, you know. That I would fail. Then, when I started getting stronger, getting the use of my leg back, I got so excited I was afraid I'd disappoint myself. Then when I started getting some confidence, I decided I would surprise you. I decided I would win for you."

I tried to dampen down the sudden leap of joy I felt.

I decided I would win for you.

But I didn't *want* him to race. Not for me, not for any reason.

"So, you don't need me to drive," I said. "Then why . . ."

"I arranged for you to be my driver on this trip, Sarah, because I wanted you to come with me."

"Why didn't you just ask me?"

"I was afraid if you knew I didn't need you to drive, you wouldn't come. Would you have?"

"I don't know."

The waiter brought the check; Gatien threw down a few bills, and we left the café.

"Do you want to take a walk?"

I nodded. We walked along the highway, which, here in the middle of this tiny hamlet on the desolate north coast of California, was an empty, silent street at nearly eleven o'clock on a cool spring night.

I had lied to Gatien when I said I didn't know if I would have gone with him. I *did* know. I had wanted him to ask me; wanting someone to ask doesn't necessarily mean the answer will be yes, but in this case, it would have been. I felt his power over me. I would always say yes.

Damn it all.

Why was he saying these things to me, as if he wanted to woo me?

He wanted me with him? Why? If not merely to drive, then why? And why did he say he wanted to win . . . for me? Why was he saying these things?

"I don't understand you!" I blurted out.

"What don't you understand?" he asked earnestly, turning toward me, making me stop on the street to answer him.

"Why don't you hug your daughter good-bye, Gatien? Why don't you tell her you love her? Why don't you show her some small shred of affection?"

He drew himself in. "Sarah, you don't understand what you're talking about." His voice was cold. "I do for May what I think is best for her."

This answer sounded so pompous to me I became infuriated and turned on him. "What you think is *best?*" I said with my most withering scorn. "Cold disinterest is best? Best for whom? For *you*, I suppose. So you don't have to think about how others might be feeling. Like your daughter. You hold her at arm's length. God forbid she should get too close. Like your best friend, you just shut him out of your life without a word, right when he needs you the most! And why can't you talk about your wife? Don't you mourn her *at all?* I'm so disoriented by you and your coldness. Toward May. Toward Paul. Toward everything in your life—"

"Including you, isn't that right?" He seized my arm. "I am much colder to you than you would like me to be." His hands were gripping my arms now, and he gave me a shake. "They all want you, every man who sees you, every man who hears your voice, they all come on to you, don't they, and it drives you crazy 'cause I don't—"

I was scared out of my head and fighting him, and yet on some level surrendering to the physical force of him, melting from the heat of the molten anger, while at the same time some very cool aspect of my being was instructing me to bring up my hands, to push against him, to fend him off. His chest was solid and immovable, and I was very much aware of the power difference between us. Male to female. Master to servant. And yet between us was an equal strength, and I knew it. We both knew it.

"Is that the only reason you want it from me?" he demanded. "Because I'm the only one who isn't offering?"

"Why are you doing this, Gatien?" I gasped.

"Which one is it?" he went on. "Is it my contractor? Or my best friend? Or is it Isaac Shipton? Which of them is the one you really want? Or do you want all of them?"

"I don't want *any* of them," I cried, "and I don't want *you*, either!" I flung his hands off me, turned proudly, and walked away down the road. I was panting, beside myself, blown away, but most of all I was thrilled to have encountered that fire in Gatien Defalle. I was scared to death of it, and I was drawn to it. I had been singed by it, felt the pleasure of that pain, and I was tempted to throw myself into it again.

I thought about all the stories that warn against losing oneself to consuming passion. It was a common mythological theme, the perils of giving in to dangerous desire. Pandora's box. Icarus and Daedalus. Adam and Eve. It never turned out happily.

I heard his footsteps behind me, and instinctively I broke into a run, but he was faster than me, and in three strides he caught me, his big warm arms around me; we stumbled together on the pavement, and he held me, kept me from falling, wouldn't let me go.

"Sarah, look at me." We were both breathless. "I'm sorry. Please. I'm sorry. I'm sorry." He crushed me against his body, hugging me tightly, his face buried in my hair.

"I'm sorry, too, Gatien."

His fingers were tangled in my hair, and when he tried to move his hand away, he pulled my hair.

"Oh, God," he said. He gently untangled his fingers from my hair, and his hands reached for mine. He entwined my fingers with his. We stood facing each other in the middle of the empty road in the darkness. "Forgive me, Sarah. I don't know why I said all those things. Yes, I do. I'm jealous. I'm so jealous of Nathan and Paul and Dimitri and Isaac and Carlos and any man or any woman for that matter who gets to be with you and talk to you and make you laugh. Anyone who isn't me."

He pulled me close to him, and his mouth was soft on my cheek as he spoke, his lips moving over my skin, and I could feel the trembling of his words, a vibration on my body and all through me, as he said in that deep voice I loved so much, "I want you just for myself, so badly."

I felt the heat of his breath on me, smelled the scent of him, breathed him in deep.

"Now I understand," he murmured, close to my ear. "I understand how a man might feel he's been enchanted. Bewitched. How he could lose all reason, and not even care."

"But you *do* care," I said, stepping away from him, but he didn't let me go. He held my hand and reeled me in close to him again.

"No. Not anymore," he said. "Not right now. Let me kiss you, Sarah. Why won't you let me kiss you?"

I kept turning my head away. "Because you know there *is* more than *right now,* Gatien. More than just us," I reminded him soberly, even as he dipped his mouth and began sliding it over my throat. My body shuddered, and he tightened his hold on me.

My God, I cried inside. *It's happening We're going to be together, tonight. . . .* And yet, there I was, sounding the voice of reason. I was the one pulling back from the edge of the precipice, with a strength I didn't think I had in me. He had always held himself as the model of decorum—well, almost always. He had let me know he did not intend to sleep with the nanny, however tempted he might be.

Never surrender to the beast.

The lines he had written in his notebook . . . *I can't make love with you, Sarah.* What was that about? It was something real enough and serious enough that he had to express himself in writing, if not to me directly. Had something changed since he had written those words?

I didn't know, and I couldn't bring myself to ask, and that was the problem. Instinctually, the urge was high to mate with this man, to become one with him in the flesh. But intellectually I could not reconcile the two of us so physically trusting of one another. With such conflicting emotions, I could not continue what we had suddenly started. I managed to slip out of his consuming grasp and I started walking quickly up the road, back toward the cottage, though why I thought I would be safer there, I have no idea.

"I WANT THIS time with you, Sarah, even if it has to be time outside of time."

He closed the door firmly behind him and stood staring at me. There was only a faint glow in the room, from the night light in the bathroom, but I could see the intensity in his eyes.

He was warning me that it would be just a temporary affair. *Time outside of time.*

I said nervously, "You said I could have the bed, and you'd take the chair. I think that was probably a good idea. But we can trade places, if you'd rather. I don't need the bed, and your legs are longer—"

"Sarah, do you really think we can both sleep in this room tonight and not be lovers?" His voice was throaty, almost a cry. "Please, you've got to tell me now. If you won't have me, I'll leave right now. I can't do it any other . . . any other way. Tell me now." He was breathing hard, as if he had been running. And at the same time, he was moving closer to me, slowly, step by step across the floor, advancing on me, not waiting for my answer. In the tiny room he was quickly upon me. I was trapped in the corner between the bed and the wall. His hands were on me, all over me, spreading over me hot and strong, stroking my belly and sliding up over my ribs, my arms, his thumbs brushing over the swelling where my breasts began.

"Let me kiss you," he whispered. He brought his hand up to guide my mouth to his. His mouth was petal softness, the kiss a shared breath.

For a moment I relaxed. *Ah,* I thought. *That's all there is to it.*

And then I dropped off the edge of the world.

I WAS SCARED. Alone with him, in this little cottage on the cliff miles from anywhere on the winding highway— it was as if he had suddenly made up his mind to have me, and have me he would, by God! He was a hungry predator, and I was the prey. My own mating instincts fled me in the face of his devouring strength, and I felt the urge to run again. I glanced at the door, uneasy, as his hands took incredible liberties with my flesh, grabbing handfuls of me, at the curve just over my hips, below my shoulders. He was bigger and stronger than me, perhaps seventy pounds heavier, and more willful. The warring desires tore me in half. *Get away from him, save myself, stop this madness—no, let him take me, take me now!*

He was kissing me again, his imperious mouth finding me with that teasing softness, lingering over my mouth, our eyes closed. I let out a deep, long, stressed sigh as we came apart. He took me by the hand and led me to the bed.

But I could not ignore what was troubling me, nagging at me, and I began to hear it louder than his breath in my ear. I kept thinking about that note I had read in his little notebook: *I can't make love with you, Sarah. . . .*

I jumped away from the bed that he had nearly laid me down upon. I walked to the door, looking back at him, with an expression that must have appeared as stricken as I felt.

"I'm sorry," I said, stumbling hoarsely over the two words. I let myself out the door and started walking down the gravel path. The waning moon was up now, just peeking over the trees, everything glowing eerily in the middle of the night. I felt the cold air against my nipples through my blouse. His hands had brushed against the sides of my breasts, but he had yet to take the forbidden fruit into his hands, into his mouth. God, I was dying for him to. Why did I leap away like a frightened rabbit?

Because of some secret allegiance he had to some other person?

Because I was May's caretaker?

Because he was my employer, and I was his employee?

Tell the truth, Sarah. Your fear really has nothing to do with any of that. It was really because I couldn't bear it if we did make love and then lived to regret it.

That would be worse than never having had it at all.

Wouldn't it?

"Sarah."

I stopped and turned, and there he was in the moonlight. I could see the evidence of his arousal in his jeans. His white shirt was unbuttoned partway down, and his hair was rumpled, like he'd just woken up. He was walking toward me with that heartbreaking limp. For a moment I thought he might fall, and I nearly ran to him.

"Please don't run away from me, Sarah."

I stepped back as he came closer, my heart beating hard. He stopped.

"Please," he said. "Come back inside."

I shook my head, staring at him, wild-eyed.

"I don't blame you for running. Look. I'm going to go sleep in the car. The room is all yours. Good night."

He turned and walked down the drive. He walked past the door of our cottage and continued on toward the parking area.

Standing there for a moment, I felt a release of tension in my body and a lessening of the constriction around my throat. *What am I doing?* I asked myself. *I'm letting him go.*

To hell with that.

I sprinted after him and caught up with him just before he got to the car.

"Gatien," I said softly. "Come back with me."

He didn't respond; he looked at me warily. He must have thought I was crazy. Maybe I was.

"Please," I said. "Come."

He walked with me back to the cottage, and we went inside.

He threw himself into the overstuffed chair and glared at me beneath fierce brows, saying nothing.

"I'm going to take a shower, okay?" I said.

I went into the bathroom and hesitated, my hand on the latch. I closed the door but left it unlocked. I slowly undressed and slipped into the shower. Standing beneath the hot rain of water, I pondered my position here, at this crossroads. I was either going to make love with the man in the next room, or I was going to run away from him again. He had asked me, plain and simple, to give ... how had he put it? Time outside of time. Nothing more. Nothing less.

Fair enough.

All I had to do was say yes. Primal instinct would see to the rest.

Why not? I wondered. What did I have to lose? It

wasn't like I wanted to marry him, as cold and arrogant as he was; we were worlds apart, besides which he wouldn't make a very good father for the children I hoped to have someday, what with his lack of warmth and spontaneity. But I did want him badly, and that was the truth of it. Would it be so wrong to enjoy this time, time out of real time, with Gatien Defalle?

May need never know. No one would ever know but the two of us.

I worried, though. Going back to a normal life afterwards . . . could it really be done? I had my doubts. And yet that was going to be a problem for me after tonight anyway, so what the hell.

I want him, I thought.

I should fly away.

I turned off the water, toweled myself dry, and wrapped the towel around me. I opened the door a crack and peeked out.

Gatien was sprawled in the chair, lying with his head back, his mouth slightly open. He was sound asleep.

I shook my head sadly and laughed at myself as I dropped the towel and climbed into bed, naked and alone.

I AWOKE TO find him on the bed beside me, lying asleep on top of the blankets. The room was very cold. He was wearing his jeans and his white oxford shirt, both partly undone. I lay there in bed for at least an hour, racked with lust, his body agonizingly near.

Just as I was dozing off, he woke up, and I heard him go into the bathroom. When he came out he murmured, "It's *freezing* in this room."

He lifted a corner of the covers and slid beneath them, careful not to touch me. I pretended to be asleep, to see what he would do. Moments passed, and he settled himself in. He stayed on his side of the bed. It was alarming and sensual, being naked in a bed with a man beside me, a fully clothed man who was being careful not to touch me, but whom I desperately wanted to be touching me. The warmth between our bodies kindled, heady, intoxicating. I drifted into sleep at last, with the incredible sensuality continuing on into my dreams.

Coming to consciousness again at dawn, I stretched without thinking, and my leg stroked against some warm, hard, clothed part of Gatien's body. I curled away from him, shy, but he moved against me, slipped his arm around me. He might have been doing this unconsciously, in his sleep. I wasn't sure. I felt the heat between us. He made no other move.

We slept together.

When I woke again, we were tangled in the sheets and tangled together, and we were already making love, his mouth on me, all over me, my hands diving into his unbuttoned jeans. He was naked against me in seconds, throwing off his clothes, flinging his fine shirt to the floor in his haste, something I never would have imagined him doing.

Chapter Twenty

FOR THE NEXT three days and nights we stayed together, all the while making love, making love, making love. The desire never seemed to be fulfilled; fulfilling the desire simply generated more desire. We were the only two in the world. No other people, no responsibilities, no obligations.

As a typical American woman of twenty-six, I'd had what I considered to be a modest number of lovers, yet not so few that I might one day feel I'd missed out, looking back in old age upon my youth. What I thought of as my perfect balance of experience left me completely unprepared for Gatien Defalle.

I had never experienced a man so accomplished in the art of lovemaking. He slid from one pleasuring motion to another without breaking rhythm, all the while bringing me along with him so skillfully I hardly realized where I was going until I found myself there. His appreciation for me and for my body was so genuine and unabashed that I truly forgot myself for the first time in my life and discovered what it was to go beyond physical pleasure into an altered state of being. He pushed past any reticence on my part with a subtle, steady deepening of intimacy of our bodies, but also of our minds and our spirits, daring me to look him in the eye when we were joined in the most intense moment. Later, when I could think again, I would pretend to myself that the energy we had exchanged was purely physical, and if his sheer technical virtuosity brought up uneasy conjecturing on my part, I told myself to get real; it would have been foolish to assume his mastery of sexual technique did not point to the vast experience he must have had with women who were similarly accomplished. For my part, I could offer no such virtuosity, but I became an eager and willing acolyte—if only one of many, as I had to remind myself.

I ruthlessly bracketed this charmed moment with the implicit understanding that it would have no future, no past, was simply for now. The deeper I dove into my passion for this man, the more I realized how hard it would be to go back to life without it, but my convictions were strengthened that I could do no differently than experience it, full on and wholly, something extraordinary and bittersweet, if fleeting and singular.

We drove on up to Mendocino and found a perfect little nest, a refurbished water tower on the grounds of an elegant old Victorian inn. Our tiny home had a sitting area and kitchen on the first floor, a steep staircase leading to the bedroom upstairs with its sloping water tower walls, views of the ocean from three small square windows, and the bed, a huge four-poster that filled the entire tower.

We strolled hand in hand through the village when the sun peeked out of the fog in the afternoon; we played together on the beach. We sat side by side on our private patio and sipped champagne as the afternoon turned to evening. We wandered in a wine- and sex-soaked bliss down to dinner at the inn or one of the other restaurants or cafés in the village.

Rather than deflating something, as is sometimes the case when desire is fulfilled, the sex seemed to charge us up to one another; we seemed to need each other more desperately as the hours and days passed. Not only physically, but emotionally, and we indulged ourselves with the hungering for knowledge of one another on every level. We talked about our lives, our childhoods, and our early experiences of love, as new lovers do. But he said little about his marriage, and I didn't ask about it. This time we had alone together was for him and for me, and right now, nothing else mattered. My instincts told me there was something amiss there, something unhealthy in that marriage of his, though I felt certain it didn't go as far as Dimitri's wild conjecturing. I could not entertain the notion that Gatien had murdered his wife. It was impossible.

And yet there was an entire aspect of him I knew nothing about. Ironically, I was getting to know him well enough to understand that. As our idyllic time together unfolded, I became more and more certain that something was missing. He was holding something back. Keeping something of himself from me. On one level it was tearing me apart, my awareness of that. On another level I was at peace with it, content with things just the way they were. Whatever his reasons for not giving his all, I felt the difficulty he had, abiding by that self-imposed rule of his, as did I, with mine. Because I was holding back something of myself, so to me it seemed only prudent that he would do the same. That's the way I wanted it. At that point, I still felt perfectly capable of not losing myself to the man, heart and soul, utterly and completely.

WE HAD TALKED about continuing on with our travels through California, driving down to Yosemite, perhaps, and then cutting back over to the coast to spend a day or two at Carmel, but we were so perfectly content there in our Mendocino water tower we stayed for three days.

"We'd better check in with the real world," I said one afternoon.

"I don't want to."

"We need to make sure May can find us if she needs us," I said.

He rolled over on top of me and laid his soft, heavy lips

on my forehead. He kissed my eyebrows, so slightly I hardly felt it. "Okay, Mother Hen," he said fondly. "I'll go see if there's a phone in the main house."

"You didn't bring your cell phone?" I asked, astonished. I had noticed he hadn't been using his phone, but I had figured he'd brought it. I had planned to bring mine, but I had forgotten it. I still wasn't used to having one.

"Nope. I didn't bring it," he said. "I didn't want anything to distract me from you." And he went out, with a lingering look over me as he let the door shut behind him.

WHEN GATIEN RETURNED from making his phone call, I jumped off the bed when I saw him. I knew something had happened; it was the look on his face, the posture of his body. He looked stunned.

"Gatien!" I demanded of him, my heart pounding. "What's *wrong?*"

He blew out a sigh, let his shoulders drop. "I gotta ride."

"You what?"

"They want me. Sabatino is out. They want me right away. They want me to drive at San Marino."

My heart was pounding, and the adrenaline was pumping. Nothing was wrong with May. That was the main thing.

"To race, you mean?"

"Yeah," he said. "To race."

"That's fantastic! I am so glad," I lied, and didn't fool him for a minute.

He looked at me, burst into a laugh. "Oh, Sarah. I don't want to go."

"You have to go right now, huh?"

He didn't answer, but looked intently at the sunlight, a perfect triangle on the floor by the window.

"You've got to go," I said.

"Come with me," he said.

My turn to laugh.

"Come with me. We'll bring May."

"Well," I said. "That's a nice fantasy, but May's got

less than two months until she finishes middle school. She's finally making friends and doing well in her classes. . . ." *And you should know that yourself, being her father,* I nearly said, but I bit back the words and felt the suppression of my anger like a weight on the bliss. I felt myself grow hot, not wanting this argument to rise between us again, but the feelings it provoked were real and hard to ignore, once ignited.

"I know you can't come with me, Sarah," he said softly. "I just *want* you to. I just wish you could. That's all I meant. I know you're going to make sure May gets everything she needs, and finishes school and does well, and I love you for it."

He sat down on the bed and pulled me against him, into his arms, and I felt him warm and solid and holding me so lovingly. So lovingly, I thought. *I love you for it,* he said. He loves me. For taking care of his daughter? He had once told me he had loved many people. Animals. Cars, even. But he had never fallen in love. Didn't believe in it. I wanted him to fall in love with me.

It was already too late for me. In love? I *had* fallen in love, I thought, a few times in my life. But no, I'd never felt like this before, not nearly, not with anyone. I thought about him in a race car. The speed. The risk. I felt his heart beating against my heart. And wondered how I would endure it.

GATIEN DROVE.

We didn't take the coast route back; we took the fastest way. He had a meeting in Nice the next afternoon. He drove expertly, as I would have expected, coaxing the car to do what he wanted it to do with a minimum of effort, the way a raptor uses the winds to soar and hardly moves his wings. An hour above San Francisco he said he was tired and asked me to take over driving.

As he pulled to the side of the road, I looked at him with concern. "How are you going to race when you're tired that easily?" I asked him.

"I'm not really that tired, Sarah. I just wanted you to drive."

"Fine."

"Okay, I just like it when you drive. I like looking at you while you drive. I like the way you handle that gearshift," he added with a mischievous grin.

I dropped him off at the airport. He didn't want to go home, didn't need anything; he said he had a place in the south of France and had everything he needed there.

This comment alone sent me into a tailspin of misery each time I played it over in my head after we had said good-bye.

He didn't need anything. He was a man who had a house in California and another one in the south of France.

I have a place in the South of France; everything I need is there. . . .

Maybe it wasn't his own house. Maybe it was his mistress's house.

He probably had a whole other life in Europe. A man like that is entitled. Entitled to the nanny, on top of everything else? Certainly, if they're both adults, if the nanny says yes. But then some would say the relationship was by its nature imbalanced, with the man, the master, in the position of dominance, the woman submissive and without real power, without real control of the situation. My friend Mallory in Santa Barbara had sent me an article she had clipped from a magazine about this very topic, because she felt it pertained to me. According to the writer, the unequal relationship is, by its nature, sexually charged. Was it some kind of a transference thing with me and my employer, like a patient falling in love with a doctor?

I couldn't complain about being used or coerced. I had wanted it as badly as he did. It was my choice. And I had accepted the terms.

Chapter Twenty-one

S O WHAT IN the heck is going on, Nathan?" I demanded. "I really need to get those books back. Your aunt was supposed to be gone a month or two; it's been much longer than that."

May wasn't supposed to come home from Santa Cruz until Sunday, and I needed to keep myself busy so I didn't go crazy thinking about Gatien. The first thing on my agenda was get those books back from Madame Curio. I drove down to her shop on Wednesday morning, only to find it was still locked up, with the same sign in the window.

I had called Nathan, who asked if I would meet him for coffee. He said there was something he had to tell me. The serious tone of his voice left me unnerved, and he did not allow me to press for more on the phone. Thirty minutes later we were at Peet's in Menlo Park, and he broke the news.

"She's dead, Sarah."

"What?"

"My aunt Edith. Madame Curio. She's dead."

"Oh my God. Nathan, I'm so sorry."

"Thanks," he said somberly.

"Oh my *God*. What happened?"

"We don't know. My dad got a call from the State Department in the middle of the night, couple days ago, told him she'd been found dead in her hotel room in France. They say it's suspicious. And it's complicated, her being in France and everything. My dad's flying out there to get things straightened out. Look, I know you're worried about your books. . . ."

"Well, I guess that's kind of trivial, all things considered."

"She wasn't that old," he said. "They're doing an autopsy. But to me . . ."

"What?"

"I don't know. It just seems wrong. She wasn't that old. She was healthy."

"Was she traveling alone?"

"We thought so. But it seems she was with a man, at some point. But he's nowhere to be found, now that some people would like to have a talk with him."

"Wow."

"Yeah. Look, I'm going to do what I can to get those books back to you. But it might take a little more time. We can't get into the safe yet; we can't even get into her shop right now. Anyway, I just thought I'd tell you in person."

"I appreciate that," I said, though I was dubious about the need to communicate in person, rather than by telephone. The memory of that awkward kiss in Madame Curio's shop seemed to intrude, made me wary of him. But he didn't make any moves that day, and as we parted I felt sad for him; he seemed so subdued. I thought about the fears I'd entertained earlier, when Madame Curio had closed up her shop and left the country. What if she had been murdered by the same people who had murdered Lisa, a murder connected to what was in her library? Surely that was simply an egocentric notion on my part, and just plain wacky, to be thinking that this woman's death was somehow connected to *my* concerns.

It might have been crazy conjecturing, but being alone

in the house for several days—Louisa and Carlos were on vacation, too—the sense of unease I felt was pervasive. I was glad when May got home Sunday night, though I had to wonder if she was safe in that house. If *we* were safe. There, or anywhere.

THE DAYS WENT by, and there was no word from Gatien, except for one broken-up phone call after he had won the Spanish Grand Prix. At the news, May and I danced around the house with great enthusiasm, and Helene took us out to dinner to celebrate. We tried to keep up with what was going on, but we didn't have cable TV, and the San Francisco papers didn't give much space to Formula One racing. May and I took to checking various Web sites on her computer to keep up with the standings. Gatien was doing very well, despite his late entry into the competition.

One Sunday afternoon Dimitri and Kate stopped by to drop off a couple things May had left when she stayed with Kate during spring break. Kate and I stood in the driveway, chatting.

"Don't go far—we can't stay," Kate called to Dimitri.

He ignored her and walked into the woods with May.

"They're so beautiful together, aren't they?" Kate said. "It's kind of scary."

"They're two very attractive young people. I've kept my eye on them," I said pointedly.

"Well, sure, I mean, especially with *her* history," Kate said, her voice suddenly hushed nearly to a whisper.

"What do you mean, her history?"

"Well, you know May was sexually abused when she was about seven years old."

From the look on my face, she saw immediately that I hadn't known. Maybe I should have known. But I didn't. It was an ugly, painful shock.

"Oh, shit," she said. "I put my foot in it big this time. I should have known better, but I thought they would have told *you,* at least. I guess it's still this big secret. That's supposedly for May's sake, I know, but I think it's dishonest, personally. But it's none of my business."

"Who was it?" I asked, shaken. "Who did that to her?"

Kate shook her head. "I'm not going there," she said curtly. "It's not my place. Sorry. And by the way, Helene doesn't know, either. Lisa never told her, didn't want her to know. May doesn't want her to know."

"You can't just drop that bombshell and not tell me who it was," I said, my voice trembling.

"I suggest you ask Gatien to tell you what happened."

"He's out of the country."

"Well, that's the usual thing for him, isn't it?" she said, and I could hear the contempt in her tone. "To tell you the truth, after Lisa died I thought he had no business having May. But that's just me! I didn't say anything. Helene was in there taking charge, arranging everything, but she doesn't know what I know. Maybe I was a coward for not saying anything. I don't know. Let him try to prove himself worthy, I decided. The child seems happy enough now. But you never know. You never know!"

"Kate—"

"Nope!" She held herself protectively. "That's all I'm going to say about it."

She went off, looking disturbed, but not nearly as disturbed as I felt.

They drove away, Kate in the driver's seat. Dimitri looked out solemnly at May and me from the passenger window, and I wondered how much I really *wanted* to know.

I realized I had to know everything. *Now.*

After May was in bed that night I went into the library, intending to look for information there. I needed to know exactly what had happened to May. I had decided not to say anything to her about it. Not until I learned more.

I needed to know about May, and I needed to know about Gatien.

If he was the one who had hurt her . . .

What was happening to me? I felt my world giving way beneath my feet. I could not contemplate the horror that had found its way into my soul. One voice in me scoffed: *inconceivable;* Gatien was no child abuser. *Child molester.* All my instincts about him cried out against it. A man who makes love with a woman so well has no interest in sex with a child, surely?

And yet . . .

Why had Kate refused to tell me who had done this thing to May?

Was it possible? How well did I really know him?

After Lisa died I thought he had no business having May. Let him try to prove himself worthy. The child seems happy enough, now. . . .

What was she saying? What had Kate been trying to tell me, without telling me? I wondered and I wondered. Was that why . . . was that why he was so strange with May? Why he didn't touch her? Why he was so stiff with her? I had sensed something wasn't right there, between the two of them. Not like a normal father and daughter.

My God, my God. If Gatien hurt that girl, I couldn't bear it. I would kill him.

I had to find out what happened.

The journals. I'll read Lisa's journals. I'll go back as far as I need to, to find out. I'll read every word until I know.

Did Gatien do this monstrous thing?

So I went into Lisa's library. I switched on the light and went to the shelf. But the journals were gone.

Chapter Twenty-two

I WAS SERIOUSLY shaken by what I had learned. And to find the journals were missing, on top of everything else—I could not fathom the meaning of this. With the break-in and ransacking of Lisa's library, someone setting fire to my cottage, and now this horrible thing that had happened in May's past come to light and this insidious suspicion of Gatien—I was literally sick, dizzy, nauseous.

The next evening I left May home alone after dark. She was nearly fourteen years old. It wasn't the first time. Still, I felt guilty, somehow. But I was on a righteous mission. I was determined to learn the truth about what had happened to May and what Gatien had to do with it. Was he some kind of incestuous monster? The word *unthinkable* came to mind, and yet, here I was, thinking it.

So I cast about for a way to find out what I needed to know. I would naturally turn to Helene, but Kate had said Helene didn't know.

If anyone knew what had happened and would tell me, it would be Paul, I thought. Gatien's best friend, a friend of the family for years. A favorite of May's. And he was my friend, too; or so I hoped. He would tell me the truth.

He would tell me if what I feared was true. I couldn't live with not knowing another minute. I could not reconcile the magical three days Gatien and I had shared and this harrowing possibility, that the man I had fallen for was a monster.

I was so nervous by the time I reached his house I was trembling, and I slammed the seat belt in the car door with a loud thwack. I opened the door, moved the seat belt out of the way, and shut the door again. The fog was in over the city, and it was a cold night, but as I walked up to the house I saw someone sitting on the porch. It was Theta.

"Hello, Sarah," she said quietly. "What a surprise."

"Is Paul here?"

"He's gone out for a few minutes. You seem disturbed. Are you all right?" She seemed genuinely concerned, which surprised me. It wasn't like her to pretend, not when we were alone.

"I just really need to talk to Paul. How long do you think he'll be?"

"Oh, I don't know. What's going on? Is May all right?"

"Yeah, well, except I just found out that she—" I stopped myself. I needed badly to talk about it, but not with her.

"Found out she . . . what?" Theta prodded.

I didn't answer her, but I saw the lightbulb going on above her head.

"Oh," she said, "you mean about how her father molested her when she was a little kid?"

The words ripped through me, and I fought the dizziness that now threatened to overwhelm me, overcome me, and pull me to the ground, unconscious or dead. I think I would have preferred death. "It's not true," I whispered.

She laughed, a mirthless, bitter bark. "I'm afraid so."

"I can't believe that of Gatien." I shook my head, incredulous, my throat so dry the words came out as a croak.

She studied me for a moment with her lips parted, and I sensed some calculation going on in her mind. But when she spoke, her voice was gentle. "I warned you, Sarah. I told you he was flawed. I warned you."

"I don't believe you," I said, and my voice must have sounded on the edge of hysteria. "You want Gatien for yourself."

"Notice he never took the bait?" She said it with a sneer, rather more at herself, it seemed, than me. "I guess that's because he prefers the young ones." She eyed me shrewdly. "Like you, I suppose. You might be just enough of a waif to interest him for awhile. Better not gain any more weight. Keep that gamine thing going. No, I only taunted him because he deserved to be taunted. Paul says we should cut him slack because he's changed. He doesn't do it anymore. But even if they just do it once . . . or twice . . . how can you ever trust them again? I don't know. It's pretty creepy. Don't you think?"

"This is unbelievable," I gasped. I felt like I couldn't breathe.

"Not what you hoped to hear, huh?" She looked at me pityingly. "I'm sorry, Sarah. Truly I am. It's a sickening thing."

I was not ready to believe this. Not out of the mouth of this one. Too much of what I'd seen and heard her say contradicted it. She only flirted with Gatien to taunt him? I had my doubts about that. But would she make such an accusation about Gatien, if it wasn't true? She might.

And yet, I had to remind myself, *she* had brought it up, hardly prompted. I had asked no leading questions. She had known about Gatien. I wanted to lash out at her, tear the knowing, pitying expression off her lush, lovely face.

"What are you doing here, anyway, Theta?"

"I live here."

I was surprised to hear it, but then it had been a while since I'd heard news of Paul. Maybe things had changed.

"So you two are back together, then?"

"That's right. As of two weeks ago."

"Well, congratulations."

"Thanks. We're trying to make it work, but it's not always easy." She shrugged. "We'll see."

"Well, good for you," I said, my voice hollow.

"May I ask what *you're* doing here, Sarah?"

"I told you. I needed to know about May. I thought Paul might help me—"

"Yes, you're right. Paul would be the one to ask. He knows all about what happened to May. If you want to wait until he comes home, I'm sure he'll be happy to talk with you. He'll confirm everything I just said."

I felt that I might throw up all over the porch if I stayed. "No," I said. "I've got to go."

"I'll tell Paul you came by."

"Yeah, all right."

"He's attracted to you, you know," said Theta. "My husband is."

I hardly heard what she was saying.

"So can I ask you a favor, Sarah? Would you keep away from my husband? At least for now? So we can try to make it work without distractions?"

"Sure, no problem," I said with a mechanical wave, as I turned to walk away. "Good luck."

I REALIZED, WHEN I had walked through the door at home, that I could not remember a single moment of the drive home. I had made the trip on automatic. I should not have been driving.

"Sarah?"

I looked up to see May standing there, at the dark mouth of the hallway, staring at me with large dark eyes.

"Are you okay, Sarah?"

"May," I cried. "You startled me. No, I'm fine. It's nothing. Go back to bed."

"Sarah. I can see there's something wrong. You've been crying."

"No, really. Please. Just go back to bed."

"Where did you go?"

"May, I can't—"

"You don't trust me, do you?"

"Oh, God, no, it's nothing to do with you, that is . . . please, just go to bed."

"It *is* about me, isn't it?" she said.

I could not deny that without lying.

She said in a cool voice: "Someone told you."

I didn't answer. We looked at each other.

"Someone told you what happened to me. When I was seven. Someone told you."

How in the hell had she guessed? I wondered vaguely. But that hardly mattered now.

"Kate told you," said May. "Right?"

"Oh, God, May. I was hoping it was a lie."

"No. It's not."

"My God. I'm *so* sorry, May."

"I don't know why she had to go and say anything. We're trying to make a new start, here."

"I guess she thought I already knew. She mentioned that you had been abused, like she thought I already knew . . . but then she wouldn't tell me more. May, now that I know, I *need* to know more. I need to know what happened. I'm so sorry. It's so unfair to you. But I need to know. I need to know who did this to you. You're the only one who can tell me the truth."

She considered this for a moment. She walked to Gatien's big chair and sat down, still thinking. "Yes," she said finally. "I'll tell you what happened. But I want to do it with Natalie."

"Who's Natalie?"

"She's a doctor. You know, a shrink. She's helped me before, and I can talk to her. If I have to talk about it, I want her to be there."

I nodded, blew out a poisoned breath. "Okay."

"I don't want to talk about it anymore. Not until we get Natalie. You can call her and make an appointment. Her name is on the list by the phone."

I nodded.

"And I don't want *you* to talk to anyone else about it. No one else. Not Kate or Helene or anybody. Not even Gato."

If he were here right now, I'd rip him open, I thought. *I'd demand to know. . . .*

I wasn't sure if I was sorry he was out of the country, or not.

"Don't talk to *anybody* about it," she said. "Do you promise me, Sarah?"

I hesitated, and I asked myself if I could make that promise in good conscience.

She watched me, wondering, I suppose, if I was trustworthy.

"I promise," I said finally. I had calculated that, because of when Gatien's next race was scheduled, there was no way he could be home within the next week. "I won't say anything about it to anyone," I said. "At least until we talk with Natalie."

She considered that response, found it satisfactory. "Okay. At least until then."

The next morning, after taking May to school, I drove straight home, found the number, and dialed the office. The earliest Natalie could see us was Friday, the receptionist said. *Friday,* I thought. Somehow I would make it until Friday.

After I made the appointment, I wandered around the house, wringing my hands. I needed to forget about it, I told myself. Get my mind off it. But how?

It was impossible.

When Nathan appeared at the door a few minutes later, I was almost glad to see him. Anything for a distraction.

But for me, it all came back to Gatien.

"I have a question for you, Nathan," I said.

"Sure. Anything."

We were leaning against the rail on the deck outside the kitchen. Louisa was in the kitchen, brewing coffee. The sky was low and gray, and there was no wind. The mountains across the bay were gone, and all the East Bay cities had vanished. There was nothing but gray. Even the waters of the bay faded into gray.

"Nathan, did you have something going on with Gatien's wife?"

He looked at me, shocked. "Well," he said. "That's something I didn't expect you to, uh, ask me."

"There are rumors, you know," I said. "I'm just curious if they're true."

"Yeah, I knew there was some talk like that. When I worked for her dad, Lisa and I got close. I mean, we became friends. She came over to her dad's a lot, visiting him. You know, they were pretty tight. We hung out. Talked. We did a lot of talking, and that's really about it. I guess I sort of got off on the perception that she was my mistress, if you will, and I never did anything to counteract those rumors. She was hot. I was flattered. But the truth is, there was nothing like that between us. Actually, I think she was pretty hung up on her husband."

I found that easy enough to understand.

"But there was some weird shit there, with them, that I never fully understood."

"Like what?" I demanded.

"She was really insecure, I think, and I probably helped her out with that. She knew I was attracted to her. She seemed a little unsatisfied with her marriage, didn't think he loved her the way she loved him, something like that."

I forced myself to keep my breathing even. Had Lisa found their marriage unsatisfactory because her husband was more interested in their child than in her? It was too horrible to contemplate. But I had to. I thought of our three days on the Mendocino coast. There was nothing in that interlude that would lead one to suspect the man preferred children. . . .

Theta's voice intruded in my consciousness. *You might be just enough of a waif to interest him for awhile.* Was I that deluded?

Nathan was still talking. "I do remember one afternoon she came to me, looking completely crushed, saying she didn't trust her own ability to judge people she thought she could trust. But you know, toward the end of the job, I thought she seemed happier with herself, and her life, and I thought things might be improving between her and Gatien. Then I heard she'd drowned, probably killed herself. I was sad to hear it. And shocked, actually. I couldn't believe she would do that."

"Helene said she wasn't surprised at all. She talks like

it was practically inevitable. She says her sister was really messed up."

He shrugged. "I don't know. She was unusual, maybe a little high strung, but she was a charmer. I really didn't know her that well, despite the rumors." He smiled. "But I didn't come here to discuss Lisa Defalle. I came here to give you something. Something I think you might be interested in having. Come look."

He had brought me back the missing books.

Chapter Twenty-three

NATHAN LEFT AN hour later, and Louisa left, too, shortly after he'd gone. I had the feeling she had been waiting for him to leave, though I couldn't imagine why. Carlos wasn't there today; maybe she had qualms about leaving me alone in the house with a man.

The doorbell rang a few minutes after Louisa had said good-bye, and I figured she had probably forgotten something and locked herself out of the house.

"Coming!" I called, and I opened the door without thinking, seeing the black hair through the curtain parted over the window on the door. But it wasn't Louisa's black hair. The two dark-eyed men who were so interested in Lisa's library stood on the step.

"Hello, miss," said the smallest of the two, looking at me earnestly from piercing black eyes set far apart in his skull. "I am Ira Meyer, and this is Moshe Yaron."

"Yes," I said. "I remember both of you."

"My friend here, Moshe Yaron, is an Israeli scholar, and I am a businessman. We have a keen interest in the library of Lisa Defalle, and we would like to talk with you for a moment."

"Okay," I said. "Come in. You can take a look in her library yourself."

They looked astonished, as though they had not even thought to ask for such a favor. Ordinarily I would never have done such a thing as inviting these two into Gatien's house, to look into Lisa's library. But that day I was feeling reckless, and I wanted to be distracted from the nightmare I was living in my mind. *Go ahead and plunder the house, take what you want, murder me, I don't give a damn!*

I led them down the hall and threw open the door of Lisa's library, and we went into the room. It smelled musty and unused. I pulled aside the drapes and opened one of the windows. I looked to the empty shelf where Lisa's journals once lived, and looked away.

"Here you have it," I said, indicating the room with a dramatic flourish of my hand. "Mrs. Defalle's library. Go ahead and have a look around."

They looked embarrassed. "Please . . . if we could explain why we are here."

"You don't want to look around?"

"Yes, but it may be that you have already found what we are looking for."

"Mr. Defalle took everything of any real value and made sure it was safely archived. I don't think what you are looking for exists. Not in Mrs. Defalle's personal effects, at any rate."

"The documents in question are potentially some of the most important and valuable of our times," Ira Meyer said earnestly, pleadingly, as if this might compel me to produce the thing he was looking for.

I looked at him, amazed at his intensity and his belief in what he was saying.

"Let me explain," he said. "You see, up until relatively recent times, the oldest copies of Hebrew scriptures were from medieval times. But in 1947, a young man tending goats in Palestine near the Dead Sea was tossing stones into a cave and heard an odd sound. He explored the cave and found a number of ancient clay jars filled with old

scrolls and leather scraps covered with strange
writings. . . ."

"The Dead Sea Scrolls."

"Ah, so you are familiar with the discovery at Qumran?
So perhaps you are aware of how much of that treasure
was damaged, and the writings lost to history because of
the way the material was initially handled, not to mention
the political and religious controversies that have ham-
pered the process of study and release of the contents of
the documents, not only to the general public, but to
scholars around the world, as well. We are greatly concerned about the preservation and study of any newly discovered texts—"

The other man, perhaps feeling his partner was getting
off the subject, interjected: "We have reason to believe
Mrs. Defalle might have come into possession of some
ancient Hebrew texts, perhaps very nearly as old as the
material from Qumran."

"That's a nice story," I said. "But I don't think there's
anything to it. At least not as far as Mrs. Defalle was concerned. She bought a bunch of Medieval stuff, and I don't
think it's what you're looking for. Wait a sec, I want to
show you something." I went out and came back a minute
later with the books Nathan had returned to me that afternoon. I cleared a place on the table and set them out, one
by one, for them to look at. "You see?" I indicated them
dramatically. "Look at these. Beautiful old things, just had
them appraised. You see, my appraiser—who incidentally
was just found dead in a hotel room in France—she says
right here in this written appraisal that these books are
valuable, because of their age, and the condition, and the
beauty, particularly this illuminated book of hours. Look,
you could buy a house with what this one is worth. Well,
maybe not a house around *here,* in this neighborhood, but
you could buy a house *somewhere* with this much money.
It's hundreds of years old. This one"—I indicated another
book—"is worth a bit less. The condition is fair and some
of the pages have been removed. It's not complete. These
old notary works are fairly valuable, too, for historical

reasons. But all in all, there's apparently nothing too unusual or earth-shatteringly important, and the value isn't that great, considering what Mrs. Defalle paid for the collection, according to the packing materials that came with the books, which lists the price of the lot!"

They nodded politely, uneasy, no doubt thinking me a raving idiot. I didn't care.

They examined the library quickly, methodically, but they didn't find anything that drew comment, and they didn't seem to have expected to, which made me wonder what they really were there for.

"Thank you, miss—"

"Logan. Sarah Logan."

Ira Meyer gave me his card. "You will call us if you find anything of interest?"

"Sure, why not?" I said.

I led the way to the entry hall to see them out.

And there was Gatien, standing in the doorway.

I was so surprised to see him I let out a cry. He looked so good. So terribly good.

"Oh, it's you," I said inanely, my hand flying up instinctively to shield my heart. How could I hold these contradictory feelings side by side; how could they coexist within me, this dread suspicion of him, and this instant thrill of desire for him that I felt the moment I saw him?

His hair swept over his forehead and down alongside his broken cheek and his gorgeous mouth, which was suspiciously loose, the intense dark eyes framed by that hair and those dark, scowling brows, as he looked at the two visitors, and then, out of the corners of those eyes, at me, his expression wary, withholding, waiting.

"I invited them in," I explained.

"Well, then," Gatien said coolly, "that's all that needs to be said." He remained still, with that vague scowl on his face.

"They're looking for ancient Hebrew scrolls. I told them we don't have anything of that sort here."

Gatien was lordly. He did not speak or make any superfluous movement, while the two other men fidgeted.

They thanked us both politely and went out, hesitating as they passed Gatien, as if afraid of what he might do to them if they got too close.

I followed them outside. Gatien's leather travel bag was sitting on the porch.

He's home, I said to myself, as a shudder ran through me. *He's home.*

WHEN THEY HAD gone, I turned to go inside, and he was there, blocking my way.

"Sarah," he said softly. "Aren't you glad to see me?"

"I am glad to see you," I replied. My own voice sounded sorrowful to me.

He moved his body so that I would have to contend with him, but he did not touch me. One hand was easy in his trousers pocket, the other relaxed at his side. If I did not know him as I did, I would not suspect the smoldering heat that lay beneath that cool exterior.

If I had hoped—or feared—that he would pretend nothing had happened during our time on the Mendocino coast, at least now I knew that he wasn't going to do that. I realized how afraid I had been that he would act as though our time out of time had never happened at all. But now I was afraid in a new way.

"You are?" he said, in the same soft voice. "You're glad to see me? I would not have guessed it."

"I didn't expect you," I said. "You're supposed to be somewhere in Austria, getting ready for the race."

"Yes, I had no time to come home, but I had to come home. To see you."

"I apologize for going against your orders," I said. "Letting those two in here."

"I will never again presume to issue orders to you, Sarah."

"Oh—congratulations on your winnings," I said, walking past him casually, ignoring the annoyance that flashed off him like heat. He trailed after me, and we walked together through the hall into the library. I was hardly thinking about where I was walking or what I was doing, his presence was so utterly disconcerting to me. He followed me into the library, and I began to put away some of the things I had taken out for Ira and Moshe. The old books Nathan had just brought back were lying on the table; I wondered if Gatien would notice them, but he seemed fixed only on me.

"I had to come home, Sarah. I couldn't go any longer without seeing you again. . . ." He made as if to take me in his arms, but I turned away from him with a fierce shake of my head.

He flinched and stepped backward as if I had raised my hand to slap him.

A pain shot through my breast, and for a moment I wondered if I might be having a heart attack.

"I was scared of this," he murmured. "All this time, without you, I imagined this moment, seeing you again. You know, I was so high, for days, just from being with you, Sarah. But then I started getting scared, wondering how it would be when I saw you again. Wondering how I could take it if you did what you just did. If you turned away from me."

"Gatien, you said . . . it was you who warned that what we had in Mendocino was something outside of reality. We went into it, both of us knowing that. 'Time out of time,' is what you said."

"Time out of time!" he scoffed. "I want you *all the time,* Sarah."

I closed my eyes. I had wanted to hear this so badly. And now I wanted to scream at him, to shut him up.

"It's time for me to leave, Gatien," I said.

My words hung in the air.

"I've got to go pick up May."

"I want to tell May," he said.

"Tell May what?" I cried, alarmed.

"I want it out in the open. I want it official. I want her to know what's going on with us."

"There's nothing going on with us," I snapped. "Don't say anything to May. Please."

He stared at me, unbelieving.

I wanted to run to him, throw my arms around him, feel my arms surrounding the lean, hard column of his body, feel the solidity of him beneath the soft, silky fabrics of his expensive, beautiful clothes. I almost didn't care if what I had heard was true. He could be a monster—if Theta was telling the truth, he was—and I almost didn't care.

Almost.

I was so frustrated with him, for the whole mess. Angry and frustrated and crazy. If he was a monster, I would have to kill him, for what he'd done to her, and what he'd done to me. If he was innocent somehow—*God, please let him be innocent*—he was still guilty, for hiding all this from me. I couldn't talk to him about it—I had promised May. I wished to God now that I hadn't, but I had, and I knew instinctively that to betray that trust would be to lose her trust altogether. I was terribly frustrated, that I couldn't say anything, yet strangely relieved, too, for I didn't know how I would begin to broach such a subject with him, even if I were able to. Perhaps I couldn't bring it up to him, but he should have brought it up with me, a long time ago. I was frustrated and angry at myself, too, for wanting him so damned badly in spite of it all.

He seemed about to speak, then thought better of it, clenched his fists, and turned to walk out. He seemed to notice the old books on the table for the first time, and he stopped short.

"I found those in the storeroom, in the garage," I said. "They arrived after your wife's death; she never even opened the box. They're valuable. You can see the written appraisal there."

"Fuck all this," he said. "You're as obsessed by this crap as *she* was." He brought his arm down across the table, sweeping the books off the table, sending the frail old things crashing to the floor.

He left the room.

In a trance, I bent down and gathered up the old books. I was offended and angry and heartsick. *This just proves it!* I told myself. *Taking his anger out on these priceless*

*old books. He's all wrong for me. Even if he's no monster,
he's still a jerk.*

I examined the books, which were somewhat worse for
the wear.

Some of the pages had come loose, and one of the notary books was a bit torn around the binding.

*You just lopped off a good percentage of your own in-
vestment, you idiot,* I silently admonished Gatien. Now
the books would have to be repaired.

I thought: *He's no monster. No. Losing your temper
that way is a human failing.*

As I picked up the last one, one of the accounting
books, as I called them, I noticed the cover was split at the
edges, and stuffing was coming out of it. Flakes fluttered
out onto the floor.

I gritted my teeth and carefully gathered up the pieces
of stuffing, which resembled the shredded newspaper you
might find in a hamster's cage. I supposed since it was so
old, it couldn't be newspaper. And, since it was so old, I'd
better save it and have it restuffed when the books were
repaired, to keep everything authentic. Carefully I put the
books and the stuffing into a cabinet, then took a deep
breath and braced myself to walk out of the room, to encounter Gatien again, perhaps—unless he'd had the good
grace to make himself disappear.

Chapter Twenty-four

H E WAS SITTING on the porch when I came out. I went to pick up May from school and left him staring after me with intense, bewildered eyes. If things had been normal for us, he would have come with me. But then, what was "normal" for us, anyway?

On the way home May and I stopped to pick up some groceries. I stalled for time, but finally I had to bring her home. As I watched May and Gatien greet one another, I studied their interactions with sick interest. All those times I had wondered at his stiffness with her, his inability to show her his love. Did a history of sexual abuse have anything to do with that?

We had a hurried supper, then it was off to Awards Night for May's school. I was grateful we had an event to occupy us that evening. May was quiet on the ride over, no doubt picking up on the tension between Gatien and me.

Gatien and I sat high up in the back of an old auditorium on the Stanford campus where the awards ceremony was taking place. It seemed every kid in the entire school was up for some award, and the event went on and on, making it alternately agonizing and tantalizing, sitting with him so close beside me.

I retired to my room soon after we got home. I heard May and Gatien talking in the living room and the occasional laughter—mostly hers.

I lay on my bed, fully dressed, tormented. If Gatien was a sick, wicked man, shouldn't I be out there, watching over May, making sure he wasn't harming her?

But I knew there was nothing like that going on between them. It was difficult, if not impossible, to entertain the possibility that there ever had been. The idea was ludicrous.

So why was I so frightened?

They watched TV together for awhile. I could hear the music, the canned laugh track, the occasional rise of voices in conversation. And then I heard May call out good night, and the snick of her door shutting when she went to bed. And sometime later, I heard a soft knocking on my own door, which I pretended not to hear. I heard the latch turn, heard the lock catch. He tried it again, to be sure. There was a moment of silence. Of stillness. And then I heard his footsteps receding from my door.

I hardly slept that night, fearing and hoping he would return and break down the barrier between us.

I WAS UP early the next morning, relieved to think he was sleeping in, but then I saw him sitting out on the deck, looking rumpled in last night's clothes, and I realized he wasn't up early; he had never gone to bed. I shepherded May out to school, and then I went out for coffee, unable to go home, knowing he was there.

This isn't working, I said to myself. I *have* to talk to May and tell her I *have* to know. I *have* to be able to talk to him. I can't *not* talk to him about it any longer. I made my decision. After I picked her up from school, I would talk to May.

Midmorning, I steeled myself to return to the house, and there I found a taxi waiting in the driveway.

Gatien was at the front door with his travel bag and another suitcase. Apparently he had packed more clothes to bring with him. He was about to leave; I had nearly missed him.

"You're not going now?" I said plaintively. "So soon?"

He must have thought I'd lost my mind. I was beginning to fear that I had.

"I shouldn't have come at all," he said without looking me in the eye. "There was no time. And no reason." He went to the taxi and loaded the bags in himself.

When he had satisfied himself that everything was properly handled, he motioned to the cabbie to give him a moment, then came back to where I was standing on the porch, waiting to watch him go away again.

He stopped a few feet away from me and looked at me long and hard, as if daring me not to feel what was there between us, snapping and alive and electric. Then he turned on his heel without saying a word and walked down the driveway to the waiting taxi. He didn't glance back at me.

I watched the taxi roll out of the drive.

IT MUST HAVE been nearly midnight that night when I found out the truth.

I was sitting in the darkness on the love seat in the guest room—my room, now—staring at the empty, dark fireplace, shaking with sobs.

I felt the gentle, firm touch of her hand on my shoulder.

"Sarah! Oh my God. Sarah, please don't cry! Sarah. Sarah, come on, you're scaring me!"

"I'm sorry, May. I am so sorry. But if he's the one who's hurt you, I'll kill him. I'll kill him."

"Would you really?" she replied, astonished. "Would you kill someone, Sarah?"

I hung my head. "No, May. When I say I'll kill him, it's like, a figure of speech. Never mind. I'm sorry. This is so unfair to you."

"Oh. Sarah . . ."

"I'm talking crazy, I know. I'm not really crazy, May. I

am very sane. But I'm not going to be able to function normally until I know . . . until I know what happened to you. I'm sorry, May. This is so unfair to you. So unfair."

"That's okay."

"No, it is *not* okay!"

"Sarah . . . I think I know what you want to know," she said gently. "You want to know if my father was the one who molested me when I was a little kid."

I nodded.

"The answer is yes," she said. "I was abused by my father when I was seven years old."

The blood in my veins flashed cold, numbing me from the inside out. I felt myself falling toward shock, so I wouldn't have to feel the shattering pain of this. *So this is what it feels like,* I thought wonderingly, *to have your whole world come down around you. It feels like nothing.* It was too horrific to feel.

"But there's something else you should know, Sarah," May went on, hastily, but too slowly for me, as if her voice was a record playing at the wrong speed. "Gatien Defalle is not my father."

I stared at her, too stunned to think.

"He's my guardian. Gato never hurt me. He's the one who *saved* me."

Too paralyzed to process this strange new information at once. As it slowly sank into my brain, what she was telling me was such a relief, I could hardly bear it. I started to cry again, in shaking, dry sobs.

"Oh, Sarah," May breathed. "I'm sorry. I should have told you. He wanted to tell you, right from the beginning. He thought you should know, but I wouldn't let him. I didn't want you to know. I didn't want anyone to know. We came here to start a new life. He's my dad, now, and I'm his daughter, and I wanted us to leave the past behind. Only a few people know what really happened. Paul and Theta know. Aunt Kate and Dimitri. Dimitri knows."

"He's not your real father. . . ."

"But he *is,* you know," she said quietly, and she sounded so mature just then, I wanted to break out in smiles and hug her so tightly. "He wants to adopt me, but my real father is against it. Gato has custody of me, but my real father has put up obstacles. It's just expensive because of the lawyers, and takes a lot of time. My real father has a lot of money, and expensive lawyers. It's been hard on Gato, but he won't give up. We have managed to get my name changed so that I'm a Defalle now. I figured, if I'm a Defalle now, why does anyone have to know about my past? But . . ."

I was blown away. I was wasted. May opened up like I'd never heard her before, talking about what had happened to her candidly and wisely, and winsomely, as was her way. My heart broke over and over again. And Friday, when we went to visit Natalie, we went even deeper.

"I'VE DECIDED SOMETHING, from all this," May said shyly to Natalie and me, toward the end of our session. "I have decided I'm no longer going to pretend it didn't happen. I'm going to face it, and deal with it, and get past it."

The psychiatrist's office was a charming Victorian house painted blue with white gingerbread trim and pale pink roses blooming in the front garden. Natalie, a regal woman with obsidian skin, dressed in flowing turquoise silk, had greeted us at the door. "Hello, May." Natalie spoke in a musical, vibrant voice. "It's good to see you again." She turned her gaze on me, long and wise and curious. I had intended to go into this meeting as something of a neutral observer, but of course it didn't work out that way at all. I hadn't been in Natalie's comfortable parlor long when I realized I was in the right place: I needed a shrink!

"One thing I think it's important to remember," said Natalie, sitting like a queen in an appropriately thronelike rattan chair. "Sexual abuse is a physical assault; you were violated physically, as well as emotionally. So it's important, when going through the process of working it out, to work it out physically as well as emotionally."

"How so?" May asked, suspicious.

"Well, any number of ways. For example, with dance. Or—well, let's see. Have you ever done yoga?"

"Yeah, a little."

"Sports? Tennis? Running? How about kickboxing?" Natalie smiled. "That's a particularly good one for getting out certain feelings."

"She sings," I said.

They looked at me, each with a different expression.

"May's singing is *incredible*. Really, she has a beautiful voice, and her pitch is dead on."

May blushed. "Thank you, Sarah."

"Singing is very important, you know," Natalie said. "I couldn't live without it. It's a way to massage yourself from the inside."

May said, "I'm learning fencing."

"Oh, like sword fighting? Well, there you go."

"I think I see what you're getting at, with this physical stuff," May said thoughtfully. "It does make you feel more . . . powerful. Actually, I play soccer, too."

"Is that so? What position?"

May smiled to herself, sat up a little straighter, and said with pride, "Forward."

After our session, I left the office with May feeling like I had been the one who had needed the therapist. I was rather ashamed of myself. May seemed so calm and steady, and I was such a mess.

"If there's someone else you need to talk to about it, Sarah," she said to me when we were driving home, "that would be all right with me."

THREE DAYS LATER I had a visit from Paul.

"Take me for a ride in that sweet little car of yours, will you, darling?" he said, throwing his arm around me. "May," he said, "you don't mind, do you? I need to talk to your Miss Logan in private."

May shrugged, hardly looked up from her book. The school year was nearly finished, and she was swamped with schoolwork—studying for finals, projects to complete. "I'm not paying any attention to either of you," she said. "But if you'd feel more comfortable driving off in the car alone together, that's fine with me."

So Paul and I drove off down Edgewood and turned onto Cañada Road, which was bucolic and deserted but for the occasional bicycle. I drove north, past 92 along the lake. I knew now this lake was the Crystal Springs Reservoir, where our drinking water was stored. It was dusk, and both of us were rather more subdued than usual.

Finally Paul came to the point. "I had to talk to you, Sarah, because I recently found out . . ." He stopped and tried again: "Theta told me you stopped by the house the other day."

I nodded, waiting for what more there was to this.

"She told me what she told you."

"Yeah . . . ?" I wondered what she'd told him she'd told me.

"It's all bullshit, Sarah."

"What did she tell you she said?"

"Well, she said she told you we were back together. Trying to make it work. We're not."

"You're not?"

"No. But that's not the main thing. She told me that she told you—well, that she led you to believe that Gatien was the guy who messed with May when she was a little kid."

"Yes. She did lead me to believe that."

"That's total bullshit, Sarah."

"I know."

"Good." He threw up his arms and breathed again. "I'm so glad you know. So you weren't duped by Theta!"

"I was completely wiped out, Paul," I said. "Until May told me the truth. I thought my world had collapsed around me."

He looked at me with piercing interest. "Took it that hard, huh?"

I nodded.

"Gatien's a lucky man."

"I came over that night," I rushed out, embarrassed, "to ask you, to find out what really happened. I had just learned May had been abused, but I didn't know who had done it to her. I came to find you, to ask you—"

"And you found Theta instead."

"Why would she *say* those things about Gatien?"

"She's jealous. She can see he wants you and not her. That pisses her off. She's accustomed to the guys wanting *her.* She said what she said just to get to you."

"But to make such horrendous accusations . . ."

"Yeah. What's ironic is, Gatien is actually the one who got that child away from her abuser."

"May's real dad."

"So you know, huh? May once asked me not to let on, and I promised I wouldn't. She wants the world to think Gatien is her real daddy."

"I know. All this time, I've been wondering why he's so cool toward May, you know, like he's this cold fish father, and it turns out he's giving her precisely the amount of physical affection he thinks she can handle, given her history. . . ."

"There was some talk of taking her away from him, after her mother died. Lisa's sister Kate, especially, was very vocal about it. She didn't know Gatien, didn't think much of him when she met him, didn't think this guy, who had been married to Lisa for what, two or three years, should automatically be handed the girl after her mother's death. He had legal custody, though. Lisa had made certain of that before she died, bless her soul. And to tell you the truth, no one else actually wanted the job. Not Helene, not Kate. The old man, May's grandpa, certainly couldn't have handled the kid. At that point there was some question that the father might regain custody, and that's when Gatien got serious and hired some hotshot lawyers. He had already moved the family from Europe, where May's father lived, to California, to get away from him and be closer to Lisa's relatives. When they moved to the area, they decided they wouldn't tell anyone that Gatien was not May's real father. Louisa doesn't even know, I don't think."

"And Helene doesn't know what happened?"

"She knows May's father was abusive, both to May and her mother. She doesn't know the extent of it, though, I don't think. Lisa didn't want her to know. She felt Helene would judge her, think she was a bad mother."

"I just can't get my brain around all this. It's just such a different way of looking at everything, everything I've questioned about Gatien and May and their relationship, all these months. I have to rearrange all my thinking."

"They should have told you, straight up, from the beginning. At least about him being her stepfather. But I guess they wanted to project what they were trying to be: a normal father and daughter trying to cope after her mom's death. They tried to keep a low profile."

"A secluded estate, unlisted phone number . . ."

"Exactly. Gatien didn't want the Lone Wolf finding them. Though of course he did, didn't he?"

"The Lone Wolf. So that was *him*. May's father. No *wonder* he looked so familiar! He's a dissipated, masculine May. He came by the house once."

"Yes, Gatien told me. Nasty character."

"I think that was around the time Gatien had the security system installed. . . . I thought that was because of the break-in, but now I think it was because May's dad had shown up. Unless the two incidents were somehow related . . ."

"May's dad isn't the kind of guy to break into a house for a bit of merry vandalism. Then again, he might be the kind of guy who would hire someone else to break into a house, if he had a reason to."

"Maybe to find documentation of some sort, to support his case? He said he would have what was *his*. . . . He must have meant May herself."

"I don't know. Anyway, Sarah, I just wanted to make sure Theta didn't do too much damage. I'm glad to find she didn't. And, though I hate to admit it, I'm glad about you and Gatien. He deserves someone as fine as you."

I blushed. "It's not like that," I said hurriedly.

"I heard the two of you went off on a road trip together during spring break," Paul said with a foxy grin.

"Who told you that?"

"A mutual friend of ours named Courtney."

"How would *she* know?" I asked, suddenly cross.

"She wanted to take him to her cabin at Tahoe that week, but he told her he was going up north with you."

"Hmm," I grumbled.

"Sticking to your story?" he prodded, with that same sly grin. "It's not *like that?*"

"We had an amazing time on that trip."

"That's what I thought."

"But that was . . ." An icy image washed through me: Gatien, the last time I had seen him. He had turned and walked away, without a word. I hadn't let him touch me, and he was too proud to try a second time.

"Oh, so it was like, a one-time fling, or something?" Paul grinned at me, a droll tease.

I slowed and turned the car around where the road dead-ended at the gates of the Hillsborough Country Club. "Gatien came home to see me the day after I had that conversation with Theta," I said. "Before I found out what really happened. I didn't know if he was the one who had done it. . . ."

Paul swore. "Perfect timing, eh? Did you confront him?"

"No. I couldn't. I had promised May I wouldn't talk about it with anyone until we had a chance to discuss it with her therapist."

"Huh. What happened?"

"He went away. I haven't heard from him since."

Chapter Twenty-five

S O I KNEW the truth, but there was nothing I could do about it. What could I do? Call Gatien on the telephone and say, hello, hey, for a while there I thought you were a child molester, but I found out you're really not. Can we go back to being lovers?

Right. I wouldn't know what to say to him even if I could call him. I had the numbers to call in an emergency, but I had never called him when he was out of the country. He rarely called home, though I could see he had been making more of a point to keep in touch with May, since I had upbraided him about it.

So I was startled to answer the phone early one afternoon, when I was expecting a call from Helene, to hear his heartbreakingly deep voice, cool and businesslike in greeting. He asked for May.

"She's at school," I said. How sarcastically I would have once said those words, because shouldn't he know that? How penitent I felt now.

"I thought it might be early day today. Isn't Thursday early day?"

"You're right, it is," I said. *So,* I thought wistfully, *he* is *aware of what May is doing.* "But she's staying after today for the fencing club."

"Oh, yeah, she told me she was doing some sword fighting." He chuckled at that, cut himself off, and said brusquely, "Speaking of which, I was calling to invite May to come to Europe as soon as school's out. I think she has a couple weeks in between school and that summer fencing class she wants to take, right?"

"Right," I said. I felt it like a sweet stab in the gut. He was sending for her, calling for her to come to him. I would be superfluous. Unnecessary. Thank you for your service, miss, but you are no longer needed here.

"Do you think she'll want to come?" he asked.

"I think she would love to."

I tried to concentrate on the words we were saying to each other, but my thoughts were crazily storming around as I groped for some way to communicate what I wanted him to know. But I could tell, by the aloof, businesslike tone I knew so well, that it was too late. He was already moving on. As for me, I had finished my job; my work was done. May was ready for high school. Technically, I had another month on my contract, but perhaps my contract would be terminated early, by mutual consent.

But gradually I became aware of what he was saying to me, and it was nothing about terminating my contract. "Can I ask you to bring May to France, Sarah? Unless you already have other plans, of course . . ."

I couldn't help laughing, I was suddenly so happy, and I found him so absurd.

"Unless I have other plans!" I cried. "I think I can fit a trip to Europe into my busy schedule," I added dryly.

"Good. I'll make the arrangements."

"Gatien . . . there's something I need to tell you. It's about last time . . . when I saw you, I—"

"There's no need." He cut me off abruptly. "Let's not speak of it again."

"There *is* need," I answered. "I need to talk to you about it, about—"

"Fine, but not on the phone." He was in a hurry to be

finished with the conversation. "If we must talk, let's do it when you come. Okay?"

"All right." *I can't wait to see you.* I nearly said it. But his cold, abrupt manner frightened me. "I'll see you soon," I said.

"Until then, Sarah," he replied, and the phone went dead.

OUR TRIP, THE journey to Gatien, as I thought of it, was fraught with misadventure and took far longer than expected. May and I were to meet him in France, but just before we left we were told there were strikes in France; everything was stopped, and if we kept to our original plan we'd only be stuck, since our connecting flight to Nice had been canceled. We were re-routed to Milan, where we were picked up and brought to Modena, and put up very comfortably in a modern high-rise apartment that belonged to a friend of Gatien's named Nicolas, who was on vacation. Everything was there for our convenience, and our driver and hostess, who was actually Nicolas's housekeeper, did everything she could to show us hospitality and kindness.

I was severely disappointed with everything. I had wanted to see France, I wanted to see Gatien race, and most of all, I wanted to see Gatien. When we were informed we were going to Italy, I told myself I should be completely happy with that; I'd always wanted to see Italy. But it meant a delay until Gatien could join us.

I felt disappointed with Italy, having seen no ancient ruins during the drive from Milan, and the overcast landscape might have been a smoggy day on Interstate 5 through California's Central Valley. When we got to the apartment, on the third floor of a boxy building that failed to meet my expectations of Italian architecture, we were shown our room, which had two single beds side by side and outdoor rolling shades that completely blocked out the light of day. This light-blocking feature was the one thing that satisfied me about the place, because though it was daytime in Modena, it was the middle of the night for May and me. We hit the beds and fell sound asleep.

I was very bad company for May during our first couple of days in Europe.

Here I am in marvelous Italy, and I only want to be somewhere else. I stewed, ashamed of myself. With an aggressive determination to enjoy this trip to Europe, I concocted a scheme with the housekeeper and her boyfriend, who drove us over the mountains to spend a day in Florence.

I remember riding in the car over the mountain pass, feeling the tension as Marco navigated the curving road through this strange and beautiful new country. Down from the mountains we dropped into fairy-tale Florence.

When we finally found a parking spot, we left the car and plunged into the city on foot. Francesca and Marco turned out to be excellent guides, enthusiastic and experienced as they were. They gave us the whirlwind tour, showing us the sights. We climbed the Duomo, astonished by its size and grandeur. We went to the Uffizi, where Venus on her shell looked down at us from the wall. We strolled the Ponte Veccio, ate panini, and listened to American rock outside the cafés. We gazed up at the statue of David, the most amazing piece of art I had ever seen. Running through those narrow gray corridors of ancient city streets, my spirit woke up, and I thought: *I'm here! I'm in Florence, Italy!* I stopped and savored it, a lifelong dream come true. Life was good. Life was an adventure.

And tomorrow, or maybe the day after, I would see Gatien again.

HE ARRIVED THAT night, in the middle of the night.

I got up out of bed in my white cotton nightshirt and drifted to the kitchen for a glass of water. I felt relaxed and uninhibited; Francesca had gone to spend the night with Marco, and May and I were alone in the apartment. I had dozed off earlier, but now that I was suddenly awake again, I was completely awake. I wondered how long it would take me to get used to local time.

As I was walking back through the main hall to my bedroom, I heard a fumbling at the front door.

A cold wash of fear ran over me; my heart began to pound. Someone was trying to break into the apartment.

I moved cautiously to the door, and I heard the soft knocking. And then I heard his voice.

"Anybody home?"

"Who is it?" I called out sharply. It had to be a coincidence that the muffled baritone behind the door sounded so much like *his*. Gatien's voice. I would know that deep, resonant sound anywhere. But he was not due until tomorrow, at the earliest.

"Sarah?"

It *was* Gatien. I sprang to the door and unlatched it, bumbling in my haste.

I got the door open, and he was standing there, shadowed by the light from the outer landing, wearing jeans and a green army coat, a duffel bag slung over his shoulder. He walked past me into the apartment like he owned the place and threw his bag on the first chair he came to.

"Were you awake?" he asked me.

"Yeah, I just woke up and came out here, and then I heard you—"

"How's May?"

"Good. Sleeping."

"Right. So you made it all right? I'm sorry you were left alone."

"We haven't been alone. We've had Francesca and Marco. They took us to Florence."

He looked surprised at that. "Well, good. How did you like it?"

"I loved it. It was like a city in a dream."

We were there in the dark apartment, alone together, and it might have been quite awkward between us, except he did not allow any silence; he asked about my trip and apologized for the problems with transportation and told me a little of what May and I might expect for the next couple of weeks. He warned me that he would be busy but that he would try to make sure we were well taken care of and would have a good time.

I listened, dutifully nodding, the governess receiving instructions from her master. His manner was formal. He was polite, but he allowed no warmth into his voice. He maintained a proper distance between us. He did not attempt to touch me. He did not leave any pause for me to fill. He finished what he had to say, then bid me a stiff good night. "Which room did she intend for me?" he asked.

"There, at the end of the hall. She said you've stayed in there before."

"Right. Good night, then."

"You surprised me," I said. "To hear your voice at the door, it was like . . . I didn't think I'd see you until . . ." I faltered; I was only trying to hold him back.

"I drove without stopping," he said coolly. *To see you.* It gleamed in his eyes when he looked at me, which he finally did now. And for a moment I thought I might have a chance to approach him, to offer something like a confession, an explanation—because I wanted so badly for him to understand why I had pulled away from him when he had come home to me, and I wanted to find out what was going on with him now. He had chilled toward me; if it wasn't in his eyes, it was there in the carriage of his body, in the distance he kept between us. He had withdrawn his suit, and he wanted me to know it. I had lost him.

Was it irrevocable? Would he listen to what I had to say? Would he forgive my suspicions, when I confessed? And how would I ever begin to say the words that needed to be said? Did they need to be said? *Yes,* I thought. There was too much there, too much between the two of us, and between Gatien and May, too much that I had misunderstood, and it affected everything that had come before. I would talk to him. I would tell him everything.

But before I could say anything more he turned away, saying casually, "I'm beat. I'll see you in the morning." He grabbed up his duffel bag and walked off to his room.

Chapter Twenty-six

IT'S HARD FOR me to remember the sequence of events in Europe that summer. Where I was, what I saw, what I was feeling, it all swirls together in my mind and my soul, a collage, a kaleidoscope, a montage set to music in a romantic movie. We had some time before the next race, and so we drove leisurely through the European country-side in yet another wonderful car—a vintage Mercedes convertible. It was not quite summer, yet it felt richer than spring, the air was so clean. This was time out of time, again, and I wondered how it would be, to live like this all the time, with Gatien and May as my own.

One afternoon we were traveling on a winding road above the sea in the south of France when Gatien sud-denly turned the car off the main road, and soon we were climbing up a gentle hill, at the top of which stood a long, low stone house surrounded by orchards and woods and vineyards. A man and a woman came from behind the house to watch us ascend the hill.

Gatien swung the car around and pulled up beside the house. The woman set a watering can down on the ground and walked toward us. She was about sixty, with a sunny complexion and white hair pinned up high. The man looked older, slender but robust; he was waving as if he expected us, but he was paying more attention to the car than to us.

"What the hell are you driving, here, G. D.?" he called out to Gatien. "This a rental?"

"Hell, no, it's no rental," Gatien shouted out the window.

I looked to Gatien, questioning, but he remained inscrutable. May wouldn't look at me, either, and by the slight curve of her lips on her pure profile, I could see she was in on the joke.

"All right," I said sternly. "What is this? Who are they?"

Gatien turned to me and smiled at me shyly, and without quite comprehending it right then, I already knew. The old man walking toward us with that long stride—even the limp was the same!

"That's my dad," Gatien said.

THE TABLE WAS long and rustic and shaded by a pergola; the warm afternoon was caressed by a perfect breeze. It was all there, the checkered tablecloth, the fat wine bottles, the dozen or so family and friends gathered round, chattering in French and English, the food so good it made you want to weep with bliss, old women and little kids hugging Gatien, taking May by the hand and leading her off to show her something in the garden. I noticed they treated May as if she were Gatien' s real daughter. They treated me with wary respect and deference.

Gatien's father was an older, less sophisticated version of Gatien. He was an American through and through, despite the exotic (from my point of view) setting in which he lived. And despite the occasional crude remark, I liked him. He seemed to like me, too. Gatien's stepmother was of a more refined stamp, with that elusive throwaway elegance I admired in Gatien. She was French and Spanish, and had been a friend of Gatien's mother. She had been married to Gatien's father for twenty years, and she maintained a proprietary air over both men, her husband and her stepson. She didn't take to me right away.

After the meal I walked into the garden, ostensibly to look for the children, but really to step away from the intense family scene, needing a moment to assimilate this new world. Such beauty—the hillsides, the vineyards, the old stone house, the healthy, vibrant, loving people—it was as if they had been called on cue to provide dimension to the man I had already fallen for. *I'm here,* I thought, *I'm in this scene, this place, this time.* It made me so happy to be alive and to see how beautiful it was, that I must remind myself to let go and live it.

And how to speak of the aching emptiness, the sore void, the wanting that came from being so close to him, and not being able to get closer? His courteous aloofness. My regret.

I WAS WANDERING through a secluded part of the garden when I encountered Zora, Gatien's stepmother, and though she appeared to be taking a casual evening stroll, as I was, I knew she had calculated this meeting. We fell into step with one another, and I caught myself before I began to chatter. I waited to see what she would have to say.

She spoke of the gardens, and the vineyards, which I gathered were a source of revenue for herself and her husband, since Gatien's father had retired from racing years earlier.

"It's difficult, you know," she said, "with some of them. They can't let go. It is like that with many athletes. They *are* athletes, you know, the drivers are. Racing is tremendously demanding, physically. As well as mentally. Rick had a hard time adjusting. He didn't want to stop, but finally, it was not up to him."

"He must be proud that his son followed in his footsteps."

"Proud, yes, but there is a rivalry there, as well. I believe Rick was hard on Gatien when he was a boy. Pressed him hard to become the best. Only the best, you see. Nothing less would do. Serves him right that Gatien surpassed him in his career. But please understand, there is undying love between the two of them. They would do anything for each other. Otherwise, why would Gatien come so often, when his father needs him? These past two years have been so difficult for everyone. Gatien has had his own problems, as everyone knows. His wife's death. The accident. Becoming a father so suddenly, and then a single father. He moved to California for the sake of that child. And yet he was here for his own father so many times this past year, helping him through his heart troubles, and the bypass surgery. I don't think Rick would have recovered so quickly if not for his son's support."

I had no idea, I thought. *Why didn't you tell me, Gatien?*

"We came very close to losing Rick; for a long time it was touch and go. I began to worry that Gatien was spending too much time here in France, when I know he has the child there in California. I suggested he move her back here, where we could look after her. But he felt it was better for her to stay there, near her mother's family. To stay in the school she's become used to. And of course the farther away from her so-called real father, the better!"

"I have noticed you treat May as one of your own," I said.

"Well, we think of her as one of our own," Zora replied. "We came to know May when they lived here in France, after Gatien and Lisa married. We've seen her grow from an introverted, wounded child into a poised young woman. I believe we have *you* to thank for that, Sarah, at least partly."

"Thank you for saying so. But it's mostly due to May herself."

"And I see the change in Gatien," said Zora, looking at me meaningfully.

"Yes, he's recovered from the accident. He's driving again. . . . He's worked hard."

"It isn't just the driving. Or recovering from the accident. He's happier. There is something less . . . restless about him, in recent months."

I squirmed uncomfortably. From something in her tone, I knew she was saying these things purposely, to ferret out some response from me.

"Sarah," she said gently. "I do feel I ought to warn you. He won't be an easy one."

"What do you mean?"

"It's the way he was raised. His parents were passionate enemies. Gatien's mother ended the war in her own way, I'm afraid. And then, Gatien's wife, well . . . do you understand what I am trying to tell you?"

I wasn't sure I did.

"I don't know you, Sarah," said Gatien's stepmother. "I don't know what you came from, or what you are going to. But I know Gatien cares for you, and so I care for you, too. And I want to warn you to be very careful, because I care for you. But I care most for my stepson, and I would protect him if I could. Do you understand what I am saying?"

"I think so."

"Good. I would have disliked you instantly if you had pretended not to. It isn't his fault. It was what he saw of his own parents."

"And yet—he also saw you and his father," I pointed out. "You have been together a long time. And you seem to have it pretty good together. Maybe he learned something from that."

She laughed suddenly. "Indeed. I suppose you're right."

Chapter Twenty-seven

THEN WE WERE in Monaco, and it was all about the racing.

Monte Carlo reminded me of Santa Barbara, with its harbor and the mountains curving around. The place was flashy and beautiful, the water so blue, the sky so blue, the scent of wealth in the air, and the incredible cars. The town was built on a hillside; fortunately my legs were primed from climbing up and down around Winding Hill. During the day the air was filled with the roar of engines and the smell of fuel, first for the practice sessions, then for the qualifying. At night the racing circuit was opened up to the public and people drove around the streets in their own cars, Ferraris and Porsches and Volkswagens. There were parties on the yachts in the harbor, in the hotels, in the beautiful houses. It was champagne and suntanned girls in bikinis and handsome, reckless boys and the most beautiful cars in the world, on the circuit, in the streets. The Monaco Grand Prix seemed to be one big excuse for partying in a major way.

I was caught up in the excitement and the glitz, thinking very well of myself for leading such a privileged life, wearing beautiful clothes and riding in beautiful cars, going to parties with beautiful people in beautiful places, though all the while I felt a deep melancholy beneath the thrilling giddiness of it all. Since we had arrived in Monte Carlo, I had seen little of Gatien, and then only in passing. I had never been more aware of our separate lives.

He took May and me down to the place they called the paddock, to see the cars, which we were only allowed to get near afler we negotiated a complicated security gauntlet involving some mean-looking bouncers and showing ourselves to be in possession of a VIP pass, which made me feel quite special to possess. Here they were, like Thoroughbreds in their stalls, the strange rocketlike Formula One cars, most of them partially dismantled. We VIPs wandered around nonchalantly, trying to pretend we weren't terribly excited to be there, and I was astonished at the atmosphere of celebrity. Every other person who walked by looked like a movie star or a supermodel and from what I heard, might well have been; I wouldn't have recognized them anyway. Apparently this car racing business was considered very glamorous. But the drivers themselves were the real celebrities. It seemed like most of the time May and I were with Gatien, we were waiting for him to finish with whomever it was he was receiving at the moment; there was always a lineup of those who wished a moment of his time: his fans, his teammates, his mechanics, his sponsors, his managers, the owners of his team, and all the pretty girls who wanted to slip him their phone numbers.

Although this whole racing world was glamorous, and exciting, and fun, it was no place for me. I tried to picture myself traveling from circuit to circuit around the world, year after year, watching races from the sidelines with a clipboard in my arm and a stopwatch in my hand, like drivers' girlfriends in racing movies. It was a rush, and I was soaking it up here in Monaco, but I had to be realistic. I knew myself well enough to know it might last a season or two, this fascination, this thrill, this glamorous, nomadic existence, but then I would be moving on. I wanted to find a home. Maybe it was for the best that Gatien and I had cooled off.

I felt the wary interest of the other women—wives and girlfriends of Gatien's teammates and manager—but it was a closed club, and they weren't about to let a newcomer in. There were no VIP passes for that gate. I couldn't really blame them; the drivers were so bombarded by demands for attention from every direction, the women probably felt they needed to circle the wagons around their men, just to protect them from the groupies, the fans, women with titles of nobility, and the bikini-clad sponsor girls.

I was there in the capacity of May's caregiver, but Gatien's parents were there, too, and they liked looking after May. The three of them seemed close. In fact, there was so little for me to do officially that I wondered if I ought to shrink away and hide in my hotel room, waiting for a summons. But everyone in the family did their best to make me feel I was one of them and treated me with friendly respect.

I couldn't say the same for others we encountered. At one party I overheard a woman say, "Her? Oh, she's just Gatien Defalle's nanny."

Well, I thought, so much for my glamorous VIP existence. What should I have expected?

Later, at the same party, I heard my name spoken in a similar tone of derision; I almost ignored it, but I looked up and there was Theta, wearing a dress the color of her own skin, spangled with coppery sequins. She looked like she was naked and sprinkled with stars.

She made her way through the crowd and joined me. "Ah," she said. "So Gatien wanted to show little May what Daddy does for a living. Can't think what else *you* would be doing here in Monaco, Sarah."

"That's me," I replied. "The governess. What's your excuse?"

"Oh, we come every year, Paul and I. That's how I met them, you know, Paul and Gatien. Gatien was racing, and I came with—well, someone else, actually, but I left with

Paul, who had come to support his friend, the great Gatien Defalle."

"His friend the child abuser," I said.

She stood there before me with her erect, beautiful figure, completely shameless. "Oh, Sarah," she said with a *tsk*. "You know all is fair in love and war."

"And you said those things about Gatien. Why, exactly? Are you at war with him?"

"In a sense, yes. Because I love him."

"You love him."

"Don't tell me that's difficult for *you* to understand, Sarah."

"I'm not even attempting to understand anything you say anymore, Theta."

"I'll explain it to you anyway, Sarah. I want Gatien. I intend to have him. And I want *you* out of the picture. *Capiche?*"

"So you said those things about him—"

"To freak you out. You're far too noble to date a child molester, aren't you, Sarah? I thought I'd head you off at the pass. I was hoping you would leave. I was hoping I wouldn't have to resort to using *dirty* tactics." She leaned closer and purred, "But I will, if necessary."

"Speaking of dirty tactics, why don't you just be yourself, see how that works?" I looked up at the stairway leading down into the ballroom and saw Paul and Gatien descending together, the bright and the dark, both dressed in tuxedos, both of them noticing Theta and me at the same time.

"They're becoming friends again," I said, but Theta had melted away into the crowd.

I was standing just outside the doorway of a very mod disco an hour later when Paul appeared at my side.

"Why aren't you dancing?" he scolded me. It seemed so strange, that he was here in Monte Carlo.

"I'm the nanny," I said. "I'm just here to watch May. She's in there dancing with a young Polish count."

"I saw her. She looks great. She's come so far, Sarah. You've done a great job with her."

"Nah," I said, tilting my head, trying to get a good shot of May, but the place was crowded. Everywhere we went, in this town, it was crowded. "May's done it all for herself."

"With your guidance."

"Thanks, Paul."

"Shall we dance, you and I? That's not against the nanny rules, is it?"

"I don't know about nanny rules, but your wife very politely asked me to stay away from you, not long ago, because the two of you were trying to make your marriage work."

"Well, forget it. My marriage is completely, irrevocably not working, and you can't change that." He grabbed up my hand and pulled me out into the heaving young crowd to dance.

"So what are you two doing here together, if it's not working?" I asked him, shouting over the pumping bass the DJ was mixing with some ethereal trance tones.

Paul leaned forward, unable to hear me, and I repeated what I said into his ear. When he eased away, I saw Gatien staring at us from the edge of the dance floor, where he was standing near Theta, who was angling to place herself at his side.

"We're not here together," Paul shouted back in reply. "She's stalking me."

I laughed. "I see. Can't shake her, huh?"

"We bought our tickets months ago. The flights, the hotel, the best racing venues. I tried to talk her out of coming, but to no avail. I almost didn't come myself, just to avoid her, but I needed to come. I needed to see my buddy Gatien."

"I saw the two of you together earlier, but I couldn't tell if you were speaking or not."

"We're speaking, but only minimally."

INTO MY LIFE came Sir Lancelot, aka Nigel Lance, a baby-faced, fortyish Brit with a blond ponytail, an overbite, and a pear-shaped body dressed down in elite hip-hop fashion. I was never quite sure what his official position with the team was, exactly, but he seemed to have been assigned to take care of May and me.

It was Nigel who guided us through Monte Carlo when Gatien was busy; it was Nigel who made sure we made it through all the pass checks, and Nigel who gave me a primer in Formula One.

"It's not like driving a car, luv, it's like piloting a rocket," he explained. "A Formula One car can accelerate to one hundred sixty kilometers per hour and stop again— in six seconds. You can imagine the stress on the driver. The G force is incredible, especially to the head during cornering, and it affects everything, blood flow to the eyes, pressures on the legs, the hips, the arms, ankles, knees. The down force can increase the weight of the car, making steering quite a feat for the hands and arms. The physical strain puts pressure on the heart, which is beating around one hundred seventy or one hundred eighty beats per minute for one and a half hours, sometimes rising to two hundred ten. And then there's the heat, dehydration— up to two pints of bodily fluid can be lost during a race —and the noise! A Formula One car on the starting grid produces one hundred twenty decibels. That's louder than a 747 at takeoff."

"I was already impressed," I said.

"You should be," said Nigel. "It all comes down to stamina and strength. Why do they do it? Imagine, if you will, sliding behind the wheel of one of the most incredible cars in the world. It's a privilege. A costly privilege, but there you are."

THE NIGHT BEFORE the race, Gatien came to my hotel room. The door was open to the hallway, and I was standing near the bed, folding some clothes. He came into the room and remained a good distance from me, pacing slowly, watching me, and I began to wonder what he had come for.

"You didn't go to the party," I said.

"No. You didn't either."

"Your Dad and Zora wanted to take May and they let me stay behind. I'm tired of parties."

"Don't you want to see and be seen at the social event of the season?"

"Not tonight. What about you?"

"I always try to sleep the night before a race. But usually I can't."

"You got a good position on the track."

"Yes. I didn't manage pole, but I'm right up there in the front."

"They say it's very important, on this circuit, to qualify well, because once the real race begins, you can't pass, the streets are so narrow."

"You've been paying attention, Governess."

"It seems very dangerous," I said with a frown, ignoring what he might have meant by using May's pet name for me, which at different times had been a term of derision as well as one of endearment.

"I can't believe you drive through these steep old winding streets at those speeds!" I said. "I just cannot believe it."

He stood in front of the window, looking down on the street below, where he would be driving so fast tomorrow.

He let the drapery fall and turned to me.

"Sarah," he said. "Paul told me something this evening. He filled me in on some things. . . . You might have tried to tell me yourself, but I think I cut you off when you did. I know I cut you off. I did it on purpose. The truth is, I was afraid you were going to justify your reasons for backing off, that day I came home to see you, after Mendocino. Well, I guess that's exactly what you were going to do. And you had a good reason to back off, or you thought you did, and you'd promised May you wouldn't talk to anyone, so you couldn't ask me about it. Paul told me. I'm sorry it's come to this, Sarah. I'm sorry you had to learn about it the way you did. I'm sorry we just didn't tell you about everything from the beginning. And I'm sorry I didn't listen to you when you tried to tell me, myself."

"It amazes me," I said. "When I learned about what happened, what really happened . . . it changed everything I thought about you and May. About everything. What you had with May, with your wife. Here I accused you of being a cold fish father, and really, you were a hero for those two."

"No." Gatien shook his head. He didn't like the idea of being a hero.

"You don't like to talk about her. Your wife."

"I will tell you about Lisa," he said. "Anything you want to know."

"Okay," I said slowly. I might not get this chance again. What did I want to know? "When you lost her, did you lose the love of your life?"

"When I lost Lisa, I lost a friend. I lost a partner. I liked Lisa. I loved her as a friend, but it was no consuming passion, Sarah. We'd been casual friends—she'd dated other drivers, guys I knew—and we started what I thought would be a brief fling. She was in a messy breakup. She was certain he had abused their little girl. That was something I admired about Lisa. As soon as she figured out something was going on, she got May away from the guy. She tried to start a new life, but he didn't like that. And he began to threaten her, and so I married her, rather impulsively, thinking I could protect her."

"Wow," I said. "That's so selfless."

"I don't think so."

"You married for May's sake," I said.

"If you say so. But I wouldn't marry for that reason again."

We were silent together, both of us suddenly embarrassed.

"I married Lisa for myself as much as for anyone else," he continued, with what I could only describe as a snarl. "We were compatible. We had fun together. Cared about each other. Good sex. I didn't have a family of my own, and May was already dear to my heart. I wanted a family. Sarah, I had no illusions that I would ever fall in love. I wanted to marry and have children of my own, but I felt that if I did, I would eventually see it break apart, because that's what happens, and I'd be the proud founder of a broken home, like my own father. At least doing it this way, I reasoned that I was taking something broken and putting it together. That was the idea."

"So how did it work?"

"I learned what it was to be a husband and father, crash course style. I realized I'd made a huge mistake, that I had no idea what I'd gotten myself into. But I was in for good; I'd made that promise. We had our problems, I can't deny that. After we got married, Lisa began to beg me to quit driving. I was astonished, wondering how she thought I had become the man I was—successful, respected, well-off—all the things she liked about me. It was only with the driving I had become those things. But it was hard on her. I traveled so much, it was hard to make a home. She was an American. She no longer wanted to live in Europe, where my family was. And there was May's father to contend with. So we bought the place in the Bay Area because it seemed so far away from May's father, and because we had friends there, and her family. But it was far away from my work, which made it difficult."

"I should think it would be hard," I said, putting myself in Lisa's place. It was hard enough for me, with him gone all the time, and I was just the nanny.

"I thought there at the end that Lisa was becoming resigned to my driving. She was starting to get involved in her own interests more. . . . She tended to get really into whatever she was into at any given time. I liked that about her, that one-pointed energy she had, but sometimes it drove me crazy, too. We did all right, for the most part. At least, I thought we did. May was growing up, moving away from the past, and I guess her mother and I were growing up, too. It might have all worked out okay, in the long run, if we'd had time. We were only married less than three years."

I walked to the window, to see what he was seeing. Below, the streets were alive. A woman we couldn't see was laughing. Somewhere, off in the darkness, a techno

beat hammered away. There was a smell of something sa-
vory cooking, and the Stones' "Gimme Shelter" wafted in
from somewhere. We were alone in the room, standing
side by side.

He looked at me somberly. "Anyway, Sarah," he said.
"Paul cleared up a few things for me tonight, and I just
wanted you to know. . . ."

"I'm glad you told me."

I thought he might kiss me, but he turned away and
looked at his watch. "I better go," he said. "Good night,
Sarah."

Chapter Twenty-eight

GATIEN WON THE Monaco Grand Prix. I saw it happen on the giant movie screen that faced into the harbor, instead of live in front of me as I had imagined it. I heard the roar of the engines. The images on the screen were vaguely ill-matching, the rapid-fire commentary in French impossible for me to comprehend. He won the race, and they were announcing it. I was still trying to understand it, though I had just seen it, though I hadn't actually witnessed it, but it was a close race, and they showed the finish again. That's when we heard the crash and the image on the screen cut to the accident.

Later I was to learn that after they had crossed the finish line, the second-place car had lost its brakes and veered into Gatien's car, sending him into a spin. But all I knew in that moment was that there had been an accident.

SEVERAL OTHER CARS were involved, they said. And one of the drivers was killed.

The American is dead.

The American—

○   ○   ○

BECAUSE OF MY special VIP status I was supposed to have a special place from which to watch the race. Gatien had told me to be waiting in the hotel lobby in the morning where I would meet with my escort, Nigel, who would provide transportation and passes and everything I needed. May was to accompany me, but plans had changed the night before, when she went to stay with her grandparents at their rented house in the high country above Monte Carlo. They had invited me, too.

"Yes, you can go with Noni and Grandpère," Gatien said loudly enough for us all to hear, when May had asked his permission. "But I want Sarah to stay at the hotel, in case I need her."

I could not fathom why on earth he would need me, since he hardly saw me or spoke to me lately, last night's conversation in my hotel room being the exception, but nobody questioned it, and I certainly didn't. Besides, though the house in the high country was beautiful—we had driven up there the day before—and it was an attractive offer, I wanted to stay at the hotel. I wanted to be near Gatien. So it was arranged that we would rendezvous before the race, May and her grandparents and me.

But the morning of the race, before I left my room to go downstairs to the lobby, I received a message to meet Nigel in a patisserie a few blocks away from the hotel. This seemed strange to me, but I did not question it at the time. I went to the patisserie and waited; it wasn't such a bad place to wait, after all.

I waited, listening to the engines revving in the distance. From seven in the morning on, each day we were in Monte Carlo, the air had been full of the throaty, roaring engines.

And I waited.

After an hour, and having spent the equivalent of nearly thirty dollars for a pastry and a cup of coffee, I walked back to the hotel and asked if there was another message. There was none. I asked if I had misunderstood the previous message; I had not. Well, who exactly was it that sent that message? The concierge had no idea. I went back up to my room. The smell of fuel filled the air now and the sound was deafening and I was growing anxious. I didn't want to miss a moment of the race. I called May's grandparents but they had long since left the villa.

I left my room and walked back to the patisserie, but my so-called escort was not there. I was getting used to the noise and the smells and the crowds, but this morning it was all more intense than ever. The preliminary races had begun; people hung off balconies and out of windows, craning to see the cars go by. I began to despair of finding my way to my VIP place. I had no pass for any of the venues today, and by now they were impossible to get. But I did know the approximate location of where I was supposed to be, and so I set off walking, hiking the steep streets.

The entire town had been readied for this very day; every detail was in place. And that meant that I couldn't see a thing. Barricades had been erected everywhere so that visual access to the circuit was blocked. Every hole had been plugged. I was beside myself. I was going to miss the race.

"MY DEAR, CONSOLE yourself!"

An effeminate scarecrow of a man stopped me outside the lobby of a posh apartment edifice, where I had stopped to catch my breath and get my bearings. I had not been able to get close to where I was supposed to be. I had been stopped, turned away, forbidden to venture further. How could I explain that I was really a VIP? Nobody would be impressed with my credentials. The man, who was dressed in a dark, ill-fitting suit rather out of keeping with the elegant, fun-in-the-sun designer attire of most of the people in the city, carried a bag with a loaf of bread sticking out of it. He shifted a bit to free up one hand, which he laid on my cheek. "Console yourself, Mademoiselle," he said again in thickly accented, elegant English.

I wiped the tears off my face and smiled, embarrassed. "How may I help you, my young damsel in distress?"

He was a comforting figure, old enough to be my grandfather and, I was fairly certain, gay.

"I don't think anyone can help me now," I said. "There was some kind of misunderstanding, and I lost touch with my friends. I was supposed to have a place to see the race, down there—" I waved my arm.

"Down there!" he exclaimed. "You can't go down there, my dear. You'd sooner secure an audience with the prince himself!"

"I know. And now I can't see anything. I can't believe I came all this way, and I won't see him race, after all! And what if he's killed?"

"Ah, but that's what they all come to see, isn't it?" The scarecrow chuckled.

I looked at him, appalled.

"Never mind, my dear, you shall have an excellent location from which to see the race. Come with me."

"Where are we going?"

He was steering me through the lobby and into an absurdly small elevator and then we were ascending floor upon floor upon floor. "You will be happy now!" he exclaimed. "I am Marco Polo."

"I'm Marie Antoinette," I replied. "Pleased to meet you."

"I took you for British, at first, but now I see you are American. I like Americans. But not so much for driving. Not so many good American Formula One drivers, I am sorry to say. You know there is an American driving today?"

"Yes, I know." I was about to tell him I knew this American driver, but then I thought that would probably sound absurd.

We emerged from the elevator and entered an apartment sixteen stories high with views of the race through the streets below. There were perhaps a dozen people already there, most of whom were out on the balcony, leaning over the railing, heads turning in unison as the cars roared by.

I got comfortable at the party, and I started to relax and

roll with the situation. I even thought I saw Gatien's car go by at one point; but then a pretty young Monegasque walked in at the precise moment her boyfriend, a gorgeous flesh-and blood version of Michaelangelo's marble David, decided he wanted to express his appreciation of my neck with his lovely cupid's bow lips. This sent her into a frenzy and, unfortunately for me, it happened to be her apartment, and so I was out on the street again.

I WALKED THROUGH the streets with a sort of blindness. All I had of the race was the sound, the vibration of it, and the smells. The bright sunny weather of the morning had suddenly turned cold and windy, and rain began to spatter down on the narrow streets. I worried for Gatien's safety as the old twisty streets turned slick.

The last part of it is hard to sort out in my memory. I walked and walked. In order to skirt the barricades, I had to climb steps, staircases three stories high, and then descend again. I met some other people who showed me where I could watch the race on a huge screen. I heard the voice of an announcer, but could hardly make out a word.

It was a close finish, but it looked to me like Gatien had won. The engines were deafening. I thought I heard Gatien Defalle' s name, but I couldn't be sure. The way the French pronounced Gatien's name, it sounded different, as if it had a *shh* in the middle of it.

"Who was it?"

Yes, they said, it was Gatien. *Gatien. My Gatien. Gatien Defalle.* He had won the race. I was thrilled, amazed, elated, and frustrated enough to explode at not having seen it for real.

But almost instantly everything changed.

An explosion ripped the air, the ground shuddered for a moment, and a plume of smoke began to rise above the city.

"Bad accident," was all I could understand.

"IT'S THE AMERICAN!" I heard the shouting. "The American is dead."

•   •   •

TURNS OUT EUROPEANS don't think of Gatien as American. Since he was half French, and they loved him, they
forgave and forgot the American part of him. Gatien Defalle was not "the American." When the scarecrow had
spoken of the American, he had been referring to Tobey
Ashcroft, a young Texan driving his first Formula One
season. Tobey was in the car that nearly beat Gatien. He
crossed the finish line a split second after Gatien, and
when his brakes failed and he lost control of his car on the
wet track, he took Gatien with him. It was Tobey who was
killed in the accident, not Gatien.

I didn't know this for something like half an hour,
forty-five minutes, I can't say for sure. The only thing I
remember with any clarity is the mindless need that drove
me to get there, to get to him, to be with him, in whatever
shape he was in. I can't remember how I made my way to
where he was, though I can still conjure up the memory of
how my lungs burned as I ran. I remember barriers were
meaningless, bouncers useless; if I was thwarted or turned
away I tried again, tried somewhere else, until I got
through the barriers and the people and the gates. I shoul-
dered my way through the crowds and eluded the officials
and I finally found him. I remember when I spotted him,
when I saw his face and he saw me, at the same moment.
I nearly cracked open from the release of tension I had
been carrying in my body, suddenly knowing he was
alive, and not even much worse for the wear, from the
look of it—just sweaty and dirty and exhausted looking.
The tears were streaming down my face unbidden and un-
noticed at that point, and when I reached him, thrusting
myself rudely past and between and through all those who
surrounded him, I threw myself against him, wrapped him
in my arms, and laid my head on his heart. I felt his hands
on me, heartbreakingly tentative. He was stunned, dazed,
from his accident, of course. We were jostled apart almost
immediately.

But he was alive. Alive. *Alive.* That's all I cared about.

•   •   •

WHEN I FINALLY met up with May and her grandparents, May and I clung to each other, shaking, tears still streaming. "He's okay, May," I said to her, a repeating mantra we both needed to hear. "He's okay." It was worse for her, in a way; she had actually seen it happen—but she had found out almost immediately that he was all right. We couldn't stop going on and on about it.

At one point I noticed Gatien's stepmother, Zora, studying me with a thoughtful look. She had remained poised; she was used to the fear. But I knew she was badly shaken, too.

Gatien was the hero of the day, surrounded by throngs of overexcited people. It was peculiar, I thought, how the congratulations and even the celebrating went on despite the death of one of the drivers. Gatien himself did not seem to be in a celebratory mood. I didn't see much of him again until later that evening, in the hotel, when he came to fetch me for a party we were going to.

The atmosphere of the night was surreal to me. A party? I was ashamed that I felt so eager to go out tonight.

"Are you ready, Sarah?" Gatien seemed distant, distracted; though I could have sworn he was just a little flustered at the sight of me in my silver cocktail dress. "Come on then," he hurried me, though he was the one who had kept May and me waiting.

"Where is May?" I asked. "I sent her to your suite to look for you."

"Yes, I know. She's gone on with my dad and Zora," he said. "She's going to spend the night with them. They're not coming with us."

"Oh!" I stood there, feeling foolish, dressed for this party without my reason to be going. I was only here in Monte Carlo to tend to May, as I constantly reminded myself. "Then there's no reason for me to go to this party," I said.

He took my arm with polite insistence and escorted me to the door. "Come on, Sarah, it's going to be fun. It's on a yacht."

Chapter Twenty-nine

EVERYONE WANTED TO greet Gatien and congratulate him and kiss him, sleep with him, or just shake
his hand. He had not only won this particular race
today, but he had achieved such success this season that,
despite his late start, he had managed to become a con-
tender for the championship. If he continued to do so well,
the ultimate prize could be his. Because he was the un-
derdog fighting from behind, coming back from a devas-
tating injury, he was particularly beloved by his fans. I
wanted to be happy for him, to sincerely urge him on to
his goal, but what I really wanted was to go home with
him and be with him in our house on Winding Hill Road.

Gatien was at the bar next to the dance floor, drinking
with some friends. The yacht was beautiful, and the swell
of the sea was exhilarating, but I felt out of place, useless
and unneeded without my charge there to anchor my reason for being. Gatien had little to say to me; all evening
long he had been broody and silent. I wandered outside
into the warm windy night. There were couples and small
groups standing on the deck near the railing. Their laugh-

ter and good-natured, drunken shouting was snatched away by the wind.

"Sarah—"

I turned to see Nigel rushing toward me, his coat flapping, his white ruffled shirt unbuttoned, his tie undone.

He stopped before me, out of breath. "Can't tell you how sorry I am about this morning, luv. Had no idea you had enemies—p'raps you should have warned me, eh? Well, you know I had no idea Theta had put me up to no good. She told me plans had changed, there was no need to meet up with you at your hotel. I swear I didn't know she was leading me wrong."

"I know." I actually felt a little sorry for him. When Gatien learned Nigel had disregarded his assignment on the basis of something Theta had told him, his cool, controlled anger reverberated through team management and was enough to make poor Sir Lancelot fear for his job.

"Really, I had no idea. Why would I doubt her? She was a friend of his, or so I thought."

"It's okay, Nigel, really," I assured him, and I moved away.

"I made sure she didn't board the yacht, this evening, if that helps—" he called after me. He wanted to keep talking about it, but I wasn't in the mood right now. I didn't care about Theta and her little tricks or Nigel's justifications. All I could think about was Gatien, and how I might have lost him for good today.

I climbed a stairway to the upper deck, where several couples huddled together in the darkness, looking off over the back of the boat at the moon. I felt awkward, self-consciously alone, but I liked the rocking of the waves, and the clean, salty taste of the air. The glamour and the adventure of it all had dulled for me since this afternoon. None of it meant anything without life. A man was dead. It might have been Gatien. It might be any of us, at any time. I felt grateful just to be there, experiencing that moment. Alive. In love. Even if it turned out to be unrequited love.

I climbed another set of stairs and arrived at a small observation deck with a bench and railing around it, so that I was all alone and high in my own little crow's nest, the wind whipping my silk wrap around me, and my hair, long enough now to blow in a breeze, flying wildly. I would look a wreck when I went back down into the party, but I didn't care; I had found my spot, and I drank in the wind, alone and high over the water.

Gatien was completely innocent, and all my hesitations about him had gone; I even understood his strange lack of physical affection for his daughter. Instead of branding him a bad parent, I had come to understand he was an exceptional one. There was nothing holding me back from him, not anymore. I would give myself completely. I suppose I already had. What a cosmic joke, that I was the one who had put an end to it when he would have pressed for more. But now our old ways had been reestablished, all formal and businesslike and separate. He even knew what had happened now, understood why I had balked, but it hadn't made any difference. My world and his were so far apart, and the longer I was with him the more I understood that. This party on this yacht, for example. I was Cinderella at the ball, but it was past midnight. I had lost my chance with him, if I'd ever had a chance. The glass slipper never did fit me, anyway.

I peered off through the wind, straining to see the horizon, distant and dark, pierced by the lights on the water and the stars in the sky. I looked up at the bowl of sky lit with constellations. I thought I still heard the roaring of the Formula One engines in my ears. I rode that way for a long time, looking out, the motion of the yacht moving through my legs. I loved the feel of it, of the wind against my skin, and the smell of the sea, the music and laughter floating up from below, the rocking of the waves, and now the metallic clang of footsteps ascending the staircase.

Someone was climbing up to me. In the darkness, I saw the bulk of his shoulders, the crazy wind-whipped hair. I leaned over to see him, my own hair thrashing madly around me. I reached out instinctively, and he took my hand as he topped the stairs. The boat lurched, throwing us together. He grabbed me and trapped me against the railing, almost hurting me with the weight of his body, like he was afraid if he let go, I'd throw myself over the railing or be tossed overboard by a wave. I held fast to him and to the railing, while he stared into my eyes, intense and serious in the dark.

"You love me, don't you, Sarah?" I heard his voice over the wind.

"Yes, I do," I answered.

"I mean you're *in love with me.*"

"How did you know?"

He sighed and pressed his forehead against mine. "I knew this afternoon, when you forced your way through the crowd to get to me. When I saw your face. That's when I knew."

He lifted his face and stared into my eyes, unsmiling.

He had nailed me; I couldn't hide it, didn't want to hide it, but I felt open and exposed and vulnerable.

"And yet, really," I teased him, to mask my overwhelming emotions, "it hasn't been so long since you didn't even exist for me, Gatien Defalle."

"A year," he said. "It was a year ago almost to the day that I first heard of you. It was late May or early June, and Helene said to me, 'I believe I've found the perfect girl for you, Gatien.'" He dipped his fingers into the hollow of my throat, traced the line along my collarbone. "And you know what? She was right."

He did not tell me he loved me back, not that I was waiting to hear it from him. I was nearly driven past thinking at that point, the way his hands were on me, except to wonder why he wasn't kissing me.

"God, I've missed you," he said. "I want to tear into you."

The strange familiarity of him! It was so good. *So good.*

We weren't holding onto the railing anymore, only to each other. We might have made love then and there, but the ship lurched, and I cried out.

"Come with me, Sarah," said Gatien with decisive

verve, taking me by the hand. I followed him down the stairs, three flights of them, down past the dance floor and the bar, slipping through the darkness outside to avoid meeting anyone, down and down to the lower deck. Gatien led me through a door from the outside deck into a quiet hallway. We could hear the party above, the laughter and music. He opened a door to a room off the hall and stood aside to let me through.

I entered tentatively. It was a stateroom, a spacious bedroom suite, all luxurious sensuality and nautical elegance, with caramel blond wood veneers and polished brass fixtures. He slid the latch on the door.

I went to the large porthole over the bed and drew the curtains, stared outside. All was blackness, except for a row of lights blinking in the distance, and all was silence but for the muffled roar of the engines, and the sound of the water lapping against the side of the yacht.

I felt Gatien's hands on my arms, his fingers spreading over me as he turned me like a dancer to face him and he gathered me in his arms, and his mouth sought mine, finally, finally, finally. I tasted the trembling hunger. His mouth on my neck, bodies arching, curving together with a gasp. We swayed together to the caressing movement of the waves.

The voice of insecurity rose in me: *Whose stateroom is this? What right have I to be in here?*

But of course *I* had no right. *He* did, however: this was the night of the Monaco Grand Prix, and Gatien Defalle was the conquering hero. He had the right to the finest suite in the house, or, in this case, the ship. My girlfriend Mallory was right; he had the power in this relationship. He had the status, he had the fame and fortune, he had the ability to make this decision now, that we be together, he and I, here on this yacht, rocking on the waves in this large, solid bed that dominated the room. He had all that, and he had a beautiful, weary body that was roused and primed to claim the spoils of his victory. And strangely, he was offering all of it to me. I sensed the generosity in him, and I sensed that when he gave, he would give it all. It was an overwhelming, luminous thing.

What did I have to give him in return? All I had to offer was myself.

The way he was kissing me now, it was like something I had once glimpsed when we kissed—it seemed so long ago now—in Mendocino. I thought of those days with tender agony, and it was with shame that I remembered deliberately hardening my emotions, regarding Gatien with a list of judgments that precluded real involvement. But even then I was falling in love with him. I couldn't help myself.

Women, as Mallory would say, are exhorted to play by the rules, to play hard to get, to conceal our feelings from our man, at least until we've caught him. And after all, there *is* something to playing hard to get; it works for men as well as women. But that night with Gatien, when he told me I was in love with him, and I had not denied it— letting go of coy pride, throwing it to the wind—I had somehow discovered the magical key that brought him home to me, and I found him here in the middle of a dark exotic sea, pressed against my heart.

The sex was different, too. I was no longer thinking of technique or his exceptional physical prowess or his experience with others, because this was something completely beyond mechanical interactions, and it was just between the two of us. This was holy communion. The sweetness of him was unbearable. When he had me completely undone, he began to whisper my name, and whisper that he loved me, in English and in French.

And unlike last time, when it was so easy with him it was like my body was an oak leaf spinning on the surface of a river, falling easily over the rapids, again and again, this time I couldn't come.

I've found my way to the sea, I thought. *I'm so deep in, there's no more falling.*

"No, you go on without me," I told him, panting, when he finally called me on it. "I can't. It's too—it's too much. I can't." My body was slick with sweat, my hair drenched, my breasts heaving. I tried to explain. "I missed that tributary half an hour ago. You kept me swirling and whirling down the river—"

He began to massage my back. I relaxed, loved the weight of him on me, on the back of my thighs. He stretched out over me and crouched down, and I felt his soft hair between my legs. Slowly he moved up between my legs, and I felt his hot mouth on me.

"I CAN'T STOP thinking about it," I said.

Gatien's hand was on my hair, stroking slowly. "Can't stop thinking about what?" he asked.

"About what happened in those cars this afternoon."

"I'd rather you couldn't stop thinking about what happened in this bed a few minutes ago," Gatien replied. He was rather pleased with himself, having made me do what I had sworn I couldn't do.

"I told myself I'd never say this," I said. "But I want to beg you not to do it again."

"To do what?" he asked, with mock alarm.

"To get into one of those rockets, and blast off, and—"

He began to laugh. "You mean to race?"

"Yes. I hate to say it, and I'm sorry. I'm just like all the rest of them, nagging you about the racing. I know you don't want to hear it from me, but there you are!"

"Sarah, you're the only woman I ever wanted to hear it from. I didn't think you cared *what* I did."

"I care too much. I have cared too much about anything you did, from the moment I met you. From *before* I met you."

"Good," he said. "I like that."

"Fine," I said, grumpy. "I'm glad you like that. But what about me and my poor heart? I thought I had lost you today. It was intolerable."

"Answer me something honestly, Sarah. What would you think of me, if I no longer raced? Would you still want me?"

"That's a ridiculous question. I think it's obvious I wanted you before I knew you could even *drive*."

"I have tried to draw the same conclusion, but I have to admit I was worried."

"Worried? Why?"

"Insecurity, I guess. A lot of my identity has been wrapped up in my driving, for a long time. After Lisa died, and I was suddenly a single father, I began to see the life just wasn't working for me anymore. Hadn't been working for awhile; Lisa was right. Without her there to challenge me on it, I stopped resisting. I noticed something had changed; it wasn't in my blood anymore, not in the same way. For some time now, even before my accident, I have been attempting to structure my life so that I could still be involved in Formula One and yet retire from driving. I've been working with some constructors, and a couple of investors, and I've been talking to some people who are trying to bring something to the Bay Area. And then after the accident, I thought the decision had been made for me, that I'd retire even earlier than I'd thought. I thought I was finished with racing. But then you came along and goaded me back to it."

"Me and my big mouth."

"I wanted to show off for you, Sarah. And I think it was good for me, and for my career in the long run, that I was able to make a comeback. It's given me something I thought I'd lost. But then I began to worry that if I did stop driving, you wouldn't want me anymore. . . . So I am asking you, now . . . how would you feel if I no longer raced?"

"I would feel relieved."

"Honestly?" He sighed. "Then I'm relieved, too."

"The only thing that worries me is, you seem to be so good at it, and so popular. . . . Do you really want to leave this life? Would you be happy without it?"

"I used to wonder the same thing. But for the past few years I have derived very little satisfaction from racing. It was one thing when I was passionate and one-pointed about driving, about winning. But at this time in my life, it's not the main thing anymore, and it's not something I want to do when I have a wife and a family. Do you understand what I am saying, Sarah?"

A wife and a family. Yes, I think I understood.

"And whenever you're ready, I want to tell May about us. Because there *is* an *us*, isn't there?"

"I read what you wrote in your notebook," I said.

"My what?"

"The day of Mr. Browning's funeral. You gave me your notebook when you went up to speak. It fell open to one particular page."

"Oh." He blushed furiously, but he kept his composure. "I think I know that page you're talking about."

"You wrote, *I can't make love with you, Sarah.*"

"Something like that," he said with dry humor.

"You couldn't make love with me, because of *her*. . . ."

"Yeah."

"You meant May."

"Right. I had to be really careful about May. In any other circumstances, Sarah, I could not have held myself back from you for so long . . . but you are her *caretaker.* How is that going to affect her? She's already messed up because a man, her father, used sex to hurt her. Do you see what I mean?"

"Of course. I have the same concerns; you know I do. But at the time, I thought *her* was Theta."

"Theta?" He looked blank.

"I thought you were having an affair with Theta."

"I've never slept with Theta," he said.

I let out what had been a tightly held breath.

"You aren't worried about Theta, are you?" He seemed both concerned and delighted by my jealousy.

"Well," I said slowly. "She's so obviously willing. And she's very beautiful."

"She has her moments, I guess. There was a time, long ago, if she hadn't been with Paul, sure, I would have gone for the offer. The ironic thing is, it's because of *him* that I never did. He was my friend. Not that she was ever that tempting to begin with."

"Come on. Must be *somewhat* tempting."

"To tell you the truth, no, it isn't tempting at all anymore. I just think of her as a pain in the ass. It's not a turn-on. I don't respect her. I don't even like her much. Mainly because of how she treated her husband. My best friend. My ex–best friend."

"You've got to get over that."

"You know why Paul and I got into it, don't you?"

"You told me he accused you of sleeping with his wife."

"Right. But things really got heated when I forbade him to sleep with *you.* I know I had no right, but I won't apologize for that."

"Seems to be something in the air. Do you know, just the other day Theta warned me to stay away from *you?*"

"Is that so?"

"Yep. In fact, she said if I didn't back off, she would have to resort to using *dirty* tactics."

"But you didn't let that stop you."

"Obviously, no, I didn't."

"There's my brave girl."

"I'm sorry about backing off from you, Gatien, when I didn't know about May. I'm sorry I thought—"

"No, I'm the one who is sorry, that I didn't tell you before it got to that point. And I'm sorry I lost my temper in the library that day. I hope those old books of yours are okay."

"They're actually yours, you know," I said drolly. "Yeah, I think they'll be okay. The binding on one of them broke, split down the spine, and the stuffing is coming out of the cover, but I think it can be repair—" I stopped, struck dumb with a new thought.

"What is it?" Gatien asked. "What is it, Sarah?"

"That just made me think of something."

"You didn't leave the coffeemaker on at home, did you?"

"I told you how I found those books in the storeroom, in the garage. The box hadn't even been opened. It was shipped from Spain, right before your wife's death—"

"Lisa was still waiting for more of that shipment when

she died, but I don't recall ever receiving anything else. I
didn't think much about it; we already knew she'd been
scammed."

"I'm not so sure she *was* scammed, Gatien."

He looked at me, waiting for me to explain that.

"What was she expecting in that shipment?" I asked.

He sighed. Clearly he was reluctant to delve into the
subject. But he could see I would not be put off this time.

"I don't know that much about it, to tell you the truth,"
he said. "It was Lisa's hobby, not mine. I thought, if she's
having fun, why not? A few months before she died, we
were in Spain, and we met this old count—he was the
grandfather of one of the drivers on my team—and when
he heard Lisa was interested in that sort of thing, ancient
manuscripts and such, he invited us up to his castle, yes,
a real castle. He told us, quite casually, about an old abbey
in Spain that was going out of business, so to say, being
dismantled and sold off, piece by piece, from the stones of
the building on down to the pews and reliquaries. Parts of
the abbey itself dated back to the middle ages, but supposedly there were manuscripts in the abbey library much
older than that. So my wife bought a portion of the abbey
library."

"A lady after my own heart,"I said.

"She bought all this stuff, sight unseen, trusting this
guy. I knew she was going to make a purchase, but I had
no idea the extent of what she had invested. I only learned
of it when Helene tried to stop the transaction; Lisa had
borrowed some money from her father, unbeknownst to
me. But Helene was too late; the sale had already gone
through. Shortly after that, we got word that the count was
dead. He was an old man, though he had seemed perfectly
healthy when we visited him. But something went off in
his heart. Well, Lisa received a couple boxes of books.
They were slow in coming, and she was supposed to re-
ceive more than what she did. She went through what she
did get, then she had some of her so-called experts go
through it, and they couldn't find anything older than
some illuminated manuscripts dating from about 1400."

"That's pretty darned old," I pointed out.

"Yeah, that's old, but not old enough or important enough to justify the price my wife paid for the lot, I'm afraid. So what's going on in that brain of yours?" he asked me fondly. "I can just see the wheels turning."

"Oh, you can, huh?" I laughed.

"Yes, I am very good at spotting wheels turning. So tell me, did you discover anything of earth-shattering importance in that box of books you found, my little snoop?"

"You know what? I'm not sure yet. I have an idea, but I need to check it out. And I can't do that until I get home. So I'll let you know. Okay?"

"I guess it's not going to do me any good at all to ask you to leave it alone."

"Probably not. But why don't you tell me why you think I *should* leave it alone? You've always been so cagey about the whole thing."

"When I got home after Lisa's funeral, I went to her library and I noticed immediately that something was different. It wasn't ransacked like it was on New Year's Eve, but I knew someone had been in there while we were gone. Lisa's computer was on, which it hadn't been when I left, and I had been in that room right before we went to the church. I was already suspicious about the whole rare-book deal, because it looked like my wife had been swindled. Then she's found dead under suspicious circumstances. The day of her funeral I come home to find someone has been in her library. And several boxes of the shipment Lisa bought are still unaccounted for, though the shipping company claims they were delivered."

"And the one I found—"

"Accounts for a small portion of what more there should be. And what she did get from that abbey, though of fine quality I'm told, was nothing of great antiquity or importance. It appears that the gallant old gent who took a fancy to my wife was actually a con artist."

"But why all the interest?" I asked. "If there was nothing to it? Isaac said there were those who would kill to get a look at Lisa's library."

"With Isaac, it was probably a figure of speech," Gatien said.

Similar to how I had declared that I would have to kill Gatien if I found out he had been the one to hurt May.

"He was the guy who appraised Lisa's stuff. He knew what she had, and what she didn't have. But the story gets out, rumors get started. Then again, I've wondered if maybe there was something to that old Spaniard. Maybe he was for real—but someone else beat us to the stuff. When I get suspicious, I start thinking like that. And I wonder about my wife's death. And I wonder who came into our house and turned on her computer when everyone who knew her was at the funeral. And I wonder what the hell happened to the rest of that shipment of stuff from that Spanish monastery. It worries me, Sarah, because it doesn't seem to let up. The library was vandalized on New Year's Eve. Then someone set fire to your cottage. We get visits from strange gentlemen—"

"Ira and Moshe," I said. "The scholar and the businessman. You know, they're actually quite sweet, the two of them."

He refused to comment on that. "Is it a pattern? I don't know. Or a random series of strange, unrelated incidents? I find that difficult to believe. Anyway, it worries me, you and May home alone. And that's really all I know, Sarah," he said to me wearily. "I don't know what to make of it. But it sure seems strange to me. And that's why I wish you would leave it alone. But you won't. You've got a hunch. . . ."

He looked at me hard. "You once said I didn't want to let you in on it, Sarah; you accused me of wanting to keep whatever it is for myself. The truth is, my main motivation for trying to keep you out of that library, out of that whole business, if I could have, was simply to protect you. I'm scared for you, Sarah. I can't prove anything, but I can't help thinking my wife died because of something she had in her library. If the same thing happened to you . . ." He stopped a moment, took a deep breath. "I have absolutely no interest in any of it myself. Sarah, I closed off the library because I don't want anything to do with it, and I don't want May, or Louisa—or you—to get involved with it, because I don't want you hurt."

"But you put my books in there," I said. "After you forbade me to go in there." It was something I'd wondered about, since he'd done it.

"I could see you loved the place, and I knew I'd only entice you further if I kept forbidding you to enter, so I thought I'd give your books a home there; then maybe you'd relax and wouldn't be so interested in poking around."

Funny, I thought. *That was kind of how it had worked, too. For a while, anyway.*

I wondered if he'd press for more information, insist I tell him my sudden insights, but he had never seemed terribly interested in anything to do with Lisa's library, and he didn't appear to be all that interested in it now. In fact, he seemed more interested in other matters, and in moments he had me giggling uncontrollably. The giggling subsided into deep, rapid breathing.

"Gatien." I sighed, drunk with his touch. "We have to stop. We have to get out of here. They're going to be looking for you. Everyone is always looking for you. *Everyone* wants you."

"To hell with everyone," he said. "I only want you."

Chapter Thirty

WELL?" SAID MAY.
I looked up at her questioningly. I was sitting on the bed in the hotel writing postcards. Her grandparents had just dropped her off; we were to meet them in a couple of hours for lunch. Gatien was at the paddock.

Her arms were folded, and she had a very demanding and determined look on her face.

"Isn't there something you'd like to tell me, Sarah?"

"What?" I asked innocently, setting down my pen.

"What?" she mimicked me. "You're crazy about him. Right? And I suppose he feels the same about *you.*"

I was speechless.

"You're not going to deny it, are you?"

"May . . . I can't deny it."

"I know you can't." She sounded angry. "So we're stuck with each other, aren't we?"

"May, I—" I was flustered. This wasn't how we'd planned to do it. "He wanted to tell you," I said. "We wanted to tell you together."

"It doesn't matter." She shrugged. "I already knew."

"What do you mean, you already knew?" I cried, righteous about this point, at least. "There was nothing to know! Not until last night, anyway," I added. "And last night, as soon as we . . . as soon as we knew, we decided to talk to you about . . . it."

"I've known about *it* from the first day I ever saw you two together, in my mother's library," May said dully.

"Really?" I was ready to argue about it, but what could I say? "Well . . . what do you think?" I asked her humbly. I felt vulnerable, for all of us.

"I think it's good. I'm not thrilled—please don't expect me to be. But I can see you make him happy, and so it would be awfully selfish of me to object, wouldn't it? I have to admit, the idea of sharing Gato with some new girlfriend has never appealed to me, though I knew, after my mom died, it was inevitable. But there's something about you, Sarah. It's like, even though I have to share him with you, you bring something out in him that opens him up to *me* more, you know what I mean? So in a way, I have more of him, since you came. I don't know if that makes any sense."

"I don't know if it does, either," I said. "But I understand what you're saying. And I thank you for it."

We heard the door to the suite open, and suddenly Gatien was there, standing in the doorway of the bedroom, looking at the two of us. We all looked at each other, and we all knew that we all knew.

"I know you wanted to tell me all about it yourself," May said to him. "But I didn't need anybody to tell me. I've got eyes, haven't I?"

"Ah, *It's a Wonderful Life*," he said. "May, I should have known you would be one step ahead of me."

"Don't worry, Gato," said May. "I think Sarah will make an okay stepmother."

"May, come on, don't scare her off," Gatien warned, catching my look of alarm. He came to us, stood by the side of the bed, and gathered us both in his embrace. "I think she will, too," he whispered loudly in May's ear.

May and I snaked arms around each other, and around

him, so that we were a circle, me sitting cross-legged on
the bed, the two of them standing beside me.

"My ladies," he said. "I can tell you honestly that being
a family will not always be an easy thing. But there's
nothing I want more than to make a go of it with the two
of you."

"Aww," said May.

SAYING GOOD-BYE TO Gatien was excruciating, and yet
it was with a certain relief that I felt the plane lift from
European soil. I was glad for the time to think, to gather
perspective, and reflect on what had happened between
Gatien and me. Besides, I was still so high from our
union I could hardly be persuaded to be sad, though I
wasn't sure when we'd see one another again. It was increasingly clear he was the driver to watch in this ongo-
ing Formula One contest, and even I could see he needed
to do his job without distraction. I wanted him to win, but
more than that, I wanted him to stay safe so he could
come back to me.

As soon as May and I were settled in at home, I pur-
sued my hunch about the old books. I called Isaac at his
studio, and when I got no answer there, I called the home
number he had once given me. I didn't get Isaac, but I did
talk to his wife, Rachel. An hour later I was driving to
their home in Palo Alto.

Rachel and I had struck up a conversation on the
phone, and I found her to be very interested in what I had
to say. Turns out she was every bit the expert that her husband was, and she invited me to come see her and show
her what I had found.

She was about thirty-five, with the sort of coloring I
had always admired: black hair and dark eyes and the kind
of skin that never flushed or burned red in the sun but only
deepened and became more lustrous.

"Come in, Sarah." She greeted me with a firm hand-
shake and a friendly smile over a bite of large white teeth.
"Isaac told me he met you, last New Year's Eve, right?
Isn't it interesting, all that mystery surrounding Lisa's li-

brary? It's so funny. She would have laughed if she'd known. Let's see what you've got there."

She showed me to her studio, a large, tree-shaded room that was obviously a later addition to the charming craftsman-style house she shared with her husband.

"We all wanted it to be something, you know?" she said as she got to work, readying the space, putting on gloves. "This thing of Lisa's. It was such a great story, and it would have been so exciting. And I would have loved it, for her sake, if it had turned out to be something. She was a friend of mine, you know."

"No, I didn't know."

There was something capable about Rachel, and I felt, for the first time since this entire old book mystery began, that I was in good hands. Or rather, the books were. I watched her with awe. She handled the books far more casually, and yet with a more careful assurance, than I had been able to do. Examining the material, her excitement became obvious.

"I think you just might have yourself something here, Sarah," she said without glancing up at me. Her entire attention was riveted on the flakes coming out of the split in the book cover. "Yes. Look, here's a nice big piece.

"In the middle ages," she explained, "book covers were often stuffed with older documents that were thought to have no value. You know, for padding, to make the book covers firm. It appears that these books are filled with fragments of something . . . it'll take some time to know more, but this appears to me to be something special."

She looked up at me at last, her eyes shining.

SEVERAL DAYS AFTER we returned to Winding Hill Road, May's father showed up at our door. He asked to see May, and I turned him down flat.

He looked mildly offended. "You don't seem to realize who I am," he said.

"I know exactly who you are," I replied. "And right now, at this time in her life, you are not to see her."

"I'm her father. She's none of your concern, whoever you are."

"On the contrary, she's entirely my concern," I said. "I'm her mother now. When she's of age, she can decide what she wants to do. She may want to see you, she may not, that's up to her, but right now I am her guardian, and I say no dice."

"I don't think you understand the situation."

"I understand enough. You messed with her, she tried to pretend it never happened and make a new life for herself, but that's worked only so well up until now, and you don't seem to want to let it go. She's not as willing to hide from what you did to her as she once was. She's been talking about pressing charges against you. I am not sure it's the right thing to do, for her sake. But if she—"

"Listen, Lady Madonna." The pockmarked face gleamed, and for the first time he was really looking at me, staring, with a calm intensity that scared me. "Don't try to threaten me. That girl is my daughter. I don't know what kind of rubbish she's been fed about me, but it's irrelevant to me what you think of me anyway. You give my regards to my daughter." And that was all he said; he turned on his heel and was off. I waited until he had passed the gate and a few moments had passed, to make sure he was really gone.

I closed the door and turned to see May standing there. She had been behind me all the time, hiding from her father, listening.

"You're not my mother," she said flatly.

I opened my mouth, too surprised and flustered to come up with an appropriate, quick response to that.

"But I appreciate you saying it," she added.

I blew out a breath of something like relief. "I'm sorry, May," I said. "I just said the first thing that came to mind. I would never try to take the place of your mother."

"Well, you got to him, I think," she said. "Especially the part about pressing charges. I don't think we'll be seeing him again anytime soon."

"If I overstepped my boundaries, saying what I said, I apologize."

"No. What you said was—it was good, Sarah. You defended me. You make me feel safe."

I shook my head, wondering. I was questioning all my perceptions these days.

"And maybe I will," she said. "Maybe I *will* press charges."

"I just said that to, you know, to scare him, but . . ."

"I know."

"And I don't think I scared him much."

"Oh, I don't know. He pretty much up and left, right after you said all that stuff."

"You know what? You're right."

"I know I'm right." She tried to suppress a giggle. It was such a strange and solemn occasion—imagine having to *hide* from your own *father*—a giggle just didn't seem proper, which was why she tried to suppress it. But the harder she tried to suppress it, the harder it became to suppress it. She lost control and snorted out a laugh. I caught it like an infection. I tried to stop it, too, but that only made it worse. We gave in to it, laughing and laughing hysterically without stopping until finally we could laugh no more.

We ended up sitting on the floor of the entry hall, cradling our sore bellies, totally spent, worn out, all the tension gone out of us, and completely bonded.

Having decided we were famished, May and I resolved to make pizza, and we were helping each other to our feet when there was another knock at the front door. We looked at each other warily. I went to the door and breathed a sigh of relief to find it was the neighbor boy, Daniel.

"Hi," he said politely. "Is May home? Oh, hi, May."

"Hi," she said.

It was an awkward moment. I wanted to invite him in, but I didn't want to upset May. He had come to see her, I thought, so I began to withdraw, to let them talk.

"Excuse me," he said. "There was something I wanted to tell both of you."

I hesitated; May and I were giving him our full attention now.

"I found out that some flowers I left on your porch one time were poisonous. I heard you almost ate one."

For a moment, May and I looked at each other, baffled.

"It was a long time ago," he explained. "But I always felt bad about it, and I wanted to tell you."

"Oh," said May, remembering.

I remembered, too. "The big white bells," I said. "Oh, don't worry about it. We wouldn't have really eaten them. They were beautiful flowers."

"Well, I just wanted to tell you I didn't mean any harm. I didn't know they were poisonous. I just wanted to give you some flowers." He was looking at May now. He added earnestly, "I am really sorry."

"That's okay, Daniel," May said. It was the most civil I had ever heard her speak to him.

"Well, that's the reason why I came," he said.

"Okay," said May.

"See you later."

"Thank you. Daniel," I said.

"No problem."

He loped off and was nearly to the end of the driveway when May called out. "Yeah, thank you, Daniel."

He didn't look back or answer, but he gave a leap as he ran along.

Chapter Thirty-one

I N THE MORNING May was up before me, doing some last-minute laundry so she could finish packing for a weekend trip with Dimitri to his mom's house. I wasn't worried about Dimitri and May anymore. Well, not as much, anyway. I knew she wouldn't trust him so completely if he had ever treated her with the slightest impropriety. It was a bittersweet occasion; it was the last of Dimitri we would see for awhile, as he was going away to college in southern California.

Before they set out, Dimitri made a point of catching me alone in the kitchen, where I was packing a small ice chest for them to take.

"This is for you," I said. "I put in some juice and some string cheese and some fruit—"

"Cool," he said. "Thanks."

"So you're heading off to school next week, I hear," I said.

"Yep. Still a few weeks before the quarter starts, but I gotta find a place to live and stuff like that."

"Helene is going to miss you, Dimitri. I mean, we *all* will—"

"I hope so."

"—but what will she do without you?"

"Yeah, she was sobbing a few minutes ago, when we left the house. I'm leaving for school from my mom's house, you know. So with Helene it was like, good-bye."

"She was really sobbing?"

"No. Cool as a cucumber, actually, but she packed us cookies, not just healthy stuff like you."

"Oh, I see how it is."

"Sarah, there's something I need to talk to you about."

"Sure, what?"

He looked down a moment, scowling. "Okay," he said. "On the day of Aunt Lisa's funeral, I had Aunt Helene's car, you know, because she had to go to the church early with the SUV, for the flowers, so she let me take the Mercedes. . . . Anyway, they had this reception after the funeral, you know, and I cut out early. I guess the whole thing was just starting to get to me, I don't know. So, anyway, on my way home, I stopped by the Defalles' because"—and now he reddened shamefacedly—"because I wanted to see if I could get back a book that I'd lent to Lisa. I didn't want to ask for the book from the family, you know, it seemed like a tacky thing to do. But I wanted it back. So I snuck into their house—everyone knew where the extra key was hidden, until Gatien had that security system installed—and I went into Lisa's library.

"Anyway, so while I'm in there, I decide to get on the computer, check my E-mail and stuff, 'cause I don't know when I'll be able to use a computer again. Helene didn't have one—we always used Lisa's. In fact, I used to think Aunt Helene used Lisa's computer more than Lisa did. Why didn't she just buy her own? It used to drive me crazy. Anyway, I fired up the computer and got on-line with Lisa's password—she'd let me use it before, because Aunt Helene didn't have a computer, like I said, so I knew it—and I checked it out.

"And all the time, I'm thinking it's weird how Lisa supposedly killed herself. I'm no psychiatrist, but she just didn't seem suicidal to me. I'm wondering, what was going on in her head? What was she thinking about? And sitting there, playing around on the computer, I find myself wondering, what were the last Internet sites she visited? Easy enough to find out. So, just out of curiosity, I pulled down the list of the most recent sites visited, and I see some sites for funeral parlors and cremation services, stuff like that. And it occurs to me that *Helene* was the last one to use the computer, not Lisa." He stopped and looked at me significantly.

"So I scroll down past the funeral stuff, and I find this."

"What is it?"

"Tide tables. You know, listing when it's going to be low tide, high tide. I printed them out. And look, here's a schedule of spring tides. That's when the tides are in really high, because of the strong gravitational pull of the moon when it's lined up with the earth and the sun. It's actually nothing to do with the time of year. But they have them all calculated. You can read these tide tables and see when the really low and really high tides are. I thought that was significant, seeing that Lisa was just found dead, washed ashore from the ocean. It just so happens that the day she was drowned, not only was it a spring tide, but the moon was at perigee—closest to earth—when its pull on the tides is the strongest."

I wasn't exactly sure what Dimitri was driving at, but one thing struck me above all else: it had been Dimitri who had come into the Defalles' during Lisa's funeral and turned on her computer. It was something as innocent as a teenage kid sneaking into his aunt's house to retrieve his own property. I felt very happy to hear this. Perhaps all the other creepy things that had happened over the past year were nothing more than these kinds of coincidences. Like Daniel leaving poisonous flowers for May, without realizing they were poisonous, or May's dad showing up out of nowhere, calling himself the Lone Wolf; an unpleasant encounter, but not part of a larger, sinister pattern.

I had the feeling Dimitri was about to say more, but at that moment his mother appeared, coming in from the dining room.

"I want you to have this, Sarah," he said quickly. "And follow up on it. Check out these sites." He thrust the rolled-up computer printout into my hand.

I recoiled slightly from the offering but accepted it meekly, like it was a doomsday tract from an evangelist on a street corner. I glanced at the material Dimitri had given me. *Tide tables,* I thought. Why would anyone need tide tables, if not for boating or fishing or beachcombing? Why would Lisa want them? Did she use them to plan the best time to get swept away by the sea?

I was surprised that Dimitri, who had been so vocal in his doubt about Lisa's death being a suicide, would at last concede that she had actually planned her own demise. But then Dimitri was growing up. He seemed far more mature than he had just a year ago, when I'd met him. He was going away to college, and obviously he was ready to be on his own. Maybe he was giving up his youthful affectations. I had always thought he used Lisa's mysterious death as a sort of shock tool when he spoke to me. It could be that he no longer had any need for such an attention-grabbing ploy.

"I won't be here to watch over you and May anymore," he said. "You be careful, Sarah."

"I will," I promised.

"So, anyway, Sarah," he said brightly, as his mother joined us. "I have yet to congratulate you on your great archeological discovery."

"The ancient manuscript fragments, yes."

"You're quite the celebrity now," said Kate, who seemed keenly interested in anything to do with the ancient manuscripts. She had been one of the most excited to hear the news of our discovery, when May and I had told the family.

"Oh yes. My fifteen minutes of fame. I have been interviewed by the *Palo Alto Daily News*, the *San Francisco Chronicle*, and *People* magazine! Oh, and there was a message from somebody who claims to represent the legal interests of the country of Spain, who is threatening to sue for repossession of the ancient Hebrew scroll fragments, saying they were illegally sold out of the country."

"How very exciting!" Kate laughed.

"Yeah," I said. "I'm having a great time. It's so incredible. We have no idea the extent of what might be there, but there's a fragment of the book of Ecclesiastes that may turn out to be older than any copy of the text in existence."

"It's incredible to think it could have lasted that long."

"I guess it's helped that the fragments have been preserved for centuries inside the leather bindings of books. Sealed from air, from light . . ."

"So how many have they found?"

"They're still uncovering them. Did Helene tell you that there were almost a dozen other boxes of books stashed around the house?"

"Yeah," Dimitri said. "She said you found a bunch of them up in the attic above the hallway."

"Well, I didn't find them. Louisa told me they were there."

"Ah, Louisa was holding out on us, huh?"

"Yeah, I guess Louisa hadn't been working here long when she received a box of books that was delivered to the house, and she didn't know what to do with it, so she had Carlos put it in the storeroom. When more were delivered, she decided to store them up in the attic to get them out of the way. There was already some old furniture up there and stuff like that, so it was a natural. Then after awhile she wondered if she'd been right to do that, but by then she didn't want to confess to what she'd done, and the master of the house didn't seem to care, anyway. But when she heard how valuable the first box of books might be, she finally admitted there were more where that came from!"

"That's great," Dimitri said, laughing. "That sounds like our Louisa."

"You know," I said. "It's a shame Lisa didn't live to see what she really had. It seems so unfair, you know, that it isn't her who gets to enjoy all this."

"Oh, I know," said Kate. "She would have been so

thrilled about it. It is so sad. I mean, everyone is just *so* excited by this discovery of yours."

"Not everybody," Dimitri remarked. "Not Aunt Helene."

"Really? What do you mean?" I asked him.

" 'Such a lot of fuss about a heap of aged paper! To think I had at last begun to feel confident the furor surrounding Lisa's library was dying down, and instead we have it reborn on a whole new level!' " Dimitri's imitation of Helene's prim, mannish voice and manner was uncannily accurate, so much so that Kate and I burst into laughter.

"I had no idea she felt that way!" I cried. "She's always seemed so supportive! And interested . . . that is, *politely* interested." I laughed again. "Oh well!"

"Helene is nothing if not polite," said Kate. "But when it comes to anything to do with Lisa, she's got her issues. She's always been jealous of Lisa."

"Really?" I was mystified. Helene had never struck me as being in any way jealous of Lisa.

"Sure," said Kate. "Well, Lisa got our mom, you know. Helene got their dad. It should have been a fair split. But you can't divide kids, when you divorce, like you divide your furniture and other possessions. Lisa resented the setup and made a point of running away to California when she was a young girl. Made a big fuss to get her father's attention. He paid attention to her, all right, but she had to go back to Las Vegas, eventually; Mom had custody. But when Mom died, Lisa was seventeen years old, and there was nothing holding her back anymore. She reached out to her dad again, and pretty soon they were as close as two peas in a pod. Lisa's dad doted on her, you know. Well, she was sweet, easy to love. He showered her with affection. Presents. Cash. Indulgences he probably shouldn't have—bailed her out of situations so she didn't get to feel the consequences, which meant it took longer for her to learn her lessons. When our mother was alive, it wasn't so much that way. Once Mom died, he kind of went overboard. Well, Helene didn't like *that* one bit."

"Helene says Lisa was a lot of trouble for their dad. Caused him lots of trauma and heartache."

"Cost him lots of money, is more like it!" laughed Kate. "It's easy for me to joke about it. He wasn't my dad, you know. I came along after the big breakup. Mom married my dad after she divorced Lisa and Helene's dad. Sure, Lisa did some wild stuff when she was younger. She had an affair with a married man, and then she got pregnant by another guy who walked out on her. I guess her dad didn't want her to give it up, and he was talking about taking in the baby and raising it himself. Helene did not approve. Well, Lisa ended up having a miscarriage, so that was that. She seemed to settle down a bit afterwards. She got involved with some guy who was supposedly European aristocracy, got married to him. They had that little girl together."

"Our May," Dimitri said.

"It wasn't a great marriage. The guy was penniless, but they lived an extravagant life in Europe, and Lisa was continually mooching off her dad just so they could maintain proper appearances in society. This drove Helene absolutely nuts. Lisa was never shy about asking her dad for a handout, but she was terrified that her older sister should find out—or so she once confided to me. And then she discovered the so-called nobleman was a sleaze. He was—" She caught herself.

"Molesting their daughter," I finished.

"Right. I see you've got the facts. Sorry I couldn't tell you myself, that day. . . . I just felt it was not my place."

"Yeah, I know," I said. *You nearly killed me,* I thought.

But Kate was already going on with her story. "So Lisa dumped Baron Von Wolfgang, or whatever his name was, and set up her own household, and of course that required even more money from dear old dad. Ironically enough, right after Lisa splits and files for divorce, his lordship comes into his big inheritance, with a fancy title and land and a nice big fat allowance to go with it. Now he's got ammo, and he tries to leverage his way into a custody battle."

"And there goes more of the Browning family fortune!" Dimitri put in.

"Then Lisa meets Gatien Defalle, the famous race car driver. We were all surprised when we heard they had married. They lived in France in those days; we'd never even met Gatien. It seemed rather sudden, and I had my doubts about it. I was worried for May's sake. It just seemed odd to me. I have to be honest with you, Sarah. After my sister died, I didn't like the idea of my niece going to her stepfather, instead of to us, her family. But it wasn't up to me. By then Gatien had legal custody of May. I actually considered challenging him on that. But at the time, I was having trouble with my own son. I didn't have much to offer as an alternative."

"Well, it seems to have worked out for May," I said.

"Yes, I guess it has. And you know you're a big part of why that's so, Sarah."

"It's nice of you to say so."

"Sure. You round out the equation." She turned to her son, who had been listening avidly to her comments regarding the family. "Don't you think?"

Dimitri nodded solemnly. "Absolutely."

"Absolutely what?" asked May, joining us in the kitchen. She had her bags packed and was ready to go.

"Sarah rounds out the equation around here," said Dimitri.

"Well, yeah," said May. "I guess she'd better, since she's going to be one of us from now on."

Kate and Dimitri glanced at each other, startled, and looked at me for confirmation. I'm sure my blush gave the whole thing away.

Dimitri was the first to speak. "Well, Gatien couldn't have made a better choice," he said graciously.

"Okay!" said Kate, drawing out the word. "Well, I—I should have put it together myself. But I had no idea!"

"Congratulations, Sarah," said Dimitri.

"I think we're getting a bit ahead of ourselves here," I said quickly. "There is nothing to congratulate me on."

But the damage—shall we say?—had been done.

Chapter Thirty-two

I THOUGHT ABOUT everything Kate had told me, and I was left perplexed. There was something about Kate that I just didn't quite trust. The things she had said about Helene had taken me by surprise, but I was pretty sure Kate had her own issues, and probably projected onto her half sister some of her own feelings of jealousy or resentment. I knew Helene wasn't as cool about the whole subject of her sister Lisa as she pretended to be, but I thought Kate might be reading more into Helene's psychology than was warranted.

And yet I was struck by Dimitri's claim that Helene wasn't thrilled about the discovery of the ancient manuscripts. That rang true to me, and when I thought back over the past, I was disappointed in myself that I hadn't realized how she felt. But she had hidden her feelings well; I had just assumed she'd be supportive of Lisa's success, even if it came about after her death. And why wouldn't she be? Kate had said that Helene was concerned about Lisa draining their father of his money; well, surely *that* wasn't at issue anymore. Mr. Browning's money and property had gone to Helene after his death, aside from a generous trust for May's education.

I decided I would talk to Helene about the subject my-self, because she had always seemed to appreciate a direct approach. And the innuendo, about Gatien and me, that had been set in motion this afternoon with Dimitri and Kate, had me worried. Word got around fast, and I didn't want Helene learning about my relationship with the mas-ter of the house through the grapevine. Of all the people we would have to let it out to, Helene probably intimi-dated me the most, and I was half-afraid she wouldn't ap-prove of me. Of *us.*

So I called her that afternoon, after May had left with Dimitri and his mom. When she didn't answer at home, I tried her mobile number and got her. We chatted about the weather for a moment, and how it was for her, with Dim-itri leaving for college. She told me she was a little sad about being an "empty nester," as she put it. Then she asked what was going on with me.

"Well," I said, "now that May is gone, I was hoping we could get together, you and me. There are some things I'd like to talk with you about."

"Are there?" She sounded so prim, I was suddenly afraid of what I was doing.

"I mean, I wanted to talk to you about the develop-ments with the old manuscripts. And also, Dimitri gave me something. I'm not quite sure what to make of it. He gave me these printouts from an Internet site that he found on the day of Lisa's funeral. They're tide tables, and he implied that they have something to do with her death. It's probably nothing, but I wanted to show them to you, to get your input. Anyway, the main thing has to do with Gatien and me, um . . ." *Shut up,* I said to myself. *Wait until you see her. Wait until you rehearse what it is you want to say.* "And so I was just hoping we could get together and talk. . . ."

Helene laughed at me gently over the line. "Of course, I would love to get together with you, Sarah, any time. But you know, right now I am up at the beach house."

"Oh, are you? Well, when you get home, then."

"Tell you what. I would love to have you come up and stay with me here for a couple days. May is with Kate, Gatien is in Europe. Why don't you come?"

"Well, it's true, May is with Kate, and there's no reason I couldn't come. . . ." I leaped at the idea; anything to keep busy, to keep from missing Gatien too badly. So we agreed; I would leave the next day. As I hung up the phone, I reflected that Dimitri had mentioned just seeing Helene at her home in Palo Alto. If that was true, there was no way Helene could be at the beach house already.

One of them was lying.

Or, as was more likely, I had misunderstood somebody. Dimitri had probably been joking. At any rate, it didn't matter. I needed to pack a few things, talk to Louisa, and call May at Kate's to let her know my plans. I was off to the beach!

WE WALKED TOGETHER down the cliff stairs, laden with gear. If it had just been me, I would have kicked my shoes off at the top of the stairs and gone down with only a bottle of water, but Helene seemed to think it necessary that we come fully equipped. She had me hauling two beach chairs and a big bag full of towels and sunscreen and snacks, and she carried another bag just as large. But I didn't mind; I was feeling very well disposed toward Helene that morning. After I had arrived at the beach house the previous night, we'd had dinner together, and I had told her about Gatien and me, and her warm, sincere acceptance of us made me happier than I would have guessed. It was a relief, I realized, because I sensed she wielded a lot of power in that family. I didn't really care so much about what she felt about the old books as I did about how she felt about Gatien and me.

In fact we had never even reached the topic of the old scroll fragments last night, so I intended that we should this afternoon.

"This is a nice spot," I said.

"Oh, but I want to show you my favorite place," she said, and we continued walking.

We came to the end of the beach and climbed up and over a tumble of rock, dropping down into another, smaller cove, a half-moon curve of steep, dark sand banked with high cliffs. At the end of the small beach, chunks of greasy, sharp boulders jutted out into the ocean. The waves were seriously impressive this afternoon, even for the north coast: high and translucent, fast-moving, and vicious-looking. I could see the rip of retreating waters rushing down the beach to meet the incoming waves. It wasn't the most relaxing sight to behold. Certainly not a beach for small children to wade.

But Helene seemed content that we had found our spot, and she set about making a place for us beneath the cliff, setting up the chair and laying out the towels and sunscreen. She had bananas and chocolate chip cookies and a thermos of coffee, which I gratefully accepted when she poured me a steaming mugful. *This* is *sweet of her,* I thought; Helene wasn't a coffee drinker, but she knew I was a coffee aficionado. I still didn't know what she had in the other bag.

I wasn't terribly comfortable sitting right beneath the cliffs, as we were. I had grown up in Santa Barbara near the ocean and I knew the cliffs were volatile. Unstable. But the beach was narrow, and I didn't want to get too close to that cold, hostile-looking surf, either, so under the cliffs we sat. It was, I thought, an odd place to choose as one's favorite spot, though after I had sipped some coffee, I began to relax a bit and it hit me that it really was quite a lovely, secluded place, and the ocean was fierce and beautiful. I felt looser, somehow; I felt at peace and delightfully uninhibited, as if I had drunk champagne. I chatted with Helene, who did not seem to follow me into my bliss but stayed rather serious, and suddenly I felt like teasing her.

"Oh, Helene," I said. "Tell me you think it's wonderful about your sister's discovery come to light. The oldest copy of the book of Ecclesiastes in existence! Don't you think that's amazing?"

She smiled with her eyes lowered and let out what might have been a chuckle, if a woman like Helene could be said to chuckle.

"Everyone else thinks it's wonderful, but you," I told her.

"Oh, you misjudge me, Sarah," she said indulgently. She had not taken offense, for which I was glad. "But you must forgive me if I try to keep things in perspective," she said.

"What sort of perspective?" I asked.

"We don't even know yet if we haven't been the victims of some elaborate hoax," she said. "Much more study is needed, years of study. Do you know how long it has taken for even a fraction of the Dead Sea Scrolls to be translated and made available to the public? The cost in dollars is astronomical, let alone the legal wrangling regarding ownership and access and the ethical questions involved when you're dealing with something of such significance and age, something belonging, quite arguably, to someone else."

"Yes," I said. "I know. Of course I've thought about all that. But isn't it exciting? What a thing to be part of! I'd like to do what I can to contribute to the study of these documents."

"You sound like her," Helene said sadly. "I think you're deluded, just as she was."

"Gatien thinks so, too," I said with a laugh. I picked up my coffee mug and took another sip, but the coffee had gone cold, and it had an acrid taste I hadn't noticed before. I set the mug down and looked up at Helene, and I noticed she was looking at me with pity, or something equally vexing. I realized she had been serious when she had used the word *deluded.* I had thought she was joking.

I was pondering this when she reached for the mystery bag and set it down on a towel beside me. "This is something I thought you might want," she said.

I leaned over and opened the bag. Inside, stacked sideways, I saw what looked to be the entire collection of Lisa's journals.

"There they are!" I said, marveling.

"Every single one of them," Helene said. "I've been through the entire dreary thing, page after page. It took far too much of my time."

"I *wondered* what happened to them," I said.

"I had already perused them myself after Lisa's death, but with you so curious about the whole affair, I decided I'd better see exactly what they had to say, these journals, and imagine my surprise and delight to find the last journal was there, with the others, all along!" She eyed me shrewdly, and unable to think of anything smart to say, I remained silent. I knew I was being accused of wrongdoing, that I should be feeling embarrassed or put on the spot, but I seemed to be floating above myself, looking down on the scene dispassionately, and I didn't feel much of anything.

"I assume you already know everything in them, just as I do," Helene said.

"Actually, no," I said. "I know very little of what's in them."

"Is this true?" she asked. "I have wondered. It seemed to me that you must have read them, though lately I'd come to the conclusion that you really don't know much at all; but it doesn't matter."

"So what did you find out?" I asked eagerly. "Did you discover anything?" I was into manuscript discoveries these days. It seemed entirely possible that something in Lisa's journals would turn out to be remarkable.

"You go ahead and look at the journals, Sarah. See for yourself. I know you want to. I'm going to take a walk." Helene stood, stretched her back. She began to walk toward the rocks, then paused. "Oh, as to my feelings regarding the old scroll fragments and life in general I suppose, Lisa quotes me on February the twenty-sixth, in her final journal. Surprisingly accurate quotes, I might add. My feelings haven't changed since the day I said what I said then."

I screwed up my eyes to see her face, but the sun was behind her, and I felt momentarily blinded. She trudged off through the sand, and I slid the last journal out of the bag. February twenty-sixth? Well, obviously she wanted me to read that page, and I was interested in what it had to say. What could it be, I wondered, that she would play this sort of game with me?

I flipped open the journal, fumbling with the pages. I was feeling increasingly drowsy and inept, and my stomach was beginning to clench. I slid from my chair to the towel, thinking I'd feel better if I could lie down. *There,* I thought. *That's an improvement.* I lifted the journal and began to read.

February 26

I suppose it was silly to think I could keep this mad caper of mine from Helene's prying and spying and oh my god why?ing. She told me flat out she would do anything and everything to keep me from spending any more of Daddy's money on my "foolish indulgences."

"I probably won't be able to get back that which you've already thrown away on your foolish indulgences," she said to me (using the term foolish indulgences several times), "though I shall certainly try. But I do assure you, Lisa, I will do everything in my power to prevent any more waste of what our father worked so hard all his life to build. You took away his peace of mind, and you took away the [I forget exactly how she said it, but what she meant was the exclusive closeness] he and I shared. You corrupted all that, and there was little I could do about it. But this is something I can do something about, and I will."

"You go on and tell Daddy," I said. "He knows why I needed the money. He believes in this. And besides, Gatien has been more than generous; most of the money was his."

"I have no intention of telling Dad anything. I'll be taking matters into my own hands, now, Lisa."

For some reason, she really struck me as creepy. I almost felt afraid of her.

I had to remind myself that what I was doing was important. I remember the look on the old count's face when he told me the story for the first time.

"I was, for many years," he said, "good friends with a man I greatly respected who happened to be abbot at a monastery in the north of Spain. Knowing my interest in such things, he told me (under the influence of some very fine wine) he had reason to believe that somewhere in the abbey library, which itself dated back to the early middle ages, there were some of the oldest existing copies of certain books of the Tanakh, or Old Testament, but try as I might, I could not get him to reveal more. Not until years later, on the night before he died, did he confide to me the location of these manuscripts, which were actually leather and papyrus scrolls, he claimed, ancient Hebrew texts as old as any in existence. I was unable to procure them; indeed, for a long time I was not even allowed to examine the library—the new abbot was not as well-disposed toward me as the previous.

"For years I despaired of learning whether my old abbot friend was suffering from delusions or had truly known where a fantastic treasure lay, hidden yet intact. Then one day I chanced to hear the abbey had closed and much of its contents were being auctioned off. And I was able to verify what he had said was true."

The count told me this fantastic story at dinner in his stone castle with footmen all around, and then he told me he wanted me to have the collection, which he warned was extensive and would be costly to own, though the price I would pay would be a fraction of its true worth when it came into the light of day. He also said there was work to be done; cataloguing the "library" would be a life's work.

"You have waited so long for this yourself," I said. "Why would you want me to have it?"

"Because, my dear, I am older than I look. There isn't much time for me."

We didn't know it then, but he had a weak heart, and he knew he was going to die. Why would he want to do me wrong?

Gatien thinks I'm probably being hornswaggled, and I didn't want to tell Helene because I knew she'd call me crazy. But I feel I'd have been crazy not to go for it.

My eyes were too heavy to manage. I let the lids slowly sink, like the sun sinks into the sea.

I began to dream, knowing I was dreaming. I heard Kate's voice, as if she was there with me, speaking. She was telling me that Helene had "issues" with her sister Lisa. Didn't like her spending their father's money. Wasn't going to allow it to continue. I tried to put her words together and make them mean something, but I lost my grasp on anything coherent, and I swirled away.

Chapter Thirty-three

I WOKE TO the frigid water lapping at me. I was lying in it, the journals turning and twirling around me, some of them already dragged away by the surf. My teeth chattered as I heaved myself to my feet, moving my stiff, aching limbs to get them warm. Stumbling, splashing, and unsteady, I vomited some foul-tasting, black coffee mess into the water. Pain saturated my being, deep into my core. I was so cold. Wet and cold. What the hell was going on? I was completely disoriented. Where was Helene? She must have decided to let me sleep out of consideration. The sun was setting, nearly dissolved into the shimmering, wet horizon. I must have slept for a long time.

I could hardly move.

I wondered if I might be dreaming. I was trying to move quickly, but I was unable to get out of slow motion. I packed up all the soggy journals I could catch, with some of the other beach stuff. It was too much for me to carry all by myself. Helene wouldn't have just left me with all this stuff, would she? I set the chair against the cliff, but the water was already beginning to touch the top of the beach. There was no saving anything from the tide, if I didn't get out of there soon; it was coming in fast. Soon the rushing waters would engulf the sand altogether. I gathered what I could and walked back toward the rocks the way we'd come in, unable to avoid stepping in the fast-moving, chilly water. I gritted my teeth and steeled myself against the bitter sting of the cold. As I waded along, I felt the water around my legs, pulling at me as it rushed back down the steep slope of the beach. Underwater, I felt the sand give way beneath my feet as I walked, creating a strange, unsettling void. It was then I realized the water had come in too far and was blocking my exit, at least in the direction we had entered the cove. So I turned around and went the other way, only to find the small beach was nearly gone and completely barred on both sides of the half-moon cove by giant waves smashing against the jagged rock ramparts.

I walked to the cliff and looked up. There was no escape that way. The unstable, sandy cliff was a sheer face rising high above me.

I waded back to my camp and stood on the highest section of the beach. I set the bag of journals down beside the chair and watched the waves come in and worry at them. I stared at the wet things, watching one of the journals float away.

I forced myself to focus. I needed to call on all my reserves to get myself out of this jam. As far as I could see, if I didn't, I was in big trouble. I called out for Helene, cursing my weak voice. I tried again; better. But there was no answer. There came no rescue from any point of the compass.

Finally, I knew there was no other alternative. The only way out was into the ocean. I would have to swim for it.

I'LL HAVE TO swim for it, I thought. Plucky. Fearless. *There's my brave girl.* I heard Gatien's voice in my head. Actually, it was more a matter of getting swept out to sea than sheer bravado. I had no choice. So I might as well embrace it. My adrenaline was pumping, an awkward,

dizzying pulse vying with the slow, languid lethargy that
had invaded my body, threatening to pull me under with
more comforting warmth than the sea. And that would be
the end of me.

I waited as long as I could, but the sun had set and light
was fading, and I would need to see what I was doing.

All of the journals, the chair, everything was submerged now, or floating away, up and over the waves. The
waves were coming fast and huge and powerful, mesmerizing to watch, frightening to contemplate. I was comfortable in the ocean: even so, I couldn't imagine swimming
out past these huge waves, but I had to, so I would. I
walked farther into the water.

The water was so cold it was numbing. But it was waking me up, deep inside. The cloud in my head was lifting.
I was going to need all my strength for this swim, I knew;
this wasn't for beginners.

But I was no beginner.

RIP CURRENT. I felt the pull now, suddenly much
stronger, and I fought the panic that triggered the fight instinct. *Stay calm stay calm stay calm.*

Relax.

Easier said than done. All my muscles were cramped
from the cold, already tired from navigating the churning
surf. *Concentrate. Let the tide take you.*

Let it take you. . . .

I FELT THE water pulling me out to sea, but first I would
have to scale the ramparts. The first wall of giant waves
was suddenly rising over me, and I felt the fear breaking
in my brain. I was amazed at the power of the current,
which was pulling me fast, inexorably toward the translucent green wall. There was no way I could fight against its
strength. But I knew what to do.

I took a deep, deep breath, and just as the wave loomed
over me, ready to hurl me back against the cliff, I dove
under it.

It seemed to take forever to traverse beneath the mass

of the wave, and I thought my cheeks would burst, my lungs fill with seawater. But suddenly the wave was gone, and I was on the surface again. I gasped for breath, but the current was still pulling me out fast toward the glowing horizon, toward another wall of waves. I repeated the trick I'd learned as a child at El Capitan State Beach, when a wave was just too big to ride. Gauge your timing, breathe deep, hold it, and plunge.

At last I was past the breakers, but the strong current kept pulling me out. Seventy-five, a hundred yards, I guessed. And still it pulled me. Again and again, I fought the urge to fight.

I treaded water. Breathed. Shook out the cramping in my muscles.

Finally, I noticed a lessening of the pull. I began to swim across the current, parallel to the shore. A few minutes later, I knew I'd done it. The watery atmosphere around me changed in temperature, direction, spirit. I'd escaped the rip current. Now all I had to do was body surf into the shore—if I could find a beach. But this part of the coast was particularly rocky, and the cliffs were high. The tide was in high, and I wasn't sure how long I would be able to survive in water this cold, with nightfall looming near. I wasn't sure how I would swim another yard, I was so wrung out and exhausted. But I kept doing it.

As I ventured toward the shore, swimming the breast stroke like the Little Mermaid, I searched the cliffs for the beach house, to get my bearings, but the terrain looked unfamiliar to me. Now I could see the bluffs protruding into the ocean, surrounded by toothy, inaccessible rocks at the base of the cliffs. No place to land.

Around the edge of the promontory the cliffs drew back, forming a little bay. It was my best hope; the light was nearly gone. I scanned the shoreline, desperate for a welcoming beacon. I became oddly aware of the safe harbor as a powerful metaphor, and quite literal in this case. There—I glimpsed the diagonal line of a stairway traversing the steep cliff face. Where there were stairways, there were beaches. Not much of a beach that I could see, but it was the best I could hope for. I let the waves carry me in.

This stretch of the beach was nearly underwater, too; the tide was high and still coming in. But I escaped being dashed into the jagged rocks or against the flat face of a cliff. I felt the sand beneath my feet and groaned out my thanks. I waded up to the bottom of the cliff where the stairs began.

I found they were abandoned, condemned, boarded off with a sign that read Danger: Cliff Collapsed. Stairs Unusable.

To hell with that! I thought. At this point, I really didn't have any choice. I was glad to feel the earth beneath my feet, but I was still up to my ankles in water. My guess was this beach would be submerged soon, just like the last one. I yanked a couple of the old boards of the caution fence aside and scrambled up the rocks to the stairs, such as they were. The sign was right: by most standards, these stairs were unusable. The cliff, indeed, had collapsed, and with it, some of the old wooden stairway. But by half-climbing and half-scrambling, I was able to make my way up the sheer face of the cliff on what was left of the rickety, splintery steps. I felt so thrilled to be back on dry land I wanted to sing, but I was shaking so hard it was all I could do to concentrate and not lose my footing. It was nearly dark, and I was not in the best physical condition at this point, exhausted by my swim, battling hypothermia and some residual fog in my muscles that had me worried.

It was a long, perilous climb but I was very nearly home free. I could see the top of the cliff, and the roots of a large cedar exposed and dangling over the edge, when suddenly the wooden supports of the stairway fell, and a chunk of the cliff disappeared beneath me. I could hear the fast roar, and a sort of implosion as rock met water below. With a gasp I lunged for the railing above me, which, to my immense relief, held fast, though everything below was gone. I pulled myself up on what remained of the steps, which were now hanging over empty space. Gingerly I continued up, and up—and my foot went through a rotten rung. I was clinging to what was left of the structure with all my strength, and my toes found a slippery hold on the cliff.

Shit, I thought. *First the ocean, and now the earth.*

I was even more scared now than when I was being swept out to sea. My muscles were trembling with the strain, and I could hear the creaking of the last remaining bit of the stairway above. I had to pull myself up fast, before the entire cliff fell away or my strength just gave out. It was now or never.

"Sarah?"

"Here!" I cried.

Was I hearing things? That sounded like Helene. I pulled myself up higher. One more rung . . .

"Sarah!" Her face appeared at the top of the cliff.

Thank God, I thought. *Thank God.*

But she merely looked down on me passively. She didn't hold out her hand to me.

"Help me, Helene," I gasped.

"Well, I didn't expect to see *you* back ashore so soon," she said. Her voice was droll.

It was then, finally, that I understood. Why it had taken me that long, I don't know. But in that moment, clinging to the crumbling cliffside, I suddenly understood. It was Helene who had lured me to my death. Except her plan that I drown, as Lisa had drowned, had failed. Suddenly I knew without a doubt that Helene had murdered her own sister. And I knew without a doubt that Helene did not intend to let me finish this climb. Because now *I knew.*

"So this is what happened to Lisa," I said, panting for breath.

"No, not exactly," Helene answered. "She didn't make it this far. She drowned almost immediately, fighting that current. I was hoping the same would be true for you, but maybe this is a better way. If both of you were drowned, it might look suspicious. As it is, it's bad enough that the both of you had to die. It won't look good for me, with two deaths on my beach, but this, at least, is probably a better way. You'll be found dashed upon the rocks, another climbing victim. You know I warned you against scrambling around on those slippery rocks. . . ." Helene's expression in the twilight was gentle, pitying. I sensed she felt no glee in doing what she thought she must do.

I had no recourse; I couldn't go back down; what little support from the cliff I had on the way up had disintegrated behind me. Falling down the cliff from this height meant death, surely. And that is what Helene intended.

"Why?" I asked, my voice surprisingly steady as I clung to the wooden rungs. I was trying to bide my time, to think of something. "Why did you do it, Helene? First your sister, now me? Why?"

"I didn't do anything to my sister," she said. "She did it all by herself."

"You lured her out there. You let her get swept away. But why? Why would you do that?"

"No, I didn't lure her. She walked right out into the water of her own free will. She loved the sea . . . but she grew up in Nevada, you know. She didn't know anything about the ocean. It was easy. But yes, when it happened, I made no move to stop it, same as I'll make no move to stop you from falling from this cliff. Because I was sick and tired of her making my father's life hell. I thought if she was out of his life for good, he could start living the life he deserved, free of all the stress and anxiety and the constant heartache she made for him."

"Didn't quite work out that way, though, did it?" I said, unable to keep the spite from tingeing my words. *Don't make it worse, Sarah,* I warned myself. But it seemed hardly to make a difference now. I wasn't going to talk my way out of this one. I could see that. She needed me dead. I knew too much now. But why had she decided to kill *me?* Up until this moment I had been completely ignorant of what had really happened. Did she simply lose her head? Crack under the strain of her secret? Obviously, she was mad.

"No," she said with a sigh. "You're right. It really didn't make much difference. She had already done the damage. I was too late. If only it had happened years ago . . . Everything I've done in my life, I've done for my dad. I thought I was making life better for him. Now he's gone. . . . I've got to start living for myself. May and Gatien . . . they should be mine, you know? I deserve a family like that, too."

For a moment she dropped out of my vision, and I felt a breath of hope, perhaps for a reprieve, but she popped up again right away, and now I could see she was holding something, a pitchfork.

"Now, Sarah," she said. "Let yourself go."

"Help me!" I screamed, as loudly as I could. If she wasn't moved, maybe someone else would hear me.

"I'll knock you clean off the cliff, Sarah, if I have to." The trembling in her voice betrayed a tenuous grip on her composure.

"But it won't look so good for you, will it, if they find my body punctured with holes. That won't go well with your she-fell-from-the-rocks-while-hiking story, will it?"

She lifted the pitchfork. I was beginning to lose my grip on the rung; my fingernails were breaking, and my feet were slipping on the rock.

Desperate, I spoke out, as strong as my voice could project: "Tell me why, Helene! Why are you doing this? I never did anything against you!"

She hesitated, let the heavy tool sag.

"Why me?" I demanded.

"It's not that complicated, Sarah. I think you've figured it out. You've been trying to work out this mystery ever since you came among us. When you brought me those tide tables, I knew you were about to confront me. You thought those tide tables were the evidence you needed."

"I thought the tide tables were the evidence of Lisa's suicide," I said. "I thought they proved she had planned it."

She looked at me oddly. "Well, now you know better," she said. "When I came back to the house with Gatien after Lisa's funeral, we saw someone had been in the library and turned on the computer. But I wasn't worried, not until you told me you were looking for clues to prove Lisa didn't kill herself."

"You were the one who ransacked Lisa's library on New Year's Eve!"

"Yes. I left my own party and no one even missed me," she said bitterly. "I had to satisfy myself that you had nothing on me."

"Well, you must have satisfied yourself, since I didn't."

"But then later, I misunderstood something you told me, and I thought you had found something. I never meant to hurt you then, Sarah. I thought you were out for the evening. I meant for the cottage to burn, along with any evidence, not *you*. Now I wonder if it hadn't been better if . . ."

"Dimitri knows!" I shouted. This was my last grasp.

And indeed, she seemed to falter at that.

"Dimitri gave me those tide tables. He told me about the spring tides. He thought I would figure it out for myself, but I was too stupid. But *he* knows. He knows it's you."

She hesitated. "Did he say that?"

"Yes," I lied.

"He didn't say that, did he?" she said triumphantly. But she seemed unsure of herself now. "Anyway, it doesn't matter. If it wasn't the tide tables, it would be something else. You were getting too close to my family, and you thought you could take my place."

"Helene, think about this—"

"No. I have done too much thinking already. The time has come for action. I waited too long with Lisa, and I'm afraid I've waited too long with you. It's nothing personal, Sarah. I liked you. I know you really did care for May and for Gatien, for all of us. If I thought you'd just move along out of our lives after your contract was up, I could let it go. I wouldn't be doing this unless I had to. But I'm not going to let you take up where Lisa left off. With Gatien and May, with those ancient scrolls, spending my father's money . . . With you out of the way, I will see to it that my sister's "collection" is put up for auction, with the proceeds from the sale going back to where they belonged in the first place."

"You mean, to *you.*"

"To my father's estate, which I am now managing, yes," she replied.

She lifted the pitchfork and studied it a moment, as if wondering whether it would be best to use the blunt end of the handle, or the end with the five sharp, rusty tines. She seemed to have picked the tine end, and she raised it higher to bring it down on me. I calculated in an instant how I might reach out and grab at the pitchfork as it descended, and perhaps deflect the blow, but it was futile, and I knew it. It was all I could do to keep myself balanced on the cliff, hanging on for dear life. (Ah, dear life!) My heart was pounding so hard I feared it would shake me off the cliff with its violence.

"Good-bye, Sarah."

"No!"

And then I heard the voice calling. Like a warning from the heavens. It sounded like my name.

And she hesitated.

I strained, clinging to the cliff, to hear the faint voice again.

I heard the voice again, nearer. But now it called another name. *"Helene . . ."* I knew that voice. It was the voice of an angel. The voice of a mighty angel, vibrating so deep and rich, but full of fear. . . .

She was breathing heavily now, the pitchfork swaying in her hands.

Was I crazy? Was I already dead? Was it only the wind? The wind was calling Helene's name with hysterical urgency. She turned, distracted, looking toward the sound.

"HELENE!" THERE WAS the voice again, louder and stronger.

He kept calling.

He's too late, I thought. *She has all the power over me.* She would finish her mission.

"Where is she, Helene?" I heard him closer now, and

he sounded scared and desperate. "Where is Sarah?" he screamed at her. "What have you done to her! *Where is she?*"

"Here!" I was yelling as loud as I could. "I'm here!"

Helene turned and looked down on me again. Her expression was one of utter defeat. I had seen that look on her face only once before, the day her father had died.

"I'm sorry," she said softly. "It was never meant to happen this way." She lifted the pitchfork again, and she was about to thrust it down on me, or so I thought, but instead she turned it and pressed the tines against her own heart. And then she let herself fall.

She fell so gracefully that it was like watching a ballet dancer, the way they seem to float in midair, for only a moment, then her body was smacking against the rocks, bouncing and tumbling all the way down the horrendous, steep cliffside. The pitchfork went tumbling after her.

Gatien was there above me. He dropped to his knees and was reaching down for me, grasping my hand, and then he was hauling me up the last few feet to the top of the cliff with one strong pull, and I was panting and crying and finally, finally safe in his arms.

Chapter Thirty-four

ALL THOSE MONTHS I had dismissed Dimitri as a bit touched, with all his wild talk about Lisa's death being a murder, and how he was watching over May and me, to protect us, and it turned out that he was right. He had done just that. He had a suspicious hunch about Helene, but without proof, he was reluctant to make any accusations. He had tried to warn me about her, in his own way, but I had not heeded his warning. Finally he had given me the tide tables to show me, but I had drawn the wrong conclusion about the meaning. Fortunately for me, Dimitri had taken it one step further. When he found out that I had gone to the beach house with Helene, he had decided to contact Gatien and voice his fears directly. Gatien was skeptical and had very nearly dismissed Dimitri, as had I, but the more he mulled it over, the more he wondered. He had always suspected foul play in his wife's death, though it never occurred to him that her sister could be the guilty one. Finally, acting on some instinct that told him to heed Dimitri's warning, he dropped everything, left the Formula One circuit—right before a race—and came to my rescue. In doing so, he forfeited his chance at the championship that season.

He's never shown the slightest regret.

I've often pondered Helene's motivations in the sad tale she left behind as her legacy. I'm not sure how much of her enmity for her sister had to do with the younger girl's stealing away their father's affections or "stealing" her father's wealth, which I have since learned (as much of it passed to May) was considerable. Kate says she thinks it was always about money, but I'm not so sure. Helene seemed to have a pathological, ingrown devotion to her father that went deeper than greed. The jealousy provoked by the emergence of a rival—her own sister— might have been deadly indeed. Maybe Helene really did feel she was protecting her father from Lisa's fumbling assault upon his peace of mind, not only, as Kate would have it, his portfolio. We would never know. Helene left behind no journals to explain her motivations.

We learned that the Spanish count was indeed legitimate; apparently he had chosen Lisa for his intellectual heir, as he had known he was dying and would not be able to complete the task himself—that of bringing the ancient scrolls into the public eye. Upon meeting her, he had congratulated himself on finding the perfect combination of enthusiasm and financial resources, just the person, he decided, to be the caretaker of such an important discovery.

Somehow Rachel Shipton and I inherited the task, for which we are both humbly grateful. I still can't decide what I want to be when I grow up, but in the meantime, I've been working with Rachel on the ancient Hebrew scrolls, researching their origins, writing grants and fundraising for them to be translated, catalogued, and preserved. I found an unexpected ally in this endeavor: Gatien's stepmother, Zora, who has excellent connections in the antiquities world.

The death of Nathan's aunt, Madame Curio, was determined to have been of "natural causes." I found out later that Ira Meyer and Moshe Yaron had been friends of hers.

After Helene's death, I learned the big payoff at the end

of my contract was in question, because it turned out that
Helene was the one who had put up such a sum, not Gatien, who didn't even know about the bonus. Gatien had
been willing to pay a generous salary to the person who
cared for his daughter, but it was Helene who had set the
bribe price for staying a year, and I believe this was due
to her sense of guilt and obligation to May and Gatien.
After all, it was she who had deprived them of a mother
and wife. Gatien insisted on paying me the money himself, when he learned of the deal, but it didn't matter anyway. We were living together as husband and wife by that
time, all our resources combined, as it were, and it would
have made no difference. When the money I was due, con-
tractually, became available to me after Helene's estate
was settled, I put it into a nonprofit foundation that Rachel
and I had created, devoted to the study and preservation of
the ancient manuscripts. Helene would have hated the
money going to such a purpose, but I had a feeling Lisa
would have approved.

Gatien did return to race in Formula One. He finished
out the season respectably, though mathematically it was
no longer possible for him to claim the top spot that year.
It was, in fact, his last season as a driver, and he's never
shown any regret for that either, which is a relief to all of
us, I think. He has enough money put by that he could live
comfortably on what he already has, but he's a natural
businessman, always involved in some deal or another,
and I tease him about having a Midas touch. He's managed to stay involved with racing, though from more of a
distance.

It wasn't easy, letting him go back to his job after my
adventures on the edge. He stayed home for a couple of
weeks, helping me recover, making sure May was handling it well. We were both afraid of how the events would
impact the girl, but in the long run it seemed to do her
good, to finally understand what had happened to her own
mother.

On the night he left, we had already said our good-byes
at the airport, and I had turned toward my car, which was

waiting at the curb, when I felt his hand on my shoulder. He turned me to face him, holding my arms tightly, his eyes ferocious on mine.

"Sarah," he said, "I want you to promise me you'll marry me someday."

I was shaken, I was touched; but I was also aware this wasn't a real proposal. "It's way too soon for that," I said, "and you know it."

He sighed. "Damn it, I knew you would say that. And I know it's ridiculous, but I just can't think of any other way to make sure you'll still be here when I get back."

"Like I'm going to leave May, just like that? Without warning?"

"You know what I'm talking about, Sarah."

I regarded him tenderly, forgiving him. The look on his face was so transparently vulnerable. "Don't worry," I said. "I *have* to stay."

He must have been thinking the same thing I was: my one-year contract was nearly fulfilled. May would soon start high school. "Why is that?" he wanted to know.

"Well, it's an old superstition, you know. I've seen it played out in the movies. If someone saves your life, you're supposed to hang around long enough to pay back your debt. I've got to save *your* life now, to make it even, you see." I tried not to smile at him. "I *have* to stay with you."

He considered that. "I'm not sure you haven't already saved my life, Sarah," he said soberly.

"Still, I owe you for at least two, don't I?"

"Two?"

"Yeah, remember the night of the fire? If it hadn't been for you . . . anyway, if you can manage to stay out of trouble, that ought to keep us going for awhile."

"I guess I'll have to be satisfied with that, for now. But I give you fair warning: I'm going to press you for more."

"More time out of time?"

"Sarah," he said, exasperated, and he kissed me hard. "Don't you get it yet? I want you for *all* time."

Continue reading for a special preview of
Vickie Taylor's novel

Carved in Stone

Coming in June 2005 from Berkley Sensation!

Prologue

"UNDER THE BED, *Daddy! Check under the bed!*"
Rachel Vandermere clutched Mr. Mott, the pink rabbit who'd been missing one ear ever since her boo-boo with Mommy's sewing scissors last year, to her chest. Her toes curled off the smooth, wood floor as she danced on the balls of her feet. The ruffle of her sleeveless nightgown bounced around her knees, and she hiked it up in one fist. It was a hot night. The smell of the rain Daddy said was coming and the rosemary bush Mommy had planted outside fluttered through her window on a breeze as sticky and sweet as cotton candy.

Daddy closed the door to her closet, having verified it as messy, but monster-free, and he knelt by her bed to inspect the dark space beneath.

Rachel giggled. She didn't really believe in monsters, but bedtime was the only time she got Daddy all to herself since her little brother Levi was born, and she wasn't ready to give him back yet.

She might give *Levi* back, though, if they would let her.

Daddy lifted the pink bed skirt and bent his head. "No monsters here, either." He stood, pulled back the pink bedspread, and patted the pink pillowcase. At six years old, Rachel was definitely into pink. She had a pink bicycle and pink roller skates. But she didn't want to go to bed yet, even if it was in a pink bed.

Instead of climbing under the covers, she jumped up in the air and landed in a fighting crouch. Feet spread, knees bent, and both arms outstretched, Mr. Mott dangling from her grip on his one remaining ear, she pointed an accusing finger at the foot of her bed. "The toy box!"

Daddy gave her a look, but opened the lid and squinted inside anyway. Rachel chewed her lip and glanced around, wondering where else monsters might hide. If there was such a thing as monsters, which there wasn't. Unless . . .

"Daddy, can monsters be invisible?"

"Invisible? No, honey-bug, there's no such thing as invisible—"

His eyes went suddenly wide. He swatted at the air, ducked and swatted again. "Hey! Stop that!" He swung at nothing, fell against the bed and staggered toward her, yelling, "No! Ahhhhhhhhhhh, no!"

Rachel's eyes stretched open until she thought they would pop out of her head. She tried to scream, but her throat stuck closed. She tried to run, but her feet froze to the floor. Daddy twirled, tripped toward her. He picked her up by her stiff arms, his face still all twisty, and—

—he tickled her.

Laughing, he dumped her on the bed and pulled the covers up to her chin.

Her throat opened. She gasped in a humongous breath and socked him in the arm. *"Daddy!"*

Daddy threw his head back and howled. "Listen up all you monsters, invisible and otherwise. I am the biggest, baddest, and *only* monster allowed in this house. All lesser creatures are hereby banished forthwith!"

Rachel wasn't sure what that last part meant, but she hoped the monsters listened.

Not that there was any such thing as monsters.

Yawning, she snuggled down in the puddle of cool sheets. Daddy tucked Mr. Mott next to her and planted a sputtery kiss on her forehead before he left. At the door, he paused and flicked off the light. "Sweet dreams."

"Don't forget to leave it open a crack." Rachel wasn't afraid of monsters, but she was afraid of the dark. She didn't have to worry, though. Daddy never forgot to leave her door open a couple of inches so the hall light could get in.

Which is why, when she woke up hours later, yawned, dug a fist in one eye and peeled back the other eyelid to find there was no reassuring glow coming from the hall, her chest turned cold and tingly and a whimper pushed up her throat.

Thunder rumbled overhead—just clouds bumping together, Daddy had told her once, but the wind was moaning tonight, too. Trees scraped against the house like bony fingers. The storm and the darkness pressed down on her. She wanted to cry out for Mommy and Daddy, but she wasn't a baby anymore. She wasn't *the* baby anymore. They had Levi now, and he did enough crying for both of them. Besides, her throat had closed up again. Dark air was harder to breathe. She could hardly make a squeak, much less yell.

A beam of light slashed across her ceiling from outside, and she heard people out there, their voices as angry-sounding as the storm.

In the hall, Mommy and Daddy shouted in loud whispers. "We have to get out."

"It's too late."

"The children—"

Footsteps pounded toward her bedroom. Rachel pulled the covers up and squeezed Mr. Mott so tight she'd have strangled him if he'd been a real bunny. Her door flung open and a dark shape loomed over her, snatched her from warm covers into damp air. She shivered, gasped, then smelled a familiar spicy smell and relaxed in the strong arms.

"Daddy—" She reached for Mr. Mott as Daddy pulled her against him, but the rabbit fell. The toe of Daddy's boot kicked him under the bed.

"Hush, baby," he said.

She bounced sleepily in his arms as he jogged through the house. In the living room, candlelight flickered on the walls. She thought he was taking her to bed with him and Mommy 'cuz the 'lectricity was out, and she smiled, 'cuz she didn't get to sleep with them much since Levi was born, but then Daddy stopped next to the little door under the stairs, almost invisible in the paneling. It was their secret place, the spot where they hid Mommy's birthday presents.

Rachel's smile crumbled as Daddy opened the creaky hatch and lowered her inside. She reached up to him, her lips trembling. "Daddy, no!"

"Please, baby. Do what I say."

Mommy leaned over with Levi in her arms. She looked at Daddy once, her eyes all shiny, and handed the baby to Rachel. "Take care of your little brother. And please, *please* don't make a sound. No matter what."

Then Daddy closed the door and left her in the musty-smelling cupboard.

In the dark.

Rachel gulped down her fear, trying not to cry and trying to remember how to cradle the baby. Mommy had never let her hold him without help before. She didn't want to break him.

Outside, thunderclaps mixed with the pounding of fists on the front door. There were shouts, men's voices, and then splintering wood. Daddy yelled for Mommy to run. Glass shattered.

Rachel wanted to scream, needed to scream, but Mommy had said to be quiet. Very quiet. Tears rolling over her eyelashes onto her cheeks, she jammed a fist into her mouth and bit down hard. The darkness in here made her ribs all sticky. She couldn't breathe. She needed light, just a little sliver.

Squatting with the baby balanced in one arm, she leaned forward and reached for the cabinet door. Her palm slid over rough, unpainted wood. She chewed her lip, her heart doing jumping jacks in her chest. The voices she'd heard outside were inside now. Saying bad things. Scary things.

But the dark in here was scary, too. Hand shaking, she pushed on the wood. The door opened an inch and candlelight slithered in. Shadows oozed like puddles of oil across the slice of dining-room wall she could see. There were three figures, her momma's shorter shape and two bigger ones, one of them she thought was her daddy.

"Get out of my house!" he yelled

There were lots of voices in the background, murmuring and hissing like snakes, but she could only make out the words from one. ". . . don't belong here."

The shadow she didn't know raised an arm, and pointed something at her daddy's shadow. Daddy's shadow jumped toward him. They mushed together into one bigger blob and crashed to the floor.

Mommy screamed. "No! Please—"

A big bang, like a firecracker, made Rachel's shoulders jerk. Mommy's shadow fell down.

For a moment all was quiet. Levi snuffled in Rachel's arms and she rocked him and waited for Mommy to get up and tell her it was okay, the bad shadow was gone, that it had all been a dream. But it wasn't a dream, because she didn't wake up.

Something screeched like a cat that got its tail caught in the door, only louder. A new shadow rose up. The dark figure was shaped like a man but huger than anyone she knew. The watery candlelight made it look like horns sprouted from each side of his head, and his fingers grew longer and longer until they looked like big claws. When he lifted his shadow arms, they weren't arms at all, but wings.

Rachel's heart tripped. She wanted to shut her eyes, but she couldn't. All she could do was squat in her hidey-hole and shake as the monster shadow rose until its feet— claws—no longer touched the floor, and then flew through the air with the slow *whump, whump, whump* of heavy wings.

Someone Rachel couldn't see screamed. Others cursed,

grunted. Footsteps scuffled across the wooden floor.
Something heavy, like a piece of furniture, fell over. For a
moment the light in the cupboard dimmed, then she heard
a whoosh, and the room got brighter again. Rachel
smelled smoke—not the waxy smell of a candle, but the
bitter burn of a real fire.

Lightning flashed through the room, and that's when
Rachel saw it—not the monster's shadow, but the real
thing.

She stopped breathing. Her heart stopped beating. She
didn't want to look at it, to look into its shiny black eyes,
but she couldn't look away. A forked tongue flicked from
its pointy beak. Blood matted the gray tips of its wings,
dripped from its claws as it swooped past her hiding place,
knocking the cupboard door shut with its scaly, three-toed
claw.

She crashed against the far wall of the cabinet,
crammed herself into the darkest, tiniest corner. Eyes
squeezed shut, ears ringing with the echoes of people
wailing and more firecrackers popping, she clutched Levi
against her chest and recited the only prayer she knew, her
lips moving but unable to make any sound come out.

*Now I lay me down to sleep, I pray the Lord my soul to
keep. If I should die before I wake . . .*

Chapter One

NOTHING REMINDED NATHAN CROSS he wasn't human so much as an attractive woman watching his every move from across a crowded room. She wasn't a regular at the Chicago Museum of Fine Art's patron's gala; if she'd attended before, he would've remembered. A woman like her made an impression on a man.

Even a man who wasn't really a man.

She had hair the color of sunshine, as light as his was dark, and she wore it rolled up in an old-fashioned chignon that lent her an air of classic elegance, yet appeared perfectly contemporary, thanks to the tendrils she'd left free to spiral around her face in spindly whorls. Her gown added to the impression of modern sophistication, flowing over her slender body like liquid emeralds, offering just enough shimmer to catch the eye without being gaudy, cut low enough to tantalize without being risqué.

But it was the slit rising above one knee, exposing a stiletto heel secured to her ankle by a single delicate strap, and her long, shapely calf that had Nathan's blood simmering as he waited for her next step . . . and his next glimpse.

Clenching his fist around the fragile stem of his wineglass so tightly he was lucky it didn't shatter, he turned his back on her.

Curse his unholy nature, making him burn for something he couldn't have. He wasn't looking for a woman tonight—any night.

Nathan had only come for the art.

In art, in the muted pastels and dark dashes of oil, the raw emotion, he celebrated mankind's greatest joys, suffered the depths of its despair.

In art, he experienced humanity.

And if art were a cold mistress, she was at least a faithful one. Nathan had been born, lived and died fourteen times, and through it all she'd remained his constant. Brought him peace in a way no woman could.

In art, he found his solace. Found his soul.

Refusing to spare the temptress in green another thought, he focused on the twelfth-century tapestry displayed in front of him. He was reading the placard detailing the history of the hanging—as if he wasn't intimately familiar with its origins—when the scent of rosemary wafted past on a puff of conditioned air. His unnaturally sharp senses identified the fragrance as uniquely hers among the other women's heavier florals and musks, and the zesty men's colognes perfuming the gallery.

Helpless to stop himself, he continued to stare at the placard, concentrating more on the shiny surface of the Plexiglas mounting than the writing beneath, until his vision blurred. The glass caught the reflection of the crystal chandelier overhead. Hundreds of individual bulbs coalesced into a single brilliant source, a midnight sun.

The sun bored a channel through time and space. Nathan swayed as his senses left his body, following the light, spilling into the tunnel of Second Sight, a kind of self-hypnosis that allowed him to see things his human eyes could not.

Within seconds the woman's image appeared in his

mind's eye. He watched as she glided across the room behind him, wending her way through the gallery with frequent smiles and interludes of small talk among clusters of patrons, stopping a uniformed server for a fresh flute of champagne. She appeared to wander in no particular direction, and yet every click of her heels on the marble floor drew her inexorably closer.

To him.

Tall and slender, she moved with cultured grace. The emerald pendant bobbing in the hollow of her throat competed with eyes the same color for brilliance—and lost. She would have been the picture of female perfection except for one detail: Above her unflawed eyes, her left eyebrow arched at a slightly higher angle than the right, giving her face a gentle, crooked look he found endearing.

In women, as in art, it was the tiny imperfection that made a good work a masterpiece.

"Magnificent, isn't it?"

Her voice at his shoulder was curiously rough, in opposition to the smooth sophistication of the rest of her. The husky timbre swept the spurious Second Sight image of her from his mind. With some difficulty, he resisted the temptation to turn his head and take a look at the real thing. Instead he studied *Le Combat de Rouen,* the medieval tapestry on loan from Museé de Cluny that he'd come to see tonight. It had been a long time since he'd laid eyes on the pictorial record of the birth of his people.

"It's amazing how clearly the artist portrays the triumph of Christianity over paganism," the woman in green continued.

Nathan rolled the stem of his wineglass between his fingers. "Is that what it portrays?"

"The symbolism is obvious. The dragon is the embodiment of the pagan belief in magic and mythical creatures. The priest kneeling in the middle is using prayer to slay the dragon. Christianity slays paganism."

"Those don't look like prayers tearing that dragon apart with their beaks and fangs and claws to me." He didn't need to look at the tapestry to imagine the beasts doing battle with the dragon. He could hear the roars, taste the blood. He hadn't been there himself, but his forefathers had passed down the memory.

They'd made sure none of his kind ever forgot.

He didn't point out to the woman that the priest knelt in a faint, but visible, pagan circle, that some of the beasts had human faces or that around the edges of the battle scene, only figures of women and children looked on from the streets of Rouen. The men were notably absent.

The woman rolled her shoulders subtly. "One might assume that the priest used prayer to call upon the beasts to do his bidding."

"One might assume that," he allowed. *If one didn't know better.*

Romanus had deceived the villagers of Rouen. Used their own magic to trick them. Their own religion to curse them.

Thanks to the bastard priest's treachery, Nathan and those like him were damned to forever carry a monster inside them, slumbering, but always ready to Awaken.

Always hungry.

Oblivious to the rage rising within him, the woman stared at him with cool green eyes. "The detail is incredible. There's not another work from this period with a range of color like this."

He calmed himself with a deep breath. Romanus was long dead and Nathan was too intrigued by a woman who recognized range of color in a medieval tapestry to ruin this night over something that had happened more than a thousand years ago.

"There is one," he said, aware of the danger of getting drawn into a conversation with her, but not able to stop himself.

"I can't imagine where."

He realized he was staring—and not at the tapestry— but he couldn't bring himself to look away from her. "Tibet."

"Doesn't count." Her eyes were as bright as her smile. "The Easterners had an unfair advantage. Silk thread."

"Unfair or not, they set a standard for color and pattern that the West wouldn't match for another two centuries."

"Three, at least."

"Perhaps."

She raised her glass in salute. "You know your hangings."

"As do you." A fact that honed a fine edge on his already-sharp awareness of her. Too many women cared only for their own beauty these days. Realizing she wasn't one of *them* had desire cracking and snapping like a whip low in his belly.

His breath deepened and the gossamer bouquet of rosemary surrounding her enveloped him, invaded him. Beneath it, his predator's senses caught another, headier scent: feminine awareness. She was interested in him.

He wheeled and strode toward the next exhibit, a gleaming broadsword with a gilded handle, before he completely gave in to this idiocy and asked her name.

Unfortunately, she followed.

She stopped too close behind his shoulder. Invaded his space. His peace of mind.

"Are you a collector or a dealer?" she asked.

"Neither." Although he sold the odd piece from time to time to make ends meet.

"You must be quite a patron of the arts to go all the way to Tibet to visit museums and look at tapestry. Do you travel a lot?"

"When it suits." He didn't bother to correct her assumption that he'd been to the museum in Tibet. The weaving he'd had in mind had hung in a great maharajah's hall; Nathan had been present when the prince unveiled the masterpiece he'd consigned specially for his maharani. But that had been many lifetimes ago. Literally.

"And does it suit often?"

"Often enough."

She frowned, a shallow furrow forming above the bridge of her impertinent nose. "Are you always so forthcoming with information?"

"Do you always ask so many questions?" Her curiosity put a chill on the heat her interest had stoked in him.

Why had a woman like her—educated, poised, socially at ease—singled out a man like him from among the wealthy, erudite snobs milling about to grace with her attention tonight? His body language had stated clearly enough that he wasn't looking for company.

"Just trying to make conversation," she said.

"I'm not much of a conversationalist."

"No kidding."

The flirtatious sheen melted from her green eyes, leaving challenge blazing in its place and confirming his suspicions. She had an agenda. He just didn't know what it was.

Or what to do about it. Especially since he found the fiery reality of the warrior unmasked even more attractive than the façade of civility she'd worn before.

Temptation raked him with her razored claws. His kind were born with two undeniable compulsions: to protect humans from evil, and to procreate.

At that moment, he didn't see anyone in need of protecting.

He clasped his hands around the stem of his glass to give them something to do other than twist in the curls that fell around her face in sunny ringlets. While he stood staring at her, the woman huffed out a breath. The furrow between her brows disappeared and her smile returned, somewhat chagrined. She wrinkled her nose ingenuously, and his body tightened like hardening clay.

She shifted her drink to her left hand and extended her right. "Well, now that we've had our first fight, I suppose I should introduce myself. I'm Rachel Vandermere."

Nathan left the delicate fingers untouched, not trusting himself to lay a hand on her. He'd always had a passion for beautiful things, and she was certainly a work of art with her golden hair and bejeweled eyes. But more than beauty drew him to her. There was something familiar about her. Something he recognized on an instinctual level, the way he'd recognized that she—unlike him—

wasn't here just for the art, or interested in him simply for his knowledge of ancient hangings.

He felt a connection with her deep inside, weak but palpable. A synchronous vibration, like two tuning forks singing the same key. He almost felt as if his mind could connect to hers if he reached out and tried, the way he could connect with others of his kind, but that was impossible.

There were none of his kind like her. No women, beautiful or otherwise.

The magic that made Nathan what he was passed only to male children. His people depended on human women to bear them sons, but female offspring possessed none of his race's unique characteristics and were considered inconsequential, while male children were highly prized, for producing a son in this life guaranteed rebirth into the next. As soon as a boy child was born and suckled first milk, males of his race left their human mates, taking their sons with them to be raised among the congregation and learn the ways of their people.

Ways no human would understand.

Nathan had lived, died, and lived again many times in this way, but no more. He would not mate in this lifetime. There would be no male child born to him, and the price for this refusal to contribute to the survival of his species would be that his essence would not reincarnate.

This life would be his last, and he would live it alone.

He dragged his shoulders back, feeling the full weight of the course he'd set for himself. Suicide of the soul.

The woman in green still held her hand out toward him. *I'm Rachel Vandermere.*

It wasn't a name he'd soon forget. No matter how hard he tried.

Cutting his gaze away from her, he downed the last of his champagne in one gulp. "And I'm late for another engagement," he said and stomped toward the exit.

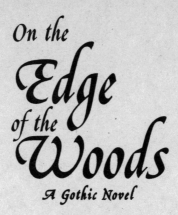

On the Edge of the Woods

A Gothic Novel

BY

DIANE TYRREL

When Stacy Addison sees a run-down
turn-of-the-century manor in the shadows of the
Sierra Nevada mountain range, she falls in
love and buys it.

But someone doesn't want Stacy in the house.
Someone wants her gone—permanently.

0-425-19477-9

**Available wherever books are sold or at
www.penguin.com**